TEAM YANKEE

TEAM YANKEE

A novel of World War III

HAROLD W. COYLE

CASEMATE

Philadelphia & Oxford

This edition published in the United States of America and Great Britain in 2018.
Reprinted in 2021 by
CASEMATE PUBLISHERS
1950 Lawrence Road, Havertown, PA 19083, USA
and
The Old Music Hall, 106–108 Cowley Road, Oxford OX4 1JE, UK

Paperback Edition: ISBN 978-1-61200-649-9

A CIP record for this book is available from the British Library

Printed and bound in the United States of America

Typeset in India by Versatile PreMedia Services. www.versatilepremedia.com

For a complete list of Casemate titles, please contact:

CASEMATE PUBLISHERS (US)
Telephone (610) 853-9131
Fax (610) 853-9146
Email: casemate@casematepublishers.com
www.casematepublishers.com

CASEMATE PUBLISHERS (UK)
Telephone (01865) 241249
Email: casemate-uk@casematepublishers.co.uk
www.casematepublishers.co.uk

Dulce Et Decorum Est
Wilfred Owen
(1893–1918)

Bent double, like old beggars under sacks,
Knocked-kneed, coughing like hags, we cursed through sludge,
Till on the haunting flares we turned our backs
And toward our distant rest began to trudge.
Men marched asleep. Many had lost their boots
But limped on, blood-shod. All went lame, all blind;
Drunk with fatigue; deaf even to the boots
Of tired, outstripped Five-Nines that dropped behind.

Gas! GAS! Quick boys! An ecstasy of fumbling,
Fitting the clumsy helmets just in time,
But someone still was yelling out and stumbling
And floundering like a man in fire lime. —
Dim through the misty panes and thick green light,
As under a green sea, I saw him drowning.

In all my dreams, before my helpless sight,
He plunges at me, guttering, choking, drowning.

If in some smothering dreams, you too could pace
Behind the wagon that we flung him in,
And watched the white eyes writhing in his face,
His hanging face, like a devil's sick of sin;
If you could hear, at every jolt, the blood
Come gargling from the froth-corrupted lungs,
Bitten as the cud

Of vile, incurable sores on innocent tongues, —
My friend, you would not tell with such high zest
The old Lie: *Dulce et decorum est*
*Pro patria mori.**

Dulce et decorum est Pro patria mori; It is sweet and fitting to die for the fatherland

Contents

Foreword

Since the end of World War II, the confrontation between the United States and the Soviet Union has dominated world affairs. While it can be argued that the issue is one of freedom versus dictatorship, capitalism versus communism, NATO versus the Warsaw Pact, in the end, the confrontation is between the two main antagonists. Issues change, locations change, supporting players change, the means of warfare change. The only fixed constant is the two main players, the United States and the Soviet Union.

There is much debate on what the final outcome of this confrontation will be. At one end of the spectrum there are the optimists who believe that the two great nations will learn to coexist and find peaceful means of resolving their disputes. At the other end are the cynics who believe that the two superpowers will destroy not only themselves, but the rest of the world as well in a nuclear holocaust. Both nations possess the means to accomplish either.

It is not the purpose of this book to debate the great issues, nor to predict how the confrontation will end. My goal is simple: to tell a story.

The story is of the men who would be called upon by the United States to decide the issue if the United States and the Soviet Union sought resolution of their difference by force of arms. More specifically, it is about one company, or team, in such a war. It is called Team Yankee, a tank-heavy combat team in West Germany. At the start of the story the Team consists of eighty-four men and a mix of modern, high-tech weaponry as well as tried and true, if somewhat outdated, equipment. Although the Team is a tank-heavy company team, it is attached to a mechanized infantry battalion.

The main character is Capt. Sean Bannon, commander of Team Yankee, a tank company which, at the start of the story, is attached to 3rd Battalion, 78th Infantry (Mechanized). Through his eyes, and those of his subordinates, a view of what modern war would look like in Europe from the standpoint of the American combat soldier is created.

Bannon is a typical American officer of the mid-1980s. Having graduated from college and having obtained a commission through the ROTC program, he has served as a tank platoon leader, a tank company executive officer and a battalion staff officer. His military education has consisted of the Armor Officer's Basic Course and the Armor Officer's Advanced Course, both at Fort Knox,

Kentucky. He is married, 27 years old, has three children, and a degree in history. He probably will never be promoted above the grade of lieutenant colonel.

The men in Team Yankee are products of the society from which they came. It was said many years ago that the soldiers of an army can only be as good as the society that produces them. This holds true in today's army. The American soldier today is a product of his society. In the next war, as in past, he will be forced to exist in a nightmare environment of mud and extremes of temperature, subsisting on cold, dehydrated meals and little sleep, faced always with the possibility of death from any quarter. These are the people who will, in war, decide its outcome and the shape of the world tomorrow.

The scenario for this fictitious war is borrowed from General Sir John Hackett's books, *The Third World War* and *The Third World War: The Untold Story*. It is the scenario of a conventional war fought in the mid-1980s. In General Sir John Hackett's books, the emphasis is on world politics and strategy. This book concerns itself with life at the other end of the spectrum as seen from the tank commander's hatch and the soldier's foxhole.

The characters are likewise fictitious. Any resemblance they have to real people is purely coincidental. The events and units involved are, of course, fictitious. Most geographical locations, towns, and areas mentioned are fictional and are not meant to resemble real places or locations. The exceptions to this are the Thüringer Wald and the Saale River, located in the southern portion of East Germany, and Berlin.

This book does not and is not meant to represent current US Army doctrine, policy, plans, or philosophy.

Addendum, 27 January 2015

When this book was written in 1985, the US military was undergoing the force modernization program initiated by President Ronald Reagan. New weapons systems, such as the M-1 Abrams tank were being fielded as quickly as they had completed their trails and were type-classified. The M-2/3 Bradley came later, as did certain support equipment such as an armored recovery vehicle that could keep pace with the faster M-1 tank. The result was a period when commanders in the field had to carry out their assigned missions using a mishmash of old and new equipment.

In writing *Team Yankee*, I used this to my advantage since I had commanded a company in which an M-113 equipped Infantry platoon was attached and was, at the time, unfamiliar with the M-2. It was not until I became the Task Force operations officer for 1-32 Armor at Fort Hood in 1988 that I had a chance to see up close and personal just what a Bradley could do.

HW Coyle

Acknowledgments

In writing this book, I owe a great deal to three soldiers and their books. The first and most influential is Charles MacDonald and his book, *Company Commander*. MacDonald was an infantry company commander in the 23rd Regiment, 2nd Infantry Division, during World War Two. After the war he wrote of his experiences as a small unit commander in that war. This excellent book has served me well in my military career and in my efforts to write this book. His assistance, kind words, and guidance have made this book possible.

The next two books, both written by Gen. Sir John Hackett, are *The Third World War* and *The Third World War: The Untold Story*. From these books I received the impetus to write *Team Yankee* and a scenario into which I could place it. The most interesting part of both books to me, as a junior officer, was Sir John's description of the war from the soldier's viewpoint. I have, with Sir John's permission, expanded upon his books, telling the story of one company team from the beginning to the end of the war. I also owe General Sir John Hackett my everlasting gratitude for reviewing the manuscript, providing me guidance, and giving me encouragement to carry on.

The fourth book, *Heights Of Glory*, written by Brig. Gen. Avigdor Kahalani, provided me with an excellent description of modern armored warfare as experienced by a tank unit commander. General Kahalani commanded the 77th tank Battalion, Israeli Defense Forces, during the Yom Kippur War in October 1973. This battalion held a portion of the Golan Heights overlooking the Valley of Tears during the first critical days of that war.

Prologue

Associated Press news story, 15 July

"Escalation of the Persian Gulf War continued today when Iranian aircraft attacked two oil tanks just outside the territorial waters of Bahrain. A ship of Dutch registry was reported sunk early this morning shortly after leaving port. At this time there are no report of survivors. The second ship, registered in Panama, was inbound to Bahrain when it was attacked by two Iranian warplanes. Casualties are reported to be high."

Television news story, 22 July

"Despite condemnation by the UN, Western European nations, Japan, and the US, Iran has pledged to continue attacks on any vessel that enters the Persian Gulf, now declared a war zone by that country. Outside the Straits of Hormuz, the entrance to the Persian Gulf, the number of tankers sitting at anchor, waiting for a break in the deadlock, continues to grow. The ships' owners and their captains feel that this deadlock will not last long. As one ship's captain stated, 'They have tried this before and have always backed off. They need us too much to keep this up for long.'"

State Department press release, 26 July

"The attack by Iranian war planes on commercial vessels in the international waters of the Indian Ocean yesterday is a threat to the security of the free world. The United States and the free world cannot allow such acts of deliberate terrorism to go unpunished. While the United States continues to pursue all available means to resolve this issue peacefully, military options are being considered."

Department of Defense press release, 27 July

"The destroyer USS *Charles Logan*, while on patrol in international waters off the Straits of Hormuz, was rammed, then fired upon by a Soviet Cruiser of the Gorki class this morning. US forces returned fire. Damage and casualties on either side are not known at this time."

TASS news release, 28 July

"A meeting of the Warsaw Pact ministers ended today with a pledge to stand together in the face of threats and increased war preparations on the part of the United States. Representatives from Poland, the German Democratic Republic, Hungary, Bulgaria, Czechoslovakia, and the Soviet Union released a joint statement pledging to meet American aggression against any member state with retaliation in kind."

White House press release, 28 July

"In view of the current crisis, the President has issued an order federalizing 100,000 Army Reserve and National Guard personnel. Personnel and units affected have been notified and are reporting to their mobilization stations."

Vatican press release, 29 July

"A request on the part of the Holy Father to travel to Moscow to talk to the Soviet premier in an attempt to find a peaceful solution to the current crisis was denied. The Holy Father calls for both sides to remember their responsibility to their people and to the world as he again offered his services in any future negotiations."

BBC news release, 30 July

"A stormy session between the French president and the Soviet foreign minister in Paris today ended when the Soviet foreign minister warned the French president that the national interests of France would best be served if that nation did not involve itself in the current crisis between the Soviet Union and the United States. In a statement immediately after the meeting, the president announced that France would stand by her treaties and do her part to defend Europe against aggression from any quarter. The president went on to announce that the French military forces, with the exception of its strategic nuclear forces, would actively cooperate with other NATO nations during the current crisis."

Television news story, 1 Aug

"We interrupt this program for a special announcement. Unconfirmed reports from Brussels, headquarters for NATO, state that the NATO nations have ordered their armed forces to mobilize and commence deployment to wartime positions along the border separating East and West Germany. While there is no official word from Washington concerning this, announcement of an address to the nation by the president at seven o'clock this morning, followed by a joint press conference by the secretaries of State and Defense seems to add credibility to these reports."

CHAPTER I

Stand-To

The noise and the metallic voice sounded as if they came from the far end of a long, dark corridor. There were no other feelings or sensations as he drifted from a dead sleep through that transitional period of half-asleep, half-awake. An inner, soothing voice on the near end of the corridor whispered, "*It's not important, go back to sleep.*" But the radio whined back to life again and the metallic voice called out unanswered.

"BRAVO 3 ROMEO 56—THIS IS KILO 8 MIKE 77. RADIO CHECK, OVER." The inner voice was silent this time. Duty called and sleep had to be abandoned.

As Captain Bannon began the grim process of waking up, other senses began to enter play. First came the aches, pains, and muscle spasms, the result of sleeping on an uneven bed of personal gear, vehicular equipment, ration boxes, ammo boxes, and other odds and ends that tend to clutter the interior of a combat vehicle. A tumbled and distorted bed made up of paraphernalia ranging from soft, to not-so-soft, to downright hard does cruel things to the human body. Only exhaustion and the desire to be near the radios whenever possible allowed Bannon to survive the ordeal of sleeping like that.

While still sorting out the waves of pains and spasms, he opened his eyes and began to search the interior of the armored personnel carrier in an effort to reestablish his orientation. The personnel carrier, or PC, was dimly lit by a dome light just above his head. It bathed everything in an eerie blue green light that reminded him of a scene from a Spielberg movie.

First Lieutenant Robert Uleski, the company executive officer, or XO, was sitting in the center of the crew compartment on a box of field rations, staring at the radio with an intense expression on his face as if he were daring it to speak to him again. Cattycorner from where Bannon was perched was the PC's driver, Sp4 James Hurly, huddled up and asleep in the driver's compartment. For a moment Bannon stared at Hurly, wondering how the boy could sleep in such a god-awful position. A twinge and a spasm from one of his contorted back muscles reminded him of his own accommodations. Perhaps, he thought, the driver wasn't in such a bad spot after all.

A static crackle, a bright orange light on the face of the radio, and the accelerating whine of a small cooling fan heralded the beginning of another incoming radio call. "BRAVO 3 ROMEO 56—BRAVO 3 ROMEO 56, THIS IS KILO 8 MIKE 77. RADIO CHECK, OVER." Without changing his expression or moving any other part of his body except his right arm and hand which held the radio hand mike, Uleski raised the mike to within an inch of his mouth, pressed the push-to-talk button, and waited a couple of seconds. The little cooling fan in the radio whined to life. When the fan reached a steady speed, he began to speak, still facing the radio without changing expression.

"KILO 8 MIKE 77, THIS IS BRAVO 3 MIKE 56. STAY OFF THE AIR. I SAY AGAIN, STAY OFF THE AIR. OUT." Releasing the push to-talk button, Uleski allowed his hand to fall slowly back into his lap. He continued to stare at the now silent radio as if he would pounce and attack it if it dared to come to life again. But it didn't.

Bannon's first effort to speak ended in an incoherent grunt due to a dry mouth and a parched throat. After summoning up what saliva he could, his second effort was slightly more successful. "Is that 3rd Platoon again?"

Still staring at the radio with the same expression, Uleski provided a short, functional, "Yes, Sir."

"What time is it?"

Uleski raised his left arm in the same slow, mechanical manner as he had used when answering the radio. Looking at his watch, he considered for a moment what he was looking at before responding in the same monotone voice, "0234 hours."

It wasn't that Lieutenant Uleski was an expressionless automaton without feelings. On the contrary, "Ski", or Lieutenant U as the enlisted men called him, was a very personable man with a good sense of humor, a sharp wit, and an enormous capacity to absorb Polish jokes and retaliate with appropriate ethnic jokes aimed at his tormentor. It's just that in the very early morning everyone tends to fall into a zombie-like state. The requirement to sit on a hard surface for hours on end, in a small, cold aluminum armored box called a PC, with two sleeping bodies as your only company with nothing better to do than stare at a radio that you did not expect, or want, to come to life only added to one's tiredness. Uleski was not an exception. Nor was Bannon.

Considering for a moment the information his XO had given him, Bannon plotted his next move. The PC was quiet, and Uleski had gone back to his silent vigil. Slowly, as his mind began to come alive, it became apparent that sitting there, watching Uleski watching the radios was definitely nonproductive. Besides, Bannon was now in too much pain to go back to sleep and movement was the only way he was going to stop the aches and spasms. It was time to make the supreme effort and get up. Besides, the Team would be having stand-to within the hour and he needed some time to get himself together. While it was permissible for everyone else to look like he had just rolled out of bed at stand-to, the Team commander, at least, had to give the appearance that he was wide awake and ready to deal with the world. The night, if four hours of sleep on a pile of assorted junk could be called a night, was over. It was time to greet a new day, another dawn, the fourth since Team Yankee had rolled out of garrison and headed for the border.

✿

Long before the tanks rolled out of the back gate toward the border, Patricia Bannon knew Sean was involved in more than another exercise. After eight years of marriage and life in the Army, Pat could read her husband's moods like a book. At first there was little change in his daily routine. The sinking of the oil tankers in the Persian Gulf by perpetually warring nations was just another story on the Armed Forces Network evening news. Life in the military community continued as usual, as did Sean's comings and goings.

It was the closing of the Straits of Hormuz and the commitment of a US carrier battle group to the area that heralded the change. The husbands began to spend more time at their units. The normal twelve-hour day that commanders and staff officers put in stretched into fourteen and fifteen hours. They tried to shrug off the extra hours as prep for an upcoming field exercise. But the wives who had been around the service for a while knew something was in the offing.

Some wives became upset and nervous. They didn't know what was happening but felt that whatever it was, it was not good. Others talked about nothing else, as if it was a challenge to find out what the big dark secret was. During the day they would gather together with the rest of the grapevine and compare notes in order to pool information they had gleaned from their husbands the night before. Pat chose to follow the lead of the older wives in the battalion. Cathy Hill, wife of the battalion commander of 1st Battalion, 4th Armor, went out of her way to carry on as if everything was business as usual. So did Mary Shell, the wife of the battalion's S-3. Pat and many of the wives followed their lead, not asking questions or nagging. They agreed that whatever was happening, nagging wives would not help the situation.

It was the public announcement that the Soviets were sending a naval battle group to the Persian Gulf to "assist in maintaining peace in the Gulf" that destroyed the last pretense of normalcy. When Pat told Sean the news after he came home from morning PT, he simply replied, "Yeah, I know." His attitude convinced Pat that he had already known about the incident and probably more. The feeling of dread and foreboding became more pronounced when word spread around the community that the training exercise the battalion had been preparing months for was suddenly canceled. In their two-and-a-half years in Germany, that had never happened before. To make matters worse, cancellation of the exercise did not change the new fourteen-hour day routine.

Over the next few days, every new deterioration in the world situation seemed to be matched with further preparations by the battalion. One night, Sean brought home his field gear and took out his old worn BDUs were replaced with newer sets. The next day, while returning from the commissary, Pat saw trucks with ammo caution signs on them in the motor pool, dropping off boxes at each of the tanks. Even the community dispensary began to pack up. The news that a US and Soviet warship in the Gulf had collided and then exchanged fire silenced the last optimist.

Pat wasn't ready for this. It suddenly dawned on her that her husband might be going to war. The possibility was always there. After all, Sean was a soldier and soldiers were expected to fight. As Sean would say on occasion, "*That's what I'm paid to do.*" Pat knew that someday it might come to that, but had never given it much thought. Now she had to. It was like a great dark abyss. She had no guidelines, no idea of what to do. The Army spent a fortune training and preparing Sean for this moment, but not a penny to prepare her, the wife of a soldier. Pat decided that the only thing she could do was to make this period as comfortable and as trouble free for Sean as possible.

Besides Sean, there were the children. Little Sean, the eldest, already knew something was not right. For a child of six, he was very perceptive and picked up on the tension and fear that both his mother and father were trying to hide. He didn't talk about it, but would show his concern by asking his father each morning if he was going to come home that night. Little Sean would stay awake until his father did come and then would get out of his bed, run to his father, and hug him with no intention of letting go, leaving the elder Sean no choice but to carry his son to bed, lay him down and talk to him for a while. Kurt, at three, was hell on wheels and just the opposite of his older brother. Their daughter Sarah, at one, was fast growing up by trying to do everything her brothers did. Her busy schedule of exploration and mischief kept her from noticing a break in routine.

∽

The transition from home and family to field and prep for war boggled Bannon's clouded mind. It was almost as if he had been moved into a different world. Pondering such deep thoughts, however, was getting him nowhere. He had to get moving and live in the present world and hope for the best in the other.

New pains and spasms were Bannon's reward for placing his body in motion. Slowly, and with great care, he moved each appendage of his body. Once in the sitting position, he stopped, rested, and considered his next move. These things can't be rushed. Minds work just as slowly as bodies do at 0234 hours.

"Well, I guess it's time for Garger's early morning ass chewing," Bannon declared grimly, more to himself than to Uleski. "You would think that after getting beaten about the head and shoulders for the same damn thing three days in a row he would learn. Lord, save me from second lieutenants."

For the first time Uleski's face showed expression as a small grin preceded a chuckle and his retort. "Yeah, especially this one."

"Don't be so smug, Ski. The only reason I like you is because I never knew you when you were a second lieutenant."

Still grinning Uleski glanced over his shoulder at Bannon. "I *never* was a second lieutenant. Wouldn't have any part of it and told the ROTC recruiter. Naturally, once they found out who I was, they agreed. So here I am, a full-grown US Army first lieutenant, guarding the frontiers of freedom and making the world safe for democracy."

Bannon groaned as he shook his head. "God, the sun isn't even up and already the bull is getting deep in here. I better get out before I drown in it."

They both chuckled. It's amazing what soldiers find humorous and amusing at 0234 hours.

"I'm going over to 3rd Platoon first to give Garger his early morning lecture on the meaning of radio listening silence. Then I'm going to swing by the Mech Platoon and see how they're doing. I expect to be back for stand-to. When was the last time you checked the batteries?"

"About twenty minutes ago. They should be good until stand-to."

"You better be right. I don't want to have the track that both the CO and XO occupied and be the only one that has to be slaved off in the morning. Bad for the image."

With a feigned look of surprise on his face, Uleski snorted, "Image? You mean we're going to start worrying about our image? Do you think the men can take it?"

"At ease there, first lieutenant. XOs as well as platoon leaders can get jacked up in the morning too, you know."

Hunching his head down between his shoulders and putting his hands up in mock surrender, Uleski feigned whimpering. "Yes, sir, yes, sir, please don't beat me too hard, sir," before turning back toward the radio with a grin on his face.

Digging through the pile of junk that had been his bed, Bannon pulled out his gear and started to get ready. Field jacket, protective mask, web gear with weapon and other assorted attached to it, and, of course, his helmet. It was a ritual that always reminded him of a matador preparing for the arena. All the gear that the well-dressed American soldier was supposed to wear was definitely not designed with the armored vehicle crewman in mind. Bannon was reminded of this when he exited the PC through the small troop door that was part of the PC's rear ramp. Climbing through this four-foot door was always a challenge. In the dark, with all one's gear on made it that much more interesting. But at that hour in the morning, the last thing he needed was a challenge.

Once on the ground, it felt good to be able to stand upright and stretch his legs. The chill and early morning mist were refreshing after being in the cramped PC for hours. It reminded Bannon, however, more of an April or early May than August, for German weather in late summer was more like a New England spring.

The chill was not all bad. It not only cleared his mind, it allowed him to focus on matters at hand. Yesterday had been hot and sunny. As there was a hint of moisture in the air, he expected the valley to the Team's front would be shrouded in a heavy fog throughout most of the morning. That meant moving a listening post down into it even though the cavalry was still deployed forward. This was the Mech Platoon's job. And though they would probably do so automatically as soon as they saw the fog rising, Bannon intended to remind them when he got there. The old saying, "*The one time you forget to remind someone of something is the one time he forgets and it is the one time it really needed to be done*," kept buzzing through his head.

Ever so slowly Bannon's eyes became accustomed to the darkness. He could now make out images of other nearby vehicles like the headquarters PC he had just exited pulled into the tree line. One track, an Improved Tow Vehicle or ITV, attached to the Team from the mech battalion to which Team Yankee was attached, sat forward at the edge of the tree line. Its camouflage net was off and the hammerhead-like launcher and sight was erect, peering down into the valley below. This track was one of the Team's OPs, or observation posts, using its thermal sight to watch the Team's sector of responsibility through the dark and now gathering fog.

Bannon walked over to the ITV to make sure the crew was awake, stumbling over roots and branches that reached up and grabbed his ankles while low branches swatted him in the face as he went. Stopping for a moment, he pushed the offending branches out of the way before going forward again, remembering this time to pick up his feet to clear the stumps and using his forearm to clear the branches. As he proceeded, Bannon decided that rather than fight the underbrush and roots on his way over to 3rd Platoon, he would skirt the tree line. This was not a good practice, but as it was dark and hostilities had not been declared yet, he decided to do it, one more time.

When he reached the ITV, the launcher's hammerhead-like turret slowly moved to the right, indicating that the crew was awake and on the job. Knowing that they would have the troop door combat-locked, Bannon took out his buck knife and rapped on the door three times. As he waited for a response, the shuffle of the crewman on duty could be heard as he climbed back over gear and other crewmen to open the door. Struggling with the door handle, the crewman rotated the lever and let the heavy door swing out. Bannon was greeted by a dark figure hanging halfway out the door and a slurred, "Waddaya want?"

"It's Captain Bannon. Anything going on down in the valley?"

When the ITV crewman realized whom he was talking to, he straightened up as much as the cramped opening he was standing in allowed. "Oh, sorry, sir, I didn't know it was you, sir. No, we ain't seen nothin' all night 'cept some jeeps and a deuce 'n a half going up to the cavalry. Been quiet. We expectin' somethin'?"

"No, at least not that I've heard. The cavalry *should* give us some warning. But just in case, I need you to stay on your toes. Checked your batteries lately?"

"Yes, sir, 'bout an hour ago we cranked her up and ran it for twenty minutes."

"Ok. Keep awake and alert. Let the XO over there know if something comes along."

After a perfunctory "Yes, sir," the crewman closed his door and locked it as Bannon turned away and walked out to the edge of the tree line. It bothered him that he didn't know the crewman's name. He'd only seen that ITV crewman for the first time three days ago after the Team had pulled into its positions. That's the trouble with attachments. You never know who you're going to get, and you

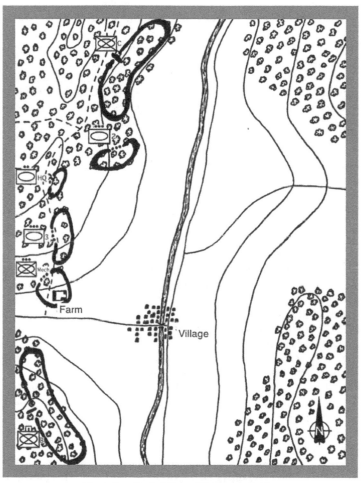

Map 1: Team Yankee's General Deployment Positions

never get a chance to know them, not like his own people. Except for the fact that he was the CO and the Team headquarters track was parked nearby, the ITV crewman didn't know much about him either. And yet, very shortly, they might have to take orders from him in combat. Bannon hoped the crew of the ITV trusted his ability to command in battle with the same blind faith that he placed in their ability to kill Russian tanks.

As he trudged over to the 3rd Platoon's positions, he reviewed the Team's dispositions and mission. The Team had gone over how it would fight its first battle time and time again using map exercises, terrain walks, battle simulations, and field training exercises, or FTXs, on similar ground. Still, Bannon was not totally satisfied that they were in the best possible positions to meet all eventualities.

Team Yankee was currently deployed on the forward slope of a large hill overlooking a river valley. The forest it was located in came halfway down the slope until it reached a point where it dropped all the way down onto the floor of the valley. That point was the Team's left flank where Bannon's 2nd Platoon was positioned. From there the platoon could fire across the face of the slope, into the valley or across the valley, toward the high ground across from them.

In the center was the Team's headquarters section, consisting of Alpha 66, which was Bannon's tank, Alpha 55 commanded by the XO's, and two ITVs from the mech battalion's antitank company. From there they had a good view of the valley, a small village situated in the valley to the right front, a north-south road on the far side of a minor river, and a second valley that ran west to east and emptied into the larger on to the team's front. This constituted the limit of the Team's battle position.

It was on the right that the Team had the greatest concentration of power, the 3rd Platoon and the Mech Platoon. The Mech Platoon attached to the Team was still equipped with M-113 armored personnel carriers and Dragon antitank guided missiles. It had been scheduled to receive Bradley fighting vehicles but, much to the chagrin of its parent battalion commander, Lieutenant Colonel Reynolds of 3rd of the 78th Infantry, that kept getting put off due to a slow down in the procurement of those powerful fighting vehicles.

The Mech Platoon was split into two elements. The dismounted element, led by the platoon leader, consisted of most of the infantrymen, two Dragons and three M60 machineguns. This element occupied a walled farmstead in the small valley on the right. The mounted element, led by the platoon sergeant, consisted of the Platoon's PCs, their crews and two more Dragons teams. They were above the same farm on the slope in the tree line. From their positions the Mech Platoon could block the small valley and keep anyone from exiting the village if and when the other people got in there.

The 3rd Platoon was located a little further behind and higher up on the slope from the Mech Platoon. From its positions there it could fire into the main valley, the small valley to its right, the village, or across the valley at the opposite heights. This platoon would also be responsible for covering the withdrawal of the Mech Platoon if that became necessary.

Bannon was not comfortable with the idea of defending on a forward slope. Should a withdrawal under fire be necessary, all the Team's vehicles would have to go uphill, at times exposed themselves to observation and fire from the enemy on the other side of the valley. In addition, the only positions from which most of the Team would be able to fire were immediately inside the tree line. This position was so obvious it hurt. Bannon could visualize some Soviet artillery officer plotting likely targets and coming across their hill during his terrain analysis. Glee would light up on the Russian's face as he told his trusted subordinate. "*There, that is where they will defend, in this tree line. Make sure we blanket that area with five, no six, battalions of artillery.*" Bannon had gone over his reservations concerning this very point with Colonel Reynolds every time they'd reviewed their go-to-war plans. On this morning, as he stood at the edge of the tree line where his Team was deployed, looking across the valley at the high ground the enemy would occupy, if, by some miracle, war was averted, he resolved he would once more push for a change in the Team's deployment. But for now he, and Team Yankee, were obliged to fight on the ground where they sat.

As Bannon approached the 3rd Platoon's position, he heard a slight rustling followed by the two low voices. He had reached the Platoon's OP/LP.

"Halt, who goes there?" came the challenge in a voice that was a little too loud and sounded surprised.

Bannon had no doubt he'd caught the soldiers manning the OP halfasleep and had startled them. The voice that had issued the challenge sounded like Private Lenard from Alpha 32, a tank commanded by SSG Joelle Blackfoot, a full-blooded Cherokee. The sentry repeated his challenge, "Halt! Who goes there?" It was Lenard.

"Captain Bannon."

"Oh, okay. You can come on in then."

While this homey invitation was a refreshing change of pace from the less-than-cheerful thoughts Bannon had been mulling over, it was definitely not the way to do business while on guard. As he approached, he could hear a second soldier telling Lenard that he had screwed up. When he was no more than arm's distance from them, the two men quietly stood up to face their commanding officer.

As they were just inside the tree line, none of them could see the other's face. But Bannon was reasonably sure there was a pained expression on Lenard's face. Not knowing which of the two forms facing him was Lenard, he directed his comments to both. "Is that the proper way to challenge someone?"

"No, sir, it's not, sir."

"How are you supposed to challenge someone when they are approaching your position?"

Without hesitation, and as if he were reading it from the soldier's handbook, Lenard went through the correct challenge and password procedures. With a plaintive voice and a few expletives, Bannon asked him why he hadn't used the correct procedures. "Because you said you were the CO and I recognized your voice, sir," came the response.

The answer was honest, but wrong. After Bannon had explained that everyone got the full treatment, Lenard, an honest, if outspoken soldier, replied he didn't understand the logic in this, but promised that he wouldn't forget the next time. As Bannon turned away and began to make his away toward 32, he could hear the second soldier berating Lenard as they settled down into their positions again. "See, I told you so."

Upon reaching Alpha 32, Bannon started climbing up on the right front fender but stopped halfway up when he heard the cocking of a .45 and a low, firm "Halt." The voice belonged to Blackfoot. Bannon had no doubt that there was a pistol cocked, loaded, and aimed at him. "Who goes there?"

"Captain Bannon."

"Advance and be recognized."

Bannon finished climbing up and moved slowly to the edge of the turret until he was able to make out the figure in the cupola with an outstretched arm holding a .45. In a lower voice, just audible to him, Blackfoot gave the challenge, "Wrinkle."

"Bait," Bannon's replied.

Satisfied with the answer, Blackfoot raised his pistol and slowly let the hammer down. "When's the war going to start, Captain?"

Pulling himself up onto the top of the turret so that he was lying across the length of it with his head near Blackfoot's, Bannon spoke to him about Lenard's failure to challenge him properly before asking how things were going with the crew's preparations for combat.

Being the thorough NCO that he was, Blackfoot informed Bannon he was not happy with the crew drill between himself and his gunner. He explained that his gunner was slow to pick up targets that he, Blackfoot, had acquired and had laid the main gun on. He wanted to spend some time someplace where they could move the tank and practice their crew drill. Bannon explained that for security reasons all vehicular movement had to be kept down to a minimum. Blackfoot, like everyone else in the Team, would just have to do the best he could from a stationary position. Blackfoot replied that he knew that, but he saw no harm in asking.

After getting the weather prediction for the day and his best guess as to when the fog would lift from Blackfoot, Bannon climbed down and proceeded to Alpha 31, Lieutenant Garger's tank, which was the next in line.

As he approached 31, Bannon began going over the *counseling* he would use with Garger this morning. All in all, Garger wasn't a bad lieutenant. In fact, he was no different from any other second lieutenant he'd ever come across known. It took time, training, and a lot of patience to develop a good tank platoon leader. For only having been in the country for three weeks, Garger wasn't doing half bad. But while half bad was acceptable during a training exercise, it wouldn't hack it in combat. The time and opportunity to teach the lieutenant everything he needed to know just wasn't there anymore. The Team was on the cusp of going into combat and Bannon had no faith in Garger's ability to perform under the stress and strain of battle.

The platoon sergeant, SFC Gary Pierson, a veteran of Vietnam and an outstanding trooper, had been doing his best to train his lieutenant when Bannon wasn't. He was also doing all he could to cover for Garger in order to keep the platoon together and functioning properly. But Pierson couldn't do it all. Either his lieutenant had to perform, or he had to go. At this late stage of the game, Bannon wasn't about to put lives in the hands of a lieutenant who had, so far, screwed up just about every task given to him. With that thought in mind, he decided to talk to the battalion commander about the matter later that day. But first, he needed to tend to the business at hand.

Climbing up onto the right front fender of Alpha 31, he was stopped as he had been on Blackfoot's tank with a "Halt, who goes there?" Only instead of using a .45 to keep the unknown intruder at bay, the figure in the cupola tried to crank his M2 machinegun down and in Bannon's direction. As the firing mechanism was part of the gun's elevation handle and was easily activated, a brief moment of panic swept over Bannon. He considered whether it would be better to jump, scream, or hope for the best. Fortunately, inept handling of the machinegun's controls frustrated the figure in the cupola, causing him to abandon it and go to his .45 instead. As the figure fumbled for his pistol, Bannon took advantage of this to identify himself and finish climbing up.

Abandoning all hopes of covering the intruder with a weapon, the figure simply called out the challenge in a most dejected and apprehensive tone of voice. Lieutenant Garger was running true to form this morning.

Crawling up onto the turret and stretching out across it, Bannon propped himself up on his elbows until he was less than a foot from Garger. "Well, what shall we talk about this morning, *Lieutenant?*"

Garger paused for a moment, not knowing if he was expected to answer, or if his team commander's question was simply a prelude to another ass chewing. Hesitantly, he replied in a half-question, half-statement, "RTO procedures, sir?"

"No, no. Close, but a no-go. How about radio listening silence? You remember our discussion on that subject yesterday morning?"

"Yes, sir."

"THEN WHY IN THE HELL DID YOU BREAK RADIO LISTENING SILENCE AGAIN TODAY? ARE YOU FUCKING STUPID, OR JUST SOFT IN THE HEAD?"

While waiting for his answer, Bannon did his best to calm down, for he had a tendency to become excited and abusive when dealing with abject stupidity, particularly when an officer was involved. He had told himself time and again in the past that it wouldn't do to get this cranked up, that he needed to be calm and logical at such times. But habits are hard to break, especially so early in the morning. There would, no doubt, be plenty more reasons for getting excited later in the day.

Falteringly, Garger replied. "No, sir. I just wanted to make sure the radios worked since we changed frequencies."

With a modicum of composure regained, Bannon continued. "Did your radio work yesterday before I chewed your ass out for breaking radio listening silence?"

"Yes, sir."

"And did your radio work the day before yesterday just before I chewed your ass out for breaking radio listening silence?"

"Yes, sir"

"Then why did you do it again? I mean, by now even *you* should be able to figure out that, *A*, your radio works every time you use it and *B*, every time you use it I am going to come down and jump in your shit. Do you understand what I'm telling you? I mean, do you really understand?"

"Yes, sir, I do, it's just that, well, I…"

Exasperated and nearing his wits end, Bannon sighed. "One more time, I swear, one more time…" Then, without finishing, he slid back off the turret and climbed down the same way he had come up. To stay any longer would not do him or his nerves any good. If the point hadn't been driven home by now, it never would be.

Bannon hadn't walked ten meters from 31 when Pierson's low, firm voice startled him. "This is starting to be a regular routine, Captain. I'm going to start setting my watch by you."

Stopping short, Bannon turned toward the shadowy figure emerging from the darkness behind him. Still riled by his *discussion* with Garger, Pierson's sudden appearance had scared the living hell out of him. As he leaned back against a nearby tree and collected his wits, he shook his head. "*The sun isn't even up and it is building up to be a real peachy day*," he thought to himself. Only when he was sure he could speak with a calm and steady voice did Bannon address the dark figure that was now standing before him. "Are you looking to give me a heart attack, or is this some type of leadership reaction course?"

"No, sir, I just wanted to come over and save our favorite lieutenant before the wolves got him. But from the growling I heard a minute ago, I figured I was too late. So I decided to wait for you here."

"You know, I could charge you with attempted murder."

"You wouldn't do that, Captain. I mean, if you did, who would you find to whip this collection of derelicts and criminals you call a tank platoon into shape?"

"You're right Sergeant Pierson. No sane man would take the job. I guess I'll have to keep you," Bannon shot back in a half-hearted attempt at humor. "But

I'm not too sure about your lieutenant," he continued in a voice that informed the NCO he was dead serious. "After stand-to and breakfast I'm going to talk to the Old Man about pulling Garger out. If I give you Williams as a loader, do you have a gunner who can take over 31 and a loader that can move into a gunner's seat?"

"Sergeant Pauly could handle the tank, and I have a couple of people who are ready to gun. But do you want to start screwing around with crews at this late stage? I mean, the lieutenant may not have all his stuff together yet, but given a little more time, I'm sure he'll catch on. You know how it was your first time out."

"Yes, Sergeant Pierson, I know what it was like. If truth be known, I really wasn't much better than Garger. But this is different. When I screwed up as a fresh face platoon leader, the worst I got was an ass chewing from the CO, a lot of smirks from the men in the platoon, and a sick feeling in the pit of my stomach. If the balloon goes up in the next couple of days and Garger blows it, he not only stands a damn good chance of losing his own behind and his crew's, but a failure on his part could cost me the whole platoon, if not more. I feel sorry for the kid, I really do. I wish I could do more for him. But I have a whole company to look out for. I'm not going to take any chances that I don't have to."

Bannon and Pierson stood there in silence, facing each other in the darkness for a minute. Neither was able to see the other's facial expression. They didn't need to. Both knew that what the other said was, to a degree, right. Pierson hated to admit defeat, the defeat of not being able to train his new lieutenant. Bannon felt the same. But they also knew that there simply was no time left, that they had to deal with bigger issues than pride. There was always the chance Garger might do well once the shooting started. Unfortunately, there was no way to tell. Bannon didn't want to take the chance. His mind was set. If he could swing it, Garger would go.

The two men exchanged a few more remarks, mostly about the condition of the platoon's vehicles, plans to improve the positions, and the training that needed to be done that day. Then they parted, Bannon proceeding around the hill to the Mech Platoon while Pierson started rousing his platoon for stand-to. The war, or at least the preparations for war, went on.

By the time Bannon had worked his way down to the walled farm where the dismounted element of the Mech Platoon was, it was getting light. Not that you could see the sun. In fact, the rising fog made it almost impossible to see anything beyond twenty meters. The Mech Platoon, led by 2nd Lt. William Harding, was already moving into its position and preparing for stand-to. Bannon decided to stay with them until after stand-to.

Harding's platoon was good. It had an unusually good combination of platoon leader, platoon sergeant, and squad leaders. Not only had Harding and his platoon sergeant, SFC Leslie Polgar, been together for almost a year, they complemented each other. Harding did the thinking, gave the orders, and led the platoon, while Polgar handled its training, which often included copious amounts of motivation and, when called for, unbridled ass kicking, which to Polgar were one and the same.

It was easy to see that Harding's grunts were well trained and confident in themselves, their weapons, and their leaders, Bannon thought as he watched them occupy their positions. Each and every man moved into them with hardly a word. Once settled in, they checked their weapons, situated themselves to cover their assigned sectors, and prepared to receive the enemy or stand down, whichever came first. By the time Bannon had arrived at the farm, a squad with two Dragons had already gone down into the village in order to establish a listening post, or LP, while keeping his other two Dragons with the mounted element.

As he leaned against the farmhouse wall, looking out of the window across from Harding, Bannon kept thinking how worthless he would be here if the other people came boiling out of the fog. Without his sixty-one-ton tank wrapped around him, he wouldn't be much good to anyone in a firefight armed only with a .45 pistol that was probably older than he was. Not that the .45 was a bad weapon. It's just that when push came to shove, Bannon wanted to have the ability to reach out and touch someone. Hand-to-hand combat, eyeball-to-eyeball brawls with the enemy might make great war movies, but it simply wasn't his idea of doing business. At the first opportunity, he resolved to secure himself an M-16 rifle. It might be a pain to carry around, but an M-16 at least provided its owner with a much greater sense of security when stumbling about in the dark alone.

By 0500 it was as light as it was going to get. With no Russians, or anyone else for that matter, in sight, Bannon told Harding to keep the squad in the village until the fog lifted and to stand down the rest of his platoon. He also reminded Harding of the 0730 platoon leaders' meeting and the weapons inspection for the Mech Platoon at 0900 hours. He knew that by the time he returned to the platoon its weapons would have already been checked for cleanliness, functioning, headspace and timing. Still, not only was it part of the routine that had been established, it gave him a chance to learn more about the men who made up Harding's platoon as well as provide them a chance to see him. In Bannon's mind it was important that attachments such as the Mech Platoon knew that their commander had high standards when it came to important items like weapons, positions, camouflage, and all those things that separated the quick from the dead.

On his way back, Bannon walked from track to track, greeting each crew as they prepared for breakfast and another day on the border. He made a few corrections, listened to a complaint or two, and generally let himself be seen.

Only when he was around Alpha 31 was his presence greeted with a proper, but chilled reception. The other crew members of 31 were in a depressed mood for they, like Pierson, did not want to be branded as failures due to the loss of their lieutenant. But they were far less sanguine than Pierson was about fighting for his retention. The crew knew if Garger screwed up in combat they would be the first to pay for it. Unlike a dismounted infantry squad where every man can go off on his own if something goes south, a tank crew is a joint venture where one's fate is welded to the actions of the other crew members. The sixty-one tons of steel that enclosed them silently bound their collective fates together. So there is a strong self-serving motivation that causes tankers to work together and ensures that each member of the crew can perform his job. At the moment, pride was running a distant second to survival for the bulk of 31's crew.

$\sim$

By the time Bannon had finished his morning rounds and returned to where the Team's headquarters element was, he found Uleski, the tank crews of the two headquarters tank, and the ITV crews were either washing and shaving or squaring away their tracks. The ITV that had been at the edge of the tree line had pulled back into its hide position and was camouflaged. Uleski was squatting next to the PC, stripped down to his waist, washing himself from a small pan of water. Looking up as Bannon approached, he grinned, "I knew you wouldn't be back by stand-to. I just didn't know what day. So," he continued with feigned gravity, "do I need to report a murder together with an emergency requisition for a second lieutenant platoon leader?"

"Come on U, I'm a nice guy. Do you for one moment think that I would bring any harm to that poor young man over in 3rd Platoon? I mean, do I look like a mean person?"

Before answering, the XO straightened up and squinted as he looked Bannon over from head to toe "Oh, sorry. I thought you were my CO, the one who isn't worth a damn in the morning until he's eaten a second lieutenant."

"Yeah, it's me alright. Only this morning a second lieutenant wasn't enough. Now I'm looking for a first lieutenant for dessert."

Uleski looked to his left, then to his right, using exaggerated movements before turning back to face Bannon. "Ain't seen any o' them 'round these parts. Y'all might try over in yonder hill cuntree," pointing east toward the border.

With the second round of poor humor decided in Uleski's favor, the Team commander and XO got down to the morning's business while Uleski finished washing and Bannon dug his shaving gear out and prepared to wash up. Uleski had a long day ahead and Bannon wanted him to get started. There were maintenance problems that needed attention and spare parts that had to be requested, borrowed, or scrounged. After that, a laundry point needed to be located and arrangements made to turn in the company's laundry. Batteries for field phones and wire to replace some that had been torn out by a cavalry track that had wandered into the Team's area had to be found. These, and many small but important tasks, were required to keep Team Yankee in business. Once the first sergeant came up to the position with breakfast, he and Uleski would divide up the list of these tasks between them and go about the day's duties.

Overall, the Team wasn't in bad shape. The last tank that had fallen out of the line of march during the movement to the border had finally closed in the previous afternoon, giving TeamYankee a total of ten tanks, two ITVs, and five M-113s, one of which was the Team's commo track where Bannon and Uleski had spent the night and Bannon worked from when not on his own tank, Alpha 66. Two of the tanks had problems with their fire control system, but nothing that would take more than a day to repair. In fact, the vehicles were in better shape than the people were.

Not that they were falling apart. Life in the field, however, wears away at soldiers unless simple creature comforts such as food, clean, dry clothes, and other such necessaries are provided. Added to the problems of living in the field was the tension caused by the alert and move to the border, the flurry of almost panicked activity during the first twenty-four hours in position, and three very long days waiting for what one wit in the 2nd Platoon called "The end of Times." This was made worse by the lack of solid news from the outside world and the concerns of the married personnel, including Bannon himself, about the evacuation of the dependents back to the States. To top it off, a number of the men had not packed extra fatigues in their go-to-war duffle bag. Some hadn't even brought a change of underwear. After three days of hot weather and hard work, the company was getting funky, which made finding a laundry and bath unit a growing necessity.

As difficult as that would be, given the muddled state of affairs among combat service support units, efforts to secure reliable news from the outside world was even more problematical. Division and Corps rear areas were in a state of panic as German civilians ignored their government's call to stay in place and instead, took to the roads leading west. The Office of Public Information, in a less than brilliant move, had taken the Armed Forces Network off the air. Censorship of the BBC and German radio only told the men in Team Yankee that NATO forces were mobilizing and deploying, something they already knew, and that negotiations between NATO and Warsaw Pact representatives were still going on at an undisclosed location. So the men were in the dark, not knowing much more than what was going on within their platoon position and unable to find out from anyone whether they were going to go home tomorrow, or be actors in the first act of World War III. The longer this situation lasted, the more it tended to erode the men's morale.

While there was nothing that Bannon could do about news or settling the dispute that started the whole thing, he and the rest of the Team's leadership could do something about the physical well-being of the men. The first sergeant, Raymond Harrert, had found a gasthaus where the men could wash up and rinse out some underwear. A schedule and transportation had been set up to rotate everyone through the first sergeant's comfort station, now being run by the company supply sergeant. The battalion had switched from a steady diet of dehydrated field rations that came in little brown plastic sacks, called MREs, to two hot meals a day, breakfast and dinner, and only one meal of MREs. A work and training schedule, which would allow theTeam to improve positions, work out any last-minute crew coordination problems, and rest the men had been instituted. In effect, the leadership was keeping their people as busy as possible doing constructive things without wearing them out. This helped somewhat by keeping their minds off the grim situation they were facing while preparing them to meet it. At the moment, it was about all that could be done.

∾

Just as Bannon finished washing up, the first sergeant arrived with breakfast. His arrival at the headquarters position meant that the rest of the Team had finished breakfast, as headquarters tanks and ITVs were always the last to eat. When the men on the position had been served, Harrert, Uleski, and Bannon took turns serving each other breakfast. It was a ritual that was not only sound from a leadership point of view, but it also provided them with an opportunity to gather around the hood of Harrert's jeep, exchange news, update each other on their activities over the past few hours, and coordinate their activities as they ate their cold powdered eggs, rubbery bacon strips, and soggy toast.

Most of the news Harrert had to share with them was bad. The evacuation of dependents, which had started only yesterday, was going slowly. German military and civilian police had set up checkpoints to stem the flow of refugees and clear the autobahns and main roads. The opposite was happening as these check points resulted in monumental traffic jams. Newspapers were scarce, with none making it farther forward than the Division's rear area. Nor was the delivery of mail of any kind sorted yet. Finally, there were no batteries or WD-1 wire to be found anywhere in the brigade.

The good news was limited but welcome. Harrert had located a quartermaster field laundry. At least, he opined, the men would be able to exchange underwear, to which Uleski commented that the Environmental Protection Agency would be glad. The maintenance contact team working for the Team had located a new laser range finder for Alpha 23 and would be up to install it that morning. While only a few problems would be solved, any forward progress was welcomed. The three agreed that, given two more days of peace, the Team would have all the big problems squared away and would be as close to one hundred percent ready as could be expected.

Bannon, Uleski, and Harrert were just finishing up their working breakfast when they were joined by the platoon leaders and the ITV section leader coming up for the 0730 meeting. The group moved over to the PC where Bannon took a seat on the end of the lowered ramp with Harrert and Uleski sitting on either side of him. Without being told, the platoon leaders dropped down on the ground facing the three men, took off their helmets, unbuckled their LBE belts, and pulled out notebooks and pencils. When he saw all were ready, Bannon began.

He didn't get much beyond *good morning* when the first sergeant nudged him and pointed off to the left. "Here comes the Old Man."

Looking over to where Harrert was pointing, Bannon caught sight of the battalion commander's jeep coming up along a logging trail that ran behind the Team's position. One could always tell Lt. Col. George Reynolds's jeep. Four antennas that were never tied down were whipping wildly as the jeep rolled down the trail. The jeep had no top and a big infantry blue license plate mounted on the front fender displaying the silver oak leaf cluster of a lieutenant colonel with a black "6" superimposed on it. This violated every security measure the Army had, but "Blue 6" didn't give a damn. He was the battalion commander, and he wanted to make sure everyone knew it.

Having no wish to keep his platoon leaders standing around waiting, Bannon turned the meeting over to Uleski, telling him to find out what the platoons needed as far as fuel and supplies were concerned before sending them back to their units. With that taken care of, he got up, put on his gear, and walked over to the trail to greet Reynolds.

The jeep hadn't stopped rolling before the colonel jumped out and started heading toward Bannon. They met halfway and exchanged salutes. Instead of "Hi, how are you?" Bannon was greeted with a gruff, "Well Bannon, how are those overpriced rattletraps of yours this morning?"

Ignoring his commanding officer's comment, Bannon smiled. "They're ready to kick ass and take names, sir. When are you going to send me some Russians?"

Falling in on the colonel's left, he and Reynolds walked up to the gathering of platoon leaders despite Bannon's best efforts to steer him clear so that Uleski could go on with the meeting. Everyone stood up, dropping notebooks and maps before scrambling to put their helmets back on. Salutes, greetings, and some one-sided small talk ate up about five minutes before Bannon could pry the colonel off to the side and let Uleski carry on.

As they walked to the tree line overlooking the valley, Bannon informed Reynolds of his intention to replace Garger. Unfortunately, the colonel took the same position that Pierson had. As war was imminent, he felt it wouldn't be a good idea to switch platoon leaders. Undeterred, Bannon went over his reasons and justification as they both watched a two-and a-half-ton truck drive down from the far side of the valley. The fog had cleared by now except along the river. The sun was bright in a cloudless sky and it was getting hot.

The colonel was about to restate his reasons for leaving things as they were when the earsplitting screech of two fast-moving jets flying at treetop level cut him off. Both Bannon and Reynolds turned in the direction of the noise just in time to see two more jets come screaming into the valley from the east, drop lower, and fly up the small valley on the right of the Team's positions. Bannon couldn't identify just what type of aircraft they were as aircraft recognition wasn't one of his strong points. But it wasn't necessary to identify their exact type. A glimpse of the red star on the fuselage told him everything that he needed to know about the two jets.

The waiting was over. The balloon had gone up. Team Yankee was at war.

∽

Despite his best efforts to give the impression that the current situation was nothing to worry about in the days leading up to his departure for the Inter Zonal Boarder that separated East and West Germany, Sean had quietly begun to make sure that his family's affairs were in order. He saw to it that Pat had her emergency evacuation kit ready with food, water, and blankets set aside. To this he added an envelope containing important family documents and a listing of things such as bank account numbers, credit card companies, the addresses of family members in the states and, most important of all, a copy of his most current last will and testament. These efforts, while possibly reassuring to Sean, were disquieting to Pat. But she said nothing, listening intently to Sean's instructions while silently praying that none of what she was hearing was going to be necessary.

Pat had known it would be Sean's last night home when he came in, for in his eyes she saw a look of disbelief that the unfolding crisis had reached a critical and unavoidable impasse. She saw the same thing in her own eyes every time she looked in the mirror. When little Sean ran up to his father, rather than taking him to bed, Sean carried him over to the sofa, pulled out the family album, and began to leaf slowly through the pages. The two sat there quietly looking at the pictures until little Sean fell asleep. It was with great reluctance that Sean put his son to bed where he lingered for the longest time. When he finally did come out of his children's room, his eyes were red and moist. For a moment he looked at Pat, then simply said that he was going to go to bed. Pat went with him.

Not long after they had gone to bed, the phone in the other room rang. Sean was up and out in a flash, as if he had never gone to sleep but had been lying there waiting for the call. When he came back, Pat watched him for a moment in the shadows of the dark bedroom as he gathered up his uniform and boots. When she spoke, she startled him. "Are you going in already?"

"Yes. Gotta. Wouldn't look good for the CO to be late, would it?"

"Will you be home for breakfast?"

"No."

"Should I hold supper for you tonight?"

"No."

With that, Pat knew. And Sean knew Pat knew. After eight years of marriage, it's hard to hide secrets, and even harder to hide feelings. Sean didn't even try. Coming over to the bed, he sat next to his wife. "Pat, the battalion is moving to the border in an hour. I don't know when we'll be back."

"Is everyone going?"

"Everyone. The NATO ministers and their governments are mobilizing. Everyone is going, including you."

"Are they really going to evacuate?"

"Starting this morning at 0900. It's no great secret. It was going to be announced later today anyway."

As he finished dressing, Pat also dressed. There was much to do. Sean was in the children's bedroom by the time she'd finished. Pausing in the door of their bedroom, she watched him for a moment before heading off to the kitchen where she fixed a bag lunch for him. As she was finishing it, all the restraint she had exercised thus far, and all her efforts to see Sean off with a cheery face and smile collapsed. She began to cry. Her husband was going out the door in a minute to fight World War III, and all she could do for him was fix him a bag lunch.

First Battle

Both Colonel Reynolds and Captain Bannon stood there transfixed, staring at the point where the two Russian jets had disappeared up the valley. Bannon's mind was almost numb. He kept trying to convince himself that maybe he hadn't really seen two Russian jets, that maybe he was mistaken. It had to be a mistake, he told himself. "*We can't really be at war. That isn't possible. We can't.*"

As if in response to Bannon's desperate effort to deny the reality of their situation, a crash and rumble like distant thunder rolled over them, causing the two commanders snapped their heads back toward the east. From where they stood, they could only see the hill across the valley. But neither man needed to see beyond that to know what the distant noise was. An endless chain of distant crashes and rumblings caused by hundreds of guns could only be the Soviets' preparatory bombardment on the cavalry's forward positions.

Bannon turned and looked at the colonel who continued to stare east as if he were trying to see through the hill across from them. The numbness and shock Bannon had felt was giving way to a sickening, sinking feeling. They had failed. The primary purpose of the US Army in Europe was to prevent war. Deterrence. That's what was supposed to happen. But it had failed. Something terrible had gone wrong, and they, NATO, the United States, the United States Army, his unit, and he had failed. Now they had to fight. They were at war. And at that moment, Bannon felt very alone, very unsure of himself, and very scared.

Eventually Reynolds turned toward Bannon and took to regarding him with an expression that betrayed nothing. If he were feeling the same things, he wasn't showing it. Reynolds, on the other hand, saw the shock and uncertainty on Bannon's face. He had seen that very same look before, in Vietnam, so Bannon's reactions didn't surprise him.

"Well, Captain, let's see if those buckets of bolts you always brag about are worth the money the government spent on them," he muttered in same gravely tone of voice he often used when addressing a subordinate. "Get your company in MOPP level II, standby to occupy your fighting positions, and stay on the net, but don't call me unless you need to. I expect the cavalry will come screaming back through that passage point like a whipped dog. Be ready to cover them and get them out of the way as fast as you can. Any questions?"

Bannon took in what the colonel was saying. What was there to question? This was what all the training was about. All their preparations were for this moment. Now all they had to do was put it into action. "No, sir, no questions."

"Well then, get moving and good hunting." Without waiting for a response, the colonel pivoted sharply on his heels and began to move back to his jeep with a quick, purposeful pace. He did not look back. Reynolds was setting the example, one he expected Bannon to follow.

As Bannon turned back toward the PC where he had left the platoon leaders, a new series of artillery concentrations could be heard impacting closer to the Team's positions. Additional Soviet artillery units were joining in, hitting the cavalry's rear positions. The latest series were coming down just behind the hill on the other side of the valley.

"Hell, the colonel could be cool and walk," Bannon muttered to himself. "This is my first war and I damn sure don't care about impressing anyone with my calm right now." With that thought in mind, he broke out into a slow run, weapon, protective mask, and canteen bouncing and banging against his body as he trotted through the trees to the PC.

As he neared the PC, Bannon could see the platoon leaders, Uleski, and the first sergeant watching the colonel's jeep go tearing down the logging trail, throwing up stones and disappearing in a cloud of dust. They too had heard the jets and the artillery and understood what they meant. Upon seeing them, Bannon slowed down to a walk, caught his breath, and moved up to them before they had a chance to shift their attention away from the cloud of dust kicked up by the colonel's jeep and over to him.

"All right, this is it," he snapped crisply in a tone of voice he hoped came across as being calm and confident. "The Russians are laying into the cavalry. When Ivan finishes with them, we're next. I want everyone in MOPP level II. Leave the nets over your tracks but clear them away from the front so that they can quickly move forward into their fighting positions. First Sergeant, take the PC and fire team from the Mech Platoon that are designated to man the passage point and get down there. Lieutenant U, you'll stay up here with the ITVs and fight them with 2nd Platoon if necessary. I'm going to move my tank down to the right of 3rd Platoon and fight from there. Other than that, we do it the way we've trained and planned. Stay off the air unless you have something really critical to report. Anyone have any questions?"

He looked into each man's eyes, just as the colonel had done to him. He saw the same dark thoughts he had reflected in their expressions. Only the first sergeant, also a Vietnam vet, wore the stern, no-nonsense look he always did. For a few moments there was silence, broken only by the continuous crash and rumble of the artillery in the distance. "All right, let's move out and make it happen." Without waiting for a response, Bannon turned and began to head slowly towards his tank. As the colonel had done for him, he was setting the example for his people. He suspected that they would do the same with their tank commanders, and their TCs would, in turn, get their people moving. At least, that's what he hoped would be happening.

∽

The drumbeat of Soviet artillery continued unabated in the distance, growing louder but less intense. The Russian gun crews had to have been getting tired of humping rounds by now, Bannon thought, for the rate of fire was slowing down. The distant rumble was joined by the noise of Team Yankee coming to life. The PC's driver cranked up its engine, revved it, and began raising the rear ramp. The crews of the ITVs and Alpha 66 were also cranking up their engines.

As he neared 66, Bannon could see Sgt. Robert Folk, his gunner, in the cupola. Folk had his combat vehicle crewman's helmet, or CVC, on and was manning the M2 machinegun, ready for action. Bannon tried to yell to him to dismount with the rest of the crew so they could tear down the net. The noise of the engine, the muffling of outside noise through his CVC, and Folk's preoccupation with trying to see what was going on to his front frustrated Bannon's efforts. It wasn't until he started climbing up onto the front right fender that Folk noticed his commander was calling out to him. Cocking his CVC off to one side in order to hear, Folk leaned forward.

"We need to get this net off!" Bannon called out over the whine of the tank's turbine engine. "You and Kelp get out here and help me with it. We're moving." Without waiting for a response, Bannon dropped back down to the ground again and began to pull down the support poles and spreaders that held the net up as Folk took off his CVC, leaned over toward the loader's hatch, and, with his left hand, slapped Kelp, the loader, on top of his CVC.

Popping his head up through the open hatch, Kelp looked over at Folk. Folk, in turn, pointed to Bannon who had already begun tearing down the net. Getting the message, Kelp also removed his CVC and climbed out to help.

"Let's get this net down and stowed, just like we do during training," Bannon called out as the two crewmen joined him. "Only let's do it a little faster this time, OK?" Neither man answered him as he saw the expression on their faces was little different than the stunned disbelief he'd seen on his platoon leaders' faces.

Folk dropped to the ground and circled the tank, pulling up the net's stakes as he went. Kelp started to pull down the supports and spreaders that were resting on the tank, taking care to keep the collapsing net from draping over the tank's nine hundred plus degree exhaust and melting it. With the stakes out and the poles down, the hard part began. The net caught on everything, including the crewmen taking it down. Tugging seldom did any good. One had to find what the net was caught on, pull it free, and roll it up until it caught again. Trying to hurry only seemed to make it worse. Despite the delays, the crew finally gathered the net up into a pile on the bustle rack and secured it. They hadn't done the neatest job of stowing it, but it was probably one of the fastest.

Before they climbed in, Bannon told his crew to pull their chemical protective suits on. This was MOPP level II. As Folk and Kelp dug their suits out of their duffle bags, Bannon walked forward to the driver's compartment and told Pfc. Joseph Ortelli, the driver, to climb out and get his suit on. As Ortelli reached over to kill the engine, Bannon stopped him, not wanting to run the risk of screwing something up. The last thing he needed was a tank that wouldn't restart. It was running, and at the moment he didn't want to mess with anything that was working properly.

As Bannon pulling his own chemical suit on, he noticed his crew was watching him. This caused him to slow down some. In part he didn't want to fumble and fall. That would have been more than embarrassing, for like the platoon leaders, they were taking their cue off of him. He had always been told that calm, like panic, was contagious. Now was a good time to find out. Besides, it had been a long time since they had trained in their chemical protective clothing and he had to figure out where all the snaps and ties went. The heavy protective clothing was a necessary evil of modern war.

When Bannon was finished, he turned to Folk. "We ready to roll, Sergeant Folk?"

Folk looked at him for a moment and blink as his expression softened a tad. "Yes, sir. We're ready."

"Are all weapons loaded and on safe?" Bannon's second question caused the relaxed look to be replaced by one of embarrassment as both Folk and Kelp stopped pulling at their suits and looked at each other. "I take it that that's a big negative on my last question."

Sheepishly, Folk replied that it hadn't occurred to him to do so because they were in an assembly area with cavalry still out in front. All the range safety briefings and all the times the men had been harangued about keeping weapons clear and elevated except when on a live fire range were coming home to haunt them. Bannon couldn't blame his crew. It was their first battle. He could only expect them to do what they were taught in training, no better, no worse, for soldiers rarely rise to the occasion. Rather, they default to their training. In the case of Alpha 66's crew, and the rest of Team Yankee for that matter, while the training had been good, it had been conducted under peacetime conditions, conditions that were now a thing of the past.

Stopping for a moment, Bannon leaned back on the side of the turret and looked at his crew. "Alright, guys, here it is. We really are at war. I don't know what's happening yet, but from the sound of that artillery, you can bet the Russians are letting the cavalry have it. The cavalry is out there to buy us some time and let us get our shit together. That's what they get paid for. When the Russians finish with the cavalry, we're next. What I want you to do is to calm down and start thinking. Remember what we did in training and do it now. Only think! There are a couple of habits we picked up in training that you're going to have to forget about. Do you understand what I'm saying?"

With a nod and a glance sideways at each other, they gave their tank and team commander a subdued but nervous, "Yes, sir."

"Alright, finish getting your suits on. We're going to move over to the right of 3rd Platoon and take up a position there. If nobody has any questions, let's get moving."

By the time the crew of 66 was finished and mounted, the rest of the crews and tracks in the headquarters position were ready. The first sergeant, having taken over the headquarters PC, had already pulled out of position and was moving down the logging trail with his jeep following. Bannon also noticed all the tracks around him, and more than likely elsewhere, were running. As the cavalry's covering force battle would last for hours, possibly even as long as a day, there was no sense in leaving the tanks running. All that would do was burn diesel, something the M-1 Abrams was very good at, and create a tremendous thermal signature, another unhealthy trait the M-1 was guilty of. The savings in diesel would be worth a small violation of radio listening silence. Besides, it might be good for the leadership of the Team to hear their commander's voice as well as give him a quick shot of confidence by seeing if they were on the ball and listening. Unless the Soviet radio direction-finding detachments were fast, Bannon figured it would do little, if any harm.

Checking first the remote box to ensure that the radio was set on the Team net, Bannon keyed the radio and paused for a moment to let the radio's small cooling fan come up to speed. "ALL BRAVO 3 ROMEO ELEMENTS, THIS IS ROMEO 25. IT'S GOING TO BE A WHILE BEFORE THOSE OTHER PEOPLE GET HERE. SHUT DOWN AND SETTLE DOWN. CHECK YOUR SYSTEMS AND LOCK AND LOAD. ACKNOWLEDGE, OVER."

One by one, the platoons checked in and acknowledged. Uleski, in Alpha 55, simply stood up in its cupola, turned toward 66, and waved, indicating that he understood. The ITVs did not respond but shut down. With nothing more to do there, Bannon turned around in the cupola and faced to the rear. Locking the push-to-talk switch on his CVC back so he could talk to the driver on the intercom while hanging on with both hands, Bannon began to back the tank onto the logging trail. As he leaned over to the right side of the cupola, watching the right rear fender as 66 moved back, Kelp popped out of the loader's hatch and leaned over to the left, watching the left rear fender. Once on the trail, the tank made a pivot turn to the right and started forward and toward 3rd Platoon.

∾

The drive down to 3rd Platoon was a short one, only about 700 meters. But it felt good to be in the tank and moving. Standing in the TC's hatch of a tank, rolling down a road or cross-country was always an exhilarating experience for Bannon. He never tired of the thrill. Despite all the pain, misery, and headaches a tank could inflict upon its crew, it was fun being a tanker. It was the little joys in life that kept a soldier like Bannon going, and right now he was in desperate need of a little joy.

As they moved along the trail, he kept an eye to the left, catching an occasional glimpse of the 3rd Platoon tanks. Their nets were still up but were propped up clear of the exhaust as well as the tank's primary sight. When 66 passed the last of 3rd Platoon's tanks, Bannon ordered Ortelli to turn left into the forest and move down a small trail cut by a combat engineer vehicle that had dug the Team's positions. As they had not planned to fight from here, 66 was taking one of the alternate firing positions from Alpha 33, now to their immediate left at about seventy-five meters. 33 would now have only its primary position to fire from and one alternate firing position to its left. 66 would not have an alternate. If 66 were detected and fired upon while in this position, the best Bannon could do would be to blow smoke grenades, back out of sight, and hope that whoever was shooting at them gave up before 66 crept forward and reoccupied the same firing position.

Unlike the other tanks in the team, rather than stay back and hide in the forest, Bannon decided to ease 66 into its firing position. From there he would be able to observe the village, the valley, and the hills across the valley. The walled farm just off to the team's extreme right was the only key piece of terrain he could not see. Satisfied with his position, he ordered Ortelli to shut the engine down and to get out with Kelp to cut some foliage and drape it across the tank as camouflage. In his place, Folk came up to the TC's position to man the M2 and monitor the radio while the rest of the crew were on the ground.

Using an ax, Ortelli began to cut some branches as Kelp and Bannon draped the camouflage net over the rear of the turret and back deck without putting up the supports or stake it down. All Bannon wanted to do was to break up some of the tank's outline. Finished with the net, the two of them began to place the branches dragged over by Ortelli on the side and front of the tank not covered by the net. They were careful to ensure that the gunners' primary sight was not blocked and that the turret could be traversed some without knocking off the foliage or snagging the net.

When they'd done as much as they could, Bannon stepped back a few meters to view their handiwork. To his eye, Alpha 66 looked like a tank covered with branches. Someone looking hard would be able to see it, no doubt about that. But, with a little luck and some harassment from the air defense artillery, any Russian pilot zooming about overhead would be moving too fast to take a hard look. Satisfied that they had done the best they could, the crew remounted and waited.

With nothing else to do for the moment, Bannon took off his CVC, laid it down on top of the turret and stood upright as he took to watching to the east. With the radio turned up so he could hear any traffic being passed, he began to listen to the noise of the battle to his front.

The rumble of impacting artillery had been joined by new sounds, chief among them was the faint crack of high velocity tank cannons firing. The cavalry, no doubt, was now fully engaged, returning artillery and tank fire. That meant the enemy was out in the open and coming on. With no way of finding out what was going on out there if he kept his radio on the team net and aux receiver on the battalion command net, Bannon was half tempted to switch his auxiliary radio receiver over to the cavalry's frequency. But doing so would have meant leaving either the battalion or the team net. Were he still up on the headquarters position, that would not have been a problem since Uleski would have been close enough to monitor the net he wasn't. After mulling the problem over without coming up with a solution, Bannon resigned himself to the fact that until the battalion started to pass information down, if they ever got around to doing so, he would just have to be like a mushroom and stay in the dark. Besides, at the moment, he felt it was more important to be near 3rd Platoon and listening to the team's command net just in case Garger had forgotten that morning's lesson on radio listening silence.

Now the waiting began. It wasn't even 0830 yet. The last hour had gone fast but had been emotionally draining. Everything had changed that morning. Wars, once started, take on a life of their own. What occurs and how they end are seldom controllable by either side. World War I, World War II, Korea, and Vietnam all took twists and turns no one foresaw. Bannon had no reason to doubt that despite all the planning and training that had gone into preparing for World War III, it wasn't going to be any different. Those thoughts were disquieting. His mind needed to be diverted to something less ominous and more comprehensible.

After pulling on his CVC, muffling most of the noise of the unseen covering force battle, he locked the push-to-talk switch back into the intercom position. "Gunner, have you run a computer check yet this morning?"

"No, sir, we haven't."

"Well, let's make sure we don't get any surprises whenever Ivan gets it in his head to pay us a visit. I intend to go home a veteran and collect some of those benefits Congress is always boasting they provide. How about you, Kelp?"

Kelp stood on the turret floor and looked up out of the opened loader's hatch at Bannon with a grin. "I'm with you. My uncle was in Nam. He's always tellin' me how rough it was. By the time we get done kickin' Russian ass, I'll be able to tell 'em what a real war was like."

Bannon left the CVC keyed to the intercom position so that the rest of the crew could hear their conversation. "Well, if Ortelli can keep this beast running, and Sergeant Folk can hit the targets I find him, you and I should do pretty well, Kelp." Both Ortelli and Folk chimed in, vowing that they were going to be the ones waiting for Bannon and Kelp. After a couple more minutes of banter, when Bannon judged that they were in a more settled state of mind, he started them on the crew checklist. With great deliberateness, he went down the checklist, item by item, watching as the crewman responsible for each item performed it. In the process, he began to feel more comfortable as he saw the initial shock slowly fade. By the time they were done, he was able to relax, both physically and mentally, for the first time that day.

Bannon took his CVC off again. To his front, off in the distance he could see pillars of black smoke rising in the sky, joining together high above the horizon before drifting away to the east. Burning tanks. There were a lot of them. No doubt about that. Hundreds of gallons of diesel, together with ammunition, rubber, oil, and the other burnable material on a tank provides plenty of fuel when a penetrating round finds its mark and turns even the most sophisticated combat vehicle into nothing more than a funeral pyre for its crew.

The noise of the battle was more varied now. The initial massive bombardment was replaced by irregular spasms of artillery fire as the artillery batteries shifted their fires to hit targets of opportunity as they presented themselves. The sharp cracks, booms, and reports of tank cannon fire were suddenly trumped by the thunderous crash of an artillery unit firing all its guns simultaneously, leaving Bannon to wonder how long the cavalry could maintain the tempo of the battle they were involved in.

Modern war consumes ammunition, material, and, worst of all, men at a frightening rate. Rapid-fire tank cannons, coupled with sophisticated computerized fire control systems and laser range finders were capable of firing up to eight aimed rounds per minute at tank sized targets at ranges in excess of 2,000 meters. Guided munitions, fired from ground mounts, vehicle launchers, or helicopters had a better than ninety percent probability of hitting a target up to 3,000 meters. Soviet multiple rocket launchers and US MLRSs could fire numerous rockets in a single volley that were capable of destroying everything within a one-by-one kilometer grid. And then there were the chemical agents produced by the Soviets, lethal concoctions capable of penetrating exposed skin and attacking the body's nervous system, crippling the victim within seconds and killing him in minutes. In the wake of World War II, all the implements of war had become more capable, more deadly. All were designed to rip, crush, cripple, dismember, incapacitate, and kill men faster and more efficiently. In all the armies arrayed across the continent, the only thing technology had not improved was the ability of the human body to absorb punishment.

Such thoughts were disquieting. The mind, left free, tends to wander into what might be and what could happen, as frightening to Bannon as the Ghost of Christmas to Come was to Scrooge. A diversion from these thoughts came from the east.

Two dots, growing rapidly into aircraft, came screaming toward the small valley from the east just as the others had this morning. Bannon hoped the Team would abide by the standard operating procedures, or SOP, and not engage them unless attacked. With only machineguns, they stood little chance of hitting fast-moving jets. The only thing that would be accomplished by opening up on them, if in fact they were Soviet, would be to give away the Team's positions.

It was a Stinger team somewhere in the cavalry's sector, however, that rose to the challenge, engaging them with two missiles. Fascinated, Bannon watched as the white smoke trail of the Stinger surface-to-air antiaircraft missiles raced up after the second jet. But it did not find its mark. The Soviet pilot popped small decoy flares and made a hard turn and dive. The missile detonated harmlessly in midair as the second jet turned to rejoin the first before both disappeared up the small valley. This reprieve was short lived as the ripping chainsaw-like report of a Vulcan 20-millimeter antiaircraft gun somewhere behind the Team's position revealed that problems for the Russian pilots were just starting. Unlike earlier in the morning, the air defense system was now alert and in action.

As if to underscore that point, two more dots emerged from the east. Apparently the Soviet Air Force was fond of this approach and were sending their aircraft through four at a time. Their heavy use of the small valley cost them this time. Two more Stinger missiles raced up to greet the next pair of Soviet jets. The pilot of the trail jet in this pair was not as quick or as lucky as the other pilots had been, for one of the Stingers managed to find its mark. With a flash and a puff of white smoke, the missile detonated, causing the jet to tumble over as if kicked from behind before disintegrating in a rolling orange ball of fire. Alerted to the danger, the first jet kicked in his afterburners, dropped lower, and kept flying west toward the waiting Vulcan.

Kelp, who had been watching the engagement, let out an "Ah, neat! Hey, Sarge, you missed it!" as if he were watching Fourth of July fireworks instead of the destruction of a pilot and a multimillion dollar aircraft. Kelp then described, in his own colorful way, the engagement to Folk. As Bannon reflected on Kelp's reaction, he, too, had to admit that it had been kind of neat.

∾

The announcement concerning the evacuation of dependents aired repeatedly on AFN TV before the network went off the air the morning 1st of the 4th Armor moved out of garrison and into its local dispersal areas. AFN radio, which stayed on the air, yielded little in the way of news or information Pat Bannon and other wives like her could use other than they were to standby to be evacuated. About the only thing it did provide concerned the closing of the commissary and the PX as well as repeated calls for all US military family members living off post to move onto US installations.

Pat was in the midst of going over her own preparations for the umpteenth time when Fran Wilson, the wife of the commander of 1st of the 4th Armor's Charlie Company, came over later in the morning. With no children of her own to distract her, Fran explained she needed to be with someone. "Sitting alone, waiting for word to leave is driving me crazy."

"I know what you mean," Pat replied sympathetically. "Between the children and the lack of any news worthy of the name, I'm half way there myself."

"If that's the case, do you mind terribly if I join you as we go crazy together?" Fran muttered half-jokingly.

"You're more than welcome. After all, misery enjoys company."

It was Fran's appearance that caused Pat to remember that Sue Garger, the wife of one of Sean's platoon leaders, was still staying in a German gasthaus in town. The Gargers, who had been in country for less than a month, had been waiting for quarters and the arrival of their car in Bremerhaven when the crisis had erupted. With children to look after and the need to keep near the phone as things steadily went from bad to worse, she had managed but a single quick visit with Sue. Afraid that the young woman might not have heard the news or, because she was new to the unit, might have been overlooked by the battalion NEO officer, Pat decided to check up on the young woman herself by calling the number listed for Garger on Sean's alert roster. The resulting call turned out to be a rather disjointed affair as Pat attempted to explain to the German who answered who she was and what she wanted using what little German she'd learned in high school from her Pennsylvania Dutch German teacher.

Eventually she did manage to get her message across, despite a number of mistranslations that caused Fran to laugh for the first time in days. When Sue finally did come to the phone, Pat could tell the young wife was just as lonely and nervous as the rest of them. Without the need to give the matter a moment's thought, she informed Sue to pack a bag. "You're staying with me until this thing blows over." With that, Pat left Fran to watch the children and headed off post.

The first obstacle she ran into was at the entrance to the housing area where an MP roadblock had been set up. Hailed down, she was informed by a young MP who came across as being just as nervous as she was that military dependents were not allowed to leave the area. When she tried to explain to him that she had to pick up a wife who was living in town, the MP held his ground, insisting that she turn around and go back. Pat, being the kind of woman who took great pleasure in defying nonsensical bureaucratic rules overseas dependents such as she were expected to adhere whenever they got in her way, decided to escalate the confrontation by informing the private she wished to speak to his superior.

Not used to being challenged by a dependent wife, and at a loss as to how best to handle this situation, the MP decided it was best if he allowed his sergeant to deal with the obnoxious woman. The sergeant, naturally, repeated the demand that Pat turn around at once and go home. "I'm sorry, miss, you can't go off post."

Having learned that there were ways of dropping Sean's rank without coming across as being a pushy bitch, Pat played her trump card. "Sergeant, like I explained to the other MP, the wife of one of my husband's platoon leaders is at a gasthaus in town and has no way of getting in. I'm simply going to get her. Now, unless you or your commander are willing to fetch her yourself, I have no choice but to do so myself."

The sergeant thought about this a moment before telling Pat to wait while he checked with his platoon leader. After a few minutes, he came back and informed her she was to go straight to the gasthaus, pick up the woman, and come straight back. "Don't stop for anyone or anything, lady. And make sure you check back with me when you return." Both the NCO's tone of voice and the precautions he took before letting her go, which included taking her name, her husband's name and unit, the make and model of the car, its license number, and someone the MPs could contact in case she didn't return in a reasonable period of time worried Pat, leaving her to wonder if this was such a good idea. But she was committed, and Sue Garger was depending on her.

As it turned out, the rush to fetch Sue Garger turned out to be unnecessary, for the old Army rule of hurry up and wait was just as applicable to military families as it was for their husbands. When it became apparent to Cathy Hall, the wife of 1st of the 4th Armor's battalion commander and Sean's peacetime superior, that they would not be evacuated for some time, she took it upon herself to call around and check on the battalion's wives and pass on whatever information she had. This included an admission by someone in the administration back in Washington that it felt there was a need to maintain the appearance of normalcy for as long as possible in order to give diplomacy a chance to work. So the evacuation of dependents was being delayed for as long as possible, causing some of the older wives to compare that decision to the Iranian hostage crisis, where the families were pulled out of Tehran only at the last minute and in great haste. Pat, in particular, was not at all pleased that she and her children were being kept in place just for appearances, but like Cathy Hall, she kept her own council. Grousing over the stupidity of such a move at a time when everyone's nerves were on edge, she reasoned, would do no one any good.

As that first day wore on and it became apparent that the families were not going to go anytime soon, the wives began to visit each other and let the children out to play. In the midst of this forced calm, Cathy Hall put out the word that she was going to host a potluck dinner for the battalion wives. Most of them, with children in tow, showed up. And even though the conversations were guarded and there was a pall on the whole affair, anything was better than sitting alone and worrying, proving there was some comfort in collective misery.

As the days wore on Pat, like most of the other wives, began to suffer from physical and mental exhaustion as more and more dependents whose husbands were part of Sean's company began to come to her seeking help, company, and solace. With no husband to help her along or buoy her flagging spirits, the pressure on her began to build. Pressure to be mother and father. Pressure to set the example for Sue and the other wives. Pressure to make sure all was ready to go the second word came. Pressure to keep from giving in and curling up in a corner and crying.

The most difficult demand she had to deal with was helping the children through it all. Sean had always been around whenever there had been a big crisis in the family, or a major decision needed to be made. Even when the battalion was in the field, he could always be reached by phone in an emergency. But now he was gone and unable to help with the biggest crisis Pat had ever faced. Having Sue Garger staying with her did help after she'd calmed down some. But Sue was even more lost than Pat, for she was new to the Army and its ways. So Pat found herself with no choice but to bottle up her fears and apprehensions and continued to stumble along the dark and twisting trail she now found herself on alone.

The second day dragged along like the first. AFN TV came back on but spent most of the time making public service announcements and broadcasting news that really didn't tell anyone anything. Even when it wasn't broadcasting public service announcements, somehow the idea of watching television shows that were months old seemed annoyingly odd. Rain in the afternoon only made the dark and apprehensive mood of the community worse.

It wasn't until that evening that official word and instructions for the evacuation of the community finally came down. When it did, it was like a vent had been opened, relieving some of the pressure that had been building up. At least now they knew for sure they would be going and had a rough idea of when. For the sixth time in two days, Pat went over the evacuation kit that had been sitting by the door. Blankets, food, water, cups, diapers, a small first-aid kit, a change of clothes for the boys, two for Sarah, a pocket knife, coloring books for the children, and other such essentials sat packed and ready to go.

All that remained now was to tell the children, a task Pat dreaded. She had put this off for as long as possible in the hope that some sanity would prevail and the whole affair would blow over. But there was no more putting it off. Before putting them to bed, she gathered them on little Sean's bed and sat down with them. She told them that tomorrow they were going to leave Germany and visit Grandma's. Kurt, a happy child who took life at face value, was overcome with joy. He jumped up and down and began to ask what toys he could take. Sarah simply looked at Pat and tried to say Grandma, a word she had heard but could not associate with an object since she had never seen her grandparents.

As anticipated, little Sean, a quiet child who thought things through before speaking, was proving to be the tough case. His first question was about his father, "Is Daddy coming with us?"

"No, Daddy's not coming with us."

"Why?"

"Daddy has to stay here and work. Remember I told you he went to the field? Well, he is still in the field with his company. He can't come with us this time."

"When will we see Daddy again?"

"Daddy will come and join us when he is finished in the field."

"When will that be?"

Exasperated by this line of questioning, Pat hesitated. She felt sorry for the boy. He was old enough to understand some of what was going on, but not yet able to make any sense of it all. That, and the way his line of questions heightened her own fears and apprehensions made their pending departure all the more difficult for Pat to come to terms with. Before she lost her restraint and began to cry, she cut short the question-and-answer period and told Sean that his father would be home as soon as he could. Though she could see it didn't satisfy him, it was the best she could do.

The morning continued with little change. The heat of the day was turning the tank into an oven. The chemical suits only made things worse. When it became clear they were in no immediate danger of attack, Bannon began to rotate his crew, letting two of them dismount at a time to stretch, smoke, cool off, and eat. During his break he walked over to check on Alpha 33, the tank nearest 66. Its TC was also rotating his crew out. Just after noon, Polgar came over to 66 from Mech Platoon's mounted element to report.

Bannon and Polgar were still conversing when they were joined by the battalion commander and S-3 who came rolling up the logging trail in the M-113 they operated out of during operations. Apparently, they were as bored as Bannon was and were getting a little antsy with nothing to do but listen to their radios, and wait. While the colonel went to visit his Mech Platoon on foot, the S-3, Maj. Frank Jordan, brought Bannon up to speed on the status of the covering force battle.

The cavalry was taking a beating and wouldn't last much longer. They'd managed to annihilate the Soviet recon element and had brought the first attacking echelon to a standstill, badly weakening it in the process. But they had paid for that success, as the parade of ambulances and evacuation of damaged vehicles coming down the opposite hill, through the village, and into the small valley to the rear indicated. As a result, brigade was anticipating a passage of lines sometime in the late afternoon. The cavalry wanted to hold on until night in order to withdraw under the cover of darkness, but Jordan informed Bannon he didn't think they'd be able to. Not long after sharing this news, the colonel rejoined Jordan and Bannon, made some small talk, and then left with the S-3.

Rather than waiting out the afternoon doing nothing, Bannon decided to follow Reynolds' example and visit the platoons to show his face, check on them to see how they were adapting to war, and to pass the word to be prepared for the passage of the cavalry. He told Folk where he was going to be and, if a call came in on the battalion net, drop to the company net and tell the XO to respond if he hadn't already done so. With helmet, pistol, and LBE, Bannon set out on his tour on foot.

As he had that morning, Bannon went from tank to tank, working his way to those elements on the left first. When he reached Alpha 31, Bannon went over the information that had been passed to him before reviewing the status of 3rd Platoon with Garger. This was followed by a review of the Team's and the platoon's responsibilities and actions during the passage and the conduct of the defense. To Bannon's surprise, Garger was able to go over each phase of the pending operations as well as each and every action his platoon was responsible for in detail and without hesitation. Either Pierson had been working overtime with the lieutenant, Bannon thought to himself, or the boy was catching on. Regardless of how this transformation had come about, Bannon was satisfied the young officer had the concept of the operation straight in his mind and was as ready as any of them were to carry it out. There was still the question, however, of whether he would be able to when the shit actually did hit the spinning propellers.

Satisfied all was as well as could be expected with the 3rd Platoon, Bannon continued on his rounds. Even in the shade of the forest, tromping up the hill in the chemical protective suit and the floppy, loose fitting chemical overshoes was brutal. By the time he reached the XO's tank, he was in need of a rest and a long, cool drink of water. As he settled down in the shade next to Alpha 55, Uleski reached down and handed him a can of Coke, a cold can of Coke. Not only did Bannon have no idea where it could possibly have come from, at that moment he had no wish to find out, for the answer to that question would more than likely entail something that was highly unauthorized.

After deciding it would be best if he set aside his curiosity over how his XO was able to chill cans of soda in the field, Bannon went over the Team's responsibilities during the passage of lines and when the Soviets finally got around to attacking them. Uleski, as the team's executive officer, would have to be able to fight the Team within the framework of the battalion's battle plan effectively if Bannon became combat ineffective, a subtle way of saying wounded or killed. Neither gave that grim possibility a second's thought, for both had been trained from Day One in the Army that everyone was expendable and replaceable. While it was not a comforting thought, it was part of the job and, in theory at least, universally understood.

Finishing with Uleski, Bannon toyed with the idea of letting the XO go over to 2nd Platoon to check on them and pass on the word about the cavalry. It was tempting. But 2nd Platoon was the one platoon he had not seen that morning. It was only proper that an effort should be made to pay a quick visit to them in order to show the flag.

As with 3rd Platoon, Bannon stopped at each tank, checked on their readiness, and exchanged small talk he hoped did something to ease the nervous tension every member of Team Yankee he came across was doing his best to hide. When he reached the platoon leader's tank, Bannon passed on word about the cavalry and reviewed the Team and platoon plan with him. No sooner had they finished then the hills across the valley erupted in a thunderclap of explosions and flames, heralding the commitment of the Soviet's second echelon. It would not be long now, Bannon reasoned as he tromped on back to 66 as fast as his floppy chemical overshoes would let him. His first battle, a term that had become as trite and over used as his own personal motto, *Steel on Target*, which he used to annoy Reynolds with every chance he had, was upon him.

∽

Just as Major Jordan had predicted, the cavalry had not lasted as long as had been expected. The fresh battalions of the Soviet's second echelon broke the worn and severely weakened cavalry like a dry twig. Thirty minutes after it had struck, it was obvious that the covering force battle was over, and the time had come for the cavalry to pass through the Team's positions. The lazy, boring late morning and early afternoon gave way to a steady buildup of tension as the cavalry began the process of handing off the battle.

The first elements to reach the passage point were the cavalry's support elements; medical, maintenance, and supply vehicles. These were followed by artillery units and squadron headquarters elements. The passage was not the neat parade like processions practiced during training. Vehicles would come down singly, in pairs, sometimes in groups as large as fifteen. Some were dragging damaged vehicles. Others limped along, wobbling on blown out tires like drunks. All showed some sign of damage. Trucks had their canvas tops shredded. Tracked vehicles that had had gear stowed on the outside now had it scrambled and tossed about on top, with articles of clothing and shreds of canvas and camouflage nets hanging from the sides. There were even a couple of trucks running on tire rims, unable or unwilling to stop to change tires. If there was any semblance of order to the cavalry unit passing through the Team, it was not evident from where Bannon was watching.

In the midst of the passage, a scout helicopter, followed by two attack helicopters, came weaving down through the valley from the north. The three slowed to a hover just in front of the Team's positions, with the scout across from Alpha 66 and an AH-1 Cobra attack helicopter on either side. The OH-58 scout slowly rose until it was just barely peering over the trees on the opposite hill. Its tail-boom moved slowly left, then right, as its observer scanned the landscape on the other side of the hill. Like a bird dog alerting, the scout suddenly froze, pointing to the northeast. The Cobra on the left then rose slowly to treetop level, hovered there for a moment, orienting in the same direction as the scout. With a flash and streak of white smoke, the Cobra let fly a TOW antitank missile. Both Cobra and scout remained in place for about fifteen seconds, then dropped down and flew a few hundred meters north to another position, preparing to fire again.

The second Cobra rose into position as soon as the first had fired. It also fired, remained locked on target for about fifteen seconds before dropping down and moving to another position just as the first had done. By that time, the first Cobra was ready to pop up from his new position and fire again. After each Cobra had fired two TOWs, they flew back up the valley behind their scout to find a new firing position.

The realization that the Soviet lead elements were now close enough to be engaged by TOWs from across the valley startled Bannon. That meant that the enemy was now within five kilometers. To add weight to that point, friendly artillery from a unit behind the Team's position came whistling overhead to the east. Once more adrenalin started to pump through Bannon's veins as the first undamaged cavalry combat vehicles came racing down off the opposite hill. M-1 tanks and M-3 Bradley cavalry vehicles, mixed together, their guns to the rear and their orange identification panels flapping as they moved, came rolling through the lanes marked in the Team's minefields and into the village.

The ordeal for the cavalry wasn't over yet. As the first vehicles entered the village, the streets erupted into a ball of flames and explosions. The Soviets were dumping at least a battalion's worth of artillery against the town in an effort to extract one last modicum of vengeance on the retreating cavalry. This initial impact was followed by a steady drumbeat of artillery as a new volley slammed home every few seconds. Bannon had no idea of the caliber of rounds they were using or how many were impacting. Not that he needed to know. Without doubt, the battalion commander was able to see it from his position. Bannon's immediate concern was his first sergeant, who was monitoring the cavalry's passage of lines, and the Mech infantry platoon's squad who were in the village in the middle of all that fire.

"ROMEO 25, THIS IS MIKE 77. SHELLREP, OVER." Garger was on the ball. Reporting per the Team SOP, the lieutenant was calling to inform him of the artillery barrage to his front. Garger hadn't considered that Bannon, from his position, would be able to see the same thing. The fact that he was at least thinking and had the presence of mind to report, however, was encouraging.

"ALL BRAVO 3 ROMEO ELEMENTS, THIS IS ROMEO 25. I CAN OBSERVE THE ACTION AT 179872. NO NEED TO REPORT THAT." Bannon let the CVC push-to-talk switch go for a few seconds to frustrate Soviet direction-finding attempts, then started again. "OCCUPY YOUR FIRING POSITIONS NOW. I SAY AGAIN, OCCUPY YOUR FIRING POSITIONS NOW. THE RUSSIANS WILL BE RIGHT BEHIND THOSE PEOPLE COMING THROUGH. ACKNOWLEDGE, OVER."

The platoons rapidly responded in turn. The tracks to the left and right of Alpha 66 cranked up and pulled forward. In their excitement, some of them forgot about their camouflage nets. Bannon watched Alpha 33 as its camo net supports tumbled and the net stretched forward as if it were a large spider web stuck to the tank. Once the stakes were yanked free, the net trailed the tank limply. In a belated plea, Bannon called over the company net to remind the platoons to remember the camo nets. Then he and Kelp jumped out, dragged theirs in, and jumped back into position.

The battalion net now came to life as the battalion Scout Platoon began to report sighting, then contact with the lead enemy element. As Team Yankee's artillery fire-support team, or FIST, was detached to the Scout Platoon while they were deployed forward, Bannon listened intently, hoping he wouldn't lose that valuable combat asset. The Scout Platoon's mission was to cover the withdrawal of the last of the cavalry, engage the enemy's lead elements in an effort to deceive them as to where the covering force area ended and the main battle area began, and then withdraw through Team Yankee.

Their fight was to be short but important. Once they became engaged, the battle more or less passed from the cavalry to the battalion. Though the last of the covering force still had to roll through sporadic artillery fire impacting in the village and up the little valley to the Team's right, the cavalry's battle was over. Team Yankee's first battle was about to begin.

The radio on the Team net came to life as First Sergeant Harrert reported in. "ROMEO 25, THIS IS ROMEO 97, OVER." He was still in the village and still alive.

∽

"ROMEO 97, THIS IS ROMEO 25. WHAT KIND OF SHAPE ARE YOU IN? OVER."

"THIS IS 97. I HAVE ONE WHISKEY INDIA ALPHA. THE NOVEMBER 8 TANGO ELEMENT HAS COMPLETED PASSAGE. WAITING ON THE TANGO 9 FOXTROT ELEMENT NOW, OVER."

"THIS IS 25. DO YOU NEED THE BAND - AID FOR THE CASUALTY? OVER."

"THIS IS 97. NEGATIVE. HE CAN WAIT, OVER."

"THIS IS 25. THE TANGO 9 FOXTROT ELEMENT IS NOW IN CONTACT. I EXPECT THEM TO START BACK WITHIN THREE ZERO MIKES. HANG IN THERE, OVER."

"THIS IS 97. WILCO, OUT."

So far everything was working according to plan. The only downside Bannon could see was that in their haste to occupy firing positions, the Team had probably screwed up most of its camo nets. But right now, that was the least of his concerns as he continued to listen to the Scout Platoon's fight, now being joined by reports from Team Bravo.

Team Bravo, occupying the hill across the small valley from Team Yankee, was under fire from several battalions' worth of Soviet artillery. The initial and frantic report from Team Bravo's commander over the battalion radio net was cut off in mid-sentence. Attempts by the battalion S-3 to reestablish contact with him went unanswered. That either meant the command track had had its antennas blown off or, it had been hit.

This caused Bannon to wonder if his 1st Platoon, attached to Team Bravo, was in the middle of the impact area. It had to be, he reasoned, judging from the fragmented report he'd monitored. Although he was concerned that some of his people were now under fire, there was nothing he could do for them. About the only thought that flashed through his mind was *Better them than me.*

In its wake, Bannon felt himself go flush with shame at the very idea that he could harbor such a selfish thought. About the only justification he could conjure up at the moment was to remind himself that he was only human. Though it was a rather piss poor rational, it was the best he could do as he turned his attention to more immediate and pressing problems.

Reports from the scouts continued to pour in over the battalion command net. One of the scout tracks had been hit, and contact with another had been lost. From the reported locations of the enemy's lead element, the scouts weren't slowing it down. Finally, the scout platoon leader requested permission to displace. Realizing that leaving the scouts out there wasn't going to do the battalion any good, Reynolds gave his permission to withdraw.

Unfortunately, this permission had come too late. The barriers and artillery that were supposed to slow the Soviet advance and allow the Scout Platoon a chance to pass through Team Yankee did little to slow the enemy, much less stop them. Ignoring losses inflicted on them by mines, artillery, and the Scout Platoon, the Soviets bulled their way forward, bloody minded and hell-bent on breaking through regardless of the price. The Scout Platoon leader informed the battalion commander that rather than try for the passage through Team Yankee, he was going to withdraw to the south and cross at an alternate passage point.

This was not a good turn of events for the Team. With the scouts went Team Yankee's artillery FIST Team. Bannon had never been keen on the idea of letting his FIST go with the scouts, pointing out that they might not be able to rejoin the Team. But he had always been reassured that the FIST track would be back long before TeamYankee had any contact with the enemy. This was one time he was sorry he had been right, for not only would he have to fight the Team, now he also had to play forward observer for his supporting artillery.

Contacting the battalion S-3, Bannon asked him if he had any bright ideas on the subject. Major Jordan informed him that Team Yankee now had priority of artillery fire and all calls for fire would be directed to the battalion fire-support officer, or FSO. Jordan also informed him that Team Bravo had taken a lot of casualties, including its commander, who was assumed to be KIA. The battalion commander was, at present, headed over to Team Bravo to attempt to rally the survivors and direct the fight from there. In the meantime, battalion was writing off Team Bravo as combat ineffective. Without having to say so, Jordan let Bannon know Team Yankee was expected to take up the slack and carry the fight.

Two company teams fighting a motorized rifle battalion would have been no problem. But one company team, even with priority of artillery fire, would be hard pressed. In the few minutes he had before that came to pass, Bannon contacted the battalion fire-support officer and made sure he had all the Team's preplanned artillery targets. The FSO responded he had them and was ready to comply with any and all requests for fire from Team Yankee.

Bannon's plan was simple. He intended to hold fire until the Soviet lead elements reached the valley floor. When that happened, the Team would engage them with both tank platoons and the ITVs simultaneously. The 2nd Platoon would engage the lead element, the 3rd Platoon would hit the enemy still on the opposite slope, and the ITVs would engage supporting vehicles such as BRDM-2s armed with anti-tank guided missiles on the far hill. He wanted the artillery to impact along the crest of the opposite hill at the same time as the Team began to fire. First, DPICM, an artillery shell that scattered many small armor-defeating bomblets, would be fired in order to take out as many Soviet PCs and self-propelled guns as possible. Then the artillery would fire high explosives and smoke rounds, laying down a smoke screen to blind any Soviet antitank system or artillery observers that might take up position there to engage the Team. That would leave the Team free to slug it out with only a portion of their force isolated from the rest. The FSO assured Bannon the artillery could handle the mission. All he needed was the word.

A sudden detonation in the village followed by the hasty retreat of a lone PC out of the village back to the Team's positions reminded Bannon that the first sergeant hadn't been told to blow the bridge in the town and withdraw. In the scramble to sort out the artillery fire plan, he had forgotten him. Fortunately, either Harrert had monitored the battalion net, figured out what was going on, and taken the initiative, or Uleski had ordered him out after hearing that the scouts would not be returning on the planned route. Either way, it worked out, and the first sergeant was headed back.

"ROMEO 25, THIS IS MIKE 77. SPOT REPORT. 5 T-72 TANKS MOVING WEST. GRID 190852. CONTINUING TO OBSERVE, OVER." Bannon snapped his head to the left. There was no need to use a map. There was only one place where the Russians would be, and that was on the hill 2,200 meters away. All the training, planning, and preparation was over. Team Yankee was about to learn if the Team's seventy-nine men and twenty-five million dollars' worth of equipment could do what they were supposed to do; close with and destroy the enemy by fire, maneuver, and shock effect.

༆

The five T-72 tanks began their descent into the valley in a line with about 100 meters between tanks. One of them had a mine roller attached to the front of its hull. He would have to be taken out in the first volley. As soon as the tanks started down, a line of Soviet armored personnel carriers, BMP-2s, appeared on the crest of the hill and followed the tanks down without hesitation. There were fifteen of these personnel carriers deployed in a rough line about one hundred meters behind the tanks. All moved down the opposite slope at a steady and somewhat restrained pace, as if they really didn't want to go into the valley or get too far ahead of follow-on elements.

A third group of follow-on vehicles appeared. These were a gaggle of dissimilar armored vehicles. As they reached the crest of the hill, they paused for a moment. Just before they started their descent, the tanks and the BMPs in front made a sharp oblique to the left and headed for the north side of the village. Consisting of one BMP, a T-72, a BTR-60, an MTU bridge tank, and a ZSU 23-4 antiaircraft gun, this detachment could only be the battalion command group.

The scene before Team Yankee was too good to be true. For some unknown reason the Team had not been hit by artillery yet. The Soviets were rolling forward as if they were on maneuvers, not attacking an enemy force hunkered down in prepared position. Even better, their change in direction offered most of the Team flank shots. And on top of that, the actions by the command group had telegraphed who they were. If luck held for another minute or two, it would be all over for this motorized rifle battalion.

"ROMEO 83, THIS IS ROMEO 25. DO YOU SEE THAT LAST GAGGLE COMING DOWN THE HILL? OVER."

"25, THIS IS 83. ROGER, OVER."

"83, THIS IS 25. THAT IS THE COMMAND GROUP. I WANT YOU AND THE TWO TRACKS YOU HAVE UP THERE TO TAKE THEM OUT. THE BMP AND TANK FIRST, OVER"

"THIS IS 83, WILCO."

༆

Uleski considered this last order before he relayed instructions to the ITVs. He paused for a moment and watched the advancing Soviets. With Alpha 55 silent except for the hum of the engine, he could feel the tension build up in himself and his crew. In the past, he had always been able to crack a joke or say something funny to lighten a tense moment. But he couldn't, not this time. It suddenly dawned upon him that this was real. The tanks and BMPs were manned with real Soviets, men who were coming his way to kill him.

Despite the heat of the day, Uleski felt a cold shiver run down his spine. His stomach began to knot up, leaving him feeling as if he were going to throw up. It was real, all real. In a minute, maybe two, all hell was going to break loose and he was right in the middle of it. Uleski's head, flooded with disjointed thoughts, began to spin, with one thought playing back over and over, "Oh God, please make this go away."

Satisfied Uleski understood what was expected of him, Bannon switched to the battalion command net and instructed the FSO to fire the prearranged artillery barrage. When the FSO acknowledged the request, Bannon dropped back down to the Team net. "ALL BRAVO 3 ROMEO ELEMENTS, UPON IMPACT OF FRIENDLY ARTILLERY, YOU WILL COMMENCE FIRING. MAINTAIN FIRE DISTRIBUTION AND GOOD SHOOTING. ROMEO 25 OUT"

This last message neither upset nor unnerved Garger. Without bothering to acknowledge the commander's orders, Garger switched to the platoon net and issued his own. The clear, sunny day, with the sun to his Platoon's back, made it all too easy. All the BMPs were exposed to the entire platoon. Garger ordered SSG Pierso, who was commander of Alpha 33 and Pierson's wingman, to engage the right half of the BMPs. Garger instructed his own wingman, Blackfoot, to begin to engage the far left BMP and then work his way toward the center of the line. He would begin in the center and work his way to the left. In this way, the platoon would avoid killing the same BMP.

With nothing to do but wait for the artillery, Garger leaned back and considered the scene before him. This was easier than the Armor School at Fort Knox. It couldn't be that simple. There had to be a catch. The Soviets were coming at them as if the Team wasn't there. Garger tried hard to think if there was something he had missed, an order that needed to be given. Something. But there wasn't. All seemed to be in order. All was ready. "What the hell," he muttered to himself. "Might as well relax and enjoy the moment."

In the Mech Platoon's positions, Sergeant First Class Polgar grasped the hand grips of his M2 machinegun as he watched the Soviets. He was amazed. When he had been a young private, Polgar had been in Vietnam two months before he had seen his first VC, and they had been very, very dead. In the first day of this war, he was looking at all the Soviets he cared to see. He looked to his left, then to his right at the line of PCs he was responsible for. The four M-113s with him weren't going to do a hell of a lot if the tanks in the Team fell flat on their ass. As the Soviets drew near, Polgar tracked the Soviets with his M2 and thought, "Those dumb-ass tankers better be as good as they think they are, or this is going to be one damned short war."

∽

The Team was charged and ready. Bannon could feel it. Having issued all the orders, he needed to for the moment, the time had come to fight his own tank.

Grabbing the TC's override, he traversed the turret, bringing the main gun to bear on his intended victim while yelling out his fire command without bothering to key the intercom. "GUNNER—SABOT—TANK WITH MINE ROLLER."

In response, Folk yelled out once he spotted the vehicle. "IDENTIFIED."

Kelp followed this with a sharp, crisp, "UP!" letting both Bannon and Folk know the main gun was loaded, armed, and he was clear of the path of recoil.

Bannon dropped down on top of his seat. Perched above the gunner and loader, he watched through the primary sight's extension as Folk tracked the T-72. Then they waited as the enemy continued to draw neared. And they waited. The line of tanks was now beginning to reach the valley floor. And they waited. The sweat was rolling down Bannon's face as he edged ever closer to losing nerve. And they waited.

"SPLASH, OVER." The FSO's call on the battalion net heralded the impact of the artillery. Across the valley, the crest of the far hill erupted as hundreds of small bomblets scattered and went off. *On target!*

"FIRE!"

"ON THE WAAAAAY!"

The image of the T-72 disappeared before Bannon's eye in a flash and cloud of smoke as Folk loosed his first round, sending the tank rocking back as the gun recoiled and spit out the spent shell casing. Without needing to be told, Kelp hit the ammo door switch with his knee, causing it to slide open with a sharp bang. He hauled out the next round, loaded the gun, and armed it even before the dust and obscuration of their first round had dissipated. When it did, the T-72 with the mine roller was stopped, broadside to Alpha 66, and was burning furiously.

"TARGET—CEASE FIRE." They had drawn their first blood. "STAND BY GUNNER."

Bannon popped his head up to get a quick overall picture of what was going on. Just as he did, Alpha 33 fired a HEAT-T round at a BMP. He watched the tracer streak towards the target and impact with a bright orange flash and black ball of smoke. The BMP lurched forward another few meters then stopped, quivered, and began to burn. Bannon next turned his attention to the valley floor and opposite slope, watching that scene repeated again and again. In the few instances when the first round missed a BMP, the BMP would turn away from the impact. This maneuver, however, only added a few more seconds to its life and that of its crew because the second round usually found its mark. He

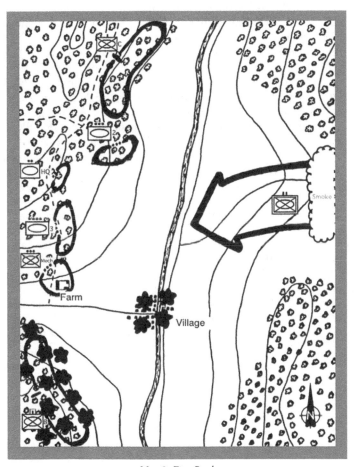

Map 2: First Battle

watched as two BMPs, madly scrambling to avoid being hit, rammed each other and stopped. This calamity only made it easier for Team Yankee's gunners, as both BMPs died within seconds of each other, locked together in a fiery death.

By now the crest of the far hill had all but disappeared from view. The smoke and DPICM were doing their jobs. So far, nothing had followed the Soviet command group down. It had scattered in an effort to avoid being hit, but to no avail. The BMP belonging to the command group was lying on its side, a track hanging off and burning. The tank that had been with it had also been hit, but had only shed its right track. It stood, immobile but defiant, returning fire towards the headquarters position. This uneven contest, however, did not last long. In return, the T-72 received a TOW missile that detonated near the turret ring. The resulting secondary detonations caused by stored onboard munitions ripped the turret off with a thunderous explosion.

"I have a BMP in my sights, can I engage?" an impatient Folk called out over the intercom.

Bannon knelt down, glanced at Kelp to ensure he was clear, checked that the gun was armed, and gave the command to fire. Folk gave an *on-the-way* and fired. As before, the rock and recoil shook the tank. A quick glance in the extension told Bannon Folk had been on the mark again. Another BMP crew and infantry squad had become heroes of the Soviet Union, posthumously. With the need to keep track of what the entire Team was doing, Bannon decided to give his gunner free rein to engage any targets he could find. "Gunner, find your own targets, if there are any left, and engage at will. Just make sure you're not killing dead tracks."

"Yes, sir!" His reply had a glee in it that reminded Bannon of a teenager who had just been given the keys to the family car.

With that taken care of, Bannon popped up again to survey the battlefield. The devastation in the valley was awesome. Over twenty armored vehicles lay strewn there, dismembered, twisted, burning hulks. Folk had nothing to engage. The lead echelon of the motorized battalion had been annihilated. Six T-72 tanks, sixteen BMPs, a BTR-60, a ZSU 23-4, and an MTU bridge launcher, along with almost two hundred Russian soldiers, were gone. The engagement had lasted less than four minutes. Team Yankee had won its first battle.

CHAPTER 3

Change of Mission

When the decision to evacuate American military dependents from Europe was finally made after countless delays and false starts, there was a rush of frantic and seemingly uncoordinated activity to get it done before hostilities broke out. The drive to Rhein-Main, which normally took one hour, took nearly four as the buses carrying Pat Bannon and her fellow evacuees from the housing area to the Air Base fought traffic on the autobahn all the way. The regular German police, reinforced with military personnel, had established checkpoints along the route where an NCO on the bus had to present his paperwork before being cleared through. At one of these stops, Pat noticed that the Germans were retaining several people. On the autobahn's median, across the roadway from where they were being guarded, was a stationary car riddled with bullet holes. Next to it a white sheet with red blotches covered a mound. No one on the bus around Pat could imagine what the car's occupants could have done to cause the Germans to fire on them. Whatever the reason, the fact that the Germans were ready to use their ever-present submachine guns highlighted the seriousness of their situation.

The last checkpoint was at the main gate of Rhein-Main. Before the bus was allowed to enter, Air Force security personnel boarded the bus and checked everyone's ID card. They, too, had their weapons at the ready. As this was going on, Pat noticed a German military policeman at the gate was questioning two women off to one side, leaving her to wonder if the women were German nationals trying to get out with the US families.

Beyond the gate, the Air Base was swarming with activity. At one intersection the bus was stopped while a line of trucks filled with American troops coming up from the flight line and heading to a back gate rolled by. They had to be reinforcements from the States, Pat reasoned, deployed to Germany as part of the REFORGER program. With luck the dependents would be flown back on the same planes that were bringing these troops in, causing her to hope this nightmare was nearing its end. At least they were now at the last stop on this side of the Atlantic.

Instead of going to the terminal, however, the buses dropped them off at the post gym, already crowded to near capacity by other dependents who had arrived there earlier. On the gym floor, rows of cots with blankets had been set up. As at the post theater back in the housing area where the wives and children belonging to her husband's unit had gathered before departing the housing area, the families were grouped by unit. Some of the women from the battalion who had come up on the first group of buses had established an area for the families from each of the units. The new arrivals were informed that since the terminal was already overflowing with evacuees, they would need to stay there until it was their turn to go. At least, Pat was told, the Air Force personnel running the evacuation were proving to be more helpful than the Army community personnel. The biggest problem they were facing was dealing with the sudden rush of families that were being dumped at Rhein-Main. One Air Force officer had told them that the people in the gym probably wouldn't leave until the morning.

The thought of this annoyed Pat. Having geared herself up for the final leap, the idea they would have to spend a night in an open gym with hundreds of other dejected and anxious people was disheartening. It seemed that every new move only added more stress and pressure. Unfortunately, however deplorable their plight was, she, like the others, had no choice but endure it as best she could. She had to. A little group that was growing was now depending on her. Jane Ortelli, the wife of Sean's tank driver had joined them at the post theater before boarding the buses. The nineteen-year-old mother had never been out of the state of New Jersey until she came over to Germany. Through the ordeal back at the post theater, during the ride to Rhein-Main, and in the gym, she clutched her four-month-old baby as a child would a teddy bear for security and comfort.

A little girl named Debby had also joined the group. Debby's only parent was a medic who had been deployed to the border with everyone else. Fran Wilson, who followed Pat everywhere she went like a stray puppy, had volunteered to escort the eight-year-old girl back to the States where her grandparents would meet her.

And then there was Sue Garger, lost, bewildered, and just as afraid and worried as the rest. The only difference between her and Pat was she made no effort to hide her feelings.

Pat and her group established themselves a little area by taking eight of the cots and pushing them together. The four adults stationed themselves on the corner cots and put the children in the middle. Jane kept her baby with her, not wanting to part for a moment with the only thing of value she had on earth. Sarah, overcoming her apprehensions, insisted on having her own cot, just like her brothers. Sean and Debby stayed together. Sean, despite being a year younger, took over the role of big brother and helped Debby. He tried to explain everything to her like his father had to him, even though he had scant idea what he was talking about. Debby would listen intently to every word as if it were gospel, then ask Sean another question. But at least Debby was talking now and seemed to be more at ease. Kurt insisted on staying near his buddy, Sue Wilson. He was enjoying all the attention she was lavished upon him and she, someone she could care for.

There was little rest that night. Fear, apprehension, discomfort, and a desire to get on with the evacuation kept the adults awake while the adventure of the trip kept the children alert and active. Some of the adults talked in hushed voices, seeking company and escape from their fears. Others simply withdrew into themselves, no longer able to cope with the grim reality they found themselves facing. Pat took solace in praying and the hope that all this would end tomorrow. It had to. There was only so much more that she could give. It had to end, soon. Otherwise she would break down and take to mewling ceaselessly like one woman, somewhere in the gym, was doing. Only exhaustion allowed her to get a few hours' sleep.

∾

Movement to the terminal began early. Groups left in the order in which they arrived. Pat and her little group had time for breakfast before their turn. Everyone was tired. It had been nearly impossible for anyone to get a good night's rest, cold meals, little sleep, overcrowded conditions, wearing the same clothes they had slept in, and the trauma of the whole ordeal had worn women and children down to the point of exhaustion. Pat could not remember a time when she had been more tired and miserable.

The passage of thousands of evacuees before them had left its mark on the terminal. The clean, modern building that had greeted Pat and Sean on their arrival in Germany was now strewn with litter, discarded blankets, clothes, and trash bins overflowing with used disposable diapers. Those who had left the gym before them were inside the terminal mixing with the evacuees that had spent the night there. Looking around as they entered, Pat decided that as miserable a night the gym had been, staying here would have been worse.

At the door, an airman took their names, gave them a roster number, and directed them to the second floor where they would wait until their numbers were called. From the second floor at least the children would be entertained, for the view beyond the plate glass windows allowed them to look out onto the airfield and watch the aircraft coming and going. Pat, eager to see an end to this ordeal, joined them.

To one side of the flight line she could see trucks and buses cued up and waiting as a C-141 transport taxied to a stop. Just as fascinated as the children, she watched as its large clamshell doors opened, reminding her of an alligator she'd seen at the Frankfort Zoo at feeding time. Only instead of consuming the waiting trucks, as soon as the cargo ramp was down, troops began to double time out and fall in on their NCOs, forming squads and platoons. Once formed, they headed toward the trucks, one platoon at a time.

While the troops were still deplaning, Air Force personnel scrambled out to service the aircraft. A fuel truck lumbered up and began to refuel the aircraft. Everyone seemed anxious to get the C-141 turned around and on its way.

Inside the terminal, a female voice began to call out roster numbers over the PA and give instructions. None of Pat's little group heard their numbers called. So they stayed where they were and watched the lucky ones move onto the airfield, form into two lines, and move out to the C-141. By the time they'd reached it, the ground crew was finishing up and moving into position to service a huge C-5 that had just landed. The sight of that plane caused excitement. Turning toward Pat, Fran said she was sure they would be able to get on that one. Pat simply smiled as she prayed they would.

For a moment there was almost total silence in the valley in front of Team Yankee's positions. It was a dull, numb silence that comes after you have endured prolonged exposure to a deafening noise. The crackle and popping of stored small arms ammunition igniting in the burning Soviet tracks, accompanied by an occasional rumble as a main gun round cooked off were the only sounds that rose from the valley. Distance and CVCs hid the moans and screams of agony of those Soviet crewman who were wounded or burning to death in their disabled tracks.

The report of a machinegun off to his right alerted Bannon to the fact that not all the Soviets were hors de combat. He watched as a stream of tracers struck short, then climbed into a group of four Russians trying to make their way back up the hill across from the Team's positions. As soon as the shooter had found the range, he let go a long killing burst in the center of the group. While many of rounds did nothing but kick up dirt, enough found their mark, sending the Russians either jerking wildly like a puppet whose strings were being yanked or simply tumbling over, head over heel.

For a moment he thought of issuing a ceasefire. The Russians had suffered enough. But just as quickly as that thought had popped up in his mind, it was replaced by cold, practical, professional considerations. If these survivors were allowed to live, they would only fall in on units that needed replacements or be issued older model equipment kept in storage and brought forward from Russia to replace that which had been lost. The odds of Team Yankee ever encountering the same Russians again were slim. But another NATO company would. That, and the wish to see the Soviets pay for a war they had started was enough to stay Bannon's hand.

One by one, reports from the platoons started to come in over the company net as other tanks continued to seek out and destroy fugitives from what had been little more than a slaughter. Both tank platoons reported in with no losses, a total main gun expenditure of thirty-seven rounds, and, as often happens in war, inflated kill reports. Only the launcher on one of the ITVs had been hit and destroyed. The ITV's crew was untouched and the track was still mechanically sound. But without its launcher and sight, the ITV was worthless to the Team. With that in mind, Bannon instructed Uleski to have that crew pass all the TOW rounds that it could off to the operational ITV, then have the damaged ITV head back to the maintenance collection point. With all the reports in and satisfied he had a handle on the team's status, he then called the battalion S-3 in order to pass the Team situation report, or SITREP, to him.

It was after Bannon had finished with his report to battalion, and while the Team was moving to its alternate firing positions that Bannon realized the third company of the Soviet motorized rifle battalion was unaccounted for. Just where it was, and what it was doing, concerned him.

The lead units, instead of having eight tanks and twenty BMPs, had had only five tanks and fifteen BMPs. Perhaps, he reasoned, the Soviet motorized rifle battalion had suffered so many losses in their fight with the cavalry that it had merged all its companies into two weak, composite companies. Or perhaps, upon witnessing the demise of the rest of his parent battalion, the commander of the third company decided he stood a better chance of standing up to his regimental commander's wrath for not pushing on than he did if he took on the Americans on his own. Of course, there was always the possibility instead of gallantly rushing down into the valley and joining his comrades in a death ride, the Soviet company commander decided to stop on the crest of the hill and engage his yet-unseen opponent in a long-range duel once the smoke cleared and while he waited for further orders. Whatever the case, the next move was his, a move Team Yankee needed to be ready to parry.

While Bannon was pondering the larger tactical questions, Kelp took advantage of the break in action to stand up on his seat and pop his head up out of his hatch. Using Bannon's binoculars, he surveyed the carnage he had helped create. Folk, slowly traversing the turret, was doing likewise. Ortelli, because the valley was hidden from his view by the berm that protected Alpha 66's hull, asked the other two crewmen to describe the scene. Talking in hushed voices so as not to disturb their commander's ruminations, Folk and Kelp described the scene in a gruesome, if colorful, manner. Folk was particularly proud of *his* destruction of the T-72 with mine roller and made sure that Kelp identified it.

Ortelli wanted to come up and see what it looked like but knew better than to ask. Instead, he dropped hints that went unanswered. At times, it was difficult to be the crew of the Team commander's tank. Bannon was seldom there to help in the maintenance of the tank or its weapons. Yet the tank, its radios, and the prodigious amount of gear Americans take to war with them always had to be ready whenever he came running up and climbed aboard or there was hell to pay. And the crew had to be straighter and more correct than the crews in other tanks. It's not that team commanders are ogres. Company commanders tend to share an easier and closer relationship with their crew than they do with other tankers in their company. But the commander is still the commander, and this thought is never far from the crew's, or commander's, minds.

∾

Uleski was only beginning to calm down. The short, sharp fight had left him drained, physically and mentally. When the ceasefire order had finally been given, it was all he could do to lift his canteen and take a mouthful of water. Swishing this around for a moment, he spat it out over the side of the tank. Still, the taste of vomit lingered.

After replacing his canteen, he sat on Alpha 55's TC seat for a moment, watching the crewmen of the ITVs move from one track to the other, transferring rounds to the undamaged vehicle. It was late afternoon; the sun was softly filtering down through the trees. Except for an occasional pop or bang from ammunition cooking off in the valley below, all was quiet, all peaceful. The XO thought how nice it would be if it could be over, just for a day, just an hour, just enough time for him to pull himself together.

That thought had no sooner come to the fore when a blinding flash and an overwhelming blast struck Uleski, knocking him back. Instinctively, he allowed himself to drop down to the turret floor as the soft green image of the forest Alpha 55 was hidden in disintegrated into flames and explosions.

∾

The Soviet major was completely flustered. Nothing, absolutely nothing had gone right that day. First, the traffic regulators had misdirected their column before the attack. It took the rest of the morning to get them turned around and back on their proper route. Then the resistance of the American cavalry proved to be far greater than anticipated. The division's second echelon, to which the major's battalion belonged, had to be committed before the division's first objective was reached. The delay required a complete revision of the plan, a plan that had been drilled and practiced for months. Artillery units were now in the wrong place and did not have the detailed fire plans needed to support a breakthrough attack properly. And to top off everything else, the major's battalion commander had managed to get himself killed, leaving him in command.

The major was in a dark mood. Not even the sight of burning vehicles belonging to the American cavalry regiment they passed as they moving forward cheered him. He had already seen far too much destroyed Soviet equipment. His new orders, issued hastily over the radio in the clear, kept running through his mind. They were simple enough. He was to cross a major valley, advance up a small side valley, and seize the regiment's objective, an intersection where two autobahns met. But the major had not been given any time to plan properly, recon, or coordinate for artillery support. The regimental commander, under pressure from his commander, merely told him to move as rapidly as possible, that all the artillery planning would be taken care of for him. Even the battalion's political officer, a man who was usually annoyingly eager to do whatever was required of him by his superiors, balked when they were told that a battalion, attacking in the same place earlier, had failed.

There was, however, nothing to do but to obey the orders he'd been given and hope for the best. To that end, the major put all his faith in the effects of the chemical weapons that were to be employed by his supporting artillery and the surprise he was trying to achieve by attacking from an unexpected direction. As they neared the line of departure, he took one more look around at the mass of vehicles huddled near his before he closed his hatch.

❧

Bannon's wandering thoughts were jarred back to the here and now by the impact of artillery to his left on Team Yankee's hill. Though he could not see where, exactly it was landing, he had no doubt that the headquarters position and possibly the 2nd Platoon's position, were under fire. A second attack was about to start.

"GAS! GAS! GAS!" The muffled cry by someone in a protective mask on the Team net electrified the crew of Alpha 66. As one, they tore open their protective mask cases and scrambled to mask. First, the CVC came off. Then the mask, chin first, was pulled up over each of their faces. Once on securely, the hood had to be pulled over the head, followed by the CVC. The final step was hooking the protective mask's microphone jack into the CVC. In training, a tank crewman was expected to accomplish this in less than twenty seconds. And though no one had a stopwatch on him, Bannon had no doubt he'd more than beat that time as he took a second to settle himself before turning his full attention back to commanding his company.

"ROMEO 25, THIS IS TANGO 77. SHELLREP, OVER."

"TANGO 77, THIS IS ROMEO 25, SEND IT."

"THIS IS TANGO 77. HE AND GAS IMPACTING FROM 190896 TO 199893. CALIBER AND NUMBER OF ROUNDS UNKNOWN, OVER."

From the coordinates given, Bannon knew that the 2nd Platoon leader, who was making the report, as well as his platoon, were safe. But the XO and the ITVs were catching hell. Because the Soviets were only firing on the hilltop and not at the actual positions of the Team's two tank platoons, it was obvious they didn't have a clear picture of where the Team was and were thus, firing blind. While that was good for the Team overall, Bannon had no doubt that that thought was cold comfort for Uleski and his people. Provided, of course, Uleski was still alive.

"TANGO 77, THIS IS ROMEO 25. I NEED AN NBC-1 REPORT AS SOON AS POSSIBLE, OVER."

"THIS IS TANGO 77. WE'RE WORKING IT UP NOW, OVER."

As he waited for an accurate NBC-1 report, Bannon began to wonder why battalion had not warned him the Soviets were using chemical weapons. While it may have been an oversight on their part, the idea that his team was the first to be hit with chemical weapons could not be totally discounted. Just in case they were, Bannon decided not to wait for the complete report from 2nd Platoon before informing battalion.

It goes without saying his report, as incomplete as it was, caused a great deal of concern on the battalion net. Judging from the pitch of the voices and the excited chatter, as best as anyone knew, Team Yankee had been the first unit within the brigade to be hit by chemical weapons. The snap analysis the battalion S-2 offered up was that the Soviets, anxious to make a breakthrough, were getting desperate.

As enlightening as this was, the chemical attack, the massive artillery barrage, and the loss of contact with the XO and the ITVs were of little comfort to Bannon, for it seemed to signal a change in the Team's fortunes.

The shadows in the valley were growing long. Early evening was upon them, and there was no end of the Soviet attack in sight. The barrage on the hill had been going on unabated for ten minutes without letup. The NBC-1 report from 2nd Platoon indicated that the Soviets were using GB, a non-persistent blood agent. While that particular agent would not last once the attack was over, GB broke down the protective mask filters rapidly, making them useless. The Team would need to change filters quickly or suffer mass casualties in the next chemical attack, provided, Bannon thought, they survived long enough after the first one to do so.

This grim thought had no sooner played itself out in his mind when, to his surprise, another Soviet artillery unit began to lay down a massive smoke screen just in front of the Team's positions. They were going to launch a full blooded attack, and soon. Bannon had expected the Soviets would wait until night and probe their positions with recon elements under the cover of darkness before attacking. That they weren't left him wondering if the S-2 was right, that they being pushed by their commanders to achieve a clean breakthrough. Not that night would have made much of a difference. The gunners in the tank platoons and those manning the Dragons in the Mech Platoon were already switching to their thermal sights. The smoke screen the Soviet gunners were arduously building would offer the attacking force scant protection, if any.

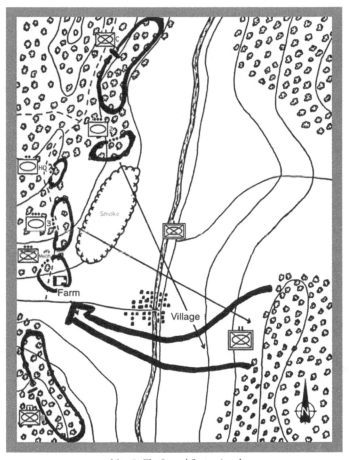

Map 3: The Second Soviet Attack

"Well, if you're gonna come, let's get this over with," Bannon muttered to himself, forgetting as he did so his intercom was keyed.

Upon hearing this, Folk nodded in response. "I'm with you on that one, sir."

∿

The 2nd Platoon reported the new attack first. At a range of 2500 meters, the advancing Soviet vehicles emerging from the tree line on the hill to the Team's right front across from Team Bravo appeared as green blobs in the thermal sights of the Team's tanks. They were either headed straight into the village, or through Team Bravo's position. Bannon informed the battalion S-3 of the enemy's appearance, direction of attack, and his thoughts on the enemy's intentions.

Major Jordan was quick to reply, informing Bannon Team Bravo was in no shape to fight. With only two functional tanks and three Dragon teams, Bravo would be hard pressed to protect itself, let alone stop a determined attack. Team Yankee, Bannon was told, would have to carry the major portion of the coming fighting.

Because of the range and the quality of the image produced on the thermal sight, it was difficult, at first, to distinguish which of the attacking blobs were tanks and which were BMPs. Bannon therefore ordered the 2nd Platoon to engage the lead vehicles with SABOT, assuming that the Soviets would follow their own tactical doctrine and lead off with tanks. The 3rd Platoon was to fire over the village at the center and rear of the attacking formation as it came out from the tree line. They would engage with HEAT on the assumption that the BMPs would be following the tanks. The Mech Platoon was instructed to stand ready to catch anything that got through. With no time left for a coordinated ambush like the one the Team had used to stop the first echelon, Bannon gave the platoons permission to fire at will before turning his full attention to working on getting some friendly artillery into the act.

As the firing commenced, Bannon fumbled with map and grease pencil in the confined space in which a tank commander has to work. The rubber gloves and the protective mask only made this more awkward, for as he searched his map for an appropriate artillery target reference point, the hose of his protective mask kept flopping down in front of him, obstructing his view of the map. To keep this from happening again, he stopped and flung the protective mask carrier, containing the filter over his shoulder in an effort to get the hose out of the way. This succeeded in clearing his view of the map, but added a new complication to his labors as the weight of the filter yanked at the hose, pulling his head over to one side. That he was able to accomplish anything amazed him. But succeeded he did in finding a suitable target reference point, contacting the FSO, and putting in a call for fire.

∿

The second attack had caught Garger by surprise. He had not expected the Soviets to be foolish enough to continue the attack in this sector. He had read that the Soviets never reinforce defeat. It was a practice in the Red Army to push everything into the attack that succeeded. They had not succeeded before, and Garger was confident they would not succeed now. Even the artillery impacting to his right, close enough so that the shock waves could be felt, did not alter his opinion. Garger listened to the Team commander's orders and acknowledged them. He sized up the Soviet force his platoon was to engage and issued his instructions to the platoon. Then he got down to the serious business of killing Russians.

⌒

With artillery on the way, Bannon turned his attention back to the battle unfolding in front of him by calling on each platoon leader and requesting a SITREP. The 2nd Platoon reported destroying six vehicles, but had been unable to stop five vehicles that had disappeared south of the village. Bannon assumed that these tracks were going to swing south, using the village for cover, and either make a run for the small valley or go up the hill where Team Bravo was. The Mech Platoon had to be ready to deal with them.

The 3rd Platoon, being at closer range, was enjoying a higher percentage of first-round hits. They had dealt easily with all the tracks that had been exposed on front slope of hill across the way and were now playing a cat-and-mouse game with Soviet tracks still emerging from the tree line. Observing through his extension, Bannon watched as the 3rd Platoon allowed two or three Soviet tracks to emerge and start down the hill. When they were 100 meters or so from any cover, the whole platoon would fire. In a flash the Soviet tracks, still appearing as green blobs in the thermal sight, would stop, then glow brighter as the heat of onboard fires provided a clearer, more intense thermal image.

A spot report from Harding, the Mech Platoon leader, alerted Bannon to the fact that the five Soviet tracks that had disappeared to the south of the village were now moving up the small valley. This small Soviet force consisted of two T-72s and three BMPs. While the voice of the platoon leader who would soon be engaging them betrayed no nervousness or confusion, Bannon became apprehensive. It would have been far better, he thought, if there were some tanks in the small valley to deal with the T-72s due to his lack of confidence in the Dragons' ability to stop tanks.

⌒

It was a disaster, a bloody disaster, and there wasn't a damned thing the Soviet major could do but carry out the insanity he found himself in to its final conclusion. A quick check revealed that only two tanks and two other BMPs had made it with him across the valley and into the mouth of the small east-to-west valley he was expected to advance up. He had no idea what in the hell he was going to do once he was in it. Figuring that out would have to wait for now. At the moment, all he wanted to do was to get out of the Americans' kill zone and find some cover. To this end, the major turned his small force toward a walled farm complex at the head of the small valley in the hoped that it would provide the tattered remnants of his battalion who were still with him with shelter from the brutal pounding his battalion was taking from the American tanks.

∾

The Mech Platoon was ready for the Soviets who were fast closing on their positon. Using sound-powered phones connected in a loop, the platoon leader passed his instructions down to Polgar and the squad leaders. The two Dragons and the dismounted infantry in the farm would take out the two T-72 tanks. Polgar, with his two Dragons and the M2 machineguns, would take on the BMPs and provide suppressive fires. For good measure, in case a Dragon missed its mark, the infantrymen in the farm had light antitank rockets, called LAWs, at the ready.

They allowed the Soviets to advance to within 300 meters of the farm before the Platoon cut loose. At that range, it was very difficult to miss with a Dragon. They didn't. On Harding's order, every machinegun and Dragon launcher in the Platoon cut loose.

The speed and accuracy with which modern weapons are capable of killing is as awesome as it is frightening. Had they survived the Dragons and the massed machineguns, the Soviets would have been most impressed by the performance of the Mech Platoon. As it was, the Soviet major had just enough time to realize his last roll of the dice had come up craps.

∾

As before, the firing died away slowly. This last fight had lasted some twenty minutes from when the enemy first vehicle had appeared, to when Bannon finally gave the order to ceasefire. Somewhere during that time, the Soviet artillery barrage on the headquarters position and to the Team's front had stopped. As the smoke screen dissipated, the shattered remains of twenty-three newly smashed and burning hulks had been added to the previous carnage in the valley to the Team's right front. The eight T-72s and fifteen BMPs amounted to more than a company, but less than a motorized rifle battalion. The why of this did not concern Bannon just then. All that was important was that the Soviets had stopped coming. Like two fighters after a round, the opponents were back in their corners, licking their wounds and eyeing each other for the next round.

Reports started to come in from the platoons, but Bannon cut them off as he tried to establish commo with Uleski. When his calls to the XO received no response, Second Lieutenant McAlister, the 2nd Platoon leader, reported that his flank tank could see a burning vehicle to its rear. Upon hearing this, Bannon immediately contacted First Sergeant Harrert and instructed him to get up to the XO's location with the M-113 ambulance attached to the Team and the M-88 recovery vehicle. As soon as the first sergeant acknowledged, Bannon pulled 66 out of position and headed up the hill to the headquarters position.

Enroute he checked in with 2nd Platoon to learn if there was still evidence of a chemical agent. McAlister reported that he had no indications of any agent at his location and requested permission to unmask. This was granted. The 3rd Platoon was instructed to do likewise after they had conducted a survey of their area for contamination. Because Alpha 66 was headed into the center of where the chemical attack had been directed, Bannon decided it was best if he and his crew remained masked.

As they neared the position, the logging trail that had run behind the position was no longer there. Shell craters, smashed and uprooted trees dimly lit by the failing light of late evening and small fires slowed their progress as Ortelli took his time carefully picking his way through the debris. Despite his skill, the craters and irregular pattern into which the trees had fallen threatened to throw one of 66's tracks as they proceeded. Through the shattered forest Bannon could make out a burning vehicle, causing his heart to sink lower than it already was. The last fight, unlike the first, had been costly.

The condition of the three tracks that had been occupying the headquarters position matched that of the shattered forest around them. One of the ITVs was lying on its side, burning. Its aluminum armor, glowing cherry red, was already collapsing into the center of the shattered remains by the time Alpha 66 came upon it. Burning rubber and diesel combined to create a thick, roiling black pillar of smoke, adding to the grim scene Bannon beheld. The TOW launcher of the second ITV was mangled, with bits and pieces of electrical components dangling by clusters of tangled wires. Between the ITVs sat Alpha 55, around which several figures could be seen moving. When Bannon saw they were unmasked, he ordered his own crew to do so as well once the tank had stopped.

Dismounting, Bannon carefully picked his way through the maze of uprooted trees and shell holes toward where Uleski was kneeling next to a figure on the ground. Upon hearing Bannon approaching, he glanced over his shoulder, but said nothing. Instead, he turned his attention back at the figure.

Besides the man Uleski was with, Bannon could see five more who were either lying on the ground or leaning up against the damaged ITV. Even from a distance, he could tell that they were all badly wounded. The temptation to go over to them and see what he could do was quelled by a compelling need to check on the condition of his XO. Besides, Alpha 55's gunner and loader were already doing all they could for the wounded despite having no idea where to start or how to properly deal with wounded men who had been as badly ripped apart as the ITV had been.

Bannon's deliberations on who needed him the most were interrupted when something underfoot gave way under his weight. Looking down in order to see what he'd stepped on, he froze, then jumped back in horror. What he had thought was a tree branch was an arm, shredded, torn, and bloody.

Horrified, Bannon just stood there, staring down at the limb he'd stepped on, unable to force himself to think, much less move. Only when Folk brushed him as he ran by with 66's first-aid kit was he able to shake off his momentary panic and continue on. Even then, he took his time, watching where he stepped. The Team's charmed life, it seemed, was over.

With more effort than such a simple act should have taken, Bannon forced himself to look at each of the wounded men as the crew of 55 and Folk tore at clothing to expose torn and burned flesh as they set about the gruesome task of tending to the wounds. One of the men had lost a foot. In horrible pain, he rolled his head from side to side, panting as if he'd just finished a race as he thrashed his arms on the ground. Another ITV crewman beside him simply lay there, not moving at all. It took a second look by Bannon to see if he was still breathing. A check of the other three showed that while not nearly as badly wounded as the other two, they were still in bad shape. Unable to do anything for them, Bannon continued on to where Uleski was.

Knelling down beside the body on the ground across from his XO, Bannon took a closer look at the still figure between them over. Only then did it dawn upon him that it was Sp4 Thomas Lorriet, the driver of Alpha 55. The twenty-year-old Indiana native's hand still grasped the hose of his protective mask as he had when he'd been fumbling to pull it free of its carrier. His mouth was opened as if he were gasping for air. The skin of his face was ashen white. His eyes were fixed and wide, but unseeing. He was dead.

Looking over at Uleski, Bannon could see his XO was shaken. Never having seen the man so despondent, he found himself at a loss as to what to say. This uneasy silence became even more unnerving when the XO, finally realizing his Team commander was staring at him, returned his gaze with a blank expression that told Bannon Uleski, like him, was having trouble coming to terms with what had happened.

Realizing they both needed to get past this awkward impasse, Bannon placed a gentle hand a hand on Uleski's shoulder and uttered one word. "Report."

After closing his eyes and swallowing hard, Uleski took in a deep breath. "The ITV crews were transferring TOW rounds when the first volley hit," he stammered. "One minute it was quiet, the next, all hell broke loose. They didn't know which way to turn. Some just flopped on the ground. Others tried for the tracks. One of them just lay where he fell, screaming for help. He kept screaming until the gas reached him. The chemical alarm went off before it was smashed."

Pausing, Uleski turned his gaze back down at Lorriet. "We all buttoned up and waited. When there was no letup, I ordered Lorriet to back it up. He didn't answer. I screamed as loud as I could, but he didn't answer. I cursed at him and called him every vile name I could think of. The whole crew started to yell at him to get the tank out of here as the impacting rounds shook the tank. By then smoke, dust and gas was seeping in as shrapnel ricocheted off the outside. All we could do was yell to Lorriet until we were hoarse. He didn't answer."

Again, Uleski paused as he started to tremble. When his eyes began to fill with tears, he turned away, either in an effort to regain his composure or to keep Bannon from seeing them. Only when he had settled down did he continue as he once more took to regarding the dead driver. "After the shelling stopped, we found him like this. His hatch was pulled over but not locked down. He never got his mask on. All the time we were yelling at him, he was dead. We didn't know," Uleski uttered mournfully. "We just didn't know." These last words trailed off into silence.

The sound of the first sergeant's M-113 and the M-113 ambulance coming up with him broke the silence. Bannon gave the shoulder he was holding a shake in an effort to make sure he was paying attention. "All right, Bob. I want you to go over to the first sergeant's track and contact the platoons on the company net. I haven't taken any SITREPs from them yet. Nor have I reported to battalion. Once you've consolidated the platoon reports, send up a Team SITREP to the S-3 and a LOGREP to the S-1 and S-4. Understand?"

For a moment Uleski looked at the Team commander as if he were speaking a foreign language. Then he blinked, acknowledging his commanding officer's instructions with nothing more than a stiff nod before slowly coming to his feet and heading over to the first sergeant's track.

As the medics, Folk, and the loader from 55 worked on the wounded, Bannon grabbed Sergeant Gwent, the gunner on 55, by the arm. "What's the condition of your tank?"

Gwent looked at him as if he were crazy. Bannon repeated his question. Ever so slowly Gwent turned his head to look at his tank for a moment, then back at Bannon.

"I... I don't know. We were so busy with the wounded and all. I don't know."

"OK, OK, I understand. But the medics and the first sergeant are here now. They can look after them. I need you to check out your tank and find out if it can still fight. The Russians may come back. If they do, the Team will need every track it's got. Grab your loader and do a thorough check, inside and out. When you're done, report back to me. Is that clear?"

Gwent looked at Bannon, looked at the tank, then nodded. "Yes, sir." With that, he called his loader over and told him what they needed to do. Together, they began to circle around their tank, checking the suspension and tracks in the gathering darkness, leaving Bannon alone for a moment to collect his own wits and decide what *he* needed to do next.

∽

As soon as the wounded were on board the ambulance, it took off for the rear, making the best possible speed. Together with the first sergeant and Folk, Bannon watched until it had disappeared in the darkness. Only when it was gone did Harrert turn to Bannon and ask him about Uleski.

Before answering, Bannon looked over at the company's M-113. He could hear the XO talking on the radio to battalion, sending up the SITREP, line by line. Uleski would be all right, he concluded and told Harrert as much before sending him to collect a dog tag from each of the bodies, if he could find one. Folk was sent over to the ITV with the damaged launcher to see if it could be driven. As they headed off to their tasks, Bannon made his way back to Alpha 66.

There he found Ortelli walking around the tank, checking the suspension and tracks. Every now and then he would stop and look closer at an end connector or pull out a clump of mud to check a bolt. Only when he was satisfied that the bolt was tight did continue on to the next one. Kelp was perched in the commander's cupola, manning the machinegun and monitoring the radio. His eyes followed the first sergeant as he went about his grim task. When Kelp saw Bannon approach, he turned his head back to the east, doing his best to pretend he'd been scanning the dark hill across the valley for signs of enemy activity the whole time.

Bannon hadn't realized how tired he was until he tried to climb up onto 66. He fell backwards when his first boost failed to get him on the tank's fender. After resting for a moment with one foot on the ground, one foot in the step loop, and both hands on the housing of 66's headlights, he took a deep breath and pulled for all he was worth. This time he made it up onto the fender where he paused, pondering his next move for a moment.

Decisions were becoming hard to make as he made his way over to the turret and sat on the gun mantlet with both feet on the main gun. Only now did he realize just how physically and mentally drained he was. So much had happened since morning. His world and the world of every man in the Team had changed. They hadn't budged an inch from where they had been, but everywhere he looked was so foreign, so strange. What had been a lush, green valley was now a charnel house. The peaceful woods he'd stepped out into just before dawn was no more. As much as he had done to prepare himself for this day, he found it hadn't been near enough. It was all too much for a tired brain to take in. Not that he tried. Instead, he let his mind go blank as he continued to sit there perched over the 105mm cannon of 66.

∽

Folk startled him. For a moment Bannon lost his balance and almost toppled off the gun mantlet. He had fallen asleep. The darkness that enveloped them told him this fearful day was finally over. That didn't mean his responsibilities were at an end.

The short nap only accentuated his exhaustion. Looking about, Bannon saw that the ITV had pretty much burned itself out, though it was still glowing red as small fires consuming the last of its rubber. Through the trees he could see smashed Soviet vehicles were also burning. Some were like the ITV, red and glowing. Others were still fully involved with angry yellow flames licking at dense black clouds of smoke rising above them and into the still night air. The shattered and skewed trees and tree trunks added to the unnatural scene.

"Captain Bannon, the battalion commander wants to see you," First Sgt. Harrert, who was standing on the ground in front of the tank, called out. The two men looked at each for a moment as Bannon collected his thoughts.

"Are you OK, Captain?"

"Yeah. Yeah, I'm OK. Give me a minute to get my shit together. Where is the Old Man?"

"He said he's back down where you last saw each other. He wasn't sure how to get in here and didn't want to throw a track finding a way in."

"Are you finished here, Sergeant?"

"Yes, sir. The other ITV was still running. Newell is going to drive it down to the maintenance collection point. We'll turn it over to the infantry there. 55 is still operational. The only real damage was to the antennas. We replaced them with the spares we carry around and made a radio check. 55's good to go."

"And the bodies?"

"Folk and I moved them over out of the way and covered them with 55's tarp. The location has been reported to S-1. We've done we can do for them. I think we're finished here, sir"

Harrert's last comment came across more like fatherly advice than a statement of fact. He was right, of course. The hilltop had been a dumb place to put a position. It took three men killed to convince Bannon of that. He had no desire to invest any more here.

Gathering himself up, Bannon came to his feet, stood upright on the front slope of the tank and stretched. Squatting down closer to the first sergeant, he then told him to pass word on to the XO to move 55 over to the 2nd Platoon position. Harrert was to follow the XO over. Once 55 was settled in, the first sergeant was to pick up the XO and the 2nd Platoon leader in the PC and bring them over to 66's position to the right of 3rd Platoon. A runner would go for the 3rd and Mech Platoon leaders. No doubt there would be some new information to pass out once he had finished with the battalion commander. There might even be a change of mission. Even if there weren't, he still wanted to gather the leadership and assess the impact of the first day's battle on them and their platoons.

∼

With nothing more to be done there, 66 pulled out of the old headquarters position and began to carefully pick its way through the debris until they reached the logging trail. Once on the trail it only took a couple of minutes to reach their former position. They did not pull all the way up to the berm this time, but stayed back in the woods about ten meters. The other tanks had also pulled back just far enough so that they could still observe their sectors without being readily visible to the other people across the valley. The battalion commander was waiting as 66 pulled in.

Not surprisingly, Bannon found he had been right on both counts. Colonel Reynolds, who had just returned from a meeting at brigade, was there to provide an update on the *big* picture and give him an order for a new mission. Rather than pull all the team commanders back to the battalion CP, he was making the rounds and passing the word out himself. Besides, Bannon suspected, like him, Reynolds wanted to gauge the impact of the first day's battle on his principle subordinates.

The first item the battalion commander covered was a rundown on the battalion's current situation. Team Yankee had been the only team to engage the enemy within the battalion task force. For a moment, Bannon wondered why the colonel bothered to inform him of that brilliant flash of the obvious. Team Bravo had been badly mauled by artillery, losing five of its ten PCs, two of the four ITVs that had been with them, and one of the four 1st Platoon tanks TeamYankee had attached to them. The destroyed tank had taken a direct hit on the top of the turret.

The armor on a tank can't be thick everywhere, and the top is about as thin as it gets. None of Alpha 12's crew survived. Of the remaining three tanks, one had lost a road wheel and hub but had been recovered and would be back up by midnight. Because of the losses, the trauma of being under artillery for so long, and the loss of its commander, Team Bravo had been pulled out of the line in order to allow them an opportunity to regroup. D Company, held back by brigade as a reserve, had moved up to replace Bravo along the front line trace.

Charlie Company, to the left of Team Yankee, had had an easy day. They hadn't seen a Russian all day. Nor had it been on the receiving end of any artillery fire. The battalion commander told Bannon that the Charlie Company commander and his men were chomping at the bit, waiting for a chance to have a whack at the Reds.

In a dry and even voice Bannon told the battalion commander that if the gentlemen in Charlie Company were so fired up for action, they were welcome to Team Yankee's position, including the bodies. This cold, cutting remark caught Reynolds off guard. He stared at Bannon for a moment before letting the matter drop by moving on to the battalion's new mission.

In the colonel's PC, Bannon received his new orders. On the wall of the PC was a map showing the brigade's sector. The battalion task force was on the brigade's left flank. 1st Brigade, to the north, had received the main Soviet attack and had lost considerable ground. The attack against the battalion, Reynolds stated glibly, had only been a supporting attack.

Bannon thought about that for a moment. The Team's fight had been a sideshow, unimportant in the *big* picture. As that thought rattled around in his exhausted mind, he felt like screaming. Here the Team had put its collective ass on the line, fought a superior foe twice, and had three men killed and five wounded in an unimportant sideshow. His ego and pride could not accept that. What was he going to tell Lorriet's mother when he wrote her? "Dear Mrs. Lorriet, your son was killed in a nameless, insignificant sideshow. Better luck next time."

Ever so slowly, he became aware Reynolds and Major Jordan were staring at him. "May I proceed?"

The battalion commander's curt question didn't require a reply, not that Bannon would have been able to give one. The irrational anger he felt over Reynolds' revelation was simply too great to allow him to do so in a manner that would have been, for lack of a better term, *civil.*

"The 1st Brigade would be hard pressed to hold another attack," the S-3 informed Bannon in a workman like manner. "Intelligence indicates that the Soviet forces in front of 1st Brigade had lost heavily and are no longer able to attack. A second echelon division, the 28th Guards Tank Division, is moving up and is expected to be in position to attack not later than dawn tomorrow. The Air Force has been pounding the 28th Guards throughout the day, but hasn't slowed it. We have the mission of attacking into the flank of the 28th Guards Division as soon as they are fully committed in the attack."

"Okay," Bannon muttered as he nodded, letting the S-3 know he was following what he was saying.

"Task Force 3rd of the 78th will pull out of the line on order, moving north, and spearhead the attack. Team Yankee will be in the lead."

Once more Bannon's mind wandered off the matter at hand. Several hours ago, somewhere in the division's rear, while Team Yankee was still knee-deep in Russians the division's commanding general had turned to his staff and pointed at a spot on the map. "*Attack there.*" While the first sergeant and Sergeant Folk had been dragging the bodies of Team Yankee's dead to an out-of-the-way spot, the brigade commander had told the battalion commander, "*Attack there.*" Now the executor of the plan, the lead element commander, the lowest ranking person in the US Army to carry the coveted title of Commander, had his marching orders.

As he received the detailed instructions from the S-3 as to routes, objectives, fire support, and coordinating instructions, they were joined by the Team's fire-support officer or FIST Team Chief, a 2nd Lt. Rodney Unger. He had finally made it back and was already familiar with the concept of the operation, so there was no need to go over anything with him. When the S-3 finished, he asked if there were any questions or anything that the Team needed. Bannon's request that the Team be pulled out of the line now to an assembly area for a rest was denied. According to Reynolds, Team Bravo needed it more than Yankee did. As Team Bravo was going to be in reserve, Bannon next requested that the 1st Tank Platoon be returned. That request was also denied. He then requested that an ITV section be attached to the Team to make good their losses. That request too was denied as the other companies without tanks needed them more than Bannon's team. Seeing that he wasn't going to get anything from battalion but a pat on the back, a pep talk, and a boot up his ass, he stopped asking. With that, the meeting came to an end. The battalion commander and the S-3 left Team Yankee to go down to Charlie Company to calm them down before they chewed through their bit.

Uleski had the platoon leaders and the first sergeant assembled in the PC by the time the battalion commander left. They were exchanging information and observations as Bannon climbed into the track. Before he discussed the new mission, he had each platoon leader update him on the status of his platoon and the condition of the men and equipment.

All came across as tired, but confident. The first day's success, it seemed, had removed many of the fears and doubts that they had had in themselves and in their men. The Team had met the Russians, laser range finder to laser range finder, and found that they could be beaten. Even Uleski came across as being more himself, which put Bannon in a far better mood. The negative thoughts that had kept clouding his mind while he had been in the battalion commander's track were fading as the quiet, calm confidence of Team Yankee's leadership gave its commander's flagging morale a much needed boost.

According to the book, a leader is supposed to use one-third of the time he has available from when he receives a mission to when he executes it for the preparation of his order. That formula is a good guide, but it seldom works out in practice. Rather than keep his platoon leaders and FIST chief waiting while he came up with his plan, Bannon gave them what information he could. As the platoon leaders copied the graphics of the operation from Bannon's map to theirs, he considered his plan of action and quickly wrote some notes for his initial briefing. This briefing included the general situation, the enemy situation, the Team's mission, routes of movement, objectives, and a simple scheme of maneuver. The Team may have done well in its first fight, but it had been an easy one, conducted from stationary positions using a plan that had been developed for months. The new mission was an attack, a short notice one at that. He didn't want to do anything fancy or complicated. Simplicity and flexibility were what he wanted.

To this end, he decided the Team would use standard battle drill and rely on their SOP. "Order of march out of the position will be the 2nd Platoon with 55 in the lead, followed by 66, the FIST track, 3rd Platoon, and the Mech Platoon," Bannon explained. "Once across the LD, we'll either move with the two tank platoons up and abreast and the Mech trailing, or in column with 3rd Platoon overwatching the advance of 2nd. This will put the majority of the Team's combat power forward while leaving me some flexibility to change formations rapidly with minimum reshuffling. Detailed instructions, the artillery fire support plans, and any new information will be provided to you prior to the move. Anyone have any questions?"

Taking his time, he looked into the eyes of each of his subordinates, waiting for them to either ask him a question or shake their head. He followed this by reminding them they needed to ensure that their platoons stayed alert and on the radio. He also stressed the need to make sure they rotated with their crews when it came to sleeping. "We need to be wide awake and alert tomorrow when the Team rolls across the LD." With that, he dismissed the platoon leaders and turned his attention over the needs of the Team and the support plan for the attack with Uleski and Harrert.

The news the first sergeant had was not good. The heavy fighting to the north had consumed huge amounts of ammunition, in particular tank main gun ammo. Because the corps ammo resupply point was still being established, division ordered the brigades to send whatever tank ammunition they had to the 1st Brigade. The result of this order meant that the rest of Team Yankee's basic load of ammunition that was supposed to be in the battalion trains area was gone, headed north to someone else's tanks. Too tired to work himself into a rage, Bannon simply sighed. The battalion commander and the S-3 had been there for over thirty minutes without bothering to inform him of that *minor* point, leaving Bannon to wonder whose side Reynolds was on. It almost seemed as if this was some kind of test to see how far Team Yankee could go on its own.

The good news was that the Team would still get a hot meal in the morning, provided there was no interference from the Russians. New protective mask filters would be passed out at that time. Harrett, who had been working on securing them since he heard the news of the chemical attack, was confident he'd have enough replacements for the entire Team by then. An additional day's worth of MREs would also be passed out to add to the two day's supply already on the Team's tracks. The Team was in good shape as far as fuel was concerned, but

Bannon wanted to be sure, asking Harrert to see if he could arrange a top-off right after breakfast, provided battalion hadn't taken the fuel too. The three of them exchanged a few sharp and humorous remarks on that subject and, with a chuckle, broke up the meeting. The first sergeant returned Uleski and McAlister to the 2nd Platoon's positions before heading back to the trains area as Bannon, together with Unger, made their way to the FIST track where they could work on a detailed fire support plan.

Second Lt. Rodney Unger was a good FIST Team chief. He still had a lot to learn about tanks and infantry, but knew artillery and how to get it. When he was first assigned to the Team as the FIST nine months before, he still had a lot of funny ideas about what his role was and how he wanted to do business. It didn't take long to convince him that a lot of what he had been taught at Fort Sill was best left there. Once that was accomplished, Bannon taught him all the bad habits FIST chiefs use in the field.

While Unger worked up his initial fire plan based on what he had been given in the first sergeant's track, Bannon sat across from him in the more spacious FIST track, going over the scheme of maneuver in more detail. He began by considering how the Soviets might be deployed to defend their flank. All likely locations and fields of fire were marked in red. Satisfied that this Russian plan of defense was plausible, Bannon took to working on the details of how the Team was going to seize its assigned objective quickly and with minimum losses. This time, he methodically went over the actions the Team had to execute in order for it to get from the line of departure to its objective. Whenever Bannon came across a Soviet field of fire he had plotted, he weighed all options before deciding how best to deal with it. If he could, he wanted to bypass them. When it wasn't possible, he had to find a way to destroy the enemy without losing the Team in the process. He kept at this until he had charted the Team's advance along the entire axis of advance he had been given.

Once Bannon finished, Unger superimposed his supporting fire plan over the scheme of maneuver. When there was a deficiency, or Bannon required a special method of engagement from the artillery in order to support his scheme of maneuver, he explained what he wanted and waited until Unger had made the changes before continuing. As most maneuver commanders are prone to do, he asked for an enormous amount of artillery-delivered smoke. If he could have, he would have moved the Team through one huge smoke screen from where they were all the way to the objective. This gave rise to a standing joke that if every company and team commander were given all the smoke he asked for, all of Germany would have been perpetually shrouded in a dense smoke screen. But reality and the constraints of the artillery basic load reduced his demands. Only when he was satisfied with the soundness of the plan did he climb out of the FIST track and return to 66, leaving Unger to rumble off into the night in his track to pass his plan on to the battalion FSE.

The high-pitched whine of the FIST's modified M-113 faded into the night and was replaced by a stillness punctured at random intervals by distant artillery fire. The moon was out and full. Its pale gray light provided near-perfect visibility of the hill across the valley. Many of the smashed Soviet vehicles were still glowing bright red. Fires in the village continued to burn, but had died down. Everything else was quiet and peaceful. The casual observer would have been hard pressed to find any sign of life in the valley. It was amazing how quiet hundreds of men, intent on killing each other, could be.

Folk was manning the 50 when Bannon reached 66. Ortelli was asleep in the driver's compartment. Kelp was lying out asleep on top of the turret. For some reason, the image of the severed arm and wounded men at 55 flashed through Bannon's mind as he took in the scene around him. Looking at Kelp lying there, exposed to artillery fire and anything else the Soviets might throw at them, he regretted not requiring the tank crews to dig foxholes. He would have to see that that was corrected in the future. At least Kelp had his protective mask on. If nothing else, he would be spared Lorriet's fate if, sometime during the night, the Soviets launched a surprise chemical attack.

With far too many things going through his head, Bannon relieved Folk and told him to get a few hours' sleep before switching places. If the lull continued after stand-to, he would issue his complete order during a working breakfast, then get some more sleep. It was a good plan, one he prayed like hell he could implement it.

For the next two hours Bannon stood there, alternately fighting sleep and boredom. He had to change his position every five minutes in order to stay awake and semi-alert. Every hour on the hour 66 and the rest of the tracks would crank up their engines to recharge their batteries. They didn't all come up together but it was close enough. If every vehicle ran its engine on its own, the Soviets would be able to pinpoint every track by the sound of the engines. By running them together, that became more difficult. Once finished, Ortelli would immediately slip back into a deep, untroubled sleep.

With nothing else to occupy his mind once he was satisfied his plan for the attack was as good as it was going to get, Bannon began to wonder what was happening on the other side of the hill. Even with the muffled rumble of artillery in the distance and the smoldering remains of combat vehicles in the valley before him, it was difficult to come to terms with the reality that they were at war. From the Baltic Sea to the Austrian border, almost three million men were facing each other just as he and his crew were, waiting for another chance to hack away at the enemy on the other side of the valley, or across the river, or in the next village.

He tried to imagine what the young Russian company commanders were doing in the 28th Guards Tank Division. No doubt they were going over in their minds how they would seize their objectives, trying to guess where their enemy would be and how they would deal with the US forces once they were encountered just as he had. He knew enough about Soviet tactics to appreciate that their company commanders had few decisions to make. The regiment made most of them. Subordinate battalions and companies simply carried out the orders using fixed formations and battle drill. That, Bannon reasoned, must have made it one hell of a lot easier on the Russian company commander. But, if the end results were attacks such as the two Team Yankee had smashed, Bannon wanted no part of a system like that. Even if he didn't get all the support he wanted, at least he had some control in deciding how to crack the nuts Team Yankee had been handed. His only worry now was whether he had guessed right and come up with the best possible plan.

At about 0130 he woke Folk. As he was giving his gunner a few minutes to get himself together, Bannon considered waking Kelp and putting him out as an OP. That, however, would have left him out there alone, violating the cardinal sin of placing only one man out on outpost duty. In the end, he abandoned the idea as being a waste since the 3rd Platoon OP to the left, and the Mech Platoon OP to the right was already covering 66. He also decided to violate the standing rule that required each tank keep half of its crew up and alert at all times. So in a moment of weakness, he let him sleep.

Once Folk was ready, they switched places. This didn't take long, for rather than Folk rolling up his sleeping bag and Bannon rolling out another, they hot bunked with Bannon using Folk's sleeping bag. It was a normal practice in a tactical environment that allowed the relieved crewman to crash without having to screw around in the dark with gear.

With pistol at arm's reach, protective mask on, and the sleeping bag pulled over but not zipped, Bannon was finally free to close his eyes and let his mind go as the enormity of the events of the day quietly slipped away. Sleep did not follow, at least not right off, as in their place personal concerns crept in, concerns and thoughts that had been pushed aside by the needs of Team Yankee. Now that they were, for the moment taken care of, Bannon's concern about the safety and welfare of his wife and three children could no longer be kept at bay. Where was his family? Had they made it out? Were the airfields still open? Was someone protecting them and caring for them? When would he find out about them? Only sleep quieted the Team commander's troubled mind.

CHAPTER 4

Into the Vacuum

The quiet chatter of the evacuees watching the loading of a C141 was drowned out by the blast of air raid sirens. Everyone froze in place, then took to frantically looking about in the hope someone, anyone, near them knew what to do.

The first to come forward was an Air Force sergeant who began to run up along the window, yelling as he went for everyone to get back away from the windows, adding that the Air Base would be under air attack in a minute.

Like a deer in a forest fire, Pat sought safety. She noticed that the stairs leading down to the flight line had a solid wall on both sides. While not offering complete cover, they would at least provide some protection from flying glass. Yelling to her group to follow her, she grabbed Sarah and ran for the stairs. At the top of them, she told everyone to go halfway down and get against the wall on the airfield side, following only when everyone with her was accounted for and on the stairs.

The children, with a look of sheer terror on their faces, huddled against the adult they were with and held their hands over their ears. Sarah and Jane's baby were crying while Kurt pleaded with his mother to make the noise stop. Pat and the other women could offer little in the way of comfort as they were barely able to hold back their own screams.

Outside the soft muffled report of large caliber air defense weapons, heard above the wailing of the siren, grew louder and closer at an alarming rate. A gun just outside the terminal that sounded like a chain saw joined in just before the first bombs hit.

A series of crashing explosions, accompanied by the sound of shattering glass and screams of women and children on the second floor filled the terminal. Now all the children were crying or screaming. Fran pulled Sean and Debby in closer. Sue, with tears running down her face, held on to Kurt, doing her best to cover his ears and face. Jane and Pat did the same with their babies. Just as the tinkling of glass and the screams from upstairs began to subside, another series of bombs went off closer to the terminal, blowing out what glass was left and causing the screams to begin anew.

We're going to die, a panicked voice in Pat's head screamed. *We're all going to die.* This trip was no longer one of inconvenience and discomfort. It had become a life and death ordeal. Any second now the next series of bombs could hit the terminal, killing them all in the blink of an eye. This thought horrified Pat. What had she ever done to deserve this? What harm had her children ever done to anyone? What purpose would their deaths serve? It wasn't fair. It wasn't right. Unable to hold back any longer, Pat began to weep as she rocked Sarah in a vain attempt to comfort her baby.

At the height of the bombing, a disheveled Air Force captain without a hat came running in from the flight line. When he turned to run up the stairs. He stopped when he saw Pat and her group. He stared at them for a moment, then started yelling. "YOU PEOPLE, FOLLOW ME. QUICKLY!"

Pat looked at the captain. The other women looked at Pat. With no time to waste trying to coax them on with persuasion or threats, he reached out and grabbed Pat's arm. "COME ON. FOLLOW ME. I'M TAKING YOU OUT OF HERE NOW."

Without the need to give the matter the thought it deserved, and realizing anywhere would be better than where they were, Pat got up and yelled to her group to follow the officer.

Fran was first to respond, pushing Sean into the officer's arms and telling him to carry the boy before picking up Debby and following. Pat was last to leave the shelter of the stairway, watching to make sure everyone in her little group was in motion.

At the bottom of the stairs, Pat flew around the corner, bringing up the rear. Only then did she realize, to her horror, that the Air Force captain had run out of the door of the terminal and onto the flight line followed by the rest of her group. *What the hell was he doing?* She asked herself as she slowed, then stopped. After a brief moment of hesitation, she continued on after them. She had to. The bastard leading them had Sean and Sue, who was on the man's heels, had Kurt.

Once outside the pop-pop-pop, the detonations, and the ripping *burr* of the gun that sounded like a chainsaw became deafening. The shattered fuselage of the giant C-5 that had been taxiing up to the terminal was engulfed in flames, its huge wings drooping down to the ground like an injured bird. The ear splitting screech of the air raid siren, the sharp report of anti-aircraft guns and the roar of explosions drowned out the captain's voice when he turned to scream something to them. Only when she looked past him did Pat see the C-141 he was running straight toward it. He was going to get them out of here.

With a sudden clarity of mind, Pat appreciated that plane represented their last chance. This was it. There was no going back, no options. Calling upon the last reserve of nerve and strength she had left, she threw herself into this one last effort. It was now all or nothing.

Onward the group ran, swerving to the left or right only to avoid shell craters and debris strewn about the flight line. As they were circling around one of the craters, Fran suddenly stopped dead, causing Sue to ram into her from behind. When the captain noticed the women behind him had stopped, he turned, and ran back. By the time he'd reached Fran, Pat caught had up enough to see what had caused Fran to stop.

Looking down, Pat's eyes fell on the remains of several bodies tossed about the flight line. The brightly colored clothing marked them as civilian, not military. No one needed to tell her they were some of the very same they had seen heading for the C-141 before the attack had been. Caught in the open, they had been killed, which was why the captain had come back for more evacuees to take their place.

Looking up, Pat saw the captain was coming back with Sean. *NO!* a voice in her head screamed. *NO!* She wasn't going to let anything go wrong this time. Every step of the way during this evacuation had been a screw up. Now, when they were only a few feet away from what she saw as their last means of salvation, Pat was determined they were going to finish this trip. Pushing Fran, she yelled at her to go. When Fran began to run, Pat turned to Sue and took to pushing her along as well. Jane, who seemed to share Pat's resolve, followed without the need for further encouragement. When he saw the women were on the move once more, the captain let Fran catch up to him, then grabbed her with one arm and began to pull her along.

Not waiting until they reached him, the crew chief of the C-141 ran down the ramp in order to helped the women up. Another airman inside pushed them over to some empty nylon seats arranged along the sides and middle of the aircraft's cavernous body. Only when they were all on board did the captain hand Sean to the crew chief who threw the boy on a seat and buckled him in. Having done all he could for Pat and her little group, the Air Force captain ran back down the ramp toward the terminal. He was halfway there when the closing ramp shut out the view of the shattered flight line.

The crew chief and airman were still hustling about buckling in the new arrivals as the plane began to roll. Above the sobs of the women and children who filled the dark cavernous interior of the transport and the sound of the air attack outside, Pat was deafened by the roar of the transport's engines as it began to pick up speed and rumble down the runway. The pilot, she appreciated, was just as anxious to leave as she was. As if to confirm this, when he did bring the transport's nose up for lift-off, the aircraft shot up at an angle that was alarmingly steep, causing a chain reaction as everyone in the cargo bay was thrown sideways into the person seated next to her.

Pat had no sooner managed to recover from this when the transport suddenly leveled off, throwing everyone in the opposite direction, back towards the front. Glancing over her shoulder and out a small porthole-like window behind her, she saw that they were skimming along at tree top level and moving fast. No doubt, she thought, the pilot had no wish to become mixed up in the air battle or be taken under fire by nervous anti-aircraft gun crews.

Only when she was sure they were well away from Rhein-Main and safe did Pat take stock of her little group. There was a blank, emotionless stare on the face of every woman and child she laid eyes on. They, like she, were drained, exhausted, and listless. The harrowing climax of their ordeal had succeeded in beating the last bit of energy and emotion out of them. If there was one thing to be said for this sad state of affairs, it was that the long flight home was made in near total silence, with only the steady drone of the engines and an occasional whimper of a child seeking what comfort its mother could give them.

∾

Bannon was not ready to wake. It was too soon, far too soon to end his escape from reality and misery. Even with the protective mask on and lying on the hard turret roof, the sleeping bag was too comfortable to surrender without a struggle. It was just too damned soon to get up.

But Folk was persistent. As soon as he registered a muffled obscenity and some independent movement on his commander's part, he gave one more shake before seeing to it the rest of the crew was stirring.

In less than thirty minutes it would be dawn. The second day of World War III, and, as far as Bannon was concerned, just as difficult to greet as the first had been. The pain from sleeping on a hostile surface, the dullness of the mind from too little sleep, and the realization that this day would be no better than the last was a poor way to begin the day.

Sitting up, he leaned forward and squinted at Folk, trying to see if he was masked. Satisfied that he wasn't, Bannon removed his protective mask and paused to relish the feeling of cool morning air hitting his face. After sweating for two hours with the rubber mask against his skin, it was a relief to be able to breath the crisp, unfiltered morning air. Looking around, he saw Kelp stowing his gear. Folk was ordering Ortelli to crank up the tank. It was 0400. All around them, in the dark forest the sound of other tracks doing likewise could be heard. At least some of the Team was awake and alert.

Only after he'd finished stowing Folk's sleeping bag and relieving himself by standing on Alpha 66's back deck and pissing off to the side did Bannon climb down to his position as Folk slid to the gunner's position. Still groggy, but at least functioning, the crew went through their checks while they waited for stand-to and the new dawn. Computer checks, weapon checks, thermal sight check, engine readings and indications, ammo stowage and count were all ticked off until Bannon was satisfied Alpha 66 was ready.

∾

Just before dawn, Lieutenant McAlister reported that he and his platoon were observing a group of six to eight personnel in the woods across the valley from them. Early morning is the best time for detecting targets with the thermal sight because the ground and trees lack any warmth from the long absent sun. McAlister requested permission to engage with the platoon's caliber .50s. which Bannon vetoed opting instead to hit the intruders with artillery. That way they would cause the same amount of damage, or more, without having any of the Team's tanks give away their positions, which was what the people McAlister had spotted were hoping to provoke. Bannon's best guess was that the dismounted intruders belonged to a recon unit that would either call in and adjust artillery on any targets they spotted or engage with antitank guided missiles if they had them. Either way, they had to go.

At Bannon's direction, McAlister contacted the FIST Team. Using a known target reference point to shift from, he provided Unger with the location of the target and what the target was. Bannon cut into the conversation and instructed Unger to fire at least three volleys of artillery with mixed fuse settings of super-quick and delayed. The super-quick fuse setting would go off as soon as the round hit the tree branches, creating an air burst effect and showering shell fragments down on exposed personnel. The delayed fuse setting would burrow into the ground, hopefully getting anyone in foxholes. The FIST replied that he would do his best to comply. Bannon urged him to try real hard, with a great deal of emphasis on the word real.

The call for fire took close to five minutes to process. At this hour, this was not surprising. Everyone waited impatiently, hoping that the Russians didn't leave before the artillery hit. It was almost as if they were preparing to spring a prank on another fraternity. They knew what was coming and the other people didn't. But this prank was deadly. In a few moments some of the other "fraternity" brothers would be dead. The more, Bannon thought, the better.

To the rear of Team Yankee, the low rumble of the firing guns could be heard as the FIST called, "SHOT, OVER" on the Team net. McAlister replied, "SHOT, OUT." Unger's call of "SPLASH, OVER" was drowned out by the detonation of the impacting rounds.

In an excited, high-pitched voice, McAlister called, "TARGET, FIRE FOR EFFECT. TARGET, FIRE FOR EFFECT." In the excitement of the moment, he forgot that they were, in fact, firing for effect. From 66, Bannon could see the impact through the trees. He wanted to move 66 forward into its firing position to observe, but knew that would serve little purpose and unnecessarily expose his tank and crew. So he sat where he was, having to content his morbid curiosity by listening to McAlister's reports.

The guns to the rear boomed again, followed by another series of impacts. The rounds with super-quick fuse settings burst high in the trees with a brilliant orange ball of fire. For a split second it lit the surrounding trees and area like a small sun. Then it died as fast as it had appeared. Anyone staring at the blast lost his night vision. In its place were bright orange dots the blasts etched in their eyes. The final volley was no less spectacular.

As Bannon waited to hear McAlister's report on the effects of the barrage, he began to hope the results would be worth the efforts of the artillery. More was involved than merely the act of making the calculations, preparing the rounds, laying the guns, and shooting twenty-four rounds. The firing battery would now have to displace. If the Russians were alert, their target acquisition people would have picked up the flight of these incoming rounds. With some calculations of their own, they would be able to locate the guns and unleash counterbattery fires. It was therefore important for the artillery to shoot 'n' scoot. In modern combat there is no middle ground, no almost. You're either quick, or you're dead.

After observing the area for ten minutes, McAlister reported that neither he nor any other tank in his platoon could detect any more movement in the target area or to the left or right. Bannon therefore reported to battalion that they had engaged and probably killed eight dismounted personnel. Whatever those people had been doing or planning to do, they weren't going to do it to Team Yankee this morning. The efforts of the cannon cockers were rewarded.

∼

The Soviets were also placing demands on their cannon cockers that morning. The American guns barely had fallen silent when the sky to the east was lit up with distant flashes, followed by the now familiar rumble of distant artillery. At first Bannon thought that it was counterbattery fire searching out the guns that had just fired for the Team. But the crash of the impacting rounds drifted down from the north, not from the rear. After watching and listening to the barrage for five minutes without any noticeable letup, it became obvious that this was more than counterbattery fire. In all likelihood, it was the preparatory fire heralding the attack of the 28th Guards Tank Division.

The night slowly gave way to the new dawn as the Soviet artillery preparation to the north continued. First Sergeant Harrert appeared with breakfast, passing the word to the track commanders to send half of their men at a time back for chow. At first Bannon was apprehensive about allowing the men to dismount for breakfast. He was fearful that the enemy would launch another holding attack against them as they had the day before. If not a ground attack, he at least expected the Soviets to pin the battalion with artillery. But nothing happened. Perhaps, he reasoned, the Soviets didn't have any more units they could throw away in useless holding attacks. Perhaps the people the Team had hit with artillery across the valley were antitank guided missile teams or artillery forward observers who had had the mission of pinning the battalion. Perhaps, perhaps, perhaps. As the platoon leaders began to gather for the early morning meeting, he gave up on the second guessing. No one was shooting at him or the Team right now and that, in Bannon's mind, was all that mattered.

∿

One by one the leadership of Team Yankee gathered around the rear of the first sergeant's PC, map case and notebook tucked under arm with breakfast and coffee in hand as they had done just twenty-four hours earlier. But this morning was different. The nervous apprehension of the previous day was gone. They still had the same slightly haggard and disheveled look from too little sleep and too much stress which all soldiers who had been in the field too long wore. That was to be expected. Today, however, there was also a look of confidence on everyone's face, a calm, steady look. In the words of Civil War veterans, they had seen the elephant and having done so, had been changed forever.

It made little difference that the Team had been incredibly lucky, that their task had been simple and straightforward. It didn't matter that the new mission was going to turn the tables around and expose the Team to the same punishment that it had given to the Soviets. What did was that they had won their first battle, erasing any doubts as to their equipment, their leadership, and their own perceived ability to face combat. The Team was ready to move forward and tackle its new mission.

The meeting started with a discussion of the previous day's action. Just as they had done numerous times after a training exercise, the officers and senior NCOs present went over step-by-step what had happened. First the platoon leaders gave their account and observations. Then Bannon gave his. This was followed by a brief discussion on what needed to be done better the next time. With that aside, Bannon issued the completed Team operations order that he had worked on earlier that morning. After he finished, Unger went over the fire-support plan in detail and answered any questions. Bannon ended his portion of the meeting by informing the platoon leaders he would visit each of them for a one-on-one brief back of their platoon plans. In the meantime, they were to prepare for the attack.

Bannon was about to turn the meeting over to the XO and first sergeant so that they could cover the Team's admin and maintenance chores when a call from battalion put an end to his plan to catch up on some sleep. There was going to be a meeting in thirty minutes at the battalion CP to go over the new mission. Not wanting to move 66 out of position, he decided to use Harrert's PC. While the platoon leaders moved and the PC prepared to roll, Bannon quickly shaved and washed his hands and face. Cleaning up was going to make him late, but it was a matter of pride that he look as sharp as possible. He might be miserable, but he didn't have to look miserable. Standards had to be preserved.

∿

The lack of change at the battalion CP struck Bannon as odd. He really couldn't say what should have been different. But something should have been. Back at TeamYankee he could feel the change that had occurred between yesterday morning and this morning. The CP, on the other hand, was still running as if it were conducting a training exercise. The M-577 command post vehicles were parked side by side with their canvas tent extensions set up and connected with a massive camouflage net covered the tracks and extensions. Around this was barbed wire with one entrance guarded by a soldier checking access passes as staff officers and other commanders entered the tactical operations center, or TOC. Somehow, this just seemed wrong to Bannon.

While the outside was quiet and peaceful, the inside was alive with the usual chaos that comes before the issuance of an operations order. At one end of the crowded space staff officers and NCOs were busily updating and preparing maps and charts for the briefing. Team commanders gathered in a corner, quietly talking amongst themselves. The XO sat with the battalion commander in the middle going over maintenance and supply matters with him. The sight of all this running around, confusion, and last-minute preparation by the staff left Bannon wondering what they had been doing all night. Not that that was hard to figure out. The lack of haggard faces and bags under the eyes of the staff officers and their NCOs betrayed the fact that late nights and little sleep were not a part of their daily routine. How long, he wondered, was that going to last.

Off to one side was First Lieutenant Peterson, formerly the XO, sitting in the seat his commanding officer should have been occupying. Dirty and disheveled, his gaunt, vacant expression stood in sharp contrast to everyone around him. Bannon watched for a few minutes while Peterson simply sat there, staring down at the map and notebook he held in his lap. Everyone in the crowded TOC was making a valiant effort to ignore him, for those who hadn't seen the elephant yet didn't know how to treat him.

Bannon felt sorry for Peterson. Yesterday had been an emotional nut roll for Team Yankee despite the fact that he had been in command for ten months and had been training his people for what happened. It must have been sheer hell for Peterson to watch his team get ripped to shreds, then be given the job of pulling what remained together. The treatment the staff was giving him was, in Bannon's opinion, beyond cold. It was downright cruel. Yet having come to that conclusion, Bannon found himself at a loss as to what he could do to help the poor bastard. In the end, despite his feelings, he did as the others were doing. He did his best to avoid Lieutenant Peterson.

∽

Major Willard, the battalion XO, began by going over the briefing sequence before turning to the intelligence officer, or S-2, who began the formal portion of the briefing. With pointer in hand and every hair in place, he went over the *big picture*, talking about how the *hostile forces* had initiated hostilities, how this combined arms army was driving here, and that combined arms army was pushing there, and some tank army was moving forward ready to exploit the penetration to our north.

The situation in NORTHAG, or Northern Army Group, was already grim according to him. Soviet airborne forces had seized Bremerhaven. Soviet ground forces were making good progress and had broken through in several areas. In CENTAG, or Central Army Group where both forward-deployed US corps were, the situation wasn't nearly as bad. While one could claim that US forces made the difference there, anyone who understood Germany's geography and Soviet strategy knew better. The terrain in NORTHAG was far more conducive to massed, mobile warfare than the hilly, heavily forested landscape of central and southern Germany. The North German Plain provided a natural highway for armies to flow from the east to the west across Germany and into Holland, Belgium, and France. By luck of the draw and post-World War II political agreements, the US had the easiest and least important area to defend.

As interesting as the overall picture was, Bannon needed to know what enemy forces were facing his Team as well as the composition, locations, and strength of the Soviet forces in the area where the battalion was going to attack. But instead of nuts and bolts, the S-2 continued to lecture them on skyscrapers. When he finished and turned to sit down without mentioning anything about the Soviet forces they would be facing, Bannon half jumped out of his seat.

"Wait a minute! What about the people across the valley from us? What are they doing now and what do you expect them to do?"

For a moment the S-2 looked at Bannon as if he didn't understand the question. "Oh. Well, I don't think they will be doing much after the pounding we gave them." With that, he continued to his seat.

Bannon was livid! The pounding *we* gave them! "What kind of a bullshit answer is that?" he growled. "And what's this *we* shit? Except for a few shots from the scouts, I only know of one team that engaged the *hostile forces* yesterday."

In a flash, the battalion commander was on his feet and staring down at Bannon. With his index finger almost touching Bannon's nose and his face contorted with rage, he laid into him. "That will be enough, Bannon. If you got a burr up your ass about something, you see me after this. We got a lot to cover and not a lot of time. Is that clear?"

Bannon had overstepped his bounds, lost his cool, and offended Colonel Reynolds and his staff. But he was in no mood to buckle under, either. The S-2 hadn't given him a single piece of useful information that would contribute to the success of the upcoming mission. He wanted that information.

"Sir, with all due respect, the S-2 hasn't told me squat about the enemy now facing me or those we will be facing when we move into the attack. I need to know what they are doing and where they are if we're going to pull that attack off."

"With all due respect, *Captain*," Reynolds snapped, "I recommend that you shut up and pay attention."

The battalion commander had spoken, and the conversation was terminated. Without waiting for any sign of acknowledgement, he turned around and resumed his seat, instructing the S-3 to proceed. With the odds being that the S-2 really didn't know what was happening, Bannon let the matter drop.

In the tense silence that followed, Major Frank Jordan stood up and took his place in front of the map displaying the graphics for the battalion's attack. Jordan was, in Bannon's opinion, an outstanding officer and a professional by any measure. In the past he had always done all he could to make up for the shortcomings of the other battalion staff officers. By doing so, he became the real driving force behind the battalion. Colonel Reynolds might make the final decisions and do the pushing in the field, but it was Jordan who developed the battalion's game plans and made all the pieces fit. He was also easy to work with, a quality that made the time Bannon spent with the 3rd of the 78th a bit more tolerable.

After waiting a moment until everyone was settled again, Jordan began his briefing. The organization of the battalion, or task force as a battalion with tanks and infantry companies combined is called, remained as it had been from the beginning. The friendly situation, or the mission of the units to the battalion's left and right as well as the mission of the battalion's higher headquarters, hadn't changed from what the S-3 had briefed the previous night. "Our mission is as follows. Task Force 3-78 Mech will attack at 0400 hours Zulu 6 August to seize the town of Arnsdorf. On order, the task force will continue the attack to the north to seize the high ground south of Unterremmbach, northeast to the bridge at Ketten am Der Hanna, or west against objects yet to be determined."

From there, Jordan went over the plan as to how the battalion would carry out its new mission step-by-step. Little had changed from what he'd told Bannon the night before. The main difference was that he tied together a lot of the loose ends and explained what would happen after the battalion got to Arnsdorf.

The operation would kick off with a relief in place that night by the divisional cavalry squadron starting at 2400 hours Zulu. Team Bravo, already out of the line, would be the first to move. Team Yankee would follow once it had been relieved in place. Next would be Charlie Company, then Delta Company. Once the battalion was closed up on Team Bravo, it would make its way north. The route the battalion would move along was not the most direct, as division wanted to deceive the Soviets as to the intent of the battalion and the point of attack for as long as possible. If all worked out as planned, they would arrive at the line of departure, or LD, at 0400 and roll straight into the attack without stopping.

The battalion would attack in columns of companies, with one company behind the other. When they approached the town of Kernsbach, they would leave the road and move cross-country. Just east of Kernsbach they would pass through the US front lines and begin to deploy. Team Bravo would move to the high ground northeast of Kernsbach and take up overwatch positions in the northern edge of the Staat Forest. From there it would cover Team Yankee's advance. Major Jordan did not expect that Team Bravo would encounter any sizable enemy forces during this maneuver. If there were any enemy force, he pointed out as a subtle sop to Bannon, they would most likely be reconnaissance elements who would give ground quickly. Once Team Bravo moved into position, Team Yankee would be in the lead.

Team Yankee's first task was the seizure of an intermediate objective called Objective LOG, which was located midway between the line of departure, Team Bravo's location, and Arnsdorf. Once it had cleared Objective LOG, Charlie

Map 4: The Battalion Plan of Attack

Company would turn west and seize the village of Vogalburg. Delta Company, the trail company, would close up behind Team Yankee once Charlie Company was out of the way. If all went without a hitch, Jordan explained, Team Yankee was to continue to move north to Hill 214, called Objective LINK, without stopping. Once on Hill 214, Team Yankee would take up positions to overwatch Delta Company, much the same as Team Bravo had done for Team Yankee before in order to cover the attack of Delta Company as they moved up and seized Arnsdorf. Once in Arnsdorf, the brigade commander would then decide where the battalion would strike. That decision would depend upon the situation at that time and the reactions of the Soviets to an attack into their flank.

As he listened, Bannon became mildly alarmed. There were aspects of the plan that made him uneasy. Chief amongst them was a total lack of information on enemy strength and disposition. From an operational stand point, the seizure of Vogalburg by Charlie Company appeared to be unnecessary and dangerous. They would be out there alone, unable to receive support from other battalion elements. The only thing that kept him from raising any objections over that issue was that their presence in Vogalburg would protect the left flank of Team Yankee as it was moving to Hill 214.

The issue he did feel strong enough about to voice his concern was the lack of artillery preparation on Objective LOG. In his mind, that hill was just too good a position not to be occupied by the Soviets. When Jordan finished and asked for questions concerning the execution of the mission, Bannon recommended that a short but violent artillery prep, followed by smoke, be put on that objective. Both the S-3 and the colonel denied the request, stating that the element of surprise would be lost. "I expect the attack to be so fast and such a surprise to the Soviets that anyone there will be unable to react in time," Reynolds pointed out. "Besides, Team Bravo will be in overwatch, ready to smother that hill with direct and indirect fire if it's needed.

This statement caused Unger and Bannon to exchange glances. The temptation to press Reynolds on this matter, in the wake of his tiff with the S-2, caused Bannon to conclude that no matter what he said, someone was bound to tell him he was wrong. He therefore kept his peace. There'd be time later, he told himself, to get together with his own FIST and make sure he drafted up a backup plan just in case Bravo failed to cover them.

The S-3 was followed by the battalion S-4 who updated the gathered commanders and staff on the current status of supply, maintenance, supply routes, and a myriad of other details. As they were all covered in a written order they had been handed, Bannon tuned him out, turning his attention, instead, to the map sitting in his lap and going over, in his mind, the operation from beginning to end in an effort to make sure he understood all of the missions and tasks Team Yankee had to perform. To him, there is nothing worse than returning to the company after a battalion briefing to give his order only to be confronted by one of his platoon leaders asking him a question he could not answer. As they were playing for keeps this time, Bannon wanted to make damn sure that he hadn't missed a thing.

The colonel's rousing "Let's go kick ass and take names," speech at the end of the briefing brought Bannon back to the here and now. Reynolds knew he had not been paying attention to the last portion of the briefing, especially to his kick ass speech. Bannon didn't really care. His Team was only an attachment, a very bothersome one at that. As such, he was expected to be somewhat different and, on occasion, a bit of a maverick. Today had been a good case in point. With the sound of Charlie Company's commander chanting an obscene Jody call, the briefing broke up.

On his way out, Bannon briefly stopped in front of the intelligence map to see if there was any useful information he could glean from it. The S-2 watched him as if he expected Bannon to turn and attack. After studying the red lines and symbols for a couple of minutes without being able to find anything of use, he gave up and left. Team Yankee would find out soon enough what was there, the hard way.

∽

The balance of the day passed rather slowly. After arriving back at the Team position, Bannon made another analysis of the terrain they would be covering. Satisfied that he had gotten as much as he could from his map, he rewrote those parts of the plan that needed to change because of the briefing at battalion and the second map study. In reality, not much had. A few new artillery targets, a better concept for crossing the stream west of the village of Lemm, and some more information on what would happen after Arnsdorf was about all. With that finished, he sent Kelp off to notify the platoon leaders that they were to assemble at 66's location at 1300 hours for an update and further instructions.

As Bannon had been going over his plan, the Team went about its business in a slow and deliberate way. After stand-to, the checks and inspections that had not been performed while waiting for the dawn were completed. All problems that turned up during them were reported to the platoon sergeants, who in turn reported them to the first sergeant, who in turn reported them to maintenance personnel.

Once all checks had been completed and requests for maintenance made, the weapons were cleaned. First came the crew-served weapons. Every tank and personnel carrier had one M2 caliber .50 machinegun, affectionately known as a Ma Duce by every generation of American service personnel from before World War II. It was the same heavy machinegun the Army had used in that war and, despite monumental leaps in weapons technology, was still considered the best heavy machinegun in the world.

Then there were two M240, 7.62mm machineguns on each tank. These were of Belgian design and, when compared to the weapon they'd replace, were good weapons. Of course, anything would have been better than the M219 machinegun which some of the old tankers claimed had been the only single-shot machinegun in the world. One of the M240s was located next to the main gun, mounted coaxially with it, hence its nickname "COAX." The second M240 was mounted on a free-swinging mount outside the loader's hatch. The loader had little need for a weapon as his primary job was to feed the main gun. But since the loader's M240 was interchangeable with the COAX, it had value. Besides, it gave the loader something to hang onto when the tank was moving.

While some of the platoon were working on the machineguns, three or four of the men went around cleaning out the main guns with a twenty-foot rammer staff topped with a bore brush. It took three to four men to maneuver the staff and then ram the tight-fitting brush down the gun tube. Rather than have each crew assemble its own staff, the platoon sergeants had one tank, usually his, put one together and then, pulling one man from each crew for the detail, had them go from tank to tank and clean all the platoon's gun tubes. It was efficiency and teamwork in action.

After the tanks and the personnel carriers with all their crew-served weapons were squared away, each man took to cleaning his own individual weapon. For the tankers, this was a caliber .45 pistol for the tank commander and the gunner. The driver and loader each had a .45 and a caliber .45 M3 submachine gun. This last weapon also was a veteran of World War II, but it had not aged as well as the M2 machinegun. Some said the M3 was worthless. Bannon always considered that rating too generous.

Only after all the equipment had been squared away were the men free to tend to their personal needs and hygiene. The Team worked under the old cavalry principle, "The horse, the saddle, the man." The men understood this and, for the most part, abided by it. None, including Bannon, had any clear idea what was going to happen next. All they knew with any degree of certainty was that their best chance of survival was to stay with the Team. They knew what the Team was doing, and that there was safety in numbers. What lay behind the hills to the front and rear was a mystery few were interested in exploring. They wanted to stay with the Team, and to stay with the Team, their track and weapons had to work. There was no false patriotism, no John Waynes in Team Yankee, only tankers and infantrymen doing their jobs in order to survive.

∾

Except for some sporadic shelling by the Soviets, the afternoon passed quietly, allowing tank commanders and squad leaders to keep half of their men on alert while the rest slept. After the 1300 hour meeting with the platoon leaders, Bannon was free to catch up on some personal needs he'd not had time for earlier. Washing from head to toe was a priority. After twenty-four hours in the chemical protective suit, he was ripe. The only reason no one else had noticed just how bad he stunk was because they were just as dirty and smelly as he was. It had only been at the battalion CP that he had noticed how filthy he was in comparison to people who were not on the battalion staff, not that he really cared if he had offended anyone on the staff. Once he'd finished washing up, he let Uleski know that he was checking out of the net and get some sleep.

This latest respite lasted a grand total of forty-five minutes, for the cavalry troop commander and his platoon leaders who would be relieving the Team that night showed up for coordination and a reconnaissance. They were from Bravo Troop, 2nd of the 14th Cavalry, the divisional cavalry squadron. Bannon had met the troop commander several times before, so he was surprised when a tall, lanky first lieutenant introduced himself as the troop commander. When he asked what had happened to Captain Farrar, Bannon was told that he was missing in action.

The former troop commander, it seemed, had given the order for the troop to withdraw, after that was not seen again. He, his personnel carrier, and its crew had all disappeared while they were moving back to their next position. This put a chill on the coordination meeting and the recon. Conversation was limited to simple questions and answers as to the positions, enemy activities, and the lay of the land. As soon as the first lieutenant was satisfied that he had all the information he needed, he and his platoon leaders left.

It wasn't until near dusk that the Soviets became restless and began a massive shelling to the rear of the Team. This sent everyone in the Team scrambling for cover in his tracks or diving for the bottom of his foxhole as scores of shells screamed overhead, blindly searching for targets in the battalion's rear. Their fears were only partially relieved by the fact that it could have been worse; those shells could be hitting the Team itself. Once crews were buttoned up and dismounted infantry were snug in their holes, all they could do was wait patiently, alert and ready for either a ground attack, or a shift in the artillery fire onto their positions.

Given a choice, the ground attack was the more inviting prospect to Bannon and the bulk of Team Yankee. At least they could do something to the attacking troops. The enemy would be in the open where he could be seen, hit, and destroyed. That wasn't true of artillery. Of course friendly artillery could direct counterbattery fires against the Soviet guns. But that wasn't the same. The Team, if it were the target, would not be able to do anything but hunker down and pray.

As it turned out, neither occurred. As the day finally came to a close, the Team began to prepare to move out. While the rest of the crew readied 66,

Bannon pondered the meaning of the prolonged artillery attack. Had the Soviets somehow gotten wind of the battalion's planned move? Had they destroyed the roads and bridges to the rear? Had Team Bravo been hit again, or had it been the turn of the battalion CP to see the elephant? Would Soviet artillery strike again while they were moving? He, of course, did not have the answers to those questions, and radio listening silence on the battalion radio net remained in force and unbroken. He therefore turned his efforts to a more useful pursuit, dinner.

At 2345 hours the Team started their engines and revved them up to as near normal operating RPMs as possible. As they were not going to have friendly artillery fire cover the noise of the movement, they hoped that by running the engines all together, the Soviets might not notice any change in the Team's established habits. Chances of that working for long were slim, however, for the high-pitched squeak of a tank's sprockets and the crunching noise of tracks in motion could not be covered by anything less than an artillery barrage. But in Bannon's mind, it was worth a try.

The cavalry troop began to arrive on schedule. They came up along a small trail that ran west to east to the rear of the 2nd Platoon. That platoon began to put the Team's relief in place by pulling back from the tree line and moving south along the trail. As soon as the 2nd was out of its position and cleared the trail junction, the first cavalry platoon moved in where 2nd Platoon had been. As the 2nd moved along the trail, Bannon counted the tanks passing 66's position. When the fourth one had passed, he gave Ortelli the order to fall in behind the last of 2nd Platoon's tank. The movement of 66, followed by Unger's FIST track passing it was the signal for the 3rd Platoon to begin its move. As with 2nd Platoon, as soon as the last 3rd Platoon tank pulled out, the second cavalry platoon began to move into 3rd Platoon's vacated positions. The process was repeated with the Mech Platoon, which followed the 3rd. In this way, two company-sized units changed places in the dark without a single word other than that between the track commanders and their drivers.

Uleski, leading the Team, hugged the tree line on the northern side of the small valley that the Soviets had tried so hard to reach. When he reached a point about three kilometers west of the village, he moved onto the road and slowly began to pick up speed at a predetermined rate. Had he gone too fast at the beginning, the Mech Platoon at the tail of the column would have been left behind, as they were still hugging the tree line. Only when the column finally reached the designated march speed and was about to hit the first checkpoint along it on time did Bannon began to relax. The relief had gone off without a hitch and the Team had gotten out of the line without drawing fire. Now, he thought, if the rest of the operation went off this well, it would be a piece of cake.

∾

The drive through the dark countryside was quiet and eerie. The only lights visible were the small pinpricks from the taillights of the tank in front and the blackout drive lights of the tank behind. The steady whine of the tank's turbine engine along with the rhythmic vibrations caused by the tracks had a hypnotic effect, forcing Bannon to make an effort to stay awake and pay attention to where they were as the column moved along. Reading a map with a red filtered flashlight on a moving tank while trying to pick out terrain features on the darkened countryside was difficult but not impossible. Although Uleski was leading, Bannon needed to monitor exactly where they were at all times as a check on Uleski's navigation and in case something unexpected popped up. The platoon leaders and platoon sergeants were expected to do the same.

On board the tank all was quiet. Both the Team and the battalion radio nets were on radio listening silence. If the radios were used freely, Soviet radio direction finding units would be able to keep track of where they were going and, if passed to their intel officers in sufficient time, figure out what they were up to. In the loader's hatch next to Bannon, Kelp was standing on his seat, halfway out of the turret and facing to the rear of the tank. He was the air guard. It was SOP that the loader would watch to the rear for air attack and any surprises from that quarter. Folk was like Bannon, fighting to stay awake. He was having little success. During a road march the gunner was supposed to cover his assigned sector of observation at all times. But when there is a whole column in front and little prospect of imminent action, it is difficult to maintain a high state of vigilance. Only Bannon's knowledge that he would be ready when he was needed allowed the gunner to doze off and remain undisturbed.

The only chatter that took place over 66's intercom was between Bannon and Ortelli. Marching in column at night, after a long day, is worst for the driver. Not only does he have to fight the hypnotic effects of the steady engine noise and vibration the rest of the crew labored under, he had to be ever vigilant least the vehicle to his front suddenly stopped or changed directions. Drivers moving in column had a tendency to stare at the taillights of the tank in their front and become mesmerized by them. When that happens, they are slow to notice a sudden change that would result in a collision. Therefore, tank commanders tried to ensure that even if no one else was fully awake and alert, the driver was.

As they moved deeper into the rear area, other traffic and friendly units began to appear. The farther back the Team went, the more numerous these run-ins became. The first formed units they came across were the combat support troops and the artillery units. At one point Team Yankee went past a self-propelled artillery battery lined up but pulled off to the side of the road as if waiting for the battalion to pass. Every now and then a single vehicle or a group of three or four trucks would pass headed in the opposite direction toward the front carrying fuel, munitions, supplies and other badly needed commodities units still needed there in order to stay in the fight. At one road junction MPs were directing traffic, alternately letting one vehicle from the battalion column proceed, then one from another column on the intersecting road go through. Occasionally the Team would come across lone vehicles on the side of the road. Some were broken down. Others had been destroyed by artillery or air attacks. A few were filled with sleeping men who, having grown too tired to continue or having become separated from their unit, decided the best thing they could do was to pull over, get some sleep, and wait for daylight before going on.

The villages the Team passed were now populated with a new class of inhabitants. Signal units, headquarters units, and support troops of every description had moved in and set up housekeeping. Night was the time when many of these units came to life and went about carrying out their assigned tasks. This was especially true of supply units. All were in a hurry to resupply the units they were supporting before the new day brought out the Soviet birds of prey that feed on supply convoys.

It was just after passing through one of these busy little hubs of nocturnal activity that the Team hit its first snag. Alpha 66 lurched to an abrupt halt without warning. At first Bannon thought they had hit something. Without waiting for Bannon to ask, Ortelli informed him that they were all right, but that the tank in front had stopped. Bannon watched its dark form for a few minutes, expecting it to move and continue the march any minute. When it didn't, he decided to dismount and walk up to the head of the column. Whatever was wrong, it wasn't serious enough to break radio listening silence. In his place Folk, wakened by the jarring stop, moved up into the commander's position.

Bannon was not happy about the disruption in the march, but was thankful for the chance to walk around some, stretch his legs, and break the monotony. It was 0345 Alpha time. They had been moving for almost three hours and were scheduled to attack in another hour and fifteen minutes. As he moved up the column, he noticed a lot of activity in front of the Team and in the fields at the side of the road. Further up ahead he could see lights a little beyond the head of the column.

Uleski was already dismounted and was talking to some people when Bannon reached Alpha 55. One of the people with the XO turned out to be an engineer officer.

"Well, Ski, what do we have?" Bannon asked as he joined them.

"Sir, this is Captain Lawson, commander of the 79th Bridge Company" Uleski informed Bannon as he motioned to a tall captain across from him. "His people put this ribbon bridge in earlier today. When Team Bravo crossed it, too many tanks got onto the bridge at once and did some damage. Captain Lawson has to close the bridge and repair it before we can pass."

"Captain Lawson, Sean Bannon, commanding Team Yankee. How long is it going to take your people to unscrew the mess some of my tanks made?"

Lawson gave him an estimate and a brief explanation of what had to be done and why the work had to be finished before he would chance having any more tanks cross. "Barring any unforeseen problems, it shouldn't take more thirty minutes." As Lawson seemed to know what he was about, and his people were hustling, Bannon asked him to keep the XO posted, excused himself and Uleski, and let Lawson get on with his work.

Both Bannon and Uleski agreed that except for the bridge, everything so far was going very well. After telling him to stay at the front and monitor the work on the bridge, Bannon was going to walk down the column and have the tanks disperse and shut down. This halt would give the people a chance to dismount, shake out their legs, and check their tracks. If the engineers finished before he returned, Uleski was to have his driver crank up 55 as a signal.

The crews were slow to respond. They were tired. Perhaps the halt was a good thing, Bannon quickly concluded. It would give everyone a break. One by one the tanks moved off the road, with every other one alternating to the left, then the right. All stopped facing out at a forty-five-degree angle. This was a formation called a herringbone, used by mechanized forces at times like this. By the time Bannon had reached the 3rd Platoon, he didn't need to tell the crews any more. The tank commanders began to move their tracks off onto the side in the alternating pattern when they saw the tanks in front of them do so. By the time he reached the Mech Platoon, the entire center of the road was cleared.

It was then that it occurred to him that something was wrong. Had Charlie Company kept to the road march timetable published by battalion, it should have been closing up behind the Team by now. But there was no one behind the Mech Platoon belonging to the battalion. The road was clear for as far as Bannon could see. When the last of the tracks had shut down their engines, he walked about a hundred meters down the road and listened for the distinctive whine of Charlie Company's personnel carriers. Still night air, an occasional rumble from distant artillery, and the pounding and yelling of the engineers working on the bridge at the head of the column was all that could be heard. After five minutes, he abandoned his vigil and began to walk back to the head of the column. He really didn't know if there was, in fact, anything wrong. Unfortunately, with radio listening silence in effect, he had no way of finding out. All he could do was hope that if something really terrible had happened to the rest of the battalion, someone would take the initiative to break radio listening silence and spread the word. But that was a hope, not a sure thing, giving rise to a bad feeling that things were not going as well as he had thought before their unscheduled halt. If something was wrong, there wasn't a damned thing he could do about it.

❧

It took Pat's parents a moment to realize that their joyous welcome wasn't evoking any response. She barely acknowledged their presence. All she did was look at them with a unblinking stare, returning their greeting with a soft, almost hesitant, "Hi Mom, Dad," as she stood there with her three children. Sarah had her arms wrapped tightly around her mother's neck as if holding on for dear life. Sean was leaning against her side, grasping one of her hands with both of his while Kurt clung to her other arm with head tucked down, sucking his thumb.

For an uncomfortable moment Pat's parents simply stood there, not knowing what to do or say. Her father broke this uncomfortable silence by offering to go get their suitcases while they waited there. Pat's simple response, "there aren't any," further ratcheted up her parents already anxiety. After her father gave her a long, hard look, he turned and went off to pull the car around to the front of the terminal.

When Pat and the children moved to leave, they moved as one, none of them wanting to let go of the other. Pat's mother continued to stare, feeling less and less at ease in the presence of her daughter. As they left the terminal, an airman took Pat's name, the children's names, her husband's name and unit, and Pat's destination. The final checklist and roster in their long odyssey.

Outside, Pat and the children climbed in the back seat of her father's car. Even in the car they continued to clutch onto each other as if fearful of letting go. Only as they were pulling away did Pat turn and watched as the terminal faded from sight. They were finally leaving military control.

She thought about that for the moment. She thought about the other wives and their children. She looked at her parents in the front seat and asked herself the same question tens of thousands of other military wives were asking themselves; Now what? The evacuation was over, but now what? There was nothing more to do. She was safe. Her children were safe. She was going back to her parent's home.

But what then? Wait? Wait for what? For the war to end? For word to come about her husband? And what kind of word would it be? Pat had listened to stories of Old Army wives who had waited while their husbands were in Vietnam. She wasn't ready for that, she told herself. Even now, safe in the US, the dark abyss of the trackless future opened before her.

Like an earthen dam that had tried to hold back more water than it could, her resolve collapsed. As she began to cry, her children silently tightened their grips on their weeping mother in an effort to comfort her as well as themselves.

In the front seat her parents, not knowing what to do or say, simply stared at the road ahead.

CHAPTER 5

Hunter and Hunted

Twenty-eight minutes from the time Bannon had talked to Captain Lawson, Alpha 55 cranked up. The bridge was opened and ready for Team Yankee. The engineers, however, made sure that the tanks didn't screw up their work again. An engineer NCO stood at the near end of the bridge, stopping each tank as it approached the ramp where he would hold it until the tank on the bridge got off on the far side of the river. When it was Alpha 66's turn at the on ramp, Lawson came up to the side of the tank.

"Right on schedule, Lawson," Bannon shouted down to him. "Your people done good. Give 'em a well-deserved atta boy for me."

"Will do," Lawson yelled. "Give the Russians hell."

With a thumbs up and a grin, 66 rolled onto the bridge as Lawson waved. The military was strange like that. In the middle of the night you run into a major problem that requires you to put your faith in someone you never met before and probably would never see again. But that person knocks himself out to do his job and helps you get on with yours. Lawson and his engineers had done their job and done it well. Now it was Team Yankee's turn to continue on and be about theirs.

Crossing one at a time was a slow process. Uleski kept the pace down until he was sure the entire Team had cleared the bridge. He then began to pick up speed slowly until he reached, then slightly exceeded, the former march speed. It was now 0330 hours Zulu and the sky in the east was becoming light.

Further back in the column, once the Team had resumed its march, Bannon checked his map and made a few quick calculations. Team Yankee was forty-five minutes behind schedule. According to the battalion's order, it was supposed to be crossing the line of departure in another thirty minutes. Even if they were to exceed the published road march speed and run flat out in an effort to make up for lost time, Bannon knew there was no way they would hit the LD as 0400. Besides, he reminded himself as he often had to when working with the infantry, the tanks could not travel at their top speed. Besides eating up copious amounts of fuel, something the M-1 tank was very good at, the personnel carriers attached to the Team would not have been able to keep up. Since crossing the LD on time without the infantry or the FIST was a nonstarter, he kept the Team together and moving at the speed prescribed in the battalion order.

What concerned Bannon more than being late, however, was the failure of Charlie Company to close up at the bridge. Even as the Team was leaving the bridge site, he couldn't resist the urge to take one more look back across the river in the gathering light, searching for a glimpse of anyone else in the battalion. But there was no sign of Charlie Company, Delta Company, the battalion CP, or trains. Charlie Company was thirty-five minutes behind schedule for some reason. Perhaps the battalion had been informed of the problem at the bridge and had sent Charlie Company along another route. If that were the case, Charlie Company could very well be in front of Team Yankee. Of course, there was always the possibility Charlie Company was lost or was being held up in a massive traffic jam in one of the small villages. All that Bannon did know for certain was that Team Bravo was in front of Team Yankee. With that as a given, all he could do was to carry on as ordered. Hopefully when they closed up on Team Bravo someone would be there who knew what was going on.

❧

By 0520 Team Yankee was only three kilometers south of Kernsbach at the point where they were to turn off the road and begin to deploy. But rather than make that turn, the tanks to his front began to deploy into another herringbone formation on alternating sides of the road. Twisting about, Bannon signaled the FIST track following 66 to pull off even as he was instructing Ortelli to drive up to the head of the column.

Not surprisingly, Bannon found Major Jordan's PC sitting on the side of the road next to Alpha 55. To prevent a cluster of parked vehicles, Bannon pulled off on the opposite side of the road. At this point they were only six kilometers from the line of departure that was, unless things had radically changed while they had been on the move, still the forward edge of the battlefield.

Bannon found Jordan standing next to Uleski, looking unhappy and impatient to be on his way. The S-3 began talking while Bannon was still making his way across the road toward him. "There has been a change in plans. You're to pull your Team into an assembly area over there in the forest and await the word to move into the attack," he called out while motioning to the northeast where a road coming out of Kernsbach disappeared into a forest between two hills. "The battalion column became separated last night. I'm going on back along the line of march to see if I can find the rest of our people."

"Any idea how long it's going to be before we move into the attack?" Bannon asked, not at all sure if he really wanted the answer.

"Before anyone goes forward, we need to get this jug fuck unscrewed. For now, the attack is on hold. Any other questions?"

"Yeah, who's here and where are they?"

"Team Bravo is exactly where it's supposed to be. Team Charlie, Task Force 2nd of the 93rd Mech is in the tree line just west of Kernsbach. The Scout Platoon from 2nd of the 93rd is in that wood lot just to the north. If you need to, contact them by radio. I gotta be rolling. Good luck."

Without waiting for further questions, Major Jordan climbed up onto his personnel carrier and took off down the road to the south as fast as his PC could roll. Bannon turned to Uleski, "Bob, go get the platoon leaders and double time them up here ASAP."

Uleski nodded "On the way."

While the XO was gathering up the platoon leaders, Bannon laid his map out on the front slope of 55 and took a moment to study the area where the Team was to go. He quickly decided to put the two tank platoons on the west, one on each side of the road where they would have good fields of fire. The Mech Platoon would go through the woods to the east side and straddle the road. His main concern was to get the Team under cover and deployed.

As soon as the platoon leaders were gathered around the map, he gave them his orders. "There has been a delay in the attack." As one, the faces of the platoon leaders lit up as if the governor had just given them a last-minute reprieve. Before any of them had a chance to ask why, Bannon continued. "We are going to move into an assembly area to the northeast. 2nd Platoon, you deploy here to the north of the road and orient to the west."

Leaning over, McAlester glanced at where Bannon was pointing at on his map. When he was sure he had the spot fixed in his head, he nodded and stepped back.

"3rd Platoon, you deploy here and orient to the northwest." Just as McAlister had, Garger looked at Bannon's map and nodded once he was sure of where he was to go.

"From those positions you should be able to cover the ground to your front with crossing fires. Be advised, there are friendly scouts and a friendly company team here and here. So don't shoot unless you're sure they're Russians."

Next Bannon turned to the Mech Platoon leader. "Lieutenant Harding, you will deploy your platoon here on either side of the road. The XO will deploy with you. Once we're under cover, check out your tanks and tracks, boresight your main guns, and feed your people. As there is no way of telling how long we'll be here, treat this as you would any defensive position. If there are no questions, let's roll."

Garger stopped Bannon as he was about to pick up his map. "I don't have a question, but I think you ought to be advised that 33 fell out about ten klicks down the road." Uleski and Bannon stopped midstride and stared at Garger as he continued. "Sergeant Pierson stopped to see if he could help. O'Dell told him he suddenly lost all power. They tried to restart 33, but the engine kept aborting. I have the grid location of where 33 is."

Bannon stifled a grunt. "Give it to the XO when we get into the assembly area. Right now all that matters is getting off this road before some Russian jet jockey makes us all grease spots." With that, the group scattered and remounted.

∾

Moving through the Staat Forest was easy. It was a typical German forest made up of straight, well-spaced trees all lined up in neat rows and crisscrossed with logging trails that were not on Bannon's map. The forest floor itself was clear of clutter as if it had just been raked. As the tanks jockeyed into positions, the forest and the hills on either side trapped the noise and caused echoes. When all were shut down, Bannon could distinctly hear the conversations of other crews as they dismounted, stretching and yawning before checking the tracks of their tanks for lose end connectors and center guides. On 66 Kelp and Ortelli tended to that while Folk and Bannon ran a check on the fire control. When they were finished with that, the two of them boresighted the main gun.

By the time Bannon was satisfied 66 was as ready as it would be, the other crews nearby were already beginning to break out their morning meal of dehydrated MREs. Folk, without needing to be told, pulled out an opened case and began to pass one out to each man. Normally there would be complaining and haggling to secure a better meal, but they were all tired. Even Bannon, who was not a big fan of MREs, was content to munch on his cold meal, popping bits of dehydrated peaches into his mouth, a practice that caused his lips to pucker as the peach drew every bit of moisture from his tongue.

In the stillness that followed, as he pondered what to do next, Bannon decided it might not be a bad idea to go up to Team Bravo's position and do a visual recon of the area they were to cross, provided the attack did eventually come off as planned. From there Objective LOG, as well as all the terrain the Team would have to cross to reach it, would be visible. When he'd finished all the MRE he cared to bother with at the moment, he stuffed the pouches of food he wanted to save for later in a pocket of his trousers. What he didn't want went into an empty sandbag tied to the side of the turret the crew of 66 was used for trash. In doing so, Bannon could not help but chuckle to himself. Policing up their litter was a habit that was pounded into every soldier that started on their Day One in the Army. Bannon found very idea that anyone would care whether he cleaned up after himself, given what his Team and the Soviets were doing to the German countryside to be beyond ludicrous. Still, tossing the empty MRE sack and unwanted food pouches over the side of the tank was something he could

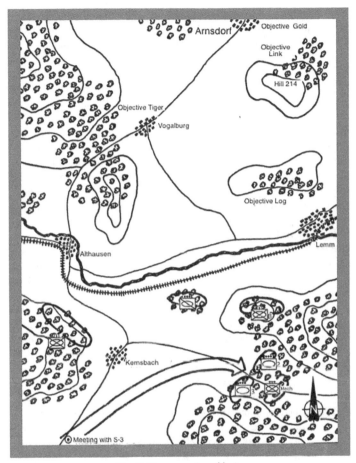

Map 5: Temporary Assembly Area

not bring himself to do. Some standards, he told himself, needed to maintained, even one as out of place as this one.

After setting that stray thought aside, he sent Kelp to fetch Lieutenant Harding with instructions that officer was to report to him with one of his platoon's PCs. Once that message was delivered, Kelp was to head over to the XO's tank and tell Uleski he would be in command while Bannon was away. Bannon himself went about on foot to collect the two tank platoon leaders and the artillery FIST.

Once everyone was gathered and mounted in the Harding's PC, they went forward, taking great care as they did so. The last thing Bannon wanted was to expose the PC in the open or come storming up behind Team Bravo and get blown away by a nervous gunner belonging to that team.

This last concern almost became a reality, for when the PC carrying Bannon and his platoon leaders did reach Team Bravo's position, they were greeted with the sight of several weapons of various calibers trained on the track and tracking them. Without having to be told, Harding, who was TC-ing the PC, stopped and identified himself. This task was made easier by the fact that even at a distance and through the woods, several of the people in Team Bravo were able to recognize Harding as well as his driver. Only when he was sure no one was going to light them up, Bannon had Harding pulling into a covered and concealed position where he, the platoon leaders, and FIST chief dismounted. From there they made their way on foot to the north edge of the tree line.

The last few yards of their trek was covered on their bellies to a spot that offered Bannon and his little gaggle cover while affording them a clear view of Objective LOG and the terrain they would need to cross to reach it. From there, Bannon took to pointing out the key terrain features to them. The village of Lemm was to the right front, the hill that was Objective LOG was directly to their front, and the village of Vogalburg was to the left front in the distance.

Bannon was in the process of explaining how the Team would deploy and maneuver once they'd crossed the LD when an infantryman from Team Bravo crawled up behind him and slapped the side of his boot. When he turned to find out what he wanted, the infantryman whispered that the colonel wanted to see him. Leaving Harding in charge of the other platoon leaders, Bannon crawled back until he felt it was safe stand upright and followed the soldier who had been sent to fetch him.

When he found Reynolds, Bannon could tell Blue Six was in rare form. Without waiting for Bannon to report, Reynolds ripped into him. "What in the hell is your company doing sitting on the fucking hill behind us and not on Hill 214?"

Dumbfounded, all Bannon could do was stare at the colonel. "I don't understand, sir. My Team is in the assembly area we were directed to occupy. I was waiting for the order to attack."

"Waiting! Waiting! Who the hell told you to wait? I've been up here for the last hour and a half waiting for *you*."

"Sir, the S-3 told me to put the Team into an assembly area behind Bravo and wait until the rest of the battalion closed up."

"I never gave such an order. What *I* want you to do is to get your people moving and get up on Hill 214 ASAP. *IS THAT CLEAR?*"

With the colonel beside himself with rage and his own anger threatening to override his ability to keep it in check, Bannon stood before Reynolds, glaring at him in silence as he struggled to calm down enough to respond. This, he realized as he was doing so, was neither the time nor place to be engaging in a pissing contest with a superior whose yelling had caused everyone in Team Bravo within ear shot to stop what they had been doing and watch.

Drawing himself up, Bannon took in a deep breath and locked eyes with Reynolds. "Am I to understand that my Team is to attack without Charlie Company in support, *sir*?"

"You let me worry about Charlie Company, *captain*. You just get those people of yours moving. *Now.*" With that, Reynolds pivoted about on his heels and stalked off, leaving Bannon standing there, unsure what to do next.

It was clear things were going to hell in a hand basket at an ever accelerating pace. The idea of starting the attack with only half of the battalion on hand was, in Bannon's mind, nothing short of insane. Yet he had been given a direct order, one that conjured up the specter of the Charge of the Light Brigade and Pickett's Charge. There had to be a way to carry out his orders without putting the lives of his people at risk in an ill-advised attack, he told himself as he turned to head back to where his platoon leaders were awaiting him. The last thing he wanted to do was to become the subject of a lesson on "*How not to conduct an attack*" at the Armor School.

❧

As Harding's PC made its way back to the Team's assembly area, Bannon's mind was racing a mile a minute in an effort to find a way out or around the dilemma he was facing. An order had been given. In his heart and mind, he knew that it was wrong for the Team to go all the way to Hill 214 on its own. Yet he couldn't get around the order. Not immediately. A partial solution slowly began to take shape. The Team could at least attack and seize LOG. Conditions for that part of the operation were still favorable. Team Bravo was in overwatch and the Team would have the full support of dedicated artillery throughout their advance. If the Team did manage to get to LOG unopposed, they could then maneuver against Hill 214 in a slow and deliberate manner. Reynolds had told him to move, but didn't say how fast. If the Team hit resistance on LOG, as the commanding officer in contact Bannon would be able to use his discretion and hold on to LOG until C Company appeared or Team Bravo moved up to support. It was decided, then. Team Yankee would comply, but with extreme caution. He was going to take this one step at a time, hoping for the best as he went.

Uleski and First Sergeant Harrert met the personnel carrier as it pulled up next to 66. "First Sergeant, when did you get here? Is C Company here too?"

"I've been here for about fifteen minutes. I haven't seen C Company since last night. In fact, after I left the column, I didn't see anyone in the battalion until I came up to Pierso and 33."

"What do you mean, you left the column? Why did you leave the column?"

"Well, sir, it's like this," Harrert began in a tone of voice that betrayed the frustration he felt over how things had played out during the road march. "We weren't on the road an hour before the company we were following made a wrong turn and began to go in circles, traveling along dirt roads, through side streets in villages where the M-88s got stuck, and on and on for two hours. At one of our halts, while we were waiting for an M-88 to back up after becoming stuck on a street that was too narrow for it to pass and find an alternate route around, I went up to the captain leading the column and asked him if he knew where he was. When he showed me a spot on his map that was two map sheets to the west of where we really were, I tried to explain to him he was wrong. Well, it had been a long, hard night for him and he wasn't about to listen to an obnoxious NCO. He told me to get back to my track and get ready to roll. That's when I said to myself, "Raymond, to hell with this shit. I'm going to find the company." So I went back, pulled my track, the ambulance track, and the M-88 out of column, and took off looking for you." Pausing, he dropped his gaze and took to shaking his head. "I'm here to tell you, sir, that boy had his head lodged so far up his third point of contact that I doubt he knows we left."

"Well, I really wish you could have brought C Company with you," Bannon opined. "Even so, it's good to have you here. You're the first good thing that's happened all day. Besides, you're just in time for the attack."

Uleski, who had been eyeing the platoon leaders and wondering why they were so glum, snapped his head around toward Bannon, "Do *what?* Attack *now?* Without the rest of the battalion?"

Bannon knew the platoon leaders had heard everything that had gone on between him and the colonel. They were now waiting to see how he was going to deal with the nightmare they'd been handed.

Bannon returned their expectant gaze with one he hoped did not betray his true feelings. It was going to take a lot of finesse to convince them and Uleski that they could pull it off. But if he could do it in the manner he had settled on without any further interference from battalion, they just might have a fighting chance. With all the positive enthusiasm he could generate, given the task ahead of him, he began issuing new orders.

"Gather around and listen up, gents, while I tell you how we're going to skin this cat," Bannon muttered with as much enthusiasm as he could muster. "The situation and the conditions for the first part of the operation, the attack on LOG, are still the same. If anything, we have improved the odds."

Ignoring the quizzical looks this comment resulted in on the face of his platoon leaders, Bannon pressed on gamely. "We've had a break, bore-sighted the guns, checked the tracks, had breakfast, and got a chance to see the objective and our axis of advance. Team Bravo is in position and ready to support us. So we will go as we had planned."

Pausing, he looked from face to face to see if his upbeat prelude had done anything to banish some of the skepticism his initial announcement had resulted in. Though he could tell none of them were totally convinced, at least they were listening.

"Lieutenant Harding, you will start the move by bringing your platoon up the road. As before, your platoon will be in the middle with my tank hanging onto your far right track. The two tank platoons will start their move when the Mech Platoon comes up even to them. Both tank platoons will move out in an echelon formation. Second Platoon, you'll refuse your right. Third Platoon, refuse your left. When we get out in the open between those two tree lines, the whole Team will pivot on 2nd Platoon, move through the gap, and head for Objective LOG. As we move on LOG, I want to give the village of Lemm a wide berth, just in case the Russians are in there. So don't crowd the 2nd Platoon."

"Lieutenant Unger, I want you to contact your guns and have them locked, loaded, and ready to pound LOG the instant we receive fire. All you should have to do is yell shoot. Don't wait for me or anyone else to tell you. Just do it."

"Lieutenant U, as 3rd Platoon is short of a tank, I want you to team up with Pierson and play wingman. That way you won't be so obvious hanging out there all by yourself in the center. Once we're on LOG, we'll size up the situation before we roll on to Objective LINK. If no one comes up to cover our move, 3rd Platoon will take up positions on the far side of LOG and over-watch the move of 2nd Platoon, followed by the Mech Platoon. We will move up onto LINK as planned with 3rd Platoon coming up on order. I'll be between the Mech and 2nd Platoon. Do you have any questions?"

The platoon leaders hesitated as they looked at Bannon, each other, then back to Bannon. As one, they all shook their heads.

"All right then, Lieutenant Harding, I want you to start your move in twenty-five minutes. I have exactly 0835 hours. Let's roll." The platoon leaders saluted and went their separate ways. The XO and first sergeant stayed.

Uleski was the first to speak. "Are we going to be able to pull this off?"

"Well Bob, like I said, as far as the first part of the attack, if anything, we're in better shape. It's the second part that's shaky. It's my intention to take my time going from LOG to LINK, if we go at all. The longer we take, the better the chances are that the rest of the battalion will close up. If we're hit hard getting onto LOG, I'm going to hold at LOG until the battalion commander either moves up Team Bravo to support, or Delta Company comes up. I think that's the only way we can play it."

"Agreed. But once we're out in the open, the other people may not like us taking one of their hills. You know how possessive the Russians are of real-estate once they take it."

"Yeah, well, that's why I said we are going to have to play it by ear. I don't intend to jump out beyond LOG on our own unless I'm sure we can do so and be around to talk about it tonight. And if it comes to pass you find yourself in command of the team, I expect you to do the same. Use your discretion. Clear?"

"Clear, boss. Got any more cheerful news you wish to share with us?"

"No, none that I can think of. If I do, you'll be the first to know."

With that, Uleski turned and headed for 55. Bannon then turned to Harrett.

"First Sergeant, there are some people over there in those woods belonging to the Scout Platoon of the 2nd of the 93rd Mech. Take your track, the medic track, and the 88 over there and let them know what we're about to do. With the way everything else has been going this morning, I doubt if anyone else has coordinated with them. If there are mines or some kind of danger that they know about that are going to cause us problems, get on the radio and call me ASAP. Stay there until we get up on LOG, then close up on us on LOG if and when you can."

"I don't have the 88 with me right now. I left it with 33. But I'll take the medic track and get moving unless you have something else."

"No, that about covers it. See you on LOG."

Bannon had little doubt his positive attitude and confident spiel did little to relieve the concerns and apprehensions his platoon leaders had about the upcoming attack. He certainly hadn't sold himself. Be that as it may, he concluded grimly, with twenty-two minutes to go before the Mech Platoon began to move, there was nothing more he could do but to mount up and wait. As he did so, the crew of 66 watched him. They had heard the orders and, like the platoon leaders, didn't look very convinced. It seemed, Bannon sighed, the old saying *You can't fool all the people* was true.

With the issue decided and the wheels set in motion, Bannon was anxious to get on with it. This wasn't going to be a peacetime training exercise. There wouldn't be an after-action critique to discuss who did well and who didn't. This was really it. The graves' registration people, either Russian or US, would be the ones sorting out the winners from the losers this time. Still, there was always the possibility that the Team just might pull this off, Bannon kept telling himself. He had to think positively, be positive. They had to go out there and make things happen. Like the roll-call sergeant on "Hill Street Blues" told his patrolman every day, *"Let's do it to them, before they do it to us."*

∾

The Mech Platoon set off as ordered. As they broke out of the tree line, they began to deploy into a wedge formation. When their last track was in the open, Bannon gave Ortelli the order to move and joined the formation to the right and a little behind the far right personnel carrier. Unger and his track did likewise behind 66. The 2nd Platoon then began to deploy, each track always a little to the right and a little farther behind the track in front. When the entire Team was deployed, it formed a large wedge that measured 700 to 800 meters at the base with a depth of 500 meters. In this formation they could deal with any threat that appeared to the front or to either flank.

When the Team began its pivot on 2nd Platoon and turn north, Bannon saw the first sergeant's track and the medic track waiting in the tree line behind the scout platoon position. Harrett stood just out from the tree line alone as he watched the Team roll into the attack. The first sergeant, whom he had known for several years, was reliable, steady, and a good man to have near in a tight spot. Bannon wondered for a moment what was going through his mind. Given the chance, he imagined Harrett would have traded places with anyone in the Team. It was his company, his people, who were going into the attack, and he was staying behind. Unable to watch, he turned and walked away, pausing once in order to glance over his shoulder before disappearing into the tree line.

The young Soviet lieutenant played with the remains of his breakfast. It wasn't fit to eat, he thought, so he might as well get some pleasure from it. Around him his men sat around finishing their meals or simply enjoying the chance to rest. The entire company, or more correctly, what was left of the company, had spent all night preparing fighting positions on the small hill overlooking a town named Lemm. Since there had been no engineer support available, all the work had been done by hand.

On the first day of the war, the company had been with the first attack echelon. Heavy losses, including all of its officers except for him, resulted in the company being pulled out on the second day. But instead of going into reserve, they had been sent to establish an outpost on the regiment's flank. The lieutenant didn't much care for the mission. With the exception of two tanks that were with him, and three in Lemm, his platoon was all alone. As he often did, he looked at the collection of tired soldiers he had and decided if a fight did come, it wouldn't last long. Letting his mind wander, he thought that things could have been worse, the regiment could have sent a political officer with him.

As the Team passed between the two tree lines and crested a small hill, the terrain beyond opened up. The hill that was Objective LOG was directly in front about four kilometers away. The German countryside here had thus far escaped the ravages of war. It was lush and green on this August morning, just like countless August mornings before. The very idea that this quiet and beautiful landscape was a battlefield seemed absurd, almost obscene to Bannon.

But it was a battlefield. As the Team left its last cover behind, all eyes for kilometers around were turning on it. The Scout Platoon to the left, and Team

Bravo on the right, watched Team Yankee as it rolled forward. Within the Team, all were as ready as they could be for whatever came their way. Guns were oriented to cover assigned sectors and all but the track commanders were buttoned up and ready for action. Like fans at a football game waiting for the opening kickoff, the officers and men of Team Bravo and the scouts watched in morbid curiosity, eager to see what would happen next, thankful that they weren't the ones out in the open.

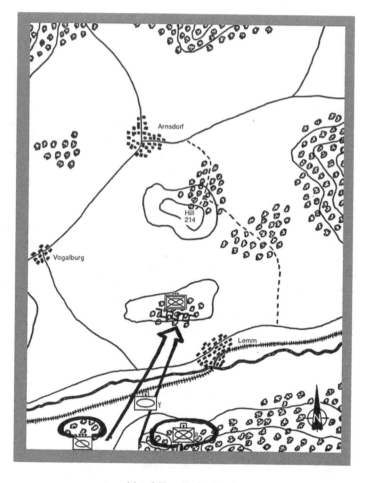

Map 6: Team Yankee Attacks

The other people, the Soviets, were also watching. Their reactions were different. To a man they scrambled to meet the American attack. Reports were flashed to their commanders. Gunners threw down their mess tins and slid into position. Loaders and ammo bearers prepared to load the next round. A new battlefield was about to mar the muchcontested Germany countryside.

∿

Team Yankee had two obstacles that had to be negotiated. The first was a railroad embankment that ran across their front. Going over it wasn't the problem. All the Team's tracks could do that with ease. The problem was that it required the Team to slow down. It would break up the formation momentarily and, as the tracks went over it, their soft underbellies would be exposed to enemy fire. If they were going to be hit, this is where Bannon expected it.

As the first track came up and began to go over, Bannon held his breath as he watched the PC crest the embankment, hang there for a moment fully exposed, then drop down to the other side. Two more PCs followed and trundled on without incident. Perhaps the Russians were waiting for the tanks, Bannon mused. Perhaps they wanted to let the PCs go over and let the embankment separate the Team before firing.

Then it was Alpha 66's turn. Ortelli slowed 66 until it made contact with the embankment. As soon as the tracks bit into it, he gunned the engine, causing 66 to rise up at a steep angle. Instinctively, Folk depressed the gun to keep it level with the far horizon. Bannon grabbed the commander's override, ready to elevate the gun once they were on the other side. If he didn't, the depressed gun would dig itself into the ground as 66 went down the other side.

As the tank crested the embankment and started down, Ortelli switched from accelerator to brake while Bannon jerked the commander's override back, elevating the gun. Folk kept fighting for control of the gun, but didn't get it back until 66 was on level ground again. Once he had control of it, he reoriented the gun and went back to searching for targets.

With the first obstacle behind 66, Bannon turned in the cupola and watched the rest of the Team's tanks make their way up and over the embankment two at a time. Satisfied that they were not going to be hit there, he faced front and eyed the next obstacle, a stream that, like the railroad embankment, ran perpendicular to their direction of travel. The first PC was already down in the stream and halfway across when he caught sight of it. The stream itself was not very wide. Centuries of erosion, however, had created a ditch some twenty meters in width with embankments a meter high. Upon reaching it, Ortelli eased 66 down into the streambed, crossed with ease, and began to climb the far bank. They were halfway up it when the shit hit the fan.

Several flashes from the hill that was Objective LOG were followed almost instantly by a thud and the appearance of a column of dirt in front of 66. "REVERSE! REVERSE! GET BACK IN THE DITCH!" The sudden change in direction threw everyone on 66 forward. Bannon reached for the smoke grenade dischargers and fired a volley. The six grenades launched and shrouded 66 in a curtain of white smoke just as the tank was settling back down in the streambed.

Grabbing the radio switch on the side of his CVC, Bannon keyed the Team net. "ALL BRAVO 3 ROMEO ELEMENTS. DEPLOY INTO LINE IN THE STREAMBED. BREAK. ZULU 77, BRING YOUR PEOPLE BACK. THIS IS ROMEO 25, OUT."

Commanders are paid to make decisions. Sometimes there is ample time to consider all the options, to analyze the situation, develop several courses of action, compare each, and then decide which alternative is best. Then there are occasions when there is no time for all that, occasions when the commander must see, decide, and act in almost the same instant. This was one of those times.

"GUNNER, STAND BY TO ENGAGE."

Bannon looked to his right and saw the FIST track halted next to his. The tanks of the 2nd Platoon were entering the streambed and nosing their way up the embankment on the far side. He turned to his left and saw two of the PCs plop back into the streambed. They had also fired their grenade launchers. He next turned back to the front. The smoke was beginning to dissipate. Off to the front left, about fifty meters from 66, a PC was still sitting in the open and on fire with one of its passengers hanging out of the troop door in the back of the vehicle. Bright flames spilled out of the door and through open hatches. Alpha 66 had been exceedingly lucky. The PC hadn't.

The turret of 66 suddenly jerked to the right as Folk yelled out an acquisition report without bothering to key the intercom. "ENEMY TANK, TWELVE O'CLOCK."

"GUNNER, SABOT, TANK." Bannon yelled in response even as he was dropping down to view through the commander's extension. He couldn't see the target.

"UP!"

Putting his trust in Folk, Bannon did not hesitate. "FIRE!"

"ON THE WAAAY!"

Alpha 66 rocked back as the main gun went off. The view to the front was obstructed by the muzzle blast and dust it created.

As soon as he could see through his sight, Folk yelled out his sensing of the round he had just fired. "TARGET!"

Bannon put his eye up to the extension and confirmed Folk's sensing. The enemy tank he had not seen before was now clearly visible as it burned. But he had a Team to run. He had no time to play tank commander right now. He had to let Folk search for his own targets and engage them when he found them. "CEASE FIRE. GUNNER, ENGAGE AT WILL."

"ROMEO 25, THIS IS TANGO 77. ON LINE AND READY, OVER." 2nd Platoon was ready.

"ROGER TANGO 77."

"ROMEO 25, THIS IS ZULU 77. READY, OVER."

"ROMEO 25, THIS IS MIKE 77. READY, OVER." The Mech and 3rd Platoons were ready.

"SPLASH, OVER."

The last voice had been Unger's. Artillery was on the way.

The hill that was Objective LOG appeared to disappear as the artillery impacted. Bits of trees and fountains of dirt rose up above the tree line. "BRAVO 3 ROMEO ELEMENTS, THIS IS ROMEO 25. MOVE! MOVE! MOVE! LIMA 61, KEEP THE ARTY COMING."

As one, Team Yankee lurched forward. For the second time 66 moved up over the stream's embankment. This time Ortelli had the accelerator to the floor. The tank flopped down on level ground with a bang and took off at a dead run. A line of three tanks and three PCs to the left of 66 were also out of the streambed and charging forward past the burning PC.

It wasn't until they were up and out in the open and Bannon was looking left, then right to see what the other tracks in his command were doing that he noticed the tank that had been to the right of 66 during the move to the stream was stopped, half hanging out of the streambed. It was burning and shuddering as its on-board ammo cooked off. Second Lieutenant McAlister was dead.

If the rest of 2nd Platoon wasn't aware they were now without a platoon leader, they weren't acting like it, for the other tank commanders in the platoon were keeping up with 66.

Within 66, Folk yelled out again. "LOADER, LOAD SABOT. TANK!"

"UP!"

"ON THE WAAAY!"

Again 66 shuddered as the main gun fired, recoiled, and spewed out a spent shell casing. This time the obscuration didn't cling to the tank as 66 rolled through the dust cloud created by the muzzle blast. Bannon turned to see what Folk had been firing at but saw only a column of dirt. He had missed whatever it was. Not that it mattered. Another tank to the left got it. A brilliant flash and a shower of sparks marked the Soviet tank that had been Folk's target.

A quick survey of Objective LOG revealed four burning vehicles, two of which were definitely tanks. The other two were partially hidden but emitting angry billows of black smoke and flames. Freshly dug dirt was now visible just inside the tree line. There were Soviet infantrymen dug in on the objective. Bannon had no intention of fighting it out with the Soviets on LOG. He did not want to dismount the Mech Platoon in the open. "BRAVO 3 ROMEO —THIS IS ROMEO 25, THERE ARE DUG-IN TROOPS ON LOG. WE WILL CONTINUE TO ATTACK THROUGH. DO NOT DISMOUNT OR STOP ON THE—"

Bannon's transmission was cut short by two huge explosions on either side of 66, causing the tank to buck violently from side to side and throwing Bannon off his perch and down onto the turret floor. Twisting about in his seat, Kelp reached down to help him as he struggled to climb back up into the commander's cupola, yelling as he did so. "ARE YOU OK?"

"Yeah. Get ready to man your machinegun!"

"Your face is bleeding."

Bannon brought one hand up and touched his face. When he pulled it away, there was blood on it. But it couldn't be too bad. He was still moving and talking. His wound could be ignored. He had to regain control of the tank and the Team. With an effort, he boosted himself up and back into place.

The scene outside was chaos. The explosions that had rocked 66 were from Soviet artillery. 66 was on the verge of rolling out of the impact area. To the right he could see there were still two tanks moving forward. One of the 2nd Platoon tanks was several hundred meters to the rear, just sitting there. The FIST track was also gone. To the left there were two other tanks closing up on 66. The missing 3rd Platoon tank was nowhere to be seen. The Mech Platoon PCs had fallen behind and, as a result, were still in the middle of where the Soviet artillery was impacting. Bannon could make out only two PCs bobbing and weaving through the columns of flame and dirt. Seven vehicles. As best he could tell, that was all the Team had left. Seven out of fourteen vehicles.

"TROOPS, TWELVE O'CLOCK! ENGAGING WITH COAX!"

Folk's call pulled Bannon's attention back to the front. They were now within three hundred meters of the objective. Several Soviet infantrymen had popped up to engage them head-on with RPGs. The total stupidity of that was, in Bannon's mind, beyond comprehension, for they were being cut down by the machine-gun fire from 66 and the surviving tanks without doing a damned bit of good. An RPG just wasn't going to stop an M-1 head-on, regardless of how brave the gunner was. Those tank commanders who could cut loose with their M-2s, adding to the mayhem. Every now and then, one of the Team's tanks would fire a HEAT round, adding to the effect of the friendly artillery that was still pounding LOG. In another minute, the four tanks that were still with 66 would be on the objective.

The destruction of the tanks and most of their BTR personnel carriers, the steady artillery fire, and the failure of their RPG gunners to stop the rush of Team Yankee proved to be too much for Soviet soldiers who had thus far survived the carnage being rained down on them. Just as the Team was about to enter the tree line, some began to take to their heels and flee.

As 66 made its way onto the objective, Bannon caught sight of a hidden Soviet BTR-60 personnel carrier beginning to back up, seeking to escape. But before he could issue a fire command and slew the main gun onto, it was taken out by a 2nd Platoon tank.

With his attention momentarily focused on the BTR, Bannon didn't notice until it was too late that a lone Soviet soldier had risen up out of a trench not twenty meters to the right of 66 and was aiming an RPG straight at him. Bannon panicked. He tried to traverse the M2 to the right to engage the Soviet but he knew in his heart he wouldn't make it in time. Calmly, the Russian took aim as he prepared to fire. He knew he had 66 and there wasn't a damned thing Bannon could do to stop him.

But luck was still with Bannon as the Russian was suddenly thrown backwards as a stream of machine-gun rounds hit him in his chest. A 2nd Platoon tank had come up, seen the RPG gunner, and fired. The relief Bannon felt was incredible. For the second time in a matter of minutes, 66 had been saved by the slimmest of margins.

❧

Overwhelmed by alternating rushes of fear, anger, and helplessness, the Soviet lieutenant watched the American tanks rumble by his position. All his efforts and those of his men had been for nothing. The American tanks had ripped through his position as if he hadn't been there. Catching his breath once they were gone, he began to survey the scene. Those of his men who had not fled or been stuck down were coming up from the bottoms of their foxholes. Looking back over the field to his front, he saw several personnel carriers closing on his positions. "Well," he thought out loud, "If we can't kill the tanks, we'll kill the American infantry." With that, he grabbed an RPG from a dead man as he prepared to rally what was left of his platoon and continue the fight.

❧

Once on Objective LOG, the five remaining tanks of Team Yankee continued on in a staggered line moving forward through the woods. Friendly artillery had stopped falling, probably as a result of a call from Team Bravo. After entering the woods a hundred meters, the tanks lost contact with the Soviets. There was also no sign of the Mech Platoon.

Deciding it would be best to wait for the Mech Platoon to catch up, Bannon ordered Ortelli to slow down as he keyed his mike to make a net call on the company net. "ALL BRAVO 3 ROMEO ELEMENTS ON LOG, STOP AND FORM A COIL. I SAY AGAIN, STOP AND FORM A COIL. WE WILL WAIT FOR THE ZULU 77 ELEMENT TO CLOSE UP, OVER."

To his utter amazement, none of the other tanks stopped. They didn't even slow down. Bannon called again, but got no response. The radio was keying, but for some reason the other tanks were not hearing his transmissions. Even worse, instead of stopping, they were beginning to speed up. He called a third time with no luck. To make matters worse, artillery began to fall all round 66. He assumed it was Soviet but couldn't tell. This caused the other TCs to crouch low in their cupolas and orient their full attention to the front as they did their best to pick their way through the woods as quickly as possible.

The ragged line of tanks that remained, with Alpha 66 trailing slightly behind the others, had just emerged from the woods on the far side of Objective LOG when 66 suddenly slid to the right and stopped with a violent jerk that sent Kelp and Bannon bouncing about from side to side. As they were struggling to regain balance, Ortelli gunned the engine. But 66 did not move. Once he'd managed to regain his footing, Bannon stuck his head out his open hatch even as Ortelli continued to gun the engine in a desperate effort to move forward.

Without having to see what was keeping them from moving forward, Bannon realized they were stuck. Even worse, the last of Team Yankee's tanks, all four of them, were continuing to roll on toward Hill 214 and there wasn't a damned thing he could do to stop them.

CHAPTER 6

On the Razor's Edge

"Lay off the accelerator, Ortelli. We aren't going anywhere and you're only making it worse."

Kelp and Folk turned and stared at Bannon wide-eyed and fearful. The expression on Ortelli's face, no doubt, was no different. All were waiting for his next brilliant idea.

"*Why me?*" he thought, "*Why in the hell me?*" He felt lost. He had managed to lose half the Team and get 66 stuck in an artillery barrage in the middle of a battle. Now his crew was looking at him expecting him to magically come up with the right answer. Maybe there was no right answer this time.

Then again, maybe there was, another part of Bannon's brain chimed.

"Okay, right," Bannon muttered, more to himself than his crew. "Listen up. I'm going to go out and see how bad off we are. Kelp, cover me with your machinegun. Sergeant Folk, be ready to give me a hand if I need you or provide suppressive fire if we're shot at. Clear?" Both nodded their heads in unison.

With that, Bannon turned, opened the TC's hatch all the way, and stuck his head out to check the situation. Alpha 66 was just on the edge of the artillery-beaten zone. Another twenty to thirty meters and they would have been in the clear. "So much for luck," he grumbled.

Ducking back down, he turned to Kelp and asked if he were ready. The loader's eyes were as big as hen's eggs and his face drawn in fear. But he was standing ready to leap into position when Bannon gave the word. With no reason to delay any further, and after unplugging his CVC cord, Bannon took a deep breath. "Alright, *let's go.*"

With that, he jumped out of the TC's hatch, rolled down the side of the turret, and dropped to the ground. The drop turned out to be more than he had anticipated. With a thud, he landed hard on his side, knocking the wind out of him. As he lay there struggling to get his breath back, he looked around. The neat German forest they had rolled through was now ripped and pockmarked by the artillery fire. Shattered branches and uprooted trees were everywhere. And the artillery wasn't finished yet, as rounds continued to impact here and there all around 66. Every now and then a loud zing or a sharp ping would cause Bannon to hunch over as a shell fragment from a near miss flew by him or ricocheted off the tank. Having no wish to stay out in the open longer than he needed to, Bannon got on with his inspection.

The track he was lying next to was still on all the road wheels and the drive sprocket. They hadn't thrown a track. Thank God for small miracles, he thought as he crawled along, keeping as close to the tank as he could for safety. Looking between the road wheels, he could see the other track was also on. When he reached the rear of the tank, he found mounds of loose dirt the tracks had been throwing up to their rear. It was clear to him both tracks had been spinning free without gaining any traction.

It wasn't until he crawled around to the rear of the tank and looked under the hull that he saw what had stopped them. The tank was hung up on a shattered tree that was still partially connected to its stump. As 66 had maneuvered through the forest, it had straddled the shattered tree and driven itself up onto the stump. To make matters worse, there was a shell crater to the right of the tank that the right track had dropped into just as 66 had bellied out on the stump.

The solution to their problem was not going to be simple. If there was another tank around, it would have been easy to hook tow cables between it and 66 and pull 66 off. But all the remaining tanks had continued onto Objective LINK.

They could sit and wait for help to come along, Bannon reasoned. Eventually, if the rest of the battalion came up, a tank in Team Bravo or an M-88 recovery vehicle could pull 66 off. But it seemed just as likely that the Russians who had survived being overrun by his Team would show up first. Odds were, he reasoned, they would be in a foul mood after being overrun.

That aside, Bannon knew sitting about, waiting there with his thumb up his ass was a non-starter. He was, after all, the team commander. He had to get back with the Team and regain control, even though the Team was now nothing more than a reinforced platoon. Besides, simply sitting there and waiting to see what happened next was not his style. A solution had to be found.

Shoveling dirt under the tracks would do no good. The tracks would simply pile it up onto the mounds they had already thrown up. It was too late to back out. Ortelli had hit the tree at a dead run and driven 66 up onto it. Something substantial had to be shoved under the right track so that it could rise up and let the hull clear the stump. But to do that would have required all of them to haul tree trunks and other rubble over to 66. The artillery would surely get some of them even if they found something they could haul before Ivan happened along.

With a sigh, Bannon did his best to remember what he had been taught at Fort Knox during the Basic Course in the vehicle recovery class. "Why in the hell didn't I pay attention to what was going on in that class instead of kicking dirt clods and bullshitting at the rear of the group," he muttered to himself. That thought, and the instructor's admonishment that someday what he was telling them could one day save their lives came back to him as if the man was standing there behind him. Well, it seemed as if today was that day.

There was something they could do, but at the moment, Bannon wasn't sure if he remembered it all. "What the hell, maybe it'll come back as we go along."

With that thought in mind, he climbed back up on the tank, staying as low and as near to the turret as possible. "Sergeant Folk, get out here and give me a hand."

As Folk was climbing out, Bannon pulled a hammer from a sponson box and threw it to the ground on the right side of the tank. He then ordered Folk help him take the tow cables off the side of the turret where they were stowed. The two men crouched down as they worked to free one tow cable, throw it to the ground near the hammer, then free the other cable and throw it down on the other side. They then leaped off the right side and took cover.

While they lay down on the ground next to the track, Bannon explained what they were going to do. The plan was to hook the tow cables together. They would then wrap the cables around the two tracks at the front of the tank so that the tow cables stretched from one track to the other. When Ortelli put 66 in forward gear, the tracks would move the cables back along the ground. In the process, the cables would catch on the stump. Hopefully, as the tracks continued to try to pull the cables back, they would stay caught on the stump and pull 66 forward and off the stump and tree.

After listening to his commander's plan, Folk nodded. "What the hell, it's worth a shot. Let's go."

With that, Bannon took the hammer and used it to get the tow hooks off the front and back of 66 while Folk dragged the two cables to the front, crawling on his hands and knees and staying as close to the tank as he could. They used one of the tow hooks to connect the cables together. Then they wrapped one end of the cables around the track on the left side and used a second tow hook to connect the loop formed around the track, doing the same on the right side. Bannon put the fourth hook and hammer to the side in case a hook broke and a second try was needed. When they were ready, he told Folk to get back in 66 and have Ortelli crank up the tank and begin to slowly move forward.

Remaining outside and a safe distance from the tank, Bannon signaled to Folk, who had Ortelli put the tank in low gear and slowly apply power. As he had hoped, the cables were dragged under and caught on the stump. When he felt them snag the tree stump, Ortelli slowly applied more power, taking the slack in the cables out until they became taut. For a moment the tracks stopped and the engine began to strain. After praying the hooks would stand the strain and not snap, Bannon signaled Folk, who ordered Ortelli to continue.

Ever so slowly, Ortelli applied more power. Grudgingly, 66 began to inch forward, moaning and screeching as the hull scraped across the stump. The cables held as 66 continued to move and rise up over the stump. Once the tank's center of gravity was past the stump, the front of 66 flopped down with a thud, allowing the tracks to bit into the ground, gain traction, and move the tank forward on its own.

When he was satisfied they were home free, Bannon signaled to Folk to have Ortelli stop. He then crawled to the rear, disconnected the cables from around the tracks, and climbed back on without bothering to recover the hooks or cables. With luck, someone could come back and get them later. At the moment, Bannon had far more important things to do, including getting out from under the Soviet artillery.

It was only as he was climbing back into the commander's cupola that Bannon noticed 66 had lost its antennas. Both had been sheared off at the base. That, he realized, explained why the other four tanks had not stopped when he had called them. The last order the Team had heard from him was to keep moving. Apparently they had thought he wanted them to keep going all the way to Hill 214. When they couldn't contact him, Uleski simply took command of what was left of the company and carried on with the last order he had received, leaving Bannon to wonder how much that misunderstanding had cost the Team as 66 left Objective LOG and made for Hill 214. Clausewitz called it the friction of war. Some called it Murphy's law. Bannon found the thought of losing what was left of the Team to a simple misunderstanding was devastating. Sixteen men and four tanks lost all because of a damned antenna was broken.

∾

Once in the open and out from under the Soviet artillery, Bannon had Ortelli move as fast as they could go. He had to find out if there were any tanks in the Team still on Hill 214. If there were, he would be able to contact battalion and find out what everyone else was doing and what the colonel wanted the Team to do. Not that there was much left to do anything with. If battalion couldn't be contacted, then the ball was back in his court. He had to decide what to do with what was left of the Team.

Bannon was fast becoming tired of making these kind of decisions. They were too expensive in terms of men and equipment. Just what would go first, he found himself wondering, the Team or his nerve.

This unwelcome thought was interrupted by the sight of three Soviet T-62 tanks off to his right. All were moving north and on an intersecting course with 66, causing Bannon to guess they had been headed to hit the tanks on Hill 214 in the rear before they had spotted 66. Grabbing the TC's override, he jerked it over as far as he could, swinging the turret toward this new threat.

"GUNNER, SABOT, 3 TANKS!"

Kelp dropped down and yelled, "HEAT LOADED, UP!"

The last round Kelp had put in the chamber had been a HEAT round. Not as good as a SABOT round when fighting a tank, but it would have to do. There was no time to switch ammunition.

"IDENTIFIED!" Folk yelled, letting Bannon know he was ready to take over.

Bannon let the override go at the same instant the lead T-62 began to traverse its turret toward 66.

"FIRE HEAT, LOAD SABOT!" At least the next round would be right.

"ON THE WAAAY!" With that, Folk fired.

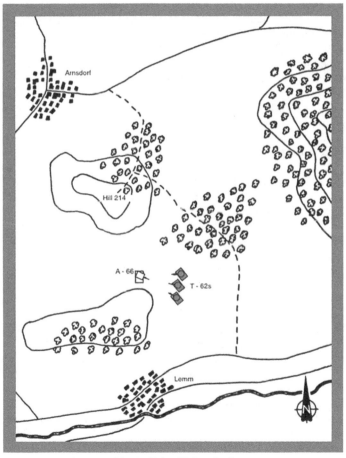

Map 7: Alpha 66's Last Battle

As if it was all one action, the main gun recoiled, causing the tank to shudder and buck. The sound of the gun firing was replaced by a highpitched scream of agony over the intercom and the hiss of the halon gas fire extinguishers discharging. The turret was instantaneously filled with the halon gas as 66 lurched to the right and staggered to a stop. It had been hit.

"What happened? Why are we stopping?" Kelp yelled in panic. He was preparing to go out through the loader's hatch when Bannon felt Folk grab at his leg to get by him and out. Over the intercom, Ortelli was screaming.

"Shut up! Everyone, shut up and stay where you are. Crew report."

"*We're on fire! Get out!*" Folk kept trying to get past.

With no other choice, Bannon raised his leg, put his foot on Folk's shoulder, and began to push him down. "GET BACK IN YOUR SEAT AND PREPARE TO ENGAGE."

For the briefest of moments, Folk stared up at him with an expression that betrayed his shock at being kept from fleeing before settling back into position.

"KELP. IS THE GUN UP?" Bannon bellowed as he looked over at the dumb-founded loader. "LOADER, LOAD SABOT, NOW!"

Though he was still stunned, Kelp turned to grab the next round.

The screaming on the intercom had been replaced by a continuous moaning from Ortelli. He had been hit. Bannon had no idea how badly his driver had been wounded. Nor could he afford to waste even a second finding out, not with enemy tanks bearing down on them. Popping his head back out, he scanned to his right in an effort to see how close the T-62s were.

There was thick column of black smoke coming from the engine compartment, blanketing 66 like a shroud. The fire extinguishers in the engine compartment had failed to put out the fire. Across the open field to his right one of theT-62s was burning and shuddering as secondary explosions rocked the derelict tank. The other two had just begun to move out again for Hill 214. Though they kept their gun tubes pointed at 66, they were not firing. Apparently, Bannon concluded, they thought 66 was finished.

"Sergeant Folk, can you see the other two tanks?"

"Yeah, I got them. They're at the edge of my sight."

"Move your turret slowly and lay on the lead tank. We don't want to let on that we're still functional. When you're on, fire. I'll hit the smoke grenades. That should cover us from return fire. Kelp, you up?"

Across the turret from Bannon, Kelp was standing with his back against the turret wall. There was a look of terror on his face, but the gun was loaded and armed. "Kelp, give me an up."

"SABOT UP."

"Anytime you're ready, gunner." With nothing more to do, Bannon watched the two T-62s through his extension. The range readout digits on the bottom of the sight changed. Folk had ranged and gotten a good range return. 950 meters.

The ready-to-fire indicator was also on. Putting his finger on the smoke grenade launcher, Bannon waited for Folk to fire.

"ON THE WAAAY!"

As the gun fired, Bannon hit the grenades, covering 66 with a curtain of white smoke. "SWITCH TO THERMAL!"

As Folk slid the sight shutter into place, the view of the smoke screen was shut out. But instead of the green thermal image, the sight remained black. "The thermal is out!"

"Switch back to the day channel and look sharp. They're going to make sure we're dead this time, so we have to get them first."

This time Kelp did not need to be told to respond when he was ready. "UP."

"STAND BY TO ENGAGE."

The fire in the engine compartment was growing. The black smoke mixed with the white smoke from the grenades. Over the intercom the sound of Ortelli's moaning was growing weaker. Within the turret there was the smell of cordite from the spent shell casing, diesel from a ruptured fuel cell, acrid smoke coming from the engine fire, and the odor of sweat from the crew lingered as they waited for the T-62s to reappear.

"IDENTIFIED!"

A T-62 was charging down on 66, gun aimed dead on them.

"FIRE!"

"ON THE WAY!"

Both tanks fired at the same time and both hit. The difference was that the Soviet round didn't penetrate the turret of 66. 66's round, on the other hand, found its mark and with telling effect. The flash of impact was followed in rapid succession by a sheet of flame that rose up out of the T-62's commander hatch, then a series of secondary explosions that ripped off its turret, flinging the fifteen tons of steel high in the air as if it was cardboard.

Bannon watched in fascination as the turret slammed on to the ground and flopped over upside down. A quick scan of the area revealed that the second T-62 Alpha 66 had engaged was smoking. Though it was not burning as the other two were, the body of the tank commander was draped over the side of the turret. Even at that range, a spattering of red on the Russian's black uniform was visible. That and the high angle of the gun tube told Bannon that it was dead. With no other threat in sight, and the fire in the engine compartment becoming larger, it was time to abandon Alpha 66.

Sometime during the engagement, Ortelli had stopped moaning. In order to check on him, Folk needed to traverse the turret until the rear of the turret was aligned with the driver's compartment. When Bannon dropped down from his TC's perch and stuck his head through the opening, he found Ortelli's crumpled body slumped over to one side, covered in diesel and blood. Reaching in, Bannon took hold of Ortelli's shoulder and held him so Kelp could lower the driver's seat back. When it was down, Bannon ease the body back onto it.

Ortelli's wounds were horrific. The right side of his face had been torn open and burned. The chest of his chemical protective suit was shredded and soaked with blood and diesel. His right sleeve ended just below the elbow in a bloody tatter. Without needing to check for a pulse, Bannon knew Ortelli was dead.

His first thought, to leave the body and abandon the tank, was discarded almost as quickly as it had come to the fore. Ortelli deserved better than that. He had been a good soldier and a loyal crewman. To leave his body in the tank and give it up to the fire that would soon engulf 66 was unthinkable. If they survived, Bannon at least wanted to be able to tell his family that they had done all they could for him, even in the end.

Bannon looked up at Kelp and Folk. "Let's get him out of here."

Working in silence, Kelp and Bannon dragged Ortelli's body out of the driver's compartment and propped it up. Folk, who had climbed out of the turret, knelt on the turret roof, reached down through the loader's hatch, and took Ortelli under the arms. As he pulled the driver's still body up, Bannon and Kelp each grabbed a leg and lifted. Before leaving the turret himself, Kelp grabbed his submachine gun and the ammo pouch. Bannon stayed behind to prepare 66 for destruction.

Though the engine compartment fire would probably finish off 66, he wanted to do everything he could to keep his tank from being displayed in Red Square as a trophy. To that end he opened the ammo ready door and locked it open. He then pulled one round out and put it halfway in the main gun's chamber as well as several more rounds on the turret floor. After turning the radio frequency knobs off of the Team's frequency, he took his CEOI, one that contained all the radio frequencies and call signs for the brigade, and tore the pages out, spreading them around the turret. Satisfied that 66 was ready, he stuffed two frag grenades and one thermite grenade in his pocket and climbed out.

Once outside, Bannon threw his CVC down into the turret, pulled on his web gear, helmet, and binoculars and grabbed his map case. Turning to Folk and Kelp, he ordered them to head for the woods to their right. Once they were on the way, he took the thermite grenade, pulled the pin let the grenade's arming spoon flip up, and dropped it in the loader's hatch among the shells on the floor. Having done all he could think of, he leaped down off the right side of the tank.

To his surprise, Bannon landed next to Ortelli. While he had been inside, Folk and Kelp had put Ortelli into a sleeping bag and laid it a few feet away from the tank. One of them had tied a tag with Ortelli's name and social security number to the zipper. They had also taken the time to place his head so that the damaged side of his face was not exposed. Except for the tag, the driver looked as if he were asleep. It seemed, Bannon told himself, Folk and Kelp had felt the same way he did about their friend. Just as they had cared and looked out for each other in life, they had done so in death.

These reflections were cut short when he heard the termite grenade pop. Having no wish to be anywhere near 66 when the main gun rounds started going off, Bannon took off to catch up with the rest of the crew. Ortelli and Alpha 66 were gone. It was time to carry on.

∽

Folk and Kelp were both lying in the tree line watching 66 burn by the time Bannon caught up. He plopped down next to them and began to watch as well. The tank was fully involved now, burning from front to rear and quivering as HE rounds cooked off and detonated. Off to the left the T-62s were also burning. That's when it struck him. For the past three days he had thought of the Soviet tanks as nothing more than objects, machines to be smashed, destroyed, or "serviced" as the Army had once referred to the act of engaging targets. But in "*servicing*" those "*things*," they had killed twelve men and had lost one of their own.

The whole scene began to seem unreal. Bannon felt detached from the horrors and the dangers that surrounded them. It was all like a bad dream, the sort you can't seem to wake up from even though you want to. Turning away from the devastation, he lay on his back, closed his eyes, and let his mind go blank. The nervous stress and the emotional strain, as well as the physical exhaustion, were catching up to him. He was thirsty but too tired to do anything about it. What he really needed was a few minutes alone to get himself together.

In the stillness that followed, Bannon listened to sounds of battle to the north drifting down from Hill 214. He listened for several minutes without thinking or moving. To the south the sounds of small-arms fire could be heard from Objective LOG. The battle there was still going on. The familiar pop-pop of M-16s firing was answered by rifle reports that were not familiar to his ears. Probably Soviet AKs, he imagined. It was the high-pitched whine of two personnel carriers approaching that finally got him to move.

Rolling over onto his stomach, he propped himself up on his elbows in time to catch sight of a pair of M-113s coming up along the same route 66 had taken. As they approached 66 from behind, they slowed down and passed it, one on each side, the TC in each track scanning the area. They turned toward the wood line and headed to where Bannon, Folk, and Kelp were. Bannon knew they hadn't seen them. All they were probably interested in was getting out of the open, using the tree line for cover. At least, Bannon mused, he and the rest of his crew would be able to ride up to Hill 214.

Without thinking, Bannon began to rise up on his knees. Just as he was about to wave down the PCs, the closest PC cut loose with a burst of machinegun fire. His wild volley ripped through the trees above him, showering Bannon with splinters and pieces of bark. As he dropped back down Folk let out a stream of obscenities while Kelp covered his head, curled up into a ball, and started to howl. "JESUS CHRIST! THE FUCKERS ARE TRYING TO KILL US!"

Still on his stomach, and with his face buried in the ground, Bannon raised his right arm and waved frantically. When the shooting stopped, he ever so carefully raised his head, looking out to see both tracks side by side headed for him, guns aimed and ready. Once more raising his arm, he continued to wave as he slowly rose, ready to go down again if they fired. This time, they didn't.

Once the commander of the lead PC was satisfied they weren't Russians, they both picked up speed and continued toward the tree line. Neither TC, however, turned his Cal .50 off Bannon. It seemed no one was taking any chances.

When the lead PC pulled up even with Bannon and stopped, its TC grinned. "Damn, sir, we thought you were dead," Polgar cried out.

"Thanks to you we almost were. Is this all that's left of your platoon?"

"No, Sir. There are a few men back on LOG with the L. T. but they're mostly wounded, including the L.T. I got most of the 2nd and the 3rd Squads with me. The 1st Squad bought it on that first volley back at the stream." Pausing, he took a quick glance over his shoulder to where Alpha 66 and the T-62s sat burning, then turned back toward Bannon. "I see you got some before you lost your tank."

"Yeah. We did. Have you been in radio contact with anyone else in the Team?"

"Yes, sir. The XO. He's up on Hill 214 with the rest of the Team. That's where we're headed now."

Bannon felt as if someone had just removed the bloody big stone that had been sitting on his heart. There still was a Team Yankee! Right now he didn't care that it wasn't much of a team. Nor did it matter that they were in the wrong place. All that was important was that there was at least something left. Despite all the foul-ups of that morning, he hadn't pissed away the whole Team.

While Folk and Kelp headed for the other PC, Bannon climbed into Polgar's track and stood up in the open cargo hatch behind the TC. Once everyone was loaded, they headed for Hill 214, hugging the tree line until they were just across from the woods of Hill 214. From there they dashed across the open area and up onto the eastern slope of Hill 214. After wandering cautiously through the forest, they came up to the four remaining tanks of the Team.

The four tanks with Bob Uleski were deployed along the tree line overlooking Arnsdorf, ready to support Delta Company's attack. As Polgar's PCs were coming to a halt about fifty meters to the rear of the tanks, Bannon caught sight of Uleski as he was dismounting from the tank in the center. Even at that distance, he could see his XO was injured. Eager to find out what was going on, Bannon clambered out of Polgar's PC and hustled over toward Uleski.

With his right arm in a sling and splint, Uleski made a show of saluting Bannon with his left hand. "Anyone else coming, sir?"

Bannon replied with nothing more than a shake of his head. "From the Team, no. As far as the battalion, I haven't a clue. Do you know where they are and what they're up to?"

Like Bannon, Uleski simply shook his head. "Battalion frequency is being jammed. I've been trying to work through it, but so far, nothing on it or the battalions alternate command frequency."

Bannon and Uleski then turned to Polgar and asked if he had made any contact with battalion before coming up to Hill 214. His reply was also negative.

"So, to the best of anyone's knowledge, battalion has no idea where we are and what we're doing," Bannon grunted.

Uleski dropped his gaze as he slowly nodded. "Looks that way, sir."

As important as it was to report to battalion that some of the Team had made it to Hill 214, as well as find out what the other companies were doing, Bannon's first priority was getting an update on what kind of condition the tanks on Hill 214 were in and what the enemy situation was. Retreating to Polgar's PC, the three of them sat down on its rear ramp once it had been dropped and the squad the PC had been carrying had deployed to the right of the tanks.

Despite the pain his arm was giving him, Uleski described how the four tanks with him had continued onto Hill 214 as Bannon had ordered. "It wasn't until we'd cleared the woods on LOG and were out from under the artillery fire that I noticed you weren't with us," Uleski explained. "When all my attempts to contact you failed, I had the remaining tanks close up, ordered the Mech Platoon, to follow up when they could, and pushed on. We reached Hill 214 without further contact and began to sweep through the Objective. As the tanks crested the hill, we ran right into the middle of a Soviet artillery battery of towed guns preparing to move." At this point, the hint of a grin began to tug at the corner of Uleski's lips. "You should have seen the faces of the Russian gunners as we were sweeping through their position, sir. It made my day."

For the briefest of moments, Uleski paused as his eyes took on a distant, almost contemplative appearance as if he was mentally replaying the scenes he'd beheld as the tanks with him overran the Soviet battery. Then, as quickly as it had come, the look was gone as he turned his full attention back to the matter at hand.

"We destroyed the guns, their prime movers and cut down anyone who wasn't quick enough to get away. Not many did," he added in a gleeful manner that sent a chill down Bannon's spine. That his XO took pride in what they had done to the Russian gunners came as no surprise to him. After watching so many of the vehicles in Team Yankee get hit, he and the tankers with him were out for blood, ready to engage in an all-out killing frenzy, one Uleski seemed to have relished.

"We literally ran down and over every Russian that got in our way. Everyone was firing whatever weapon he could bring to bear as we hunted the Soviet gunners down, sometimes one at a time. Four of the little shits made it to a house on the edge of Arnsdorf. The last man in closed the door as if that would keep the tank that was pursuing them out. It didn't. The tank just drove up to the house, rammed its main gun through the door, and fired a HEAT round. When the house burst into flames, the tank backed up a few meters and waited. When two Russians came out, the tank cut them down."

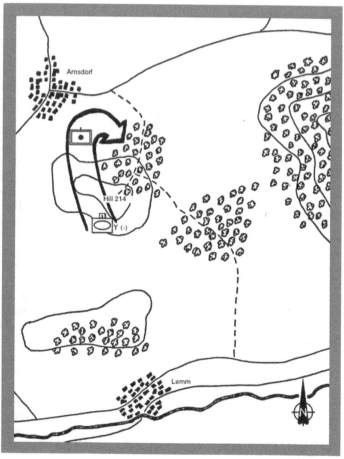

Map 8: Revenge

Throughout this story, Uleski's face betrayed neither revulsion nor regret. His eyes, set in a steady gaze, cut through Bannon like fingernails being scraped across a chalkboard. Three days of war had done much to harden Bob Uleski. As Bannon watched his XO's face and listened to his story in silence, he could not help but wonder just how much he had changed.

Uleski paused for a moment after finishing his report on the action against the battery, using the silence that followed to mentally set that incident aside before moving on to filling Bannon in on the Team's current status. "After the tanks were finished with the Russian battery, we withdrew up the hill and occupied the positions they're currently in. There were several minor wounds that had required tending, but nothing critical. Ammo has been counted and is being redistributed as we speak. Main gun rounds are the big problem. Each of the tanks here is down to ten rounds of SABOT and six rounds of HEAT. If and when the Soviets got serious about counterattacking, I fear we're going to run out."

"Personnel?" Bannon asked crisply.

"Not much better," Uleski shot back without hesitation. "Unless you know something I don't, the dead and missing include Unger and his entire FIST team, Sergeant Pierson and the 34 tank, and Lieutenant Harding who was wounded as he was rolling through on LOG. That leaves me with the Alpha 55, Garger with 31, Sergeant First Class Hebrock with 24 and Staff Sergeant Rhoads with 22."

Turning to Polgar, Bannon cocked a brow. "What about you? What kind of shape is your platoon in?"

Easing back, Polgar sighed. "Well, there's the 23 track with Staff Sergeant Flurer and 2nd Squad and my own track with Staff Sergeant Jefferson and the 3rd Squad. All told, I've seventeen men, two tracks, and two Dragon trackers with three missiles for each."

It didn't take long for Bannon to do the math. Team Yankee was now down to four tanks, two PCs, two Dragons, and thirty-five men. Even worse, he had no idea where anyone else in the battalion was or what the battalion was doing. For all he knew, 3rd of the 78th Infantry no longer existed. And even if it did, it was in no position to help him. He and the rump of Team Yankee were on their own.

The one bright spot Bannon could latch onto was that the enemy had yet to react to the loss of Hill 214. After destroying the artillery battery, the tanks had had no contact with the Russians. It was, however, only a matter of time before they did. The presence of Team Yankee on Hill 214 or in the area had to be known. Why else would the three tanks Alpha 66 had encountered have been pulled out of their positions and sent backpedaling in the middle of a battle?

Also on the plus side was Bannon's doubt that the Soviets knew how much, or how little, was on 214. If the Russians stayed true to form, before they did anything they would send in a small recon element to locate the Team to ascertain their size, composition and, if possible, pin them. Once they had done that, the Soviets would strike and strike hard.

While Uleski and Polgar were gathering up all the track commanders, Bannon weighed his options. They could withdraw. As there had been no contact with battalion since the attack had begun, and there was little prospect of making contact anytime soon, withdrawal would be acceptable. Because of its losses, Team Yankee was no longer able to perform a Team-sized mission. Added to that, ammunition was becoming critically low. Finally, he had no idea when, or even if, battalion would link up. Although Polgar had informed him that LOG had been cleared, only Harding and a few wounded had been left to hold that hill while they waited for Team Bravo to move up. If the Soviets wanted to, they'd be able to reoccupy it with ease. All in all, Bannon concluded, remaining on Hill 214, knowing full well that the Soviets would be back, made no sense.

But neither did withdraw. While there was almost no hope of holding Hill 214 against a determined counterattack given the Team's current strength, there was no guarantee that the Russians would, or could, counterattack in strength. There was always the possibility that they were in just as bad shape as the Team was and didn't have the wherewithal on hand to launch a counterattack. The fact that the Russians had been forced to throw three T-62s that had been in reserve unit or part of the security screen to sort out their rear area seemed to buttress this possibility. To withdraw his Team only to learn later that there had been no threat would ensure the losses they'd suffered taking Hill 214 would have been in vain.

Finally, Bannon could not discount the possibility that the rest of the battalion would finally get its act together and continue with the mission. It would be humiliating to be in the process of withdrawing against an imagined foe only to run head-on into the rest of the battalion as it advanced up to Hill 214. Not that pride and humiliation were of prime concern to Bannon at the moment. It was just that such a possibility was as likely as any of the others he could come up with. Besides, the order to seize Hill 214 was still in effect.

It was decided, then. Team Yankee had taken this hill and was going to keep it until ordered elsewhere or thrown off. Only now did Bannon begin to appreciate the old saying that once soldiers had paid for a piece of ground with the blood of their comrades, the value of that land transcended what cold logic would otherwise calculate was true. For Team Yankee, the ground they were standing on was now the most important piece of real estate in Germany, a hill they would hold, consequences be damned.

With that, Bannon turned his full attention to how they would hold Hill 214. With four tanks, two squads of infantry, and two PCs, the Team could hold four to five hundred meters of front. Unfortunately, the Team was on its own. Somehow, the Team needed to secure its flanks and rear, not just its front. The Soviets might try a frontal attack once, but Bannon doubted they would do it twice. Besides, they might try holding the Team's attention to the front while maneuvering infantry through the woods to hit them in the rear. Flank and rear security were therefore critical.

"Well Bannon," he muttered to himself as he walked out into the middle of the small laager the Team was currently occupying, "Let's see how you're gonna go about skinning this cat."

∾

While Sean Bannon was doing all he could to see to it that Team Yankee was ready for whatever came its way, Lt. Col. Yuri Potecknov was preparing to execute his new mission in the exact, scientific manner that he had been taught at the Frunze Military Academy and had used in Afghanistan. It was a simple mission and well within the capabilities of his unit. A small probing attack by some American tanks had penetrated the thin security screen on the Army's flank and was threatening a critical town named Arnsdorf. Colonel Potecknov's orders were to wipe out the enemy force and restore the security screen.

While he was unhappy that his motorized rifle battalion was being diverted from the main effort of the army, Potecknov rationalized that it was for the better. His troops were still untried by battle. So far all they'd done since the commencement of hostilities was follow the division's lead, waiting for the chance to pour through a breach in the American lines that never came. By sweeping up the enemy force at Arnsdorf, the colonel could blood his troops. A cheap victory would not only instill confidence in the officers and men of his battalion, it would provide him with an opportunity to see how well those officers performed under fire. This would be nothing more than a live-fire exercise with a few targets that fired back.

∾

With Team Yankee's leadership assembled, Bannon went over their current situation, what he expected the enemy would do, and how they were going to hold Hill 214. They didn't have a lot to work with. What they did have had to be stretched to cover threats from any direction. The result was not the soundest plan he had ever come up with, for it violated just about every tactical principle in the book. But, given the situation and time, it was the best he could do. Once the orders were out, the Team began to deploy and dig in.

The tanks still constituted their major firepower. Initially, they would fight from their present positions, which would allow them to parry an attack from Arnsdorf. They also needed to be ready to occupy two other positions in case the Soviets attacked elsewhere. The first was on the eastern side of the woods covering the open space between Hill 214 and a wooded lot to the southeast. A Soviet commander could use those woods as a staging area before rushing across the open area and onto Hill 214. The second position was on the crest of Hill 214 facing south. The Soviet's might decide to seal off the Team's routes of escape, then hit it from that direction.

The Mech Platoon was broken up into three elements. The two rifle squads dismounted and established an ambush along a north-south trail that ran through the center of the woods north of Hill 214. This protected the Team from a dismounted attack coming through the woods from the north, provided the Soviet commander making that attack used the trail to guide him. The two PCs with only the drivers and track commanders under Uleski established an outpost on the crest of Hill 214 covering the southern portion of the hill. The third element was a two-man OP on the east side of the woods watching the southeast wooded lot. Bannon hoped that if the Soviets came from the south or from the east, that OP and the one manned by the tanks would be able to give the tanks sufficient warning and time to switch to the alternate positions.

It was the attack through the woods from the north that was, in Bannon's mind, the greatest threat. Polgar had a total of thirteen men to cover that area. This number included Folk and Kelp, for there were no vacant slots due to casualties on the tanks they needed to fill. The distance from the west edge to the east edge of the wooded lot was just a little over one thousand meters. With two men per foxhole and ten meters between foxholes, the most Polgar could cover was sixty meters. That left a very large gap on either side that the Soviet commander could move whole companies through, if he knew where Polgar's people were. In all likelihood, however, a commander conducting a night attack through unfamiliar woods would stick to or near the trail, if for no other reason than to maintain orientation. If that happened, Polgar was ready and waiting with one of their Dragons, two M60 machineguns, two grenade launchers, and his riflemen. To provide an additional edge, antitank and antipersonnel mines, as well as field expedient booby traps using grenades, were deployed to the front and flanks of the infantry positions.

Command and control of the Team would be simple. First, there wasn't that much to command or control. Second, all radios were put on the company net. Bannon took over Alpha 55, the XO's tank and stayed with the tanks. With his arm injured, Uleski could not fight with 55. Besides, Bannon wanted someone dependable with the PCs covering the south. After the run-in with the T-62s in the morning, he was paranoid about the southern side of Hill 214. An OP sent out to the front of the tanks and manned by two crewmen who had a sound-powered phone running back to 55 would be able to pass information straight back to Bannon. The OP on the east side was also using sound-powered phones to maintain contact. Their phone line ran back to Polgar who, in turn, maintained contact with Bannon via a portable PRC-77 radio on the Team net. With the exception of Polgar, who had to run his dismounted infantry using voice commands, everyone in the Team could contact everyone else.

∾

The afternoon passed in a strange and unnerving silence. The distant rumble of artillery hitting someone else had become so common that unless an effort was made, no one noticed it anymore. That didn't mean anyone was becoming lax or blasé. Everyone was nervous and on edge. At the slightest sound or movement out of the ordinary, the men would stop work and grab their weapons. Since the war had begun no one in the Team had had much of a chance for a decent, uninterrupted sleep. In the last thirty-six hours, Bannon had had no more than two hours of sleep total.

While it was noticeable on everyone, this lack of sleep had its most telling effect on him and his leaders. Because of this, Bannon found he often had to repeat his orders to them two or three times. When the orders were being issued for the defense of Hill 214, one of the tank commanders had actually fallen asleep. Uleski wasn't in much better shape. As he was telling the men who would be with him what they needed to do to prepare, he stopped in mid-sentence, unable to remember what he had intended to say next. The only way Bannon kept going was by constantly moving around. Even then, he sometimes had to stop and try hard to remember what it was he had been doing. It didn't take long for Bannon to realize the Team could not go on like this for much longer. Unless something changed real soon, by tomorrow, he reasoned, they would be at the end of their ability to endure and function.

As he was going over this in his mind, he decided, despite his previous resolve, that if they had no contact with anyone from battalion or brigade by 0300 the following morning, he would take Team Yankee off Hill 214 and, under the cover of darkness, reenter friendly lines to the south. If someone was coming, they would be there by then. To try and hold on for another day would stretch those who were with him on Hill 214 beyond their physical capability. He could only ask so much of the men.

It was during the last hour of daylight that the Russians came.

It began when a column of four T-72s and eight BTR-60PBs rolled down the road into Arnsdorf from the northwest as if Team Yankee were a thousand miles away. Garger, Hebrock, and Bannon crawled out to the OP manned by the tankers to watch this column as it entered the town. Both its size and its behavior told Bannon they were from a different regiment, possibly even a different division than the Soviet units the Team had overrun that morning. The theory that the Russians had shoved everything forward and had left their flanks flapping in the breeze seemed to be spot on. Their coming from the northwest pointed to the fact that they were either part of the operational reserve, or the Russians were having to strip detachments from front line units in order to secure their rear areas. If the latter were true, then Team Yankee's attack had achieved some measure of success in that it was causing the Soviets to divert forces from their attack to the west.

As they continued to watch the motorized rifle company and tanks move into Arnsdorf, Bannon asked if anyone knew how many men a BTR-60 could carry. Without hesitating, Garger informed him that it could carry twelve passengers and a crew of two. For a moment Bannon lowered his binoculars and looked over at the young lieutenant. In the past three days he had done exceedingly well. His performance had been on par with that of McAlister and Harding. The fact that he had made it this far was a testament to his ability as a tank commander. Bannon had often heard stories about men who came across as complete zeros in

Map 9: The Defense of Hill 214

peacetime but turned into tigers in war. That Garger seemed to be one of them made him glad circumstances had prevented him replacing him.

Not long after entering Arnsdorf, all vehicles in the Soviet column cut off their engines. In the silence that followed, Bannon could hear Russian officers somewhere in the town shouting orders.

SFC Hebrock broke the silence. "Well sir, what do you think?"

Bannon thought for a moment. "If I were in command down there, I'd wait until dark before trying anything. First, I'd send out some dismounted infantry to conduct a thorough recon of this hill. Only when I had a firm grasp of what I was facing would I launch an all-out attack."

Hebrock grunted. "Let's hope the Russian down there who's doing all the yelling isn't as smart or as cautious as you are."

Yeah, Bannon thought to himself as he glanced over toward the west, wondering if the red setting sun was an omen of things to come. *Let's hope he's not.*

From the edge of Arnsdorf, Colonel Potecknov, his deputy, his operations officer, and his political officer surveyed the hill to the southeast. They could see the debris of the artillery battery that had been caught in the open as well as the track marks gouged out by the American tanks that had destroyed it. He tried to listen for any telltale signs of activity from the hill, but couldn't hear a thing due to the noise his own men were making in the town. If there were still Americans on the hill, and if they were watching, which the colonel had no doubt they were, they weren't showing themselves. "Very well," he declared as he was turning to his operations officer. "If the Americans won't show themselves, we will go in and find them. Prepare a patrol."

As the operations officer scurried off to issue the necessary orders, the colonel went back to studying the hill in the failing light. "A simple exercise," the battle hardened veteran of the war in Afghanistan muttered to no one in particular. "We shall squeeze this hill like a grape and see what comes out."

While they continued to watch Arnsdorf in the failing light, 55's loader crawled up beside Bannon and informed him that Polgar had received a report from the OP on the east side. Apparently they had heard the sound of vehicles moving through the woods to the southeast.

"Looks like the Soviets intend to hit the Team from both sides at once," he informed Garger and Hebrock. "Best we head back and get ready for 'em."

Bannon used the time it took them to crawl back to the tanks to figure out how the Team was going to deal with this new threat. He had no doubt the Team could easily handle one attack. Two, coming from entirely different directions, was a whole different kettle of fish. There was always the possibility the motorized rifle company and tanks that had put on quite a show while entering Arnsdorf were nothing more than a deception intended to mask the approach of units that would launch the main attack from the east. As there was less open ground to cover from that direction, this made sense.

Once back at 55, Bannon radioed Uleski. He ordered the XO to move from the hilltop and go over to where the infantry OP was sited on the east side. He informed him he was also sending the two 2nd Platoon tanks over. Uleski was to organize the defense there but was to be prepared to send the tanks back if they were needed. Polgar and his men were to stay put for now, but he was to be prepared to reinforce either Bannon or the XO.

Bannon's final instructions to the Team reflected the pessimism he could do little to mask. "If it looks like we're going to be overrun, break contact and make your way back to friendly lines as best you can with as many men as you can."

After everyone on the net had acknowledged this last message, Bannon went over his plan in his mind one last time. The odds were not good. The other people had at least four tanks in support of two hundred or more infantry. It was too late to have second thoughts about fighting or fleeing. The Team was committed. With the last light of day gone, all that was left for the Team to do was wait for the Russians to come.

They didn't have long to wait.

CHAPTER 7

Check and Checkmate

It was Sergeant Polgar and his thin line of infantry that were hit first. Just after 2300, movement was detected to their front. The first indication they had that they were about to be attacked was the faint rustling of leaves and sound of a twig snapping. Neither was sufficient to tell Polgar or his people just how many Russians were coming or what direction they were coming from. Soon, however, the infantrymen, using their night vision devices, began to make out a line of figures slowly advancing in a staggered column on either side of the trail.

Upon hearing this, Polgar smiled to himself. The Russian formation and direction their attack was coming from could not have been any better as far as he was concerned. As planned, he intended to allow whoever was leading them to get within ten meters of his foxhole before giving his own people the order to fire.

As he waited for them, Polgar's pulse began to beat harder and faster. The fear of premature disclosure of his position by one of his men ratcheted up his nervous anxiety, causing him to glance to the left, down his line of positions, then right, and back to the left. His platoon, clearly visible through his night vision goggles, were ready and, like himself, eager to fire.

When he turned his full attention back to the front, Polgar saw the Russians had stopped thirty meters short of his positions, causing his heart to skip a beat. Had they been discovered? Had he lost the element of surprise? One of the two lead Soviet soldiers, now fully exposed and clearly visible, glanced back over his shoulder. Another figure, ten meters behind them, waved a pistol and pointed it forward, whispering a command of some type. Turning his head back to the front, the man who'd looked behind used his head to indicate to his comrade they were to proceed. They, Polgar told himself, were the point element. And the one with the pistol was obviously the officer in charge, the man he personally would take out.

Only when the point element was within ten meters did Polgar slowly released the safety his M-16, take aim on the Russian officer, and fire.

His single shot unleashed the well-rehearsed and deadly ambush drill. His two squad leaders detonated a pair of Claymore mines that sent thousands of one-eighth-inch steel balls ripping through the Soviet column. Machinegunners laid down a withering crossfire that cut down those still standing after the mines had detonated. The grenadiers added to this mayhem by methodically plunking 40mm grenades wherever they spotted two or more Russians gathered in a cluster. The riflemen, like the grenadiers, scanned their designated sectors, seeking out targets and taking them out one by one.

The violence and shock of the ambush was overwhelming. The Russian officer never had the chance to utter a single command before he was cut down. The deadly and accurate point-blank fire that pelted any Russian who survived the initial volley ensured that any movement by him was his last. The darkness, the violence of execution, the loss of their leaders, and the resulting confusion proved to be too much. Those who had been fortunate enough to be in the rear of the column withdrew back down the trail, pursued by a hail of bullets.

Only when he determined they'd inflicted all the damage on the Russians they were going to did Polgar give the order to ceasefire. As quickly as it had started, the firing stopped and quiet returned. The report he passed back to Bannon was matter-of-fact, accurate, and succinct. In his opinion, the Russians that had hit his position had been a platoon sized patrol looking to find out where the Team's positions were. That discovery had been costly for the Russians. But they could afford the price.

While the Team awaited the next Soviet move, Polgar shifted his men back several meters to a new line of positions. If the Soviets decided to hit the Team in all directions, the survivors would surely lead the next group back to the point of the ambush. No doubt they would be in attack formation and ready to launch a full blooded assault. By dropping back, the next Soviet attack would hit an empty sack. If the Soviets didn't catch on to this right off and instead, began to mill about checking out the abandoned positions, some of which were booby trapped, Polgar just might catch them off guard again. With so few men, he needed every advantage he could get.

About forty-five minutes after the firefight in the woods, two of the tanks in the village of Arnsdorf cranked up and began to move to where the trail entered the wooded lot. The slowness of their progress gave Bannon the impression the Russians were trying to hide this move. Since any movement by a tank is very difficult to hide, he wondered if they were a decoy, sent out to draw the Team's fire and, in doing so, betray the position of his tanks. Since they could be on their way to support another attack on Polgar's position, Bannon informed Polgar he needed to be ready for tanks. Smugly, Polgar simply replied, "Send 'em. We're ready."

As the pair of Soviet tanks continued to creep along the road across the Team's front, the OP in front of the Team Yankee's tanks reported it could hear the sound of many engines cranking up and vehicles moving about just inside that part of

Arnsdorf that faced Hill 214. When Bannon radioed to Polgar that he thought both the tanks and infantry positions would be hit at the same time, Uleski also reported movement to his front. The Russians were putting on a full court press. The moment of truth was at hand. After ordering the OP in front of the tanks to pull back, Bannon instructed Garger in Alpha 31 to move up as soon as he heard 55 crank up. As he was waiting for his loader to return from the OP, Bannon wondered if the next move the Russians made would be check, or checkmate.

The barrage that hit Alpha 55 and 31 was not preceded by the whine of artillery Bannon was becoming painfully accustomed to. Incoming mortar rounds simply begin to explode. Instinctively, Bannon dropped all the way down into the tank and masked. Specialist 4 Newman, 55's loader, was already masked and looking over at Bannon. "Those don't sound like the shells we were hit with the other day," he stated in a matter-of-fact manner as if he was discussing sports or the weather. "There's no whine before they impact."

"Mortars. They must be firing mortars," Bannon informed him as he was fumbling with his mask. "Probably 120mm mortars from the battalion's mortar battery. They can't do much to us." At least, Bannon hoped, they couldn't.

Once masked and hooked into the intercom, Bannon had the driver crank up the tank and move up to its fighting position. As they were doing so, he popped his head up and surveyed the scene. The mortar rounds were falling just to the rear of the tanks. The volume of fire was impressive, but doing little more than making noise and tearing up more trees. A check with Polgar and Uleski revealed that 55 and 31 were the only ones being shelled, causing Bannon to guess the Soviet commander was attempting to draw their attention to the sector facing Arnsdorf.

Once in position, 55 and 31's gunners watched as a line of fifty or more Russian soldiers emerged from the village, deployed into line, and begin to advance toward the hill on foot. They were followed by four BTR-60s and two tanks. Behind them came another line of troops followed by their BTRs. The Russians were coming in force this time.

Bannon ordered 31 to engage the T-72 on the left on order. 55 would take out the one on the right. They would hit the T-72 with head-on frontal shots. Bannon wondered if the 105mm rounds of the M-1 would penetrate the front slope of those tanks. He therefore instructed Garger to continue to engage until it burned. There was no time for second-guessing. The last thing he wanted was to have some Russian do to them what he had done to the trio of T-62s he'd met earlier in the day.

Once the T-72s were destroyed, Garger was instructed to concentrate on suppressing the infantry while 55 took out the BTRs. Not that a BTR was particularly dangerous to a tank. With only a 14.5mm gun in its turret, the most the BTRs could do to an M-1 was tear up the crew's gear and punch holes in its front fenders. But the destruction of the tanks, the methodical destruction of their BTRs, and a steady stream of lead pinning them to the ground in the darkness, compounded by the confusion that often is part and parcel of a night attack, would have a devastating psychological impact on the individual Russian soldier. Bannon hoped that it would discourage them from rushing forward to become a Hero of the Soviet Union.

∽

As the tanks were preparing to meet the attack coming from Arnsdorf, Polgar came up on the net and reported that he could hear tanks coming down the trail toward his positions. No sooner had Bannon given him a "ROGER, OUT," than

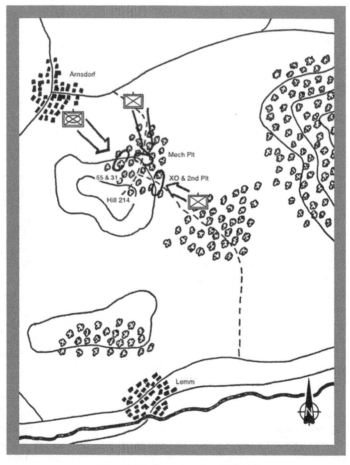

Map 10: The Soviet Attack on Hill 214

Uleski reported there were about one hundred dismounted infantry advancing toward him in a column formation, confirming Bannon's fear the Russians were going all out this time. It seemed they wanted to hold the Team's attention in the front, pin the infantry their recon element had stumbled upon in the woods with a secondary attack, and sneak up behind. Team Yankee was in check.

∽

The infantry were the first to engage. The Russian lead tank, slowly trundling along the wooded trail, hit one of the antitank mines Polgar's people had put out. This was followed by a wild volley of small-arms fire from the accompanying Soviet infantry who took to firing wildly in whatever direction they'd been facing when the tank had hit the mine. To a man, they simply dropped down wherever and continued to fire. Polgar, on the other hand, managed to keep his men in check and quiet. He wanted to suck the Russians in before they opened fire.

When it became apparent that the lead tank was crippled, unable to move forward, and blocking the advance of the second tank, the Russian leading the infantry shouted out a series of commands that quelled their panicked shooting and got them back up on their feet. Once he had his men sorted out, he led them forward.

This time, as the Russians advanced in a line perpendicular to and straddling the trail, they fired from the hip and yelled in an effort to psych themselves up. Their firing was, as before, wild and of more danger to themselves than to Polgar and his men. The only thing it did was to allow Polgar to keep track of the progress of their advance.

Step by step the line of Russian infantry came on. When they reached the line of deserted foxholes, some of the Russians began to throw grenades in the foxholes they stumbled upon and increase their rate of fire. As it became obvious that there was no one there, the Russian officers began to shout orders in attempt to regain control of their men. It was while they were milling about in an effort to reorganize and reorient for their next move that Polgar hit them.

As before, the infantry set off several Claymore antipersonnel mines, followed by machine-gun and automatic-rifle fire. With the Russians haphazardly arrayed in a line parallel to the new infantry position rather than perpendicular as the first group of Russians had been, the effects of the fire Polgar's men were hitting them with was far more devastating, killing many of the officers. Again, individual soldiers scattered, dropping to the ground, or sought cover before engaging in a desultory exchange of small arms fire with Polgar's infantry. The disabled tank, unable to maneuver, did its best to provide support from where it was by firing its main gun.

There then began a deadly game of hide and seek. The Russians, lacking night vision devices, waited until an American infantryman fired. When he fired his first few shots, the Russian would orient his weapon to the general location that he had seen the muzzle flash. If the American did not move before he fired again, the Russian would take aim and fire a burst. Doing this, however, exposed the Russians to the same risks and results. In this way, the infantry battle bogged down into a series of sporadic and violent exchanges of gunfire punctuated by brief pauses as both sides tried to find and fix new targets. This was followed by a fresh eruption of small arms fire as someone found a mark and opened up.

∼

Just as the infantry fight reached this standoff, a volley of Soviet artillery hit the trail junction in the center of the wood lot. Its purpose, Bannon guessed, was to isolate each element of the Team and keep it from shifting to reinforce an endangered sector.

Upon hearing the impact of their artillery, the infantry advancing on 55 and 31 began to pick up their pace. As they were not masked, Bannon ordered the crews of 55 and 31 to unmask and prepare to fire when the T-72s were at 700 meters. He then quietly issued his own fire command, watching through his extension as Sgt. Gwent, his gunner laid on the T-72 to the right. When he saw how large it was in the sight, he grinned. Hitting it would not be the problem. Killing it was the concern.

The first time Gwent hit his laser range finder button with his thumb, the range return digits in the bottom of Bannon's extension showed 750 meters. In silence the two of them watched as the T-72 continued to rumble along, straining to hold back behind the line of infantry. The next time Gwent ranged to it, the display read 720 meters. "Almost there," Bannon muttered.

The tank, growing larger and more menacing by the second, continued to advance. It had but a single purpose, to kill Americans.

Gwent ranged again. 690 meters!

"FIRE!"

"ON THE WAAY!"

The flash, the recoil, and the sharp report of 55's main gun broke the silence. Target! But the Russian kept coming, turning his gun toward 55. "TARGET! REENGAGE—FIRE!"

"UP!"

"ON THE WAY!"

Again the flash, the recoil, and the blast announced the firing of a main gun round. Again 55 hit the T-72. Not only did it keep coming, it was returning fire. 55 shuddered in almost the same instant that the T-72 fired. 55 had been hit.

Startled, Newman, the loader, looked over at Bannon. "WHAT'S THAT?"

"NEVER MIND. ARE YOU UP?"

"UP!"

"FIRE!"

"ON THE WAY!"

This time 55's efforts were rewarded. The third round found its mark. In a quick, blinding flash, the commander's hatch of the T-72 was blown open, emitting a blinding sheet of flame that lit up the battlefield. This was followed by a series of internal explosions that caused the T-72 to shudder. The T-72 was dead. The range showing at the bottom of extension was 610 meters.

Relieved, Bannon stuck his head out of the hatch to see what 31 was up to. Its T-72 was also burning. Steady streams of tracers from 31's COAX, loader's machinegun and caliber .50 were raking the line of Soviet infantry. Already most of them had gone to ground, either dead or trying to keep from becoming that way. When he saw two of the BTRs open fire on 31, Bannon decided to take them out first. Grabbing the override, he slued the turret to the left.

"GUNNER, HEAT, TWO BTRS, LEFT BTR!"

"UP!"

"IDENTIFIED!"

"FIRE!"

The first HEAT round found its mark just below the small turret on the BTR. The impact and the internal explosions caused the BTR to swerve to the left and out of the battle. Both the gunner and Bannon yelled target at the same instant. Without waiting, Gwent laid his sights on the next BTR and gave a quick, "IDENTIFIED!"

Once Newman had replied with an "UP," Bannon gave the command to fire, dispatching a second BTR in less than a minute.

Over on 31, Garger paused to survey the scene before him as he was reloading his .50. This, he thought to himself, was becoming all too easy. Both 55 and 31 were just sitting there as if they were on a gunnery range firing at cardboard and plywood targets instead of real people and vehicles. Both his gunner and his loader were firing their machineguns, each covering a different area. The flames from the burning T-72s and BTRs were lighting up the entire area between 31 and the village of Arnsdorf, allowing the loader and gunner to fire without needing to use night vision devices.

The sight of a small group of Russians inching their way forward, moving from cover to cover, caused Garger to slew his cupola around toward them and open fire on them with the .50. When they went to ground, he took to systematically beating the hedges and brush they'd ducked behind with ten to fifteen round bursts of fire. While he imagined some of them were already dead, he continued to hack away at them, doing his best to make sure those who weren't joined those who were. Like his commanding officer, he was in no mood to take any chances.

It took the sound of heavy caliber rounds pinging off the front slope of his tank to draw Garger's attention away from what was left of the Russian infantry he'd been shredding and over to the BTR that was firing on 31 with KPV heavy machinegun. The first thought that popped in to the young officer's mind was not the sort of thing most people would have imagined. Rather than fear or anger, Garger saw the opportunity to take on the armored personnel carrier as something of a challenge. At Knox he had been taught that a caliber .50 could take out a BTR. Here, he thought, was the perfect opportunity to find out if that was true.

As Bannon was preparing to engage his next target, he noticed that 31 was engaging a BTR with the caliber .50. It was clear from what he was seeing that though the rounds were hitting the BTR, they were causing little, if any serious damage. As a way of reminding Garger to get back to concentrating on pinning the infantry, he turned 55's main gun on the BTR that the lieutenant was engaging. One HEAT round was all it took.

In the wake of this, Newman informed Bannon 55 was out of HEAT and down to nine SABOT rounds. Since he didn't want to waste any of them on BTRs, he ordered the loader to load a SABOT round, but not to arm the gun. Then he ordered 31 to switch roles with 55. Garger was to work on the last of the BTRs while 55 would fire on the infantry. Garger's reply betrayed his joy. As 31 had, Bannon assigned his gunner and loader a different sector to concentrate their fire on. The gunner engaged the troops to the front and right. The loader, manning his machinegun, fired at any troops he could spot to the left. When he was satisfied they understood his orders and were complying, Bannon called Uleski and Polgar for an update.

∽

This request for a SITREP caught the infantry in a standoff. The exchange of fire ebbed and flowed. Every time a Russian officer or NCO managed get some of their troops up and moving, a volley of fire from Polgar's infantry would drive them back to ground. Hiding behind whatever cover they could find, the pinned Russians would return fire as those officers and NCOs who were still able to go about doing all they could to get them back on their feet and advancing.

Eager to end this deadlock, Polgar decided to send a Dragon gunner on a wide sweep around the flank to destroy the two Russian tanks that were doing their best to support the beleaguered infantry. Two other men, each carrying an extra Dragon round, went with the Dragon gunner to provide cover or, if he was hit before he was able to take out the tanks, take over from him. One of them was Kelp, who volunteered when he heard Polgar giving the order to the Dragon gunner.

Before going forward, the three-man team dropped back a short distance while the rest of the infantry line increased their fire to cover the move. The Dragon gunner, a Specialist 4 named Sanders, led the other two as they circled around the firefight, using the sound and the gun flashes to guide them. Whenever the Soviet tank fired, Sanders would reorient himself on it before continuing. They were going to go for the second tank first since it was still fully capable and therefore more dangerous. The crippled tank could be dispatched at their leisure.

Taking their time and taking care they didn't run across any Russians who were in the process of making their end run to the rear of the Mech platoon's positions, they closed in on the second tank from behind. To Sanders' relief, he saw that it was wedged in between some trees, unable to move forward or backwards. After looking and listening for a moment to make sure there were no stray Russian soldiers around, he moved to a spot where he was fairly sure the trees and branches between him and the tank would not interfere with his wire-guided missile. Once he'd reach the spot he'd picked, he carefully set up his weapon as if he was on a shooting range, laying the tracker's aim point on the rear of the Soviet-tank. After giving Kelp and the other man with him a heads-up that he was about to fire, the gunner let fly.

The missile left the tube with a blinding flash and *whoosh*. This was followed by the sound of the Dragon's rocket and a series of *pop-pop-popping* sounds as the small guidance jets ignited, keeping the missile on track. The impact lit up the surrounding area and immediately ignited fires in the tank's engine compartment.

"One down, one to go," Sanders muttered as he began to head off in search of a new firing position from which he could take out the other tank.

The three of them were in the process of creeping up on the crippled tank when a lone figure stood up in front of Sanders at a distance of five meters and fired his AK into his chest. Without a second's hesitation, Kelp leveled his submachine gun and cut down the lone figure. Both Kelp and the other infantryman, a private no older than Kelp by the name of McCauley, remained rooted to the spot as they waited to see if any other Russians popped up. Once they were satisfied that the Russian had been stray, the two knelt beside Sanders' body.

In the darkness Kelp felt for his pulse, first on his wrist, then in his neck. There was none. "He's dead."

"How do you know?" asked McCauley.

"I know. He's dead." At nineteen, Kelp was fast becoming an expert on death. "Do you know how to work that thing?"

"Yeah. We had a class on it once. I think I can do it. But I'm not sure how we're going to get around to the other tank. There may be more Russians."

"You just get that thing there and follow ole Kelp here. I'll get you to the Russians' back door."

With that, the two privates made their way through the dark.

∾

The rattle of small arms fire from the infantry's firefight, the crash of artillery behind him, and the sharp crack of 55's and 31's main guns was unnerving to Uleski. It wasn't easy to wait there in the dark, listening to the sounds of a battle all around him while watching a hundred trained soldiers whose sole intent was to kill you calmly advance on your position. Not that Uleski had any doubt about the outcome. Unless there were tanks in the far tree line, the infantry would be no match for the tanks and PCs with him. Uleski was simply getting impatient. Like everyone else in Team Yankee, he wanted to get on with it. Now.

The nausea and fear that had crippled him during the first battle were not present this time. Instead, a seething hatred welled up. As he watched the Soviet infantry advance ever closer to his small detachment's position, he subconsciously took to pounding the fist of his good hand against the roof of the PC. The image of dead and wounded men scattered about 55 after the second attack on the first day flashed through his mind, fanning his hatred into an open rage. "Come on, you motherfuckers," the XO softly muttered. "Come on and die."

As eager as he was to engage the enemy to his front, Uleski watched and waited as the Russian company began to deploy into platoon columns, maintaining a nice steady walking pace as they came on. They were in no hurry to join the chaos in the woods on which they were advancing. It seemed to Uleski as he watched them these Russians would be just as happy if they arrived in time to help with the body count and not a minute sooner. There was definitely a lack of gung-ho spirit here.

Uleski had parked the PC he was on sideways in a depression near the tree line. One of the infantrymen who had been on the OP and the PC driver were standing up in the open cargo hatch next to him with their M-16s resting on the side of the PC. The PC commander had the caliber .50 pointed over the side, locked and loaded with several boxes of additional ammunition opened and ready at an arm's distance. A loaded M-16 he'd gotten from Polgar lay on the roof of the PC next to Uleski's good arm. When the time came, he had every intention of joining the killing.

The other PC with the second man from the OP was also ready, in position to the left of Uleski. Alpha 22 and 24 were deployed to the right of the PCs, ready to engage the infantry and any tanks as yet unseen that might suddenly emerge from the darkness and surprise them.

When the Russians were about two hundred meters from the PCs, Uleski gave the order to fire. Eight machineguns and four M-16s cut loose, unleashing a hail of tracers and lead that tore into the Russians while they were still in the process of deploying. For a moment most of them stood there transfixed, unable to comprehend what was happening to them. Uleski watched through his night vision goggles as some of the Russians first ran one way, then the other as if seeking someplace to hide before giving up and going to ground. Officers could be seen here and there doing all they could to rally their men and drive them on before they were cut down as the machineguns from the tanks and PC's raked the area with steady, measured bursts of fire.

It didn't take Uleski long to conclude that this was a green unit and tonight was its baptism by fire. A smile slowly crossed his face. "So be it," he whispered quietly to himself as he picked up the M-16. "You shall be baptized in blood." In the space of three days, Robert Uleski had made the journey from being good-natured Ski to a man who was a cold, hard killer.

As with the infantry firefight, once the Russians went to ground, an impasse seemed to settle in. The Russians stayed where they were while the PCs and tanks did their best to find and finish the prone figures off. Too impatient to allow this to continue, after emptying the magazine of the M-16, Uleski decided to break the deadlock by ordering Alpha 22 and 24 to move out and make a sweep of the area where the Russians were pinned. Hebrock protested that there could be tanks or antitank guided missile teams in the woods across the way. Uleski, however, was insistent. He wanted the Russians swept away and swept away now. Besides, he reasoned, if there had been tanks or antitank guided missiles in support of the attack, they would have fired by now.

Reluctantly, Hebrock and the Alpha 22 cranked up and moved out. Swinging out wide before turning north, the two tanks slowly began to advance side by side, beating the ground before them with their machineguns as if they were spraying for insects. The violence and terror of being in their first firefight, coupled with the irresistible advance of the steel monsters proved to be too much for some of the Russians. Rather than stay where they were, or follow their officers, they began to break and run. From their positions, the crews of the PCs watched, waiting for targets. Every time a Russian in their sector of fire got up, the riflemen and machine gunners cut him down before he managed to take two steps. When the tanks reached the end of the area where the Russians had gone to ground and began to mask the fire of the PCs, they swung around and went back through the area again, searching out those who had survived the first run. A few, who had managed to keep their wits about them played dead, waited for the first chance that came their way before crawling away and out of the line of fire.

With no more targets, Uleski ordered 22 and 24 to move to their alternate positions. He also moved the two PCs. Once this repositioning was finished and quiet returned to his sector, he reported the status of his element to Bannon.

◡

Potecknov was not at all pleased with the progress, or more correctly, the lack of progress that his companies were making. From the second floor window of a house on the edge of Arnsdorf, he watched the destruction of the tanks and BTRs, followed by the methodical massacre of his troops. Although he could see officers here and there attempting to get their men up and moving, their efforts accomplished little more than adding to the carnage he was witnessing.

Making matters worse, Potecknov had lost contact with the company on the far side of the hill following an initial and incomplete report that they were in contact. Only the company commander in the woods attacking from the east had reported that he was making progress. As if to confirm this, Potecknov could hear the report of the T-72's cannon and see an occasional flash. Deciding that the attack offered the best chance of success, he turned to his deputy and ordered him to stay there with the political officer. They were to do all they could to reorganize the unit to their front while he went around to east and pushed the attack through the woods. Without further ado, Potecknov ran down the stairs and into the street to his vehicle. He was determined to win, regardless of the cost.

◡

Uleski's report found 55 and 31 in the same type of stalemate that he had been in before the sweep by 22 and 24. As Bannon monitored that action, he considered doing the same thing. Thus far, Alpha 55 and 31 had destroyed six BTRs in addition to the two tanks. Two BTRs and some of the infantry in the second line had managed to pull back into the village. Those Russians who had been in first-line had scattered and gone to ground. Some, who had taken cover near the burning vehicles, used every opportunity that came their way to crawl away from the light and heat thrown off by the burning vehicles. Sometimes they misjudged, as they quickly learned when their efforts were rewarded by a burst of fire from either 55 or 31. A few stout-hearted souls, realizing they were going to die anyway, even attempted to engage 55 and 31 with RPGs. Their efforts to crawl close enough to engage the American tanks were quickly and effectively dealt with by the tanks.

While there was no longer any return fire from the line of pinned Russian infantry, Bannon knew there were many of them who were still alive. If they were allowed to stay where they were or managed to make it back to Arnsdorf, they would be of no immediate concern. But if some of their officers were able to rally a few men and slip around to the rear, 55 and 31 would be in danger.

The shifting of the barrage that had been pelting the trail junction to the tree line where 55 and 31 were located decided Bannon's next move. Rather than sit there and be pounded, 55 and 31 were going to attack.

"MIKE 77, THIS IS ROMEO 25, OVER."

"THIS IS MIKE 77."

"THIS IS 25, WE ARE GOING TO ATTACK. WE WILL ADVANCE ABREAST TOWARD THE VILLAGE AT 10 MILES PER HOUR. ONCE

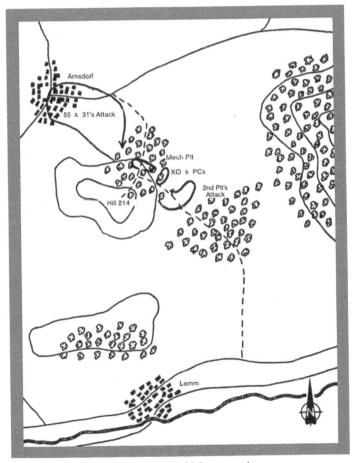

Map 11: The Tanks' Counterattack

WE REACH THE VILLAGE WE WILL GO UP THE STREET THE BTRS
WENT UP. FALL IN BEHIND ME AS WE GO THROUGH THE VILLAGE
AND COVER OUR REAR. HOW COPY SO FAR? OVER."

"THIS IS 77. GOOD COPY. OVER."

"THIS IS 25. ONCE IN THE VILLAGE WE WILL TURN RIGHT ON
THE MAIN ROAD AND GO NORTH OUT OF THE VILLAGE. FROM
THERE FOLLOW ME. I'M NOT SURE WHERE WE WILL GO, OVER."

"THIS IS 77. WILCO. OVER."

"THIS IS 25, LET'S ROLL."

"THIS IS 77. I HEARD THAT."

Garger didn't have to tell his driver twice. He was just as anxious to get out
from under the artillery fire as his lieutenant was. As 31 broke the tree line,
Garger could see 55 illuminated by the fires of the burning Russian vehicles. Both
he and his loader increased their rates of fire as they began to indiscriminately
spray the ground before them with machinegun fire without slowing down.

The sudden appearance of the American tanks proved to be too much for
many of the survivors still lying on the ground between the village and the tree
line. First there had been the battle between the tanks, which their tanks had lost.
Then there had been the accurate and deadly machinegun fire that had cut down
their comrades, their officers, and anyone who was foolish enough to move. Their
BTRs had been reduced to burning hulks that were incinerating their crews and
lighting up the area round them, leaving them exposed. Everywhere they looked
their eyes fell upon a fresh vision of horror, burning vehicles, and scores of dead
and wounded comrades, creating a growing sense in each man that he was alone.
All this pushed the green Russian soldiers to the limit of their endurance. The
appearance of the American tanks closing on them, indiscriminately spewing
death as they came, pushed them beyond it.

❧

Alpha 55 and 31 had no sooner cleared the tree line and gotten out from under the
artillery when individual Russian soldiers began to jump up and flee. Lorriet, 55's
driver, fought the urge to go faster than ten miles an hour. Bannon, the loader, and
the gunner each covered a different sector, engaging Russians as they came across
them. Newman was oriented to the left flank, Gwent the center, and Bannon the
right. Those who were smart and not in the direct path of the advancing tanks
stayed put and played dead. There were few smart Russians that night.

Slowly the tanks converged on the village. At the edge of it, Alpha 31's driver
slowed down in order to allow Alpha 55 to take the lead. Before plunging into
the narrow streets of Arnsdorf, Garger traversed its turret around and over his
tank's rear deck, taking every opportunity that came his way to fire on Russians
who were attempting to flee the carnage.

When Alpha 55 reached the first corner in the village and turned, it was greeted by a BTR at a range of twenty meters that was frantically trying to back up and get out of the way. Both the BTR commander and Bannon looked at each other for the briefest of moments before they began to issue frantic orders.

"GUNNER, BATTLESIGHT, BTR!"

The shock of seeing a target so close caused the gunner to raise the level of his reply several decibels.

"IDENTIFIED!"

"SABOT LOADED UP!"

"FIRE!"

At this range, and with the speed of the SABOT round, firing and impact were almost simultaneous. Bannon felt heat of the impact on his face. The brilliant flash of contact and the shower of sparks lit up the street and momentarily blinded him. The SABOT round, designed to penetrate the thick frontal armor of tanks, cut through the center of the BTR and continued down the street behind the BTR and into a building. The BTR burst into flames and staggered to a stop.

For a moment, 55 stood there with its gun tube almost touching the BTR. All action seemed to stop. It was as if everyone had to pause and catch his breath. Carefully, Bannon guided 55 around the burning BTR and continued down the street. As 31 followed, Garger and his loader had to shield themselves from the heat of the flames roiling up out of hatches that had been blown open by internal explosions. Once clear of the BTR, 31 continued on behind 55, searching for new targets.

∽

Taking their time, Kelp and McCauley carefully picked their way through the forest toward the crippled T-72. When they finally found a position to the rear of it that afforded them a clear shot and the two privates were settled, McCauley took to fumbling about as he struggled to affix the Dragon sight to a new round by the light burning T-72 tank.

Kelp, growing impatient with McCauley's when he saw the difficulties that soldier was having, jabbed him in the ribs with his elbow. "I thought you said you knew how to use that thing," he hissed as loud as he dared least he attracted the attention of any Russians who might be lurking about nearby.

"I told you, I only had one class on it, and that was a long time ago. Give me a break, will ya? I'm doin' the best I can."

"Well, do your best faster, damn it." For a moment their exchange reminded Kelp of countless times in the past when Sergeant Folk resorted to prodding him along using the exact same words he had used to motivate the hapless grunt. As he watched McCauley fumble with the sight, Kelp finally realized why Folk had been so hard on him. He owed Folk a huge apology.

"Got it!"

"About time. Let's do it."

With the launcher resting on his shoulder, McCauley braced himself as he had seen the other gunner do while Kelp scooted over to one side and scanned the area for Russian soldiers.

"Here goes."

The shock of firing the weapon for the first time made McCauley jump as the missile left the tube. It flew but a few meters before brushing against a tree, causing it to veer off course and hit the ground where it spun madly around as the rocket motor burned and sputtered.

"SHIT! GET THE OTHER ROUND!" McCauley cried out in panic as he scrambled to detach the sight from the expended launcher tube.

Alerted by the missile launch, the TC of the crippled T-72 rose up out of his hatch and looked to the rear to where the first missile's rocket motor was still burning. Realizing he was in danger, the Russian began to traverse the turret to the rear.

McCauley became frantic as he waited for Kelp to pass him the last missile. "SHIT! HURRY OR WE'RE DEAD MEAT!"

Fear and the specter of imminent death were all the motivation McCauley needed to move as quickly as he could and attach the sight to the new round the first time.

Kelp could do little to help as he kept glancing back and forth between the T-72 and McCauley. It was a race that would have horrible consequences for the loser.

Equally panicked, T-72's commander was on the verge of bringing its main gun to bear on the two privates when the long gun tube slammed into a tree. Frantically, he yelled an order to his gunner who traversed the turret back a few meters toward the front, then quickly slew it around as fast as he could toward Kelp and McCauley in an effort to knock the tree down using the gun tube. But the tree proved to be too thick and deeply rooted. When the tank commander saw they were not going to be able to get the turret around, he unlocked his 12.7mm machinegun, trained it in their direction, and fired. His first burst was wild, flying harmlessly over the heads of the two privates.

Kelp, determined to buy McCauley the time he needed to finish what he was doing, brought his submachine gun up to his shoulder and fired an equally harmless burst at the Russian tank commander. Both Kelp and the Russian were in the midst of adjusting their aim when McCauley let loose with the second missile. The flash and whoosh of launch, the burn of the rocket motor, and the detonation of impact put an end to this desperate contest.

∿

The sound of small arms fire to their rear and the destruction of the second tank took whatever fight the Soviet infantry facing Polgar still had left out of them. Individually and in small groups, they began to drift back along the trail and away from the American positions. At first Polgar thought the Russians were thinning their line in order to form up for an end run. But as the Russian return fire slackened, then ceased, he knew the truth. The shadows created by the Russians as they drew back past the burning tanks kept moving north. For the second time that night, the order to ceasefire rang out through the wooded lot.

～

The firing to his front began to slacken, then stop even as Colonel Potecknov was making his way down the trail on foot. At first he was elated. They had succeeded in breaking the American line. That assumption was quickly put to pay when he heard the sound of orders being shouted out in English further up the trail, followed by the sudden appearance of his own men streaming back toward him. Realizing that success had not been his, Potecknov broke out into a trot, calling out to his men, ordering them to turn around and go back as he went.

～

The relief and elation over their victory against the T-72 was shortlived. Kelp and McCauley had just begun to carefully pick their way back to rejoin Polgar when several figures came toward them from the direction of the infantry positions. Both of them took refuge behind a tree, back to back. At first Kelp thought the Russians were looking for them. But the figures running past were in a hurry. They were making no effort to search the bushes for the tank killers. That was when it dawned upon him that the Russians were retreating. That was good. Unfortunately, they were right in the middle of the Russians' path of retreat.

The two soldiers continued to huddle behind the tree, each facing out with their weapons at the ready. Kelp watched as the number of Russians increased. It hadn't occurred to him that there were so many of the bastards, causing him to wonder how the handful of men with Sergeant Polgar had not only managed to hold, but had caused the Russians to flee.

He was watching this flood of refugees when a lone figure came running south down the trail, waving a pistol over his head and shouting. Had to be an officer, Kelp thought. The dumb bastard was trying to stop the retreat. For a moment he wondered if he should kill the officer. But that feat of heroism on his part was not needed.

Kelp watched as the officer stopped a group of three retreating soldiers and tried to push them back. To Kelp's surprise, one of the three leveled his AK, stuck it into the officer's stomach, and let go with a burst. The officer fell over backwards, flopping to the ground like a rag doll. The one who had fired the AK said something in Russian before the trio continued their flight north. As one of them was stepping over the dead officer, he kicked the officer in the head. "Looks like they've had enough for one night," Kelp whispered to McCauley.

No sooner had he said this than his attention was suddenly drawn to his front as a Russian stumbled and fell right next to him. Both Kelp and the Russian stared at each other for a moment before they realized that they were looking eyeball to eyeball at the enemy. As the Russian opened his mouth to let out a scream, Kelp leaped on to the Russian's chest, wrapping one hand around the Russian's throat and the other over his mouth. In response, the Russian grabbed the hand Kelp had over his mouth with both hands and tried to pry it off, causing Kelp to push down as hard as he could to keep the grip he had from slipping.

Just as the Russian succeeded in prying Kelp's hand off his mouth, he went stiff and let go of Kelp's hand. Glancing over his shoulder, he watched as McCauley jab his bayonet into the Russian's stomach a second, then a third time. When he felt Russian go limp, Kelp released the grip he had on him. Gripping McCauley's arm, he stopped the frenzied infantryman from stabbing the Russian a fifth time. After looking at each other, two privates resumed their back-to-back position behind the tree as the last of the Russians went by without ever taking note of the small battle that had occurred in the dark.

❧

Colonel Potecknov lay on the trail, unable to move. If there was pain, he didn't feel it. What he could feel was the cold, which he thought odd, given that it had been a warm summer evening when his attack had begun. That he was bleeding to death never occurred to him. In his last minutes, his thoughts were not on death or fear of the unknown fate that awaited him. Rather, he was puzzled and bewildered. His battalion should have succeeded. He had done everything right. The plan had been a good one. What had gone wrong? Why hadn't it worked? The Russian colonel sought answers for these questions until darkness swept over him.

❧

Alpha 55 was just entering the village square when Bannon received Polgar's report that the Russians had broken contact and had withdrawn to the north. The run through the village so far had been quick and dirty. After the BTR Alpha 55 had run into had been destroyed, everyone and everything scattered up alleys or into houses. In the town square there were several trucks and two BTRs with soldiers scrambling to board them in an effort to flee.

When 55 rolled into the square, the trucks began to pull away with troops hanging half in, half out. One of the BTR drivers panicked and backed up over a group of soldiers that had run behind it for cover. A truck driver watching 55 and not paying attention to where he was going ran over an officer waving him down before crashing through a store window at the edge of the square. All this confusion was created just by 55's appearance. When 31 pulled up next to 55, and both tanks began to fire with main guns and machineguns, the situation really went to hell.

༠༢

Satisfied that all the Russians were gone, Kelp and McCauley began to cautiously make their way back. After what they had gone through, the last thing Kelp wanted was to get blown away by his own side. As he moved forward, he stepped onto a piece of metal. Looking down, he was overpowered by a sudden surge of fear. In the faint light from the burning tanks, Kelp saw that he was standing on one of the antitank mines they had put out earlier. He knew he was dead.

But nothing happened. Ever so slowly it dawned upon him that he was not heavy enough to set off the mine. Even so, when he was finally able to mustered the courage to remove his foot, he did so with the greatest of care. Sweat rolled down his face as he stood there, breathlessly fighting to catch his breath and calm down before moving on. There were too many ways to get killed out here, he told himself. He wanted his tank back. This infantry shit was for the birds.

When he thought that they were close enough to the infantry positions, Kelp called out to let the infantry platoon sergeant know they were coming back. Polgar, unfamiliar with Kelp's voice, ordered them to advance and be recognized. When they were in the open, Polgar gave them the challenge. Only after Kelp gave the proper password were the two tank killers welcomed back into the fold.

༠༢

Once the tanks were clear of the village, Bannon ordered 31 to move up to the right of 55. As they were starting to swing south to return to their positions, they ran into the Russian infantry that had just broken contact with Polgar. Only then did it occur to Bannon the Russians who had been attacking Polgar's positions had not heard of the run through the village by 55 and 31. Thinking they were their own tanks, the Russians simply stood aside to let them pass. Only when the tanks cut loose with machineguns did they realize their mistake, shattering the last semblance of order as the Russians scattered to the four winds. The battle for Hill 214 was over, for now. Checkmate.

༠༢

In silence, Alpha 55 and 31 followed the tree line as they moved back toward their original position. The only sound, other than the whine of engines and squeak of tracks being pulled around each tank's drive sprocket, was Bannon's voice as he radioed Uleski and Polgar. Satisfied there would be a pause before the next Soviet attack came, he ordered them to pull their people back to the trail junction and form a coil. Polgar and his men would cover the north, Uleski and his element would cover the east and south, and 55 and 31 face out west. When everyone was in, they were to meet him at the trail junction.

Bannon was the last to arrive. Uleski, Polgar, Jefferson, and Hebrock greeted Garger and him with nothing more than a nod. With not so much as a word of greeting, he simply asked, "Ok, what do we have?"

Uleski had suffered only one wounded, a PC driver who had been hit in the shoulder. Though the man had lost a lot of blood, he was in stable condition. Both the PCs and the 2nd Platoon tanks had ample ammo on hand. Polgar's dismounted element had suffered two killed, including the Dragon gunner, and four wounded, two of them seriously. Although his people had been running low on ammunition, now that they were with the PCs, the dismounts who had been with him could replenish their ammo pouches from ammunition stored on the PCs. The only casualty between 55 and 31 had been 31's loader. He had been hit in the face by a bullet during the run through the village. Though he was in a lot of pain and was missing several teeth, he would survive. For the price of two dead and six wounded, Team Yankee had held.

But the Team had reached the end of its rope. Even as they stood there, Bannon could tell that the stress and strain of this last fight had used up every man's final reserve of energy. They had done their best and done well. But they had nothing more to give. Besides the exhaustion, the tanks were down to a grand total of thirty-one main gun rounds and four thousand rounds for the COAX and loader's machinegun. Even if the men could hold up under another attack, which was impossible, the ammunition couldn't.

Bannon informed the Team's leadership that at 0330 they would leave Hill 214 and move south in order to reenter friendly lines. There was no need to explain. There were no protests or speeches. Everyone understood the situation and knew there was nothing more to be gained here. Now the Team's mission was to save what was left for another day.

To prepare for the move, the wounded were loaded onto the PCs, three in each. Folk, who could drive a PC, took the place of the wounded PC driver. Kelp took the place of the wounded loader on 31. Uleski would command one of the PCs and half of the infantry while Polgar took the other PC and the other half of the infantry. The tank crews redistributed the ammunition between the tanks. When all was ready, the Team settled in to wait until 0330 and move out.

Deep inside, Bannon wanted to believe that at the last minute the battalion would come forward and link up. He was going to give them another hour and a half. If they didn't arrive by then, he was going to save as much of Team Yankee as he could.

CHAPTER 8

R and R

The damned fly kept bothering him. It wasn't the buzzing so much. Bannon could block that out. It was the fact that the bastard kept landing on the cut on the side of his face and irritating it. He'd no sooner shoo it away with a halfhearted wave of his hand then it would come back and land. How could he get any sleep with that damned fly bothering him. Sleep.

"*SLEEP! MY GOD, I'VE FALLEN ASLEEP!*" The thought stunned Bannon. Shooting upright and opening his eyes, he greeted by the sight of a bright, morning sun. Instinctively his right arm shot up to check the time on his watch. 0548. The Team had missed its move-out time by over two hours! Even worse, the opportunity to slip away under the cover of darkness was gone.

Looking over and down into the loader's hatch, he saw Newman slouched over in his seat, leaning against the turret wall sound asleep. A quick scan of the tight circle of tank and PCs failed to reveal any sign of movement. Instead of being alert and watching their sectors, track commanders were slumped across their machineguns asleep. Scattered about their tracks, infantrymen lay curled up on the ground asleep where they had fallen. Even the wounded were quiet. The calamity was complete. To a man, Team Yankee had dozed off.

Dropping down, Bannon took to waking the crew of 55 starting with the gunner, who was lying up against the main gun. "Sergeant GWENT! Sergeant GWENT! WAKE UP!"

Startled, Gwent sat up, shook his head before jerking upright in his seat when he realized he had fallen asleep. "Oh shit! I fell asleep. Goddamn, I'm sorry sir."

"Well, don't feel like the Lone Ranger. Everyone is asleep." It took a second for Gwent to appreciate what Bannon was saying. When he did, his eyes grew as big as hen's eggs, "You mean we didn't pull off that hill yet? We're still behind enemy lines?"

"Target. Now, get the rest of the crew up while I wake the Team up. AND DON'T CRANK THE TANK."

Without waiting for a response, Bannon scrambled out his hatch and began to dismount the tank, forgetting in his haste that the spaghetti cord connecting his CVC to the intercom was still plugged in. Only when he felt his head jerk backwards did he pause long enough to disconnect it before jumping off 55. Once on the ground, he headed for the track nearest Alpha 55 first.

There he found the Mech Infantry platoon sergeant leaning against the side of a tree with his M-16 cradled in his arms, asleep. After being shaken a moment, Polgar eyes opened into narrow slits, looked to the left, then to the right, and finally at Bannon. Just as Bannon before him, when he realized what had happened, his eyes flew wide open. "SHIT! I fell asleep."

"Well, Sergeant Polgar, you ain't alone. Wake up the XO and your people while I get the tank crews. Gather the leadership at 55 when they're up. AND DON'T START ANY ENGINES. Clear?"

"Clear." With that, Polgar was up in a flash, hustling from body to body, waking each one up with kicks, shakes, and curses while Bannon trotted over to 31.

Garger was leaning over backwards in the open hatch of his tank, asleep. With his arms extended off to the side and stiff, he looked as if he had been shot. "Gerry! Gerry! Lieutenant Garger! WAKE UP!"

His eyes opened in tiny slits. Like Polgar, he looked at Bannon for a moment, then jumped upright. "OH SHIT!"

It occurred to Bannon that instead of good morning, "Oh shit!" was fast becoming the standard greeting for the Team. He imagined had their predicament not been as serious as it was, this whole situation would have been comical.

"Gerry, get the rest of the tank crews up and have the TCs meet me over at 55. And tell the TCs not to crank the tanks." As Bannon was getting off, Garger scootched down and gave his gunner a swift kick between his shoulder blades, yelling for him to wake up as he did so.

As he headed back to 55, Bannon began to work on a way out of this one. There would be no slipping away unseen, not in broad daylight. That thought was disturbing. But staying here to face a new series of Russian attacks was equally distasteful. The collapse of the Team's security confirmed his belief that it was at the end of its tether. The Russians were sure to come back with more people and tanks, sooner rather than later. Bannon didn't dare face a wounded bear with a handful of punch-drunk tankers and grunts who were running low on ammunition of all types. They had to pull out.

Once the leaders were together, he issued his orders. The Team would go out the way they had planned. Since the Soviets had not hit them from the south, that was the direction the Team would take. Alpha 55 and 31 would lead, traveling abreast once they were in the open. The PCs would come next, followed by 24 and 22. The Team would move around the west side of the hill that had been Objective LOG and go back into friendly lines the same way they had come out. The only difference in the plan was that rather than creep along in an effort to sneak out, they would roll as fast as the PCs would allow. In addition, the tanks would fire up their smoke generators and blow smoke the entire way back. While 55 and 31 would be exposed to the front and flanks, the PCs and the other two tanks would be hidden in a rolling cloud of smoke.

As they were about to break up and return to their vehicles, a volley of artillery fire impacted to the south in the vicinity of Hill 214. As one, everyone's head snapped in that direction. When a second volley confirmed their fears, all eyes turned back on Bannon. They had been too late. The Russians were coming back.

"All right, Sergeant Polgar, you come with me. We're going to go up there and see what's going on. Bob, you're in charge while we're gone. Be ready to crank up and roll if the Russians come. Until then, stay alert and keep quiet. If the Russians come before we're back, leave without us. Move in the opposite direction of the Russian attack until you're in the open. Then carry out the plan as we have discussed. Any questions?"

There were none. What else could they do? Bannon turned to Polgar, "Do you have an extra M-16?"

"Yes, sir. I can take one from one of the wounded."

"Good, get me one, a couple of magazines, and meet me back here, pronto." Polgar nodded before hustling over to one of the tracks. Bannon turned to Uleski. "Bob, no heroics. If there's trouble and we're not back, get out of here. Clear?"

"Clear."

By the time Polgar had returned with the rifle, Bannon had his helmet and web gear on. After inserting a magazine and chambering a round, the two turned and started to head south. Polgar followed Bannon at a distance of five meters and a little to his right. The assembled leaders watched them go. When they were no longer in sight, Uleski turned back to face the track commanders with him and ordered them to mount up and be ready to move.

◠

Bannon and Polgar had gone about a hundred meters when the artillery stopped. Pausing, they both squatted down and took to listening for a moment. In the silence that followed, the distinct sound of tracked vehicles moving could be heard to the south. Taking the lead, Bannon motioned to Polgar to follow.

It wasn't until they were nearing the crest of the hill and the tree line that Bannon caught sight of movement to his front. Instinctively, he dropped into a prone firing position behind the nearest tree. Both he and Polgar watched and waited.

To the left Bannon noticed a movement. Then he noticed there was more to the front at a distance of fifty meters. As they watched, a line of figures approached through the woods. He turned to Polgar and whispered, "When I start shooting, run like hell back to the XO and tell him to go east out of here."

Polgar thought about it. "You're the Team commander, I'll cover you. You go back and tell the XO."

"Damn it, Sergeant, I gave you an order. You better be ready to move when I let go. Clear?" Polgar didn't reply. He only nodded.

Turning his attention back to front, Bannon watched the line of figures continue forward. Slowly he raised the M-16 up to his shoulder and began to sight in on the nearest figure. This was going to be a very short fight.

As Bannon watched the lead figure in his sight, it occurred to him that the uniform was very familiar. It was camouflaged. So far the Russians they had faced weren't wearing camouflage. Then he noticed the rifle. It was an M-16. They were Americans. "They're ours," he whispered to Polgar.

Upon hearing this, Polgar stuck his head up a little higher, looked, and then smiled.

Remembering what had occurred the day before when he was a bit too hasty in trying to get Polgar's attention after he'd abandoned 66, Bannon was a little more circumspect in letting the advancing infantry know he was there and he was friendly. He let the line of infantry get within twenty meters before he bellowed out "HALT!"

The line of infantry froze where they stood, ready to drop and fire. Heads slowly turned to find the origin of the voice.

"Advance and be recognized."

This time, all heads snapped as one to where Bannon was. Ever so slowly, one of them rose up to the kneeling position while keeping his rifle trained on Bannon. When he was sure the wasn't going to be shot, the lead infantryman began to move toward Bannon.

When he was close enough, Bannon repeated the order, "Halt." At that point, he found he was unable to recall the challenge and password. He had to do something fast before the people in front of him got excited and fired. "We're Team Yankee, Task Force 3rd of the 78th. We were cut off. Who are you?"

"What's the challenge?"

"I don't know. We were cut off yesterday. I'm Captain Bannon, the team commander."

As this exchange was taking place, Bannon noticed the line of infantry was slowly beginning to spread out. Things were not working out well at all.

From behind, Polgar called out, "Hey, Kerch. Is that your mob of dirt bags out there?"

The infantryman in front of Bannon straightened up, let the muzzle of his rifle drop some, and turned toward Polgar's voice. "Polgar, is that you?"

"Yeah, it's me, you worthless sack of shit. Now tell your thugs to ease up so the captain and I can get up." With that, Polgar stood up and began to come over to where Sergeant First Class Kerch, A Company 3rd of the 78th Mechanized

Infantry and Bannon had been holding each other at gunpoint. Team Yankee had been relieved.

∾

Polgar led Kerch and his people through the woods to where Team Yankee was located. Bannon made his way up to the top of Hill 214 where he was told the battalion command group was. It occurred to him as he was doing so that while he'd been here for over twenty hours, had fought for the hill, and done his damnedest to hold it, he had never been on top of it. He was finally going to see what the Team had paid for so dearly.

At the wood line he passed the tracks from a platoon of the 3rd of the 78th that had been attached to the 1st of the 4th Armor. They were waiting for word to go in and pick up the dismounted element he and Polgar had encountered. Just below the crest of the hill, two tanks and a PC sat, peering over the top toward Arnsdorf below. Three officers were standing next to the PC looking at a map board. When one of them saw Bannon approaching, he motioned to him to join them. The other two looked up, put down the map board, and started towards him. They were the battalion commander, XO, and S-3 of the 1st Battalion, 4th Armor, Team Yankee's parent battalion.

As he closed, Bannon saluted and, as nonchalantly as possible, greeted Team Yankee's saviors. "Well, fancy meeting you here, sir."

Surprised but pleased, LTC Hall extended a welcoming hand to Bannon. "Sean, Colonel Reynolds told us you had been wiped out last night."

"Sir, the news of our demise has been greatly exaggerated. Alpha Company is reporting for duty." Not that they could do anything given how little of it that was left, but what the hell, it sounded good.

Maj. Frank Shell, the S-3, looked him over for a moment, then turned to the battalion commander. "If the rest of his people look as bad as Sean, the infantry was right, Team Yankee was wiped out." Then he turned back to Bannon and, seriously this time, asked if the rest of the Team did look like him.

Bannon's eyes were bloodshot and had dark circles around them. Every exposed patch of skin was filthy. He had two-days growth of beard. The cut on the side of his face had become swollen from infection, and there was dried blood on his face, neck and around his collar. There was also dried blood on the chest and sleeves of his chemical suit from pulling Ortelli from 66. This was mixed with diesel and oil stains. Without needing to see what he actually looked like, Bannon guessed he couldn't have looked much worse.

As they walked over to the PC Colonel Hall was using as a command track, Bannon explained the Team's situation and requested that an ambulance be sent immediately to the trail junction to bring out the wounded. The battalion XO got on it and had an M-113 ambulance rumbling down to the Team in minutes. Stopping when they'd reached the tanks where Colonel Hall was, Bannon and Major Shell looked down into Arnsdorf. There were still wisps of smoke rising from some of the burned-out Soviet vehicles. Scores of dead Russians and smashed vehicles littered the field. The battalion commander looked at Bannon, "I take it you did that last night."

In the clear light of day, the scene before Bannon seemed so unreal, so foreign. He had difficulty equating what he was looking at with the horror show he and his Team had been through but a few short hours ago. Tilting his head back, Bannon gazed up at the clear blue morning sky, then across the valley to the green hill to the north, and finally over at the battalion commander before replying. "Yes, sir. We did that, and more."

∽

After the battalion commander and XO left to go down into Arnsdorf and follow the attack, Major Shell updated Bannon on what had happened since yesterday morning and how 1st of the 4th had come into play. The Mech Battalion that Team Yankee was part of had become scattered throughout the division's rear area during the night road march. While passing through one of the larger towns, part of the column had taken a wrong turn. The people leading the two line companies, Charlie and Delta, the battalion trains, and the battalion CP all realized their mistakes at different times and tried to get back onto the proper route on their own without bothering to inform any of the units following them or battalion that was what they were doing. This led to confusion and more errors, just as First Sergeant Harrert had reported.

Delta Company was the first to show up and join Team Bravo on its overwatch position at 1730 hours. Charlie Company didn't turn around until after it had wandered into the rear areas of the German panzer division that was to the south. By then, it was running low on fuel. By the time a division staff officer managed to collect Charlie and lead it back, the division commander decided to hang onto it as a reserve. And though the battalion trains finally managed to make it to where they were supposed to go sometime in middle of the night, they never told anyone. When Major Jordan found them by accident, the S-4, in charge of the trains, told him he thought the battalion was still under radio listening silence, never realizing the net had been jammed, and the battalion had moved to another frequency. Team Bravo, which had been in position to supportYankee, moved up to LOG but was thrown off it by a dismounted counterattack from Lemm after Team Yankee had taken Hill 214.

When all this had been sorted out by the battalion and brigade commanders, it was decided to pull the 3rd of the 78th Mech out and throw in the 1st of the 4th Armor. As Team Bravo was combat ineffective, and everyone thought that, except for recovered tracks, Team Yankee was gone, the 3rd of the 78th was sent to the rear to reconstitute and act as reserve. The 1st of the 4th relieved the Mech Battalion at 0300 and went into the attack at 0530, just before the Team woke up.

"We, the commander, the XO, and I were trying to figure out what had happened to all the Russians that the 3rd of the 78th had reported and who had done all the damage in Arnsdorf when you showed up," Major Shell explained. "I expect the good news is that Bravo, 3rd of the 78th held LOG long enough for First Sergeant Harrert to gather up the Team's wounded and recover those tracks that had only been damaged."

To Bannon's surprise, Shell went on to inform Bannon that his first sergeant had four tanks and two PCs, including the HQ PC, most in varying states of repair, with him.

Exhausted and somewhat frazzled, it took Bannon a minute or two to realize that the attack against LOG had cost his Team only two tanks totally destroyed, 21 and 66, one PC, the 1st Squad of the Mech Platoon, and the FIST track. Casualties, not counting the men who were killed on Hill 214, amounted to fifteen killed and six wounded, which at first seemed to be out of proportion. Only when he thought about it did it make sense. Alpha 21, the infantry PC and the squad that was aboard it alone accounted for thirteen of the dead.

While Bannon was mulling these revelations over, Major Shell contacted brigade, informed them they'd found Team Yankee and asked if they had orders for them. The Team, Shell was told, was to road march to the rear and rejoin the 3rd of the 78th in reserve. After getting the location of the Mech Battalion's new CP in the rear and the route the Team was to use from Major Shell, Bannon asked for and received permission to stop by the 1st of the 4th's combat trains and top-off the tracks with him. With that, the S-3 wish Bannon luck, mounted his PC, and headed down into Arnsdorf to join his commander, leaving Bannon free to make his way back to Team Yankee, relieved in every sense of the word.

With the formal portion of the morning briefing at the Tenth Corps Headquarters over, the commanding general rose from his seat and walked over to the two maps that were displayed before him. The large-scale map displayed the overall situation facing NATO throughout Germany. It was not good. Up in NORTHAG's AO Hamburg and Bremerhaven had fallen. Though there had not been a breakthrough, several portions of the front were threatened with collapse as the Soviets prepared to continue their drive to the Dutch border. Already two corps commanders had requested the release of tactical nuclear weapons in order to break up concentrations of follow-on Soviet, Polish, and East German units that were moving toward the front to resume the attack.

In the CENTAG area of operations, where the Tenth Corps was, the situation was much better. The terrain there was not the best for armored warfare. In addition, French forces were readily at hand and beginning to reach the front.

Turning to his small-scale map that depicted the corps' area of operation and current situation, the Corps commander began to run his finger along the front line trace of his units, stopping every so often to study Warsaw Pact forces that were opposing the corps. At one point, he stopped with his finger resting on a map symbol that represented a group of Soviet units and turned to his G-2. "George, these people here, you said that they are continuing west?"

"Yes, sir. We expect them to be in the vicinity of Kassel by tomorrow morning at the latest unless we can get the Air Force to slow them down some."

"What's coming up behind them? Who is going to be in the Leipzig area two to four days from now?"

"Well sir, as best we can tell, no one. There is one Polish division here that could be in that area," the Corps G-2 informed his commander as he pointed to the map symbol representing the Pols. "But as of now, that's about it."

Without turning away from the map, and motioning with his hand as he spoke, the general began to issue instructions to his operations officer. "Frank, get your plans people to work on an attack centered around the 21st Panzer Division. As soon as the French relieve it, I want the 21st to move here and attack north into the Thuringer Wald. The mission of the 21st is to breach the Soviet security screen and then cross the IZB here. The second phase of the operation will be a passage of lines by either the 52nd or 54th Division with orders to continue the attack north across the Saale River towards Leipzig. I want this operation to commence in three days. Have your people prepared to present me a decision briefing by 1800 hours tonight. What are your questions?"

The operations officer studied the map for a moment, then turned to the general. "Sir, can I plan on using the 25th Armored Division? Also, how far do you want us to plan after we reach Leipzig?"

"Frank, I want you to use everything we've got. For planning purposes you will consider our axis of advance from where we are to Leipzig, Berlin, and finally the Baltic coast. If I can convince the CINC, I intend to go for broke. Until one of the Jedi knights in the G-3 Plans section comes up with a more fearsome name, we're calling this operation Winner Take All."

Having grown used to their commanding general's aggressive nature and willingness to take risks, the briefing broke up without further ado. With all the initial planning guidance they needed in hand, the staff officers scattered to prepare for the evening briefing.

✺

This road march was, for the most part, uneventful. Team Yankee had forty-five kilometers to cover and could have done it in an hour had it not been for the traffic. As it was going to the rear this time, and its movement had not been scheduled or coordinated by the division's movement control center, it was bumped by higher priority traffic going to the front, or forced to yield the road in order to allow wounded headed for the rear to get by.

After spending most of the last few days along the forward edge of the division's sector, Bannon was amazed at just how many vehicles there were driving around in division's rear. As they sat on the side of the road waiting for a convoy to go by before the Team could move again, Garger wondered if someone was really in charge of all this. There were long convoys made up of supply and fuel trucks, artillery batteries, columns of ambulances with wounded aboard moving rearward while others were making a return trip to pick up more, a field hospital moving forward, engineers everywhere you looked, and equipment he had never seen before and whose purpose he had no idea what it did. That anyone could bring order out of this apparent chaos, keep people fed, vehicles fueled, and units arriving at the right place at the right time was a source of wonder to him.

The biggest problem Bannon had during the long pauses while the Team waited for a break in the traffic was waking everyone up when it was time to move again. It seemed that each time they stopped, the drivers, and more than a few TCs, slumped down in their seats and fell asleep. Once, when a break in the traffic appeared, it took so long to wake everyone up that by the time they were ready to roll, a new convoy came by, leaving the Team no choice but to wait for it to pass. Naturally the men immediately went back to sleep.

The worst part of the march was seeing the suffering the local Germans who had stayed in place were having to endure. As the Team rolled past them, the few who bothered to look up at the passing American tanks and PCs regarded the men belonging to Team Yankee with blank stares. Bannon shuddered to think what was going through their minds, especially those of the old people. For them, this was the second time in their lives they had seen war. In one village the Team passed through, an old woman who bore an eerie resemblance to his own mother stopped pushing a cart and watched. Bannon could see tears running down her cheeks as Alpha 55 went by. He would never know for whom she was crying. Not that it mattered. By the time this war was over, he expected there would be many a tear shed, and not just for the dead.

It was the sight of the children that bothered him the most. During peacetime maneuvers through the German countryside they would wave and laugh as they ran along the side of the tanks, yelling to the soldiers to throw them candy or rations. American soldiers often did. But now the children didn't come. Instead, when they heard the rumble of the tanks, they ran and hid. Only a few of the bolder ones peeked to see whose tanks they were. Even when they saw that the tanks were American, their eyes betrayed the terror and fear they felt.

Such scenes allowed Bannon to understand for the first time why the pacifist movement had been so large in Europe. The children of the last war, who had witnessed his uncle's Sherman tank roll through their villages had not wanted their children to experience the same horror. Unfortunately, the good intentions of those parents were no match for the intentions of the Russian leaders. As had happened too often in the past, well-meaning people who desired peace at any price were no match for cold steel and people willing to use it.

Inevitably, the children he saw caused Bannon to wonder about his own. He still didn't know if all the families had made it out before hostilities. It was the nagging fear that they hadn't, and what he would do if that proved to be the case, that caused him to begin to turn away whenever he saw a child, for the thoughts they evoked were simply too painful.

༈

It was near noon when Team Yankee finally rolled into the town where the 3rd of the 78th was supposed to be. As the Team entered it, they passed a group of American soldiers sitting in front of a house cleaning their weapons. All were stripped down to their T-shirts or bare chests, enjoying the weather and in no hurry to finish the tasks at hand. Some of the men didn't even have their boots on. A PC Bannon assumed was theirs was parked in an alley. Clothes and towels were draped all over it to dry. A shirt was even hanging on the barrel of the caliber .50.

Bannon stopped Alpha 55 and signaled the rest of the column to halt. Turning to the group of soldiers, he called out, "Who's in charge here?"

A couple of the soldiers looked up at Bannon before chattering among themselves. One young soldier finally turned and yelled back. "Who the fuck wants to know?"

Garger later told Bannon that he had never seen him move so fast. When the soldier gave him that reply, he was up and out of the turret of 55 and on the ground headed for the man at a dead run all in one motion. "ON YOUR FEET, YOU SORRY SON-OF-A-BITCH! ALL OF YOU! YOU TOO!" he added, thrusting his arm out at a soldier who wasn't moving fast enough.

Suddenly realizing that perhaps they were talking to an officer, they came to their feet. Not that there was any way they could tell Bannon was an officer. About the only thing different about him since his meeting with the Tank Battalion command group that morning had been the cleaning of the wound on the side of his face.

"All right, soldier, I'll ask you one more time," Bannon growled as he shoved his face into the face of the man who'd spoken out. "And before you answer," he added as he narrowed his eyes, "if you give me a smartass answer like you just did, they'll be sending your remains home in a very small envelope. Is that clear?"

The soldier took stock of this god-awful looking and foul smelling figure before him. Taking no more chances, he came to attention. "Sir, our squad leader is not here."

"That's not what I asked you, soldier. I asked you who is in charge. There is someone in charge of this cluster fuck, isn't there?"

"I guess I am, sir."

"YOU GUESS! YOU GUESS! DON'T YOU KNOW?"

"Yes, sir, I am in charge, sir."

"What unit are you soldier?"

"Charlie Company sir."

"Good, great! You wouldn't happen to know what battalion you belong to, would you?"

"Sir, the Fighting Third of the 78th, sir."

By this time, the tracks in Team Yankee had shut down and were listening to the conversation. When the soldier Bannon was dressing down came out with the fighting third comment, everyone in the Team broke out in uproarious laughter. From struggling to keep his rage in check, Bannon suddenly found himself fighting to hold back his laughter as well. He lost. Now it was the turn of the Charlie Company soldiers to become peeved over being the object of laughter. Wisely, none of them said or did a thing. They were not about to tempt the wrath of a column of soldiers who looked no different than Bannon. They simply stood at attention and bit their tongues.

After regaining control of himself, barely, Bannon continued, "All right, soldier. Where is your Battalion CP?" The soldier informed him that it was in a school just down the street and how to get there. With that, Bannon turned and climbed aboard 55, gave the hand and arm signal to crank up and move out, then led Team Yankee at a dead run to the headquarters of the Fighting Third.

∽

As Bannon and Uleski walked down the corridors of the German school, Bannon was overcome with the odd feeling he was out of place here. In the field he felt at ease. They belonged in the field. That was where they worked. But this was a school, a place where young children came to learn about the world and to prepare for the future. Bannon was a soldier whose job was to close with and destroy the enemy by fire, maneuver, and shock effect. In short, to kill. He had no business here, in a place dedicated to the future. With that thought in mind, the two hurried down the corridors in silence so as not to offend the spirit of the school.

When they entered the classroom where the battalion staff and company commanders were having a command and staff briefing, they felt even more out of place. Though hard to imagine, the battalion staff appeared to be even cleaner than they had been two days ago, when the order to take Hill 214 had been given. It could have been that Bannon was just dirtier.

Both he and the XO had gone tromping into the room like two men storming into a strange bar looking to pick a fight with the first man who said boo. They stood just inside the room for a moment, surveying the assembled group who returned their stares. It reminded Bannon of a scene from a B-grade western. He looked at Uleski, who seemed to be thinking the same thing, causing him to stifle a snicker.

Major Jordan was the first to come over and greeted them with a sincere smile and a handshake as if they were long-lost cousins. The battalion commander and the other company commanders followed. Only the Charlie Company commander hung back. Bannon imagined it was from embarrassment. When the greetings were over, Colonel Reynolds took him to the front of the group and sat him on the seat next to his, displacing the Charlie Company commander. This move shocked Bannon since Captain Cravin, commander of Charlie Company, had always been Colonel Reynolds's fair-haired boy. Whatever Cravin did was good and right. Major Jordan, who didn't think much of Cravin or his company, smiled at the sight of the colonel's wunderkind being taken down a notch.

As the meeting continued, Reynolds would stop, turn to Bannon, and ask what Team Yankee needed from the battalion motor officer, the S-4, the S-1, and so on. It quickly became apparent that the colonel was prepared to give Team Yankee first choice of whatever was available. Given the opportunity, Bannon grabbed it and ran. When the S-1 wanted to know about personnel needs, Bannon told him that the Team needed eighteen infantrymen to replace Polgar's losses. The S-1 stated that it would not be possible to replace them now. Upon hearing this, Bannon turned to the battalion commander and told him that since Charlie and Delta companies were still up to strength, if each of their squads gave up one man, Polgar could easily be brought up to strength. He had meant this as a cheap shot at the two companies. To his surprise, the colonel told the S-1 to see that this was done and to ensure that only the best soldiers went. He then turned to the S-4 and told him that if the S-4 couldn't get another PC for Polgar right away, Charlie Company was to turn one over to Team Yankee.

At the end of the meeting Bannon and Uleski briefed the colonel and the S-3 on what had happened after Team Yankee had crossed the line of departure. The Colonel and S-3 frequently stopped them and asked questions about certain aspects of the operation, effects of weapons, where their soldiers seemed to be wanting, how the Soviets had reacted, and so on. At the conclusion of Bannon's impromptu update, Major Jordan recommended that the leadership of Team Yankee prepare a briefing for the officers and NCOs of the battalion. He pointed out that this way, lessons learned at such a high cost could be passed on to those officers and senior NCOs who had yet seen any action. Reynolds endorsed the idea without hesitation.

After being given the location where the first sergeant had the rest of Team Yankee and congratulating both him and Uleski on a job well done, both Reynolds and Jordan left in order to make it to a another meeting.

When they were gone, Bannon and Uleski sat in the silent room, staring at the floor in front of them. Without looking up, Uleski quietly asked, "Did we really do as well as they seem to think we did?"

Bannon thought for a moment. In the discussion, it had all seemed so easy. It was as if they had been discussing a tactical exercise at Fort Knox, not a battle that had meant life and death for the thirty-five men that had set out to defend Hill 214 yesterday. Their discussion had covered the effects of weapons, the deployment of forces, and the application of firepower. In the cool, quiet setting of the German classroom it all seemed to make sense, to fit together. The dread and fear of dying was absent. The stinging, cutting emotional pain he had felt as the crew of 66 removed Ortelli's shattered body from the burning tank had not been covered. The disgust and anger he had experienced when it seemed that Team Yankee had been wiped out was not important to their discussion. The battle they had talked about and the one Team Yankee had fought were not the same, and never would be. At least not for those who had been there.

Bannon turned to Uleski, "What do you think, Bob?"

The XO stared at Bannon for a moment before answering, "I think we were lucky. Damned lucky."

"You know, Bob, I think you're right." With that, they left the classroom and went about rebuilding the Team.

❧

Over the next three days Team Yankee licked its wounds and pulled itself back together in an assembly area a kilometer outside of town First Sergeant Harrert had found and claimed. Soon after arriving, Bannon found out why he had picked it.

In the center of a well-tended patch of forest was a small gasthaus where Germans taking long weekend walks through the forest had frequented before the war. The old man and woman who ran the place were indifferent to the Team at first. That quickly changed when the old woman discovered First Sergeant Harriet was more than ready to see to it she and her husband got whatever he could spare in the way of food, fuel, and the use of a generator Harrert had "found" during his forays through the Division's rear area. By end of the second day, the old woman was cooking for them and doing their laundry. She said that since she couldn't take care of her son, and since their mothers couldn't take care of them, she would. After the old man finally warmed up to the Americans, he told them his son was a panzer trooper like them before regaling anyone who would listen of his own experiences in what he called *The Last War*, taking care to make sure they understood he'd only fought the Russians, never the Americans.

Replacements arrived in dribs and drabs in for men, equipment, ammunition, uniforms, weapons, radios, and a myriad of other things modern war required. The first people they got were the infantrymen stripped from the other companies. While the Team didn't exactly get the pick of the litter, those they were sent were at least competent and reliable according to Polgar. The first thing he did whenever a new batch of fresh faced grunts reported to him was to lay down the law according to Polgar. The first rule he made sure they understood was that they were never to forget they now belonged to Team Yankee. The emphasis he put on this at first struck Bannon a little odd. In the past, a mech platoon belonging to 3rd of the 78ᵗʰ Infantry that was attached to Bannon's company considered that assignment akin to being exiled to Siberia. Now, it was a matter of pride. As one of the new men who volunteered to come over to Team Yankee told Polgar when asked why he had done so, regarded Polgar as if he'd just been asked the dumbest question he'd ever heard. "If I have to be in this war," the soldier replied. "I wanted to be with people who know what they're doing."

The Team was not as fortunate in the replacements they received for the tank crews. Most of them came straight from the advanced individual training course at Fort Knox. Some had never even been in a tank when a round had been fired. Bob Uleski was only half joking when he told Bannon they, the Team, were fortunate that most of the newbies were at least able to recognize a tank two out of three times. Given that sad state of affairs, the Team's number-one priority became integrating them into the crews as quickly as possible and training them as best the tank commanders could in what little time they had.

One of the most interesting transitions that had occurred in the Team that Bannon could not help but take note of was in the way Pfc. Richard Kelp went about his duties. Before the war he had always been an average soldier, nothing more, nothing less. Since the Team had come off Hill 214, however, he had become a man possessed. When they picked up a replacement tank from war stocks, Kelp was the first man on it. Instead of Folk having to keep on him to stay on task, it was Folk who now found he was having to scramble to keep up with him.

With the new Alpha 66 came a new man. As it is easier to train a loader, Kelp was reassigned as the driver and given the mission of training Pvt. Leo Dowd as the loader. After conducting several hours of crew drills on the second day, Bannon asked Dowd how things were going. At first the street smart African-American Chicago native was reluctant to say anything. When he finally did after some coxing, he informed Bannon that he thought Kelp was being too hard on him. "I'm doing the best I can, but that is never good enough to Kelp."

Stifling an urge to chuckle, Bannon put on his official company commander's face and told Dowd that everything Kelp was doing was for his own good. He added that if Dowd paid attention to everything Kelp was telling him, maybe, just maybe he would make it out of this war alive. "The one thing I've been told there's no shortage of is body bags," Bannon concluded. "So unless you're in a hurry to fill one of them, do what you're told." After that, there were no more complaints, at least not any that Dowd shared with his tank commander.

Along with his new direction in life, Kelp received official recognition for his efforts in the defense of Hill 214. After questioning both of the privates who had come back from the tank-killing detail that night, Polgar put each of them in for Bronze Stars with V device. As the Dragon gunner who had been killed had led the group out and had taken out the first tank, Bannon added him for a posthumous award. By the time the citations made it to division level, the efforts of the three men took on epic proportions. The story was enhanced ever so slightly until the killing of the two tanks became the pivotal event for the battle of Hill 214 that caused the whole Soviet battalion to withdraw. In reality, things weren't that clear cut, but Bannon went along with it since it expedited the awards.

One change had taken place that was not to Bannon's liking at all. It concerned the outlook on life Bob Uleski had adopted. The injury to his arm had been minor, a dislocated shoulder that was easily tended to without his needing to go any further than 1st of the 4th Armor's aid station where the battalion physician's assistant had popped it back into place while the cut on Bannon's face was being cleaned and dressed by a medic. Despite a recommendation that Uleski be allowed to spend a few days in a field hospital in order to give his arm a chance to heal properly, he refused. As the Team was short of officers, Bannon did not object, allowing him to stay with the Team as long as he could perform his duties.

For the most part, the XO reverted back to being his usual, good natured self. That façade, however, quickly gave way to a very different demeanor, for he was now unable to tolerate even the slightest error or any action that was not up to his standard, whether it concerned training or carrying out routine maintenance on the Team's vehicles. When drilling his crew, he would turn on them with a vengeance if their times or actions were not to his liking. When Bannon made mention of this to him, Uleski simply shrugged it off as nerves. Bannon, of course, knew there was more to his XO's behavior than nerves. Everyone who had started out with the Team and had made it this far had changed, including him. The problem was, in Bannon's opinion, Uleski's had not been for the better. With that in mind, he made a point of watching his XO more closely.

One of the duties that Bannon had dreaded most began the first night in the assembly area. After the Team had stood down for the night, and only those personnel required for minimal security were posted, he sat alone at a table in the gasthaus. In the quiet of the night, with no noise but the hiss of the Coleman lantern to distract him, he began to write letters to the families of those who had died.

> *"Dear Mrs. McAlister, I was your son's company commander. You have been informed, I am sure, by this time, of the death of your son John. While this is small consolation for the grief that you must feel, I want you to know that your son died performing his duties in a manner befitting the fine officer he was. His absence..."*
>
> *"Dear Mrs. Ortelli, as you know, I was your husband's company commander and tank commander. You have been informed, I am sure, by this time, of Joseph's death. While this is..."*
>
> *"Dear Mr. and Mrs. Lorriet, I was..."*

As he wrote the letters, the images of those who had been lost came back. In his mind's eye he could see 21 hanging on the edge of the ditch, burning and shaking as onboard ammo cooked off and detonated. The sight of Ortelli, wrapped in his sleeping bag as if he were sleeping was as clear to him as he sat there as it had been that day. Lorriet's eyes, eyes that stared up at him but did not see caused him to shudder every time he thought of him. His memories of the severed arm belonging to a soldier Bannon didn't even know that he stepped on were just as repulsive now as they had been when he had looked down and saw it. Those images, and so many more came flooding back to him as he wrote each and every letter to parents, wives, and loved ones who had yet to learn what had happened to the men he had been responsible for. In all his readings, in all the classes he had attended, nothing had prepared him for this. Each commander was left to deal with the images of the dead in his own way.

"Dear Mr. and Mrs...."

∾

On the afternoon of the second day the first sergeant returned to the Team's assembly area from a scavenging foray with 2nd Lt. Randall Avery in tow. As he was hauling his gear out of the first sergeant's vehicle, Avery noticed Garger going through a sand table exercise with his tank commanders. As the two lieutenants had both been in the same officer basic course at Fort Knox, Avery was thrilled to see a familiar face in the sea of strangers he had been swept up in. Eager to let him know he was there, he called out to Garger.

To Avery's surprise, instead of setting aside what he was doing and coming over to greet him, Garger merely acknowledged the new lieutenant's presence with an expressionless nod before turning his full attention back to what he had been doing. Taken aback by this cold reception, Avery wondered if the stories he'd often read about concerning the way veterans treated replacements were true. The reception he got from Bannon further reinforced his apprehensions on this matter.

Bannon and Uleski sitting at a table on the terrace in front of the gasthaus going over the next day's schedule of training and maintenance when Harrert brought Avery over. "Captain Bannon, this is Lieutenant Avery," Harrert declared matter-of-factly as he waved his hands at the young officer next to him. "He's straight out of Knox and has been assigned to take over the 2nd Platoon."

With that introduction, Avery came to attention, saluted, and reported as he had taught to do during his four years as an ROTC cadet and at Fort Knox. "Sir, Second Lieutenant Avery reporting for duty."

Before responding in any way, Bannon and Uleski glanced at each other, then over at the first sergeant before Bannon took to eyeing Avery from head to toe. With nothing more than a nod, he acknowledged the lieutenant's salute, leaving Avery standing there and unsure what to do.

Realizing the young officer was flummoxed, Bannon sighed. "At ease, Lieutenant. We don't do much saluting in the company area, or anywhere else for that matter. Where is it you said you were coming from?"

"Fort Knox, sir. I was attending the motor officers' course after AOB when things started to get serious over here."

Unable to help himself, Uleski glanced over at Bannon. "Serious?"

"I think he's talking about the war, U," Bannon replied with a straight face.

"Oh yeah, that. I guess you could say that was serious. What do you think, First Sergeant?"

"It's serious enough for me, sir," Harrert replied in an off handed manner.

Ignoring Uleski's attempt to have some fun at his expense, and eager to get on with the task of reporting in, Avery latched onto to the first thing that popped in his head. "I was in the same AOB class as Gerry, I mean Lieutenant Garger. We were friends, sir."

Again Bannon and Uleski exchanged glances. "That's nice. What college did you graduate from?"

"Texas A and M, sir."

Uleski couldn't help himself as he let out three loud whoops. Neither First Sergeant Harrert nor Bannon could keep from breaking out in laughter. Though he didn't much like being the butt of the XO's joke, Avery appreciated he wasn't in a position to do anything about it.

Seeing the lieutenant's discomfort, Bannon put his official, no bullshit company commander's face back on. "You're going to the 2nd Platoon," he informed Avery in an even tone of voice. "The man you are replacing was a damned good platoon leader who was killed four days ago. I hope you have better luck."

After allowing this grim thought to linger in the young officer's mind a moment, Bannon continued. "Your platoon sergeant is Sergeant First Class Hebrock. He's been running the platoon since Lieutenant McAlister was killed. *Your* only hope of surviving this folderol is to listen to what that man says and tells you what you need to do. Since I haven't a clue as to how much time we'll have before we move out and head off back into the meat grinder, my advice to you, *lieutenant*, is not to waste a second of it. Is that clear?"

Taken aback by this cheerless how-do-you-do, Avery simply replied, "Yes, sir," and waited for the next shock.

Closing his notebook, Bannon turned to the XO. "Bob, we'll finish this up later during the evening meal. In the meantime, take the lieutenant down to 2nd Platoon and turn him over to Sergeant Hebrock. Then you best get down to battalion CP and check on the replacement for our FIST track. I damned sure don't want to let battalion let that one slip."

"OK. You need anything else from battalion while I'm there?"

"Just the usual. Mail, if there is such a thing, and a fresh can of givea-shit. The one I have is almost empty."

With a straight face, Uleski got up, gathered up his notebook and map, and took off at a fast pace. "Come on Avery, this way."

After giving Bannon a quick salute, Avery gathered up his gear and took off at a trot to catch up to Uleski who was already thirty meters away, thinking as he went that his greeting to Team Yankee and the attitude of its commanding officer was not at all what he had been expecting. This sent his mind racing off in all different directions as he tried to figure out what was going to happen next.

∾

It wasn't until the evening meal that Avery had a chance to talk to Gerry Garger. The whole afternoon had been one rude shock after another. The greeting from the Team commander had been warm compared to that received from the platoon. Although Randy Avery was no fool and knew not to expect open arms and warm smiles, he had at least thought he'd be greeted with a handshake and a welcome aboard. What he got instead was a reception that ranged from indifferent to almost hostile. Sergeant First Class Hebrock had been proper, but short, following the same line that the Team commander had taken. "We've a lot to do and not much time, so you need to pay attention, *sir*." The sir had been added almost as an afterthought and in a manner that Avery thought to be as surly as a soldier could get without crossing the line that separated proper military protocol and disrespect. Hebrock then continued with the training under way.

Sergeant Tessman, the gunner on 21, was less than happy to see the new TC and made little effort to hide it. Even the tank was not what he had expected. Unlike the new Alpha 66, which had been drawn from war stocks, the new Alpha 21 had belonged to another unit, had been damaged on the opening day of the war, repaired, and reissued. Inside the turret there were still burn marks and blackened areas. The welds to repair the damage had been done quickly, crudely, and had not been painted. Tessman made a special effort to show his new TC the stains where the former TC had bled all over the tank commander's seat.

Even Gerry Garger came across as standoffish when they finally got together late in the afternoon and acknowledged him with an offhanded hello while they ate their evening meal. He showed little interest in talking about the Team, what it had done to date, and what combat was really like. Whenever Avery asked him about the war and his thoughts on it, Garger would give simple, short answers, such as, "*It's hard*" or "*It's not at all like our training at Knox.*" By the end of the day, Randall Avery was feeling alone, confused, and very apprehensive.

∾

Uleski returned from battalion with something that was almost as valuable as news that the war was over, the first letters from families in the States. The announcement that there was news from home brought everything to a stop. Even Bannon could not hide his excitement and hopes, hope that he had a letter, just one letter. This was counterbalanced by a fear there wouldn't be one for him.

Knowing full well what a letter to his commanding officer would mean to him, Uleski wasted no time in handing Bannon his. After giving silent thanks to God, the Postmaster General, the Division Postal Detachment, and anyone he could think, he headed off in search of a quiet spot where he could be alone for a few minutes, taking no notice of those who still stood gathered around the XO in silence, waiting to see if they, too, would be lucky.

Pat and the children were safe and staying with her parents. He read that line four times before he went on. It was as if nothing else mattered. His family was safe. After having experienced emotional highs and lows in rapid succession over the past six days, the elation he felt over this news set an all-time high. Not even the ending of the war could have boosted him any higher. It was because of that elation that Bannon did not detect the subtle implications in what his wife wrote until he had read the letter for the sixth time the next day. In reading it more carefully, what she didn't tell him spoke louder than what she had. Not all was well with her or the children. This realization dulled his joy, giving rise to new apprehensions. Even though they were safe, something terrible had happened. It would be weeks before Pat would be able to bring herself to fully recount the story of their departure from Europe. In that time, the war rolled on, taking new and ominous turns no one could foresee or predict, just as all wars have a tendency to do.

CHAPTER 9

Deep Attack

After two days with Team Yankee, Avery came to realize that the cold reception he had received had not been personal. That is, he had not been the only one who was being like the red headed stepchild at the family picnic. All the newly assigned personnel that had been fed into the Team had received the same treatment. At first he resented this fact. He looked upon it as if it were some kind of planned initiation, behavior he thought to be offensive and inappropriate. When he mentioned this to a man he had thought was his friend and the only person in Team Yankee he felt he could share his thoughts with, Garger looked at him, and thought about the question for a moment before telling Avery he had no idea what he was talking about. He went on to tell the new platoon leader that as far as he was concerned, everyone in the Team got along exceptionally well. "You're being overly sensitive," he added. "This isn't a fraternity or a social club. My advice to you is to settle down and get on with the business at hand." Then, without so much as a see you later, Garger turned and walked away.

It didn't take Avery long to understand what the difference between the newly assigned personnel and the original members of Team Yankee was when the CO authorized the tank commanders to paint kill rings on the gun tubes of the Team's tanks. It had been the old German who owned the gasthaus that had made the suggestion that the Team do what the German panzertruppen had done in World War II. "We painted a ring on the tank's gun tube for every enemy tank destroyed by that crew," he told Bannon one night as the two were sharing a warm glass of beer. The idea was quickly adopted and proved to be popular. Before these rings could be painted on a tank's gun tube, they had to be confirmed. Only the first sergeant, who didn't have a tank, could authorize the kill rings if, in his opinion, there were sufficient evidence to support a crew's claim. The kill rings were to be one-inch black rings, one for each kill, painted on the gun tube just forward of the bore evacuator. A three-inch black ring was used to denote five kills.

Once the kill rings had been painted on the tanks, the tank commanders and gunners went around to see who the top gun was. To Avery's surprise, it was Garger. His Alpha 31 tank sported eleven rings. The CO's tank, the new Alpha 66, had seven. Hebrock told Avery that the CO could have claimed six more kills, but instead allowed them to go on 55, the tank that he had been commanding at the time the kills had been made. Of the ten tanks in Team Yankee, only Avery's tank, 21, had a clean gun tube.

It suddenly dawned upon him that since his arrival in the Team, no one had talked about what they had done in the war. Every time he asked questions about the engagements the Team had been in when talking to Garger, his friend would move on to another subject. When the CO, XO, and Polgar took to discussing lessons learned thus far in the war with a gathering of the officers and NCOs, they went over it in a very impersonal and academic manner. At times, it struck Avery that they were talking about another unit, not the one he had joined. It was as if there was a secret fellowship that only those members of the Team that had been in combat could belong to.

As if by mutual agreement, even the tankers refrained from bragging about their deeds. It was as if they felt doing so would somehow be disrespectful of those who were no longer with them. The kill rings, however, gave them a chance to show what they had done without the need to go about, blowing their own horn. When this finally dawned upon him, Avery found himself wanting to go into combat. This revelation came as something of a shock, for the motivation that was behind this desire to see combat had nothing to do with defending freedom or doing his duty to God and country. The reason that drove this desire was a longing to belong to the Team as an equal, to be accepted. Avery wanted kill rings.

The battalion, Uleski often opined to Bannon, seemed to have a knack for screwing up breakfasts, a point Bannon could not argue when, on the morning of the fourth day in the assembly area, word of the pending change in mission came. This unwelcomed interruption arrived as Bannon, his platoon leaders, the XO, the first sergeant, and the Team's new FIST chief, a second lieutenant by the name of Plesset, were having a working breakfast. After finishing green eggs that had once been warm, bacon strips that were as crispy as soggy noodles, and toast that could have doubled as roofing shingles, Bannon told the gathering they were to put off whatever training they'd been planning and instead, conduct pre-combat check. "You have as much idea as I have as to when we'll be moving or where we're going," he told the Team's leadership. "But wherever it is, the odds are we won't be leaving here until late afternoon, at the earliest. So once you're satisfied your people are ready to move on a moment's notice, see to it everyone, including yourselves, get some rest."

Uleski and the Plesset, who went to the meeting with Bannon, arrived a few minutes before the briefing was scheduled to start. As they waited for the battalion XO to begin it, Bannon made his way to the front of the classroom that served as the battalion's conference room to where Major Jordan was talking to Colonel Reynolds.

When he joined them, after a quick round of perfunctory greetings, the three of them turned their attention to the battalion operations map. The graphics depicting the new mission were posted on it, ready for the briefing. A chill went down Bannon's spine when he saw that it was another attack. While the Team had made great strides in recovering from the last attack it had participated in, Bannon had his doubts if those who had made it were mentally prepared to be part of another. This was especially true of himself. He wasn't sure if he could deal with another horror show like the last one as images of the dead and dying flashed through his mind.

A quick glance at the map and the graphics displayed on it showed it was an ambitious plan, aimed at crossing the IZB, into East Germany, and driving deep into the enemy's rear. The arrows depicting the axis of advance the brigade would be using went through a German panzergrenadier battalion that was already well across the border that had separated East and West Germany since the end of World War II. Once the brigade had passed through the Germans, it would advance up a narrow valley in the Thuringer Wald in the direction of Leipzig, north of the Thuringer Wald, and out onto the North German Plain. Where it would go after that could not be displayed on the map the battalion was using as it was too small to show the ultimate objective. Not that Bannon needed to see what lay just beyond the northern edge of the battalion's map. Berlin, the heart of East Germany and center of communications, was, he imagined, the real objective they were aiming for.

When Colonel Reynolds turned his attention to the commander of Team Bravo, the S-3 sidled up next to Bannon. "Well, what do you think?"

"Let's see if I can guess who's leading?" Bannon mused without taking his eyes off the map. "Charlie Company?"

"Sean, you know damned well who's going to lead the attack, at least initially. Team Yankee is the best company we have, and you have most of our armor. It would be beyond stupid to put anyone else in the lead."

Bannon took a moment mull his response over in his mind before responding. "Sir, are you attempting to win me over with logic, or butter me up with flattery?"

"A little of both, I guess."

Before Bannon could say another word, the battalion XO called for everyone to take their seats. When Colonel Reynolds motioned to Bannon he was to sit next to him, the battalion commander's friendly attitude and smile reminded Bannon of the grinning cat who praised the canary for his beautiful song before eating him. When everyone was settled and ready, the battalion XO nodded to the S-2 to start.

The last six days of war had done nothing to improve the intel officer's skills in preparing a useful briefing. He started by summarizing the progress of the war to date and the gains the Soviets had made in the north. Those gains were impressive. Denmark was isolated. Despite the efforts of NORTHAG, the Dutch border had been reached. Most of the German seacoast was in Soviet hands. Further south, in central and southern Germany, German, French, and American forces had held the Soviets to minor gains. Only in one area, where a German panzer division had found a weak point at the boundary between two Soviet armies, had NATO forces been able to enjoy any offensive success. That division had managed to trust into East Germany before the drive spent itself. It was this toehold in the enemy rear that would provide the springboard for the attack the battalion was about to undertake.

The S-3, as usual, provided the meat of the briefing. The entire division would be involved in this effort. Brigade would lead off, widening the breach the Germans had made as it advanced north into the enemy rear. French units deploying from the interior of France were replacing those divisional units still in contact as well as another US division that would follow. If the brigade and then the rest of the division were successful in widening the breach, eventually, the attack would be expanded into a corps-size operation.

The specifics of the operation were rather straightforward. The brigade would advance along two axes that ran through two north-south valleys. The 1st of the 98th Mech would lead the attack up one valley to the west while 3rd of the 78th Mech, followed by 1st of the 4th Armor, would advance up a valley called the Nebal Valley. The battalion's scheme of maneuver called for two company teams to lead the attack, Team Yankee on the right, and Team Bravo on the left. The two infantry pure companies, Charlie and Delta, would follow with Charlie Company behind Team Yankee. At this point in the briefing, the urge to take a cheap shot at Charlie Company was too strong to suppress. Bannon interrupted Major Jordan.

"Excuse me, sir, but I seem to remember trying that before. I don't know if TeamYankee is ready to be supported by Charlie Company again."

Bannon's comment was followed by a moment of stunned silence. Everyone looked at Bannon, then at the battalion commander, waiting for his reaction. Colonel Reynolds, ignoring everyone else in the room, exchanged glances with the S-3, then smiled before turning to face Bannon. "Captain Bannon, I can assure you, there will be no rat fucks like the last time. As I will be with Charlie Company, you can rest assured they will be right where they are supposed to be." He then turned to Captain Cravin, the Charlie Company commander, and gave him a look that would have peeled paint off a wall.

Cravin, smarting from the exchange, averted his gaze as he responded with nothing more than a simple "Yes" in a low voice. During this exchange, Major Jordan winked when he and Bannon exchanged glances before Jordan continued with his portion of the briefing.

The battalion, it seemed to Bannon, had learned its lessons from the last attack. While it was moving at night, as before, it would temporarily occupy an assembly area to the rear of the German unit it was to pass through before going into the attack. There they would sort out any last-minute changes, refuel, allow the accompanying artillery time to deploy, and conduct last-minute preparations. From there they would be led through the German lines by a liaison officer from the panzergrenadier battalion they would be passing through. To expedite the actions in the assembly area, the battalion XO would leave at noon with representatives from each company, the battalion's Scout Platoon, and the fuel trucks. The scouts would be posted along the route to serve as road guides where needed.

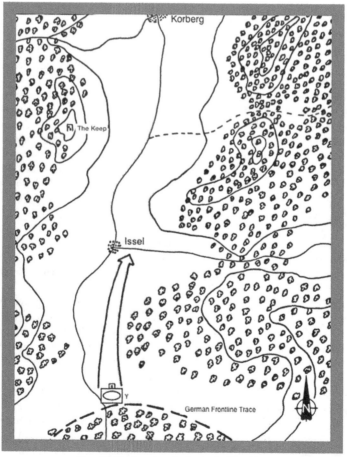

Map 12: The Attack to the Saale, the First Phase

When the S-3 finished and before the S-4 took his place at the map, the colonel got up and emphasized certain points that he felt were critical. The first one was that the battalion was going for the deep objective, Leipzig. Any resistance that could not be overcome in the first rush was to be bypassed. The second was that he wanted to keep the battalion closed up and tight so that if they did encounter major enemy forces, the full weight of the battalion could be brought to bear on the enemy rapidly and with maximum violence. The last point he made was that there would be no tolerance for a repeat of the screw-ups that had hamstrung the last operation. He was looking straight at Cravin as he made that point.

As usual, Bannon's mind turned to the new mission as the S-4, S-1, and other staff officers covered their areas. Uleski would catch any important information that might accidentally add to what had already been briefed. Tuning everyone else out, Bannon studied the map on his lap as he ran a finger along the battalion's projected axis of advance. There would be more than enough room to maneuver the Team in the valley they would be moving through. There were several choke points, but nothing of any significance. In his opinion, the greatest threat would come from the hills to the east. He began to draw goose eggs around those spots that struck him as being ideal for defense or from which a counterattack might come. When this was done, he assigned each one a letter before turning his attention to plotting the best route the Team would need to take to pass through the choke points he'd marked and deal with any threats that came their way. Without needing to give the matter all that much thought, he quickly concluded the ideal formation appeared to be an inverted wedge, with the two tank platoons deployed forward and the Mech taking up the rear.

The conclusion of the briefing interrupted his ruminations. After a brief huddle with Uleski and his FIST, he gave each one some items to cover with various staff officers before seeking out the S-3 in order to clarify some points and make some recommendations. When all his questions had been answered to the best of Major Jordan's ability and he was satisfied he, the XO and his first sergeant had everything they needed to get started with their own planning and preparation, the three of them headed back to the Team's assembly area.

The Team received the news of the new mission with the same dread that Bannon had. While they knew that they could do their part, they had no confidence in the rest of the battalion. The thought of another fight like that for Hill 214 was not a pleasant one to contemplate. Only Avery seemed anxious to get on with the attack, an attitude Bannon passed off as foolish naiveté. No doubt he would lose his enthusiasm the first time he had to collect the dog tags from one of his people. Provided he made it that far.

The balance of the day passed quickly. Bannon issued the Team order at noon, just prior to the departure of Uleski, who would be in charge of the Team's quartering party. He took with him one man from each tank platoon and an infantry squad to provide security and serve as guides once the Team reached its designated assembly area. He was also to go as far forward as possible to recon the routes through the German lines and coordinate with the Germans for fire support and cover during the passage through their lines. As he had little doubt the Soviets saw the danger that the German penetration presented, Bannon expected them to rush everything they could to seal it off or eliminate it. The only question that mattered was who would get there first.

After receiving a brief-back from each of the platoon leaders later in the afternoon on how they were going to perform their assigned tasks and satisfying himself that they were ready, Bannon decided to get some sleep. To this end he made his way to the gasthaus where he borrowed one of the rooms where he could have a few uninterrupted hours. After having slept on the ground or the turret of his tank for eleven days, the sensation of sleeping between clean sheets on a soft bed was sinfully foreign, but welcomed.

The easy manner with which the other platoon leaders and Hebrock went about preparing for the attack amazed Avery. They all were going about their business as if this were a tactical exercise at Fort Knox, not an attack that would take them deep into enemy territory. As hard as he tried, he could not settle down. His mind kept racing, pinging from one thought to another as he did his best to remember everything he had been taught at the Armor School as he prepared to issue his platoon order and make sure his own tank and its crew was ready.

Had he taken a moment to slow down, he would have realized he had little need to worry. Hebrock was always a step ahead of him, issuing orders and checking out the tanks with a quiet efficiency that was reassuring to the platoon. When Avery came to him and told him he was ready to issue his order to the tank commanders, Hebrock suggested that he allow him to look it over. Recalling the team commander's admonishment concerning listening to his platoon sergeant, Avery agreed. Together the two of them went over the order, item by item, crossing out those parts that Hebrock thought were not needed while adding a few things Avery had overlooked. Hebrock did his best to be diplomatic and patient as he *advised* his platoon leader on what he needed to do and say when the time came to issue his order.

When the revised order had been issued and the Team commander was satisfied with the brief-back Avery gave him, Hebrock told his lieutenant he needed to get some sleep. At first the young officer balked, claiming that he was fine. Only after the platoon sergeant assured him that there was nothing more to be done and all but insisted that he do so did Avery make the attempt.

An attempt was about all he could manage. As he lay on the turret roof of his tank, Avery's mind was cluttered with a deluge of thoughts, fears, and problems, real and imagined. Did he cover everything in his order? What if they got lost during the road march? How would he know when they were through the German lines? Would he be able to recall all of his crew and platoon fire commands and issue them in a clear and understandable manner when they made contact? Would he be alive tomorrow? Try as hard as he could to banish these and a whole host of other concerns, his mind refused to slow down, let alone stop dredging up new worries and disquieting doubts. Sleep never came.

The Team began its move at 1800 hours. The old German and his wife watched as they rolled out. First Sergeant Harrert left them two weeks' worth of rations, an envelope with dollars and Deutsch marks that he had collected, a first-aid kit, two cans of gasoline and the generator, which was safely hidden away in a small shed. In order to keep them from having any trouble with German or US authorities, a receipt with Bannon's signature, in English and German, identified those items left as payment in kind for services rendered by the old couple. The old woman cried, and the old man saluted as the tanks went past them. Bannon returned the salute. Watching them as 66 moved off made him think of his own parents, thanking God they did not have to suffer as these people were.

Once the Team was on the route of march and he was satisfied his tanks were at the proper march speed and interval, Garger leaned back in Alpha 31's cupola and relaxed. With little to occupy his thoughts of any great importance and no need to tell his driver what to do so long as nothing untoward happened during the road march, he took to going over the last twelve days and the changes that had occurred in him and the Team. The loss of his platoon sergeant was regrettable. Sergeant First Class Pierson had taught him a lot and had been very patient with him. Had it not been for Pierson, Garger knew he would have been relieved long before the first shot had been fired. The thought of such a disgrace had been more terrifying to him than the prospect of combat.

Even more importantly, Garger realized that it was due to Pierson's efforts that he had not only survived thus far, but had come to discover he had a natural talent for tanking and combat. The panic, the tenseness, the sick feeling in his stomach, the stammering he had experienced at Fort Knox and during his first weeks in the unit were gone. When the firing had started, everything seemed to fall in place. There was no panic, no fear. In the midst of even the most trying moments of combat, he experienced a clarity of mind that was, in retrospect, nothing short of amazing to him. There was still much he needed to learn, he admitted to himself. But learn he would, if he lived long enough, he reminded himself. Eventually he would master company tactics and all the ins and outs of staff work, just as he had succeeded in achieving an acceptable level of proficiency as a platoon leader. That he was sure of.

The road march to the forward assembly area was a hard and wearing one for Avery. His inability to sleep that afternoon exacerbated his apprehensions and nervousness. Gerry Garger had told him before they left that he was going to have to lighten up or he would have a nervous breakdown before the first Russian got a chance to blow him away. His friend had done his best to couch this sage advice as lightheartedly as he could. Unfortunately, it had the opposite effect, for the more Avery tried to relax without being able to do so, the more he worried that he just might be on the verge of a nervous breakdown. That would be disastrous, he concluded. At least he could live with a wound. Wounds were noble, a red badge of courage no one could argue with. Evacuation because of a nervous breakdown before the first battle, on the other hand, would be a disgrace too terrible to contemplate. Only the sudden realization that he no longer knew where he was because he hadn't been following the Team's progress on his map caused Avery to divert his attention from his fears of suffering a nervous breakdown to his fear that he wouldn't be able to find his location again on the map if something terrible happened before they reached their forward assembly area.

Shortly after 2200 hours, the Team pulled into that assembly area. The movement in and occupation of the marked positions went like clockwork. In peacetime maneuvers the Team had never had such a smooth road march and assembly area occupation. Greeted by Uleski as he dismounted from Alpha 66, Bannon gave his XO a broad smile and a well-deserved atta boy. "Well Bob, you done good. Real good. Have you been able to coordinate with the people we'll be passing through?"

"Yes, sir. I was forward this afternoon in their positions and have gone over the route several times. It's a piece of cake."

"What about the Russians? Does Herman have any information concerning Ivan?"

"Well, first off, they're not Russians. They're Poles. The Poles hit the Germans just after I arrived there. The German officer I spoke to said it looked as if the Russians never told them where his unit was because the Poles just rolled right up to the German positions in column formation. His commanding officer let them come into their positions before he cut loose. The Poles never had much of a chance. They were cut to pieces. The officer's commander was killed but his XO took over and is still holding. Our battalion XO passed word down to us that the German battalion commander believes the Poles will make another try sometime tonight."

"What kind of units are we facing?"

"Tanks so far, T-55s. Real second-class stuff."

"Hey, that's OK by me. I get paid the same amount for blowing away old tanks as I do for tangling with tanks that don't want to die. Tell me, do you have any qualms about going up against your own people, Bob?"

"Sir, those aren't my people. They're as red as the Russians. Though I confess I'd rather be killing Russian Communists, in the end it makes no never mind to me they're Polish Communists. A red is a red, and a red that's a Pole and is dead smells as sweet to me as any other."

Uleski's cold, unfeeling remark sent a chill down Bannon's spine. The dark side of First Lieutenant Uleski had come out again, the side that worried him, leaving him to wonder if his hatred would cloud his judgment. He hoped not. For his sake and his crew's, he hoped not.

"Okay Bob, make sure all the people that came with you make it back to where they belong. Then gather up the leadership and have them meet me here."

The battalion S-3 came into the company area while Uleski was filling in the Team's leaders on what he knew of the situation to their front. Major Jordan waited until Uleski was finished before he shared his information them. "The battalion is closed up and ready," he stated, taking care to make sure he didn't add any unnecessarily snide comments concerning Charlie Company. "The 1st of the 4th Armor, as well as the artillery battalions that will be supporting us are expected to be in place and set as planned. So far, everything has gone well. As far as anyone can tell, the Polish unit to our front doesn't know we're here and hasn't been reinforced. We will therefore proceed as planned."

"Team Yankee will begin its move at 0330 hours," Jordan continued. "At 0350, two battalions of US and one battalion of German artillery will fire a ten-minute preparation on the Polish forward positions, both identified and suspected. At 0400 hours, Team Yankee's lead element will pass through the German positions and begin the attack."

Looking over at Garger, Bannon gave him a nod before turning his attention back to Jordan. "That'll be my 3rd Platoon."

Jordan acknowledged this by giving Garger a nod before continuing. "If all goes well, the battalion will be on the Saale River by early afternoon, ready to pass 1st of the 4th Armor through us and drive on to Leipzig."

"Provided the Soviets don't object to our doing so," Bannon interjected.

"There's always that possibility," Jordan intoned.

"What do we know about Ivan and what he's up to?" Bannon asked.

"We do know he'll do his damnedest to keep us from crossing the Saale. They're already dropping brigades on that river just in case the Poles don't hold. Of course," Jordan quickly added, "there's always the possibility that maybe, just maybe, this time the plan will work."

"Care to place a wager on that, sir?" Bannon offered.

Jordan shook his head. "Captain, I'm shocked, shocked to find gambling going on here."

After sharing a halfhearted chuckle with the gathering, Jordan asked if Bannon had any questions. When he responded in the negative, the S-3 left, leaving Bannon to cover all the last-minute details he felt needed to be addressed, ask for and answer any questions, then dismiss his officers and senior NCO. When everyone was gone, Bannon made his way back to Alpha 66, clambered aboard, and informed Folk they would split guard duty. "Seeing how you slept during the road march, you get to pull first shift," Bannon informed his gunner. Then, without further ado, Bannon rolled out his sleeping bag on top of the turret, laid on top of it, and fell asleep in minutes.

∾

After Avery and Hebrock finished putting out the information they had to the other TCs, Hebrock told his platoon leader to forget about pulling any duty between now and when it was time to move-out and instead, get some sleep. Avery was too far gone to argue. By now, having come as close to worrying himself to death, it took every bit of effort he had left to keep his eyes open. While the lieutenant leaned against Alpha 21 for support, Tessman threw a sleeping bag down to Hebrock who spread it out next to the track. Avery didn't even bother to take his boots off. He simply flopped down, wrapped one side of the sleeping bag over himself, and passed put from exhaustion. He stayed in the same position until he was roused at 0310 hours.

∾

Team Yankee missed colliding head-on with the expected Polish attack by fifteen minutes. Again the fortunes of war smiled on the Team. Instead of having to go forward and dig out the Polish tank and motorized infantry from their hastily prepared defensive positions, the Poles were smashed by the combined weight of the German defensive fires and the artillery that was already scheduled to fire in support of 3rd of the 78th's attack. In war, one's good fortune is sometimes nothing more than a matter of timing, being at the right place at the right time.

Had a staff officer or the brigade commander set the time of attack at 0330, it would have been the Poles enjoying the advantage. As it was, Team Yankee gained a double advantage. Not only did the Poles impale themselves on the German's defenses and save the Team the trouble of seeking them out, they allowed the Team to get an extra half-hour's sleep.

The din of the raging battle to their front, the eerie shadows caused by the illumination rounds floating down to earth, and the flash of artillery impacting lighting up the night sky made Team Yankee's crossing of the East German border seem unreal. It stuck Bannon as looking more like a scene from a cheap science-fiction movie than war. Moments like this, when one is not actually involved in the fight, but close enough to see and hear it, are when fear reaches a peak. The fear of failure, the fear of being ripped apart by artillery, the fear of death run through the mind as a soldier moves toward a battle already in progress. Only when he is actually engaged in the fight himself does training and instinct take over. Fear is pushed aside by the need to fight or die. It's the before, the time when a soldier is little more than a spectator and there is still the chance to back out, that the rational mind pleads for reason, to stop, to turn back, to quit before it is too late. The tank, however, keeps going forward, ignoring the rational mind of its occupants, taking them ever closer to where they will have little choice but to join the mayhem and carnage.

∿

As Sergeant Polgar's personnel carrier eased down into the anti-vehicle ditch that ran along the East German border, he became elated. After being in the Army for sixteen years, something he was doing was making sense. He recalled how, as a private in Vietnam, he and his buddies felt frustrated and betrayed when they had to break off pursuit of the North Vietnamese as soon as they came up to the Vietnamese border with Cambodia. They were never allowed to go all the way in and finish the enemy. He felt the same frustration when, while serving in Korea in 1977, two American officers were hacked to death with axes in broad daylight by North Korean soldiers and no action was taken to retaliate. And then there were the 444 days of embarrassment when the Iranians held Americans hostage without any fear of being brought to account. Like others in the military, the half-measures and restrictions placed on the US military didn't make sense to him.

This attack, however, did. For the first time in his military career he was carrying the war into the enemy's homeland. He and his platoon were going to be given a chance to strike at the heart of the enemy. No more running up to an imaginary line and then stopping while some politician reflected on what move would come out best on the next public opinion poll. No more letting the enemy run across an imaginary line where he'd be able to lick his wounds and come back at a time and place of his choosing only when he was ready. The Army was going to rip out the enemy's heart and drink his blood. That made sense to Polgar. It was, in his mind, the only way to fight a war.

∼

For a moment Colonel Reynolds considered halting the attack to allow the Germans to sort out the situation before the battalion passed. When he called Bannon and told him to be prepared to halt in place, Bannon immediately called back and ask that he let the Team go. The Poles were reeling from the bloody nose the Germans had given them. This was the ideal time to strike, while they were still confused. The enemy obviously didn't know the battalion was coming, he pointed out, otherwise they would not have attacked. "Those people have T-55s with old sights," he added as Reynolds was mulling over Bannon's request to continue. "We have thermal sights. Now is the time to speed up, not slow down."

In the end, the colonel agreed, ordering him to go for it. When Bannon dropped to the Team net and ordered Garger to pick up speed, hit hard, and keep rolling, all he got back from 3rd Platoon was a simple "I heard that."

∼

The 3rd Platoon rolled through the German positions without slowing down, deploying into a wedge as they went and engaging the fleeing Poles on the fly. The surprise was complete. Some of the Polish tanks attempted to return fire. Unlike the M-1, they had to stop to shoot, telegraphing their intentions and making it easier for 3rd's Platoon's gunners to single out which tanks posed the greatest threats to them. Other Polish tanks simply picked up speed and swerved left or right in an attempt to get out of the way. Most failed. For once, the Americans had better and faster tanks. Without needing to break stride, 3rd Platoon pressed home its attack.

Following close on 3rd Platoon's heels, Bannon directed the FIST to shift the artillery fires to the left and the right of the Team's axis of advance. This would keep the Polish infantry pinned in their defensive positions as the Team passed through their front line. Once Team Yankee was in their rear, those Poles still facing the Germans would be obliged to either retreat or surrender.

The speed with which the 3rd Platoon was attaching was causing the Team to become spread out. While the 2nd Platoon, which was behind 66, would have no difficulty keeping up as it shook out of its column formation and into its attack formation, the PCs in the Mech Platoon would soon be falling behind if the lead elements of the Team continued at the pace they were going. Reluctantly, he ordered the 3rd Platoon to slow down in order to allow the rest of the Team time to deploy and assume their position. Having no wish to tempt the fates by madly rushing forward as quickly as he could a second time as he had on Hill 214, Bannon made sure the whole Team stayed together and under his control.

Once the tanks in front of Alpha 66 began to slow, Bannon instructed Kelp to angle over to the left of 3rd Platoon. Once he was satisfied Kelp knew where he was headed, he ordered the 2nd Platoon to pick up speed and deploy to the left of 66. When he saw that platoon's lead tank take up station to his left, Bannon turned his full attention to his front.

❧

The scene that Avery beheld as his tank pulled made its way through the German positions was incredible. Dante's Inferno could not have been more terrible. In his wildest dreams he could not have imagined such chaos and pandemonium. Artillery was landing here and there with no rhyme or reason he could discern. The exchange of fire between the lead tanks and the Poles continued unabated. Colored star clusters were popping overhead. And there were burning tanks everywhere, lit up by mortar and artillery illumination rounds that cast a sickly pale light on everything.

The bucking and jolting of 21 running at full throttle to catch up with the CO's tank tossed Avery about in the cupola as he struggled to respond to Bannon's order to deploy to his left. Having no clear idea where he was, and even less idea where the CO was, the best Avery could do was give a "ROGER, OUT" on the radio and order his drive to keep heading in the direction that the CO's tank had been heading the last time he had seen it.

As Alpha 21 crested a hill in search of Alpha 66 and the 3rd Platoon, it almost collided with another tank that suddenly appeared to its left. Only a quick order to the driver to go right prevented a collision with it. The TC in the other tank, apparently, had also realized he was about to collide with Alpha 21 at the last minute and had swung to the left to avoid 21. The two tanks then straightened out and began to run side by side at a distance of twenty meters.

The relief Avery felt at having found the CO's tank was short lived. Just as he was about to key the net to order his platoon to begin to deploy, it dawned upon him that the direction the tank to his left was moving in didn't make sense. Alpha 66 should have been to his right, not to the left. In an effort to verify that the other tank was Alpha 66, Avery leaned over as far as he could, squinted his eyes, and took a better look at the tank to his left.

A T-55! It was a *goddamned T-55!* The sudden realization that he was running side by side with a Polish tank was numbing. It was the sensation of urine running down his leg that galvanized Avery into action.

Grabbing the TC override, he began to slew the turret even as he was issuing a frantic fire command.

"GUNNERBATTLESIGHTTANK!"

The loader had no need to discern exactly what his TC was saying. Avery's high pitched voice was enough to tell him they were about to engage. After throwing the arming lever out and pressing himself up against the turret wall on his side of the tank, he shouted out clear enough to be heard by the gunner without the need of the intercom. "UP!"

The target was so near and the thermal sight image so uniformly green that Tessman didn't recognize the object in his sight as a tank. "CANNOT IDENTIFY!"

The belligerent move by Alpha 21 caused the Polish tank commander to give 21 a closer look. He too realized his error and began to lay his gun. Tessman repeated his call, "CANNOT IDENTIFY!"

"FROM MY POSITION—ON THE WAY!"

Without bothering to drop down and look through his extension, Avery fired the main gun from his override. The report of 21's main gun and the impact of steel on target were as one, sending the T-55 staggering off to the left a few meters before coming to a stop.

For the longest time Avery could do little but stand there and watch the T-55 erupt in flames as 21 continued to roll forward. It was the cry of the loader reporting he'd reloaded the main gun and had armed it that snapped Avery out of his trance and croak out an order to ceasefire.

～

The retreat of the Poles turned into a rout. Polish tanks were everywhere. Most of them were gone, destroyed or scattered. Garger and his platoon now found themselves coming across trucks and personnel carriers. As the platoon crested one knoll, they came face to face with a battery of heavy mortars. Without slowing down one bit, the tanks of 3rd Platoon simply continued to roll through them, firing on the mortarmen with machineguns and crushing their mortars under their tracks. In the midst of this carnage, all Garger could do was wonder when he'd receive permission to pick up his speed again. The whole Polish rear area was in an uproar. He wanted to finish them before they were able to reorganize.

His platoon had no sooner left the shattered remains of the Polish mortar battery behind when Bannon came up on the net and ordered him to deploy his platoon into a right echelon. After quickly acknowledging Bannon's command, Garger passed the order onto his platoon, watching as the tanks to his right dropped back and took up their assigned stations, swinging their guns to cover the Team's right flank as they went. It was only then that he noticed it was beginning to become light.

Twisting around in the cupola, he watched as Alpha 66 come up on his left. Behind 66 he could make out the forms of the 2nd Platoon tanks coming on fast. Once they were up, the Team would be set to continue on. Unless something terrible happened, he expected they would reach the Saale River that afternoon with ease.

～

With Alpha 66 finally in sight, Avery allowed himself a sigh of relief. He hadn't lost the Team. It was then that the first humorous thought that he had had since his arrival in Germany suddenly popped in his head. This made the second time that morning that he had been relieved, he thought to himself as he recalled what had happened during his near brush with the T-55. This led to his appreciation that while hip shooting a tank main gun was not in the book, any book, it had worked. Alpha 21 had killed the Pole, saving his hide and earning it its first kill ring.

CHAPTER 10

Red Dawn

Just prior to dawn, Colonel Reynolds accomplished what the Poles had not been able to; stop Team Yankee. As much as he would have liked to maintain the momentum of the attack, just as Bannon had been compelled to rein in Garger and 3rd Platoon as it had forged out ahead of the Team, Reynolds need to put the brakes on Bannon.

No one needed to explain why this was necessary. In listening to the traffic on the battalion net when not otherwise fighting his tank and maintaining control of his platoons, Bannon appreciated that while Team Yankee had been able to brush aside the Polish units directly to its front, those Poles who had been to the left and right of the penetration did not panic or flee. Instead, they attempted to close off the penetration as soon as Team Yankee and Team Bravo had passed through. Charlie and Delta companies' lack of tanks encouraged the Poles to try. Their initial efforts proved to be devastatingly successful as they pelted the two mech infantry companies with a deadly crossfire as they emerged from the cover of the German positions and before they had a chance to fully deploy. The garbled and fragmented reports over the battalion net from Charlie Company, which had not expected to meet any resistance, betrayed the confusion and panic the follow-on company commanders were having to wrestle with.

The battalion XO, who had been following Charlie Company took a hand in sorting out this mess, reporting the situation as best he could and his actions to the colonel. Delta Company, the last of 3rd of the 78th's line companies, was deployed into positions from which they could support Charlie Company. The XO who was still in contact with the German battalion, was able to get them to add their support to the roiling battle taking place well behind Team Yankee. Once a firm base of fire had been established and friendly artillery had been brought to bear, he moved forward to rally Charlie Company and reopen the breach.

His efforts, however, were rewarded with a direct hit on his track when it reached the place where Charlie Company had gone to ground. The Delta Company commander reported the loss of the battalion XO to Reynolds. He then informed the battalion commander that he would continue to do all he could to support Charlie Company, but, he added, at the moment there wasn't much he could do other than engage the Poles to his front with the few long range systems that he had.

Unable to contact the Charlie Company commander, and sensing that the entire operation was in jeopardy, Colonel Reynolds ordered Team Yankee to stop where it was and instructed Major Jordan to stay forward with Team Yankee. He then turned Team Bravo around and led them back to hit the Poles in the rear. The day that had begun so well appeared to be turning against the battalion.

∿

The order to halt and take up hasty defensive positions threw Sergeant Polgar. For a minute he thought that the Team Commander had made a mistake. Garger thought the same, for no sooner had Bannon stopped talking, than he came back and asked him to repeat his last transmission. A little agitated at having his orders questioned, Bannon made it a point to repeat his instructions slowly, in such a way as to ensure that they not only were understood, but Garger got the message he'd managed to push the wrong button.

As each of the platoon leaders were acknowledging Bannon's order, Polgar couldn't help but take note of the difference between the two tank platoon leaders. The 3rd Platoon leader was clearly upset with his commander for stopping the mad dash he had been leading. Polgar wanted to get on with the attack himself, especially since they had such a clear advantage over the enemy. But he was an old soldier who guessed that Bannon would not have stopped their advance unless there was a damned good reason to do so.

The platoon leader with the 2nd Platoon, on the other hand, sounded as if he were relieved to get the order to halt. Not that Avery could be blamed. The US Army had a tradition of being rough on second lieutenants. It had to be hell on that officer, Polgar reasoned, being assigned to a unit in the middle of a war and then going right into an attack like this before he had a chance to figure out which end was up. And though he was trying his best, so far the poor bastard hadn't impressed anyone, especially the captain. If any further proof was needed that there was an overall lack of confidence in the man, one of the NCOs in his own platoon had started a lottery in which NCOs and enlisted men in the Team placed bets on how long the new lieutenant would last once they went into action. The big money was on two days. Some bet it would be hours. Polgar had been one of the more optimistic. He had his bet riding on three and a half days.

∿

The Team was settling into positions along an east-west road just as the sun was beginning to peek over the high ground to the east. Bannon watched as the sky slowly changed from near pitch black to a deep, crimson red, reminding him of the old nautical saying, *"Red sun at night, sailor's delight. Red run in the morning, sailor take warning."* The sun that was greeting Team Yankee this morning was blood red. Watching the great red solar orb as it began its laborious ascent, he uttered a silent prayer that the sun he was watching rise in the east was not an ill omen.

After setting that thought aside, and once he was satisfied with the way the Team was deployed, Bannon turned his attention listening in on the battalion net. The colonel, he gathered, was preparing to hit the Poles with everything he had available. First he called the battalion's artillery fire-support officer and designated targets he wanted hit and when they were to be hit. He next instructed the Delta Company commander to get with the Germans and see if they could increase the amount of direct fire support they were already contributing. Finally, based on information provided by the Delta Company commander, he gave Team Bravo and Delta Company their orders.

His plan was a simple hammer and anvil operation. While holding the attention of the Poles to their front with Delta Company and the Germans and pinning the Poles with artillery, he would be hitting them from behind with Team Bravo.

The plan proved to be as effective as it was simple. The devastating fire that had smashed their ill-fated predawn attack, their failure to destroy C Company, the weight of the firepower of Delta Company, the Germans, and the artillery heaped upon them and the violence of Team Bravo's attack to their rear finally broke the Poles. One of the surviving Poles who was taken prisoner would later observe that the Americans and Germans had used so much firepower that even the sun was bleeding.

∾

Forty kilometers east of Team Yankee's hastily assumed positions, a Soviet tank company commander was about to finish briefing his platoon leaders when he noticed how red the morning sun was. For a brief moment he reflected on its significance.

Pointing to it, he told his gathered platoon leaders that the Motherland to the east was sending a red sun as an omen to them. He promised his gathered officers that if they performed their duties as they had been trained and adhered to the great truths that were the pillars of strength to true Communists, the red dawn they were witnessing would herald the end of the imperialist dreams in Europe and the beginning of a new socialist era. Dismissing them with a salute, the company commander turned away and headed to his own tank.

As he was doing so, he wondered if any of his platoon leaders had believed the line of horseshit he had just served them. Stopping, he turned and looked up at the red sun that was still hovering just above the horizon. After a moment, he heaved a great sigh. It wasn't important if they did or not. The political commissar had been pleased with his outpouring of socialist propaganda. Perhaps that miserable party hack would stay out of his way for the rest of the morning, leaving the serious business of killing Americans in the hands of the professional soldiers. This thought caused the Soviet captain to smile. The political commissar was happy, his company was finally going to get a chance to kill some Americans, and, if they were lucky, the Poles would get in its way, allowing him to run the worthless shits down. This, he concluded, *was* shaping up to be a great day.

∽

The end of the Poles did not signal an immediate resumption of the battalion's attack. This had been Charlie Company's first time under fire, and the experience had been shattering. Like Bannon, Reynolds had no wish to press deeper into the enemy's rear strung out and piecemeal. With the need to sort out the tangled mess that the three trailing companies were in, he advised Bannon to hold his current positions until he could get everyone on the right track. Reynolds went on to advise him that the divisional air cavalry troop was going to be operating between Team Yankee's current positions and the Saale. That suited Bannon just fine. He was becoming tired of stumbling around like a blind man waiting for the Soviets to hit the Team. Let the cavalry earn their pay.

As it was now obvious that the Team would need to hold their current positions longer than he had initially thought, Bannon began to take a closer look at the lay of the land to his front and flanks and, if necessary, reposition his platoons. Ahead, across the road embankment they were deployed along was a valley about ten kilometers wide flanked by wooded hills that rose sharply on either side. Immediately to the Team's left was a small town named Issel. As he looked at the town through his binoculars, Bannon could see no sign that it was occupied. There was the possibility that the Soviets had cleared the village of civilians prior to the attack in order to maintain operational security. There also was the possibility it was occupied either by combat service support units or security troops responsible for rear area who were, at that very minute, reporting Team Yankee's positions back to their higher ups. It was this second possibility that worried him.

After a quick consultation with Major Jordan on the battalion net, Bannon ordered the 2nd Platoon to move into a position from which they could place effective fire onto the town. As they were preparing to do so, he dismounted and made his way over to Polgar's track to give him his instructions.

With the tanks overwatching his move, Polgar was to take his platoon into the town and check it out. While he appreciated the Mech Platoon didn't have the manpower to do a thorough job of clearing the town, building by building, they at least could check out the more obvious places and, if the town was occupied, keep anyone they came across busy until one of the pure infantry companies came up and took over for them. Besides, he added as an aside, at least this way some of the Team would be doing something useful. This last point was most appealing to Polgar who didn't like the idea of sitting out in the open waiting for some hotshot Russian pilot to come along and fire up his platoon.

○⌀◡

Since there was no chance for surprise, Polgar stormed into the town mounted. The four PCs rolled into the center of the town square where the infantry dismounted and began to conduct a systematic search of the buildings. Working in three-man groups, with one group on each side of a street and their PC following down the middle and a little behind, ready to support them with machinegun fire if they ran into trouble, the infantry began to make their sweep.

The teams conducting the search all followed the same pattern when they entered a building. One of the soldiers would peep into a window to see if there were any obvious signs of occupants. Once they had done so, the three would converge on the door through which they would enter. Leaving one outside, keeping an eye on the street and the house across from his group lest they become so preoccupied with the building they were about to enter that an unseen enemy came up from behind and surprised them, the other two would kick open the door and rush in. It didn't take Polgar's men long to find out throwing themselves against a stout, unyielding door could be a painful experience. After bouncing off of a few doors that refused to give, they all began to try the doorknobs first, a technique that was surprisingly successful and infinitely less bruising.

This had been going on for thirty minutes when Polgar, who had remained in the town center monitoring the progress of his squads, heard the muffled report of a Soviet AK followed by the detonation of a grenade. Making his way to where the shots had come from as quickly as he dared, he was greeted by the sight of two of his men coming out of a house dragging a third. The TC of the personnel carrier that had been overwatching this team, after having his track roar up to the front of the house, was systematically peppering the windows along the second floor with machinegun fire. Polgar, stopping behind this PC, covered the three men as they made for the rear of the PC.

Once safely behind the PC, the two men that had been fired on watched for a moment as a medic who'd followed Polgar ripped open their wounded comrade's chemical protective suit and tore away the T-shirt to get at the wound. A quick check showed that the man had taken two rounds in his left shoulder. The wound was painful and bloody, but wouldn't be fatal.

When they were satisfied their friend was in good hands, they reported to Polgar. "McGill was on point," one of the trio, a young corporal by the name of Cooper explained between desperate gulps of breath. "After we'd cleared the ground floor and found nothing there, McGill started up the stairs to check out the second floor. That was when the shooting started. The first volley caught McGill on the stairs, sending him tumbling back down them. Hector covered me while I ran out and dragged him back. Once I had McGill out of the way, Hector threw a grenade onto the second floor to cover our withdrawal. None of us saw who was doing the shooting or how many of the bastards are in there."

By this time the squad leader of the trio who'd been ambushed had joined Polgar with the rest of his squad. After assessing the situation and deciding he needed to clear the house, if for no other reason than to find out who'd been shooting at them and what strength they were in, he directed the squad leader and one of the teams to circle around back and cover the rear of the house in case someone tried to slip out. He then ordered the TC and driver of the PC to cover the front of the building. He would personally lead the two men who had first entered the house back in to deal with the unseen enemy.

After getting a rundown on the layout of the ground floor, this three-man assault party rushed the front door. Once there, Polgar stationed himself on one side of the door, opposite Hector. This time, however, Hector leaned over and threw a grenade into the opened door before they entered. As soon as the grenade went off, Cooper, followed by Polgar, went charging into the house, guns leveled and blazing away. Once inside, the two of them sought the nearest cover available and waited to see what happened.

When nothing did, Polgar signaled for Hector to enter and cover him as he approached the stairs. When Hector was set, Polgar slowly began to climb the stairs, craning his neck in an effort to see up and over onto the second floor. When he was halfway up the stairs, Polgar halted, took a grenade off of his web gear, pulled the pin, and threw it into the room at the head of the stairs. As soon as this grenade detonated, he charged to the top of the stairs, taking two steps at a time and firing as he went. Once he reached the head of the stairs, he threw himself into the room he'd thrown the grenade and, as before, sought cover.

Just as Polgar began to get up, a yell to halt came from the portion of the squad that was outside at the rear of the building. This was followed by the sound of M-16s firing. In an instant, he realized that the people they were looking for had tried to slip out through the rear and had been caught by the team sent to the back of the house. As Cooper and Hector came up and began to check out the other rooms on the second floor, Polgar went to a window overlooking the rear of the house and peered out.

In the small yard below, two of his men were standing over the body of a young German boy sprawled in a flowerbed bleeding from several wounds. An AK was lying beside him. For a brief, sickening moment, it reminded Polgar of a similar scene in Vietnam some fifteen years earlier. One of his first firefights had involved a VC unit that consisted mainly of fourteen and fifteen-year-old boys. It was an experience that often haunted his dreams. Knowing exactly what his men were thinking, he did what his sergeant had done on that day. "Is he dead?" Polgar barked gruffly.

One of the soldiers standing over the body looked up and saw Polgar looking down at him. "Yeah. Kind of young to be running around shooting at people, Sarge."

"Just remember Patterson, that sorry piece of trash was old enough to put two holes in McGill. Given a chance, he would have done the same to you."

Patterson looked at his platoon sergeant for a moment, then down at the dead German boy. After another moment of reflection, he reached down, picked up the AK, and went around to the front to continue the house-by-house search.

∽

Polgar's report on the Mech Platoon's contact didn't surprise Bannon at all. His only regret was the discovery that the town's total population seemed to consist of a lone fanatic who couldn't have hurt the Team had cost him a WIA he could ill afford.

Anxious to find out how much longer they were going to sit there, Bannon dismounted and walked over to where the battalion S-3's track had pulled in to find out what Jordan's best guess was. Major Jordan's track was nestled up against a large hedgerow that separated two fields. The troop door on the back ramp was open as was the cargo hatch on top. Stopping at the door Bannon stuck his head inside.

Major Jordan, seated across from his radios, had arms folded with chin resting on his chest, giving all the appearances of being asleep.

"Must be nice to have a cushy staff job where you can take a nap three times a day."

"Bannon, someday when you grow up, and I trust you will, you'll come to appreciate the fact that we grown-ups need to conserve our energy if we're going to be able to keep up with you kids," Jordan replied without moving a muscle or opening his eyes.

"Oh, is that what you call it? Conserving energy? Back home we call it sleep."

"Shit, don't they teach you tread-heads anything at Fort Knox?"

"Sure they do, Major. And someday, when Infantry Branch authorizes you to use multi-syllable words, I'll tell you all about it."

"I'm sure there's a reason you came over here other than to harass me Bannon. Hopefully, it has to do with that shooting in the town you haven't reported to me yet."

"That was a small affair. Some hyped-up commie high school kid wanted to play Rambo. He wounded one of Sergeant Polgar's men before he got his ass blown away. So far, that's all we've come across. What I really came over here for is to find out when we're going to get this circus moving again. If it's going to be awhile, I want permission to move up onto the high ground to the northeast where we can get under some cover. I'm not thrilled about sitting out here lined up along this road trying to hide my tanks behind these damned bushes."

"I expect we'll be moving soon. The brigade commander just got off the radio with Colonel Reynolds. Colonel Brunn was all over the Old Man. Told him that if he couldn't get the battalion moving, brigade was prepared to pass the 1st of the 4th through us to continue the attack."

"Sir, pardon me if I seem like an underachiever, but, if the brigade commander wants to let the 1st of the 4th take the lead, that's fine by me. I could use to playing second team real fast."

Upon hearing this, Jordan sat up and leaned closer to Bannon. When he spoke, he did so in low, hushed tones. "This is not for general distribution," he began as he scotched closer to Bannon. "Colonel Brunn was a hair's breadth away from relieving Reynolds after the Hill 214 debacle. The only reason he didn't was because there didn't happen to be any spare lieutenant colonels laying around at the time. If the battalion screws the pooch on this operation, the Old Man is gone. The battalion has to succeed."

"Well, sir, between you, me, and that dumb bush your track is using for concealment, even if what you say is true, I have no intention of taking any undue risks simply to save someone's reputation. Colonel Reynolds is a fine officer and, under the right circumstances, a great guy, but his reputation isn't worth a single unnecessary casualty in Team Yankee."

"I don't think we need to worry about that. The colonel is too much of a professional to do anything dumb simply to save face."

"God, I hope you're right, sir."

Having no wish to dwell on that subject any longer, Jordan took to discussing the battalion's next move. The air cavalry, he informed Bannon, had come across some trucks and reconnaissance vehicles as they roamed out to the front, scattering the trucks and destroying the recon vehicles as they went. Unfortunately, the cavalry scouts could not tell if they were Polish or belonged to someone else. A scout helicopter had tried to land near one of the destroyed vehicles to check this out, but had drawn fire from a concealed ZSU-23-4. Not being able to obtain this information, and confident that the front would be clear for a while, Major Jordan had requested that the air cav troop shift over to the east and cover the battalion's right frank. The response from brigade was a "*wait, out.*"

When Jordan relayed Bannon's request that he be allowed to move his Team, Reynolds replied that he wanted Team Yankee to press on, but at a slower pace, adding that the rest of the battalion would be moving out momentarily and would be able to catch up, provided Team Yankee didn't get carried away again. After acknowledging the order, Jordan looked at Bannon and grinned. As soon as the transmission ended, Jordan asked if Bannon had any questions. "That's a negative."

"Okay, move out when you're ready. I'll be right behind you."

With that, Bannon made his way back to Alpha 66 and issued the Team its new orders over the Team net.

∿

Orders to stop clearing the town came none too soon as far as Sergeant Polgar was concerned. The house-to-house search was getting old. He didn't want to lose any more of his people to some runny-nosed commie who hadn't even begun to shave yet. Besides, this kind of work was hard. When he had charged the stairs and thrown himself into the room in the house where the sniper had been, he had landed flat on his chest, forgetting there were still grenades hanging on his web gear. The force of the fall had knocked the wind out of him as the grenades and other assorted items attached to his web gear dug into his chest, leaving bruises he could feel.

As his tracks were pulling out of town, he decided that he was getting too old to be running around playing John Wayne. In the future, he was going to leave the gung-ho stuff to the young kids in his platoon. He also decided that in the next war, he was going to find himself a nice cushy staff job at the Pentagon, fixing coffee for the generals. His campaigning days were over. War, thought Polgar, belongs to the young, the strong, and the naive.

∿

Avery had mixed feelings about moving again. While sitting in this semi-exposed position was dangerous, moving out into the open, this time in broad daylight with high ground to both sides of the Team, was downright unnerving. As before, his platoon deployed in echelon to the left of Alpha 66. With his own tank in the lead and the rest of the platoon trailing off to the left and behind him, he felt exposed and vulnerable. The presence of Alpha 66 to his immediate right at a distance of fifty meters, 3rd Platoon visible a little farther to the right, and the Mech Platoon bringing up the rear did little to alleviate his anxieties. The only thing his tank was missing, he mused, was a big red and white target painted on the left side of his turret.

Distracted by such concerns, Avery was finding it difficult to keep track of where they were on the map he had laid out before him, direct his driver, and keep one eye on his platoon, and the other on Alpha 66. Controlling 21, let alone the platoon, was proving to be a challenge he wasn't quite up to yet. This need to multitask was made even more difficult by the way the tank kept bucking as it made its way across plowed fields against the furrows that were separated by drainage ditches. It seemed that every time he looked down at his map in an effort to figure out where they were, the driver would hit a ditch, catching the young lieutenant by surprise and sending him rattling around in the cupola. There had to be a way to manage all of this with some degree of efficiency, he told himself. Just how the Captain and Gerry Garger were able to manage this multitude of tasks was very much a mystery he'd yet to solve.

∾

The pilot of the MI-24D Hind was taking his time as he slowly eased his attack helicopter into position just to the right of an old keep sitting atop a hill overlooking the valley below. With a little luck, their target would be just over the rise to their front. They were lucky to have made it this far. The lead Hind had barely avoided an enemy scout helicopter on their run in. Although the weapons operator had felt confident that they could have taken out the frail scout, tangling with enemy air reconnaissance units was not their responsibility. Someone else would deal with the bothersome scout. They were hunting tanks.

With well-practiced ease, the pair of Hinds positioned themselves on either side of the ancient Keep they were using as their rally point and for reference. If the reports were correct, when they popped up over the trees, there would be a town southeast of the Keep and a group of tanks sitting stationary east of it.

As soon as the pilot of the lead Hind signaled he was set, both attack helicopters slowly rose above the masking terrain they'd been using to hide behind until the weapons operator's field of vision was clear. The pilot, seated behind and a little higher than the weapons operator, saw the town first. Once he had the town in sight, he began to search to the east of the town for the enemy tanks that were supposed to be deployed along a road. When he didn't see any sign of them, he ordered the weapons operator to search the area with his sight.

As the weapons operator was doing so, movement just north of the town caught the pilot's eye. Twisting his head about, he spotted several vehicles moving in a northerly direction. Keying the intercom, he informed the weapons operator of his sighting even as he was bringing his aircraft to bear until the weapons operator called out he had the enemy tanks in his sights. While his own weapons operator prepared to engage, the pilot reported his sighting to his flight leader who quickly shifted his orientation.

Like great cats preparing to pounce, the two Soviet MI-24D attack helicopters crouched in the lee of the Keep studying their quarry. A call from the flight leader asking if the pilot or the weapons operator of the trailing Hind had observed any antiaircraft guns or missile launchers caused the weapons operator of that aircraft to scan the area for any trace of a ADA system while the pilot checked his radar warning device to ensure that it was functioning and had not detected any enemy search radars. Only when both were sure they would not be challenged by either surface-to-air missiles or AAA guns did the pilot report

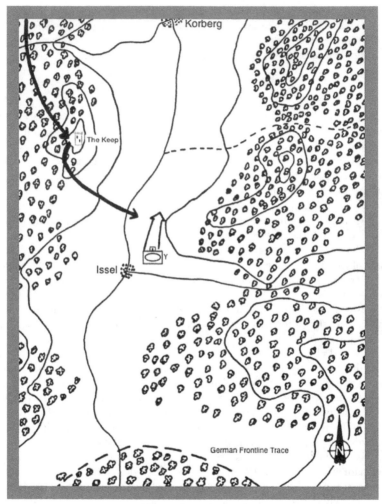

Map 13: Soviet Air Attack

back to his flight leader that all was clear before going back to tracking the American tanks, which, at the moment, were out of range.

Only when he was sure both aircraft were set and ready did the flight leader give the order to attack. It would be a standard attack, one they had practiced many times before. As one, they would swoop down on the tanks at high speed. The leader would go for the far tanks while the trailing Hind would attack the near tanks. They were not concerned with the personnel carriers. The American tanks constituted the greatest threat to Soviet ground forces and, as such, made the risk of making two passes, one west-to-east, followed immediately by another east-to-west after looping around, before rallying at the Keep.

With the cry of "*Urah*" shouted out over the radio, the flight leader signaled the start of the attack.

∾

Avery was hanging on to the machine-gun mount with one hand to steady himself while he ran his finger along his map trying desperately to find a landmark he could use as a reference when the cry of "HELICOPTERS, NINE O'CLOCK," followed by "MISSILE! MISSILE! MISSILE!" caught him by surprise.

Instinctively he looked up and to his front. There was nothing there. He then turned to his right to look at the Team commander's tank to see what he was doing. For a moment, Avery watched as Alpha 66 began to spew out clouds of white smoke from its exhaust before making a sharp turn to the right, disappearing behind the smoke. It wasn't until 66 and 3rd Platoon tanks began to fire wildly above his head that it suddenly dawned upon him what was happening.

∾

The pilot of the trailing Hind was surprised at the speed with which the tanks reacted. Almost as one, they had turned and begun to blow huge clouds of white smoke from their engines. Those that could were firing on his aircraft as they madly weaved this way and that. And though their shooting was wild and totally inaccurate, it was extremely disconcerting to see angry red tracers rising up toward him. A couple of the tanks were even firing their cannons. He had force himself to ignore his natural instincts to break off the attack and focus his full, undivided attention on closing on their target.

One of the lead tanks had not turned or cut on its smoke generator. The pilot quickly oriented on this stray even as he was ordering his weapons operator to engage it. Already tracking the tank his pilot selected as their first target, the weapons operator let fly a 9M17 antitank guided missile.

There followed several tense moments as the attention of both Soviet aviators remained riveted on that one tank, ignoring as best they could the hail of ground fire being thrown up at them. They were committed, and nothing short of divine intervention or a golden BB was going to stop them.

∾

2nd Lieutenant Randall Avery, a distinguished military graduate fresh out of Fort Knox's Armored Officer's Basic Course, had just enough time to catch a quick glimpse of the hideous attack helicopter bearing down on him and the fiery blur of a round object proceeding it before the Russian antitank guided missile struck home.

∾

The second their missile hit the tank they'd engaged, the pilot jerked his joystick to the left, increased his speed, and made a run to the north. He wasn't about to try for a second shot on this run. One hit was good enough.

As he was bringing his aircraft around, a fast-moving object caught his attention. Looking up, he was startled to see an American attack helicopter bearing down on him from the north. It must have been with the scout they had seen before. The weapons operator saw it at the same instant. Without hesitation, he began to lay the 12.7mm Gatling gun mounted in a chin turret on the enemy aircraft. He was just about to fire when his pilot jerked his joystick to the left again in a desperate effort to evade. This did him little good. The American easily adjusted his aim and fired.

A violent shudder and the sight of his weapons operator to his front disappearing in a rapid series of small explosions was all the pilot of the trailing Hind saw as 20mm cannon shells ripped into his aircraft as the cockpit began to fill with smoke.

The Hind pilot was still struggling with the controls of his aircraft, trying to escape the hail of cannon rounds pelting it when it was consumed in a ball of fire that scattered its fragments across the Germany countryside.

∾

"WE GOT 'EM! WE GOT 'EM!"

Bannon turned around to see what his loader was yelling about. Dowd was hanging onto his machinegun with one hand and pointing to the north with the other. In the distance, Bannon could see a fire and black smoke. Dowd, with a grin from ear to ear, turned back to view the conflagration he was sure he had contributed to.

"Forget him. He's gone. Keep your eyes open for the other son-of-abitch," Bannon yelled before ordering Kelp to cut the smoke generator off, but to be ready to kick it back on. He then called to the platoon leaders for a SITREP. Garger quickly came back with the report that two of his tanks had observed the second Hind disappear to the east, chased by a pair of AH-1 attack helicopters, which Bannon guessed belonged to the air cav troop that had been reconning to their front. For once, he reflected as his eyes turned skyward, someone up there was looking out for the Team.

Believing the air attack had accomplished little more than scattering the Team, he ordered the platoon leaders to rally their tracks, then form up on Alpha 66. As the smoke and confusion caused by the Hinds had not cleared, it would take a few minutes to sort things out. With that in mind, he ordered Kelp to find some cover and stop. It was only then that Bannon realized Avery hadn't replied to his call for SITREP. It was Hebrock, coming up on the Team net to report that Alpha 21 had been hit during the attack that provided him with the reason that officer hadn't.

"Damn!" Bannon thought as he mentally amended his earlier assessment. Not everyone could be lucky. By now he had come to accept the cruel fact that in war, people died. What irked him at the moment was the way second lieutenants assigned to the 2nd platoon seemed to be making a habit of it.

With nothing to do as he waited for his platoons to rally, Bannon stood upright and took to looking around to see if he could spot Alpha 21. His efforts to spot the crippled tank were hindered by the lingering clouds of the smoke that had been thrown up by the tanks, leaving him little choice but to call Hebrock and request further details. In response, Hebrock replied he'd let him know how bad things were as soon as he reached 21's position and had a chance to assess the situation there.

∾

As Alpha 24 closed on the smoking hulk of 21, Hebrock was convinced that everyone in the crew was dead. Main gun rounds in the turret's ammo storage compartment were still cooking off, throwing great balls of flame and smoke into the air. The blow-off panels, designed to vent the force of stored main gun rounds set off by a hit up and away from the crew, were lying fifty meters away from where 21 sat. After bringing his own tank to within forty meters of 21, he ordered his driver to stop. From there both he and his loader watched in silence as they waited for the last of the onboard ammo to cook off.

Just as he was about to report to the Team commander that 21 was a write off, the loader's hatch on 21 swung open. Hebrock watched for a moment. To his amazement, he saw 21's loader climb out. Turning around, he reached down to help someone else who was down inside the turret behind him. On seeing this, Hebrock ordered his driver to pull up next to 21, then made a call over the company net to the first sergeant, telling him they needed the ambulance ASAP.

∾

The air attack had given the rest of the battalion a chance to catch up. As the follow on companies were about to reach Team Yankee, Colonel Reynolds called to ask if the Team could continue in the lead, or if he needed to pass Charlie Company forward. Bannon replied that wouldn't be necessary as his platoon leaders had been able to rally their people with no trouble, with 2nd Platoon using the shattered 21 as their rally point.

Bannon waited until he saw the lead vehicles of Charlie Company closing up on his Mech platoon before ordering Hebrock to leave the recovery of 21's wounded to the first sergeant, take over the platoon, again, and resume his place in formation.

Only after Hebrock had acknowledged his transmission did Bannon realize just how cold such an order must seem to an outsider. He had no doubt that every man in the 2nd Platoon wanted to help their buddies in 21. Within the platoons there was a strong personal bond that held the men together. It was not only natural, it was necessary, for the bonds that bound a soldier to the other men in his crew, squad, or platoon are often the only thing that keeps a unit from buckling under the stress and horrors of war. So is the need to carry on in the face of a tragedy such as the one that had befallen Alpha 21's crew. It was unfortunate that lieutenant what's-his-name had been hit and could very well be dead. That happened in war. Seeing to those who had fallen, however, was now somebody else's responsibility. It was Bannon's, as well as what was left of 2nd Platoon, to continue their mission. They could not stop each time a tank was hit or a man was hit. Not only would that hinder the accomplishment of their mission, doing so would place other personnel belonging to the Team in jeopardy. As much as he didn't like the thought of rolling away and leaving the crew of Alpha 21 to fend for themselves until the medic track arrived, Bannon had his orders and the responsibility of seeing to it they were carried out, regardless of the cost.

Team Yankee, having collected itself, moved forward again. This time, however, they were not alone. Far to the left Bannon could catch glimpses of some of Team Bravo's tracks. They were now abreast of the Team and moving north. To his rear, he could make out tracks of the battalion command group, followed by Charlie Company. Satisfied that all was back on track within the Team and the battalion, he turned his attention to the town of Korberg just to the north. That, and the valley to the east of it, would be the next critical point he needed to pay attention to, for if there were any Soviet or Polish forces in the area, that was where he expected they would be.

☙

As his track, accompanied by the ambulance, closed on 21, First Sergeant Harrett could feel his stomach begin to knot up. He knew that he wasn't going to see anything new. Two tours in Vietnam, training accidents, and the first few days of this war had exposed him to many such scenes. Once he was there and doing something, he'd be all right. It was the anticipation that bothered him the most. How bad was it this time? How many? Was there something he could do, or was this just another case of bagging and tagging what was left of men he'd known? Did he know their wives, their children? Would they be able to identify the bodies? First sergeants are supposed to be detached, able to handle these things without a second thought. But first sergeants are also human.

It was with great relief that Harrert found there had been only one casualty. Tessman, who greeted Harrert, led him and the medic to where the lieutenant was lying.

While the medic began to work on Avery, Tessman explained what had happened. "The LT had been standing up in the cupola when the missile hit the rear of the turret, setting off the ammo back there. The rest of us came out of it without a scratch," he stated as he gave a quick nod of his head over to where his driver and loader were sitting. "The LT wasn't so lucky. The force of the explosion from the main gun rounds set off by the missile hit him squarely in the head and back."

Pausing, Tessman glanced over his shoulder to where the medic was working on Avery. "If the ballistic doors that separated us from the stored ammunition had been open, we'd all be dead."

"Well, you're not," Harrert replied. "How bad is the lieutenant?"

The answer to this question was supplied by the medic. "He is in bad shape, first sergeant. He has massive wounds and severe burns on his back and head. If we're going to save him, we need to evac most Ricky-tick."

"Okay, get him loaded up then," Harrert sighed as he turned to the crew and ordered them to help the medics place Avery on a stretcher and carry him over to the medic track. When it was gone, the first sergeant and Tessman began to look over 21. They had the driver try to start the engine but to no avail. Alpha 21 would have to be towed back to the battalion maintenance collection point by the M-88 recovery vehicle.

As he was waiting for the 88 to come up, Harrert looked up at the burned out ammo storage compartment. "I expect they'll be able to get this tank back in action within two days, three at the most."

Tessman, observing that this was the second time that this tank had been hit, dryly replied that they should retire it and use it for spare parts. Harrert agreed, but added the Army was fast running out of tanks and couldn't afford to throw them away simply because they had had a run of bad luck. To that, Tessman offered 21 to the first sergeant after it had been repaired. The first sergeant had to stop and think about that one. Maybe this tank should be scrapped.

∽

The Soviet tank company commander did not like the idea of moving through the woods in single file. He would have preferred to have gone north past the town of Langen. By doing that his company and the battalion following it would have been able to deploy into combat formation before making contact with the Americans. The regimental commander, however, had vetoed that idea because of the presence of American scout helicopters. To have gone through the Langen Gap would have left them open to observation from the air. Not only would the regiment lose the element of surprise, they would also be open to attack by enemy attack helicopters and ground attack aircraft. Instead, the lead tank battalion was reduced to winding its way along narrow, twisting trails through the woods.

There were few options open to the Soviet company commander. Once his tanks began coming out of the woods high on the hill, they would be visible to everyone in the valley. After they had been observed, there would be little time to take advantage of their surprise. Therefore, rather than have the three tanks of his lead platoon, the regiment's combat patrol, go out on their own, he had them pull back with the rest of the company. To succeed, they had to take risks. He gambled that his commander would not find out that he had pulled in the combat patrol and, in doing so, risked the possibility they would stumble into an ambush before they emerged from they woods.

In addition to pulling the battalion's lead element back, the Russian captain ordered his tanks to close up until they were almost fenderto-fender. With his entire company bunched up in this manner, the company would be able to quickly burst out of the woods and deploy into a tight battle formation. It was a good plan, one he was sure would work.

The only thing that could possibly go wrong now was the presence of an antitank ambush along the trail they were on. If the lead tank was hit, the others would be unable to bypass it or fight. The thought of such a thing gave the Russian chills. As far as he was concerned, the sooner he was out of these damned woods and in the open where he could maneuver, the better.

Counterattack

Air Force Maj. Orrin "The Snowman" Snow was pissed. As he led his wingman to where their two A-10s were to loiter and wait for good targets, he was fast coming to the realization the people running Flight Operations didn't have a clue as to what they were doing. He could understand how the Army pukes could screw up. Hell, most of them couldn't tell the difference between their planes and the Russians', let alone what to do with them. But getting the royal weenie from your own people was too much. It was bad enough that they had had to fight their way through enemy flak that wasn't supposed to be there to get at the target. But then to discover that the target wasn't there either, if it ever had been, was too much.

Now the two A-10s, having barely made it back from behind the enemy lines, were being diverted into a holding pattern where they would wait until a new target was nominated. At least that made sense. It would have been dumb to send the aircraft back to the airfield loaded with ordnance. But Snowman, fuming over the way they'd put their butts on the line going after a non-existent target wasn't much interested in logic. What he wanted to do was kill something, anything. And if someone on the ground didn't come up with a good mission fast, he was going to lead the other A-10 back to Flight Ops and bomb *it*, just for the hell of it.

The Team was making good progress, too good. Once more Reynolds called Bannon and ordered him to slow down. Charlie Company, it seemed, was having a hard time keeping up, creating a large gap between it and Team Yankee. "I want to keep the companies together," he told Bannon.

Twisting about in the cupola, Bannon glanced back over his shoulder to where the Mech Platoon was. From what he could see, their PCs were having no problem keeping up with his tanks, leading him to wonder what Charlie Company's problem was.

Folk, who enjoyed listening to the exchanges that took place on the battalion net, couldn't help but chuckle, adding his own opinion on the matter. "Those boys sure are having a rough morning."

"Not as rough as it's going to get if they don't pull their fifth point of contact out of their third," Bannon replied dryly as he took to surveying the area to their front to see if there was a covered position up ahead where the Team could pause while waiting for Charlie to close up.

As he was preparing to give the necessary orders to slow their rate of advance, a thought occurred to him. The longer he took to give the order to slow down, the second in less than as many hours, the farther they would go. At their current speed, every second he delayed meant the Team advanced another meter. The faster they went, the less time the Soviets had to throw something at them. By now he appreciated just how important a few extra minutes, even seconds, could be in combat. Pressing on without pause could make all the difference between seizing a bridge over the Saale intact, or finding every one of them down. Of course, speed and time could just as easily work against the Team. If it got far ahead of the other companies and ran into trouble, the rest of the battalion might not be able to catch up in time to pull its chestnuts out of the fire.

In the end, Bannon decided orders were orders. Besides, discretion, he was always told, was the better part of valor. With that thought in mind, he gave the order to slow down.

❧

As his tanks began to spill out of the woods onto the slope overlooking the valley, the Soviet tank company commander gave one short command. Like the well-drilled machine it was, the company rapidly deployed. Once all his tanks were on line, he gave the order to pick up speed and search for targets.

From their vantage point, this was not a difficult task. Before them, deployed in a great vee on the valley floor was a company of American armored personnel carriers and TOW vehicles being led by a small gaggle of three more personnel carriers. A quick count revealed that there were at least fifteen, maybe as many as twenty vehicles to their front at a range of less than 4,000 meters.

The only thing that bothered him was the absence of American tanks. The reports his commander had passed down to him had all mentioned tanks. He would have liked to have destroyed the tanks right off. They were the greatest threat to his company. But there were none in sight.

His concern over this point was quickly offset by the fact the personnel carriers before him were M-113s and not the new Bradleys. Even better, as best he could tell, they hadn't spotted him yet. With the distance between his company and the enemy formation his company was boring down on rapidly diminishing, the Russian captain decided he had no choice but to engage it, hoping as he prepared to give the order to open fire that the enemy tanks that were nowhere to be seen weren't sitting in ambush, waiting to surprise him, rather than the other way around.

∿

Even with his CVC on and 66's engine running, the sharp crack of tank cannons firing was clearly audible to Bannon as the sound reverberated down the valley. Automatically, he straightened up and looked around to see who was under fire. When he saw there were no telltale puffs of smoke or dust clouds kicked up by tank fire to the front or to his immediate left or right, he looked behind him to see if the Mech platoon was under fire. On seeing they were still with him and not being engaged, Bannon turned to his left, then to his right in search of who the hell was shooting. When he still saw nothing, he made a call over the company net, hoping one of his platoon leaders was in a position to enlighten him.

"BRAVO 3 ROMEO, THIS IS ROMEO 25—WHO'S TAKING FIRE AND WHERE'S IT COMING FROM? OVER."

Both tank platoons rapidly reported back that they were not under fire. It was the Mech Platoon that provided the answer.

"ROMEO 25, THIS IS ZULU 77. THE PEOPLE THAT WERE FOLLOWING US ARE UNDER ATTACK. I CAN SEE SEVERAL FIRES BEHIND US, OVER."

On hearing Polgar's report, Bannon spun about and stood on his seat as high as he could. Sure enough, off in the distance and to the rear of the Mech Platoon he could clearly see four pillars of black smoke rising into the air. Charlie Company had been hit. But from where? By whom? And why no reports from battalion?

Dropping down, he switched to the battalion net in order to contact the battalion commander. When he didn't receive any response, Bannon tried to contact the S-3. Still no luck.

It was the Delta Company commander who told him what was going on. In rapid-fire bursts, he reported that Charlie Company was under attack from Soviet tanks coming from the east. He went on to inform Bannon that he was deploying his company into a hasty defense along the road running north from Issel to Korberg. With that, he dropped off the net and stayed off despite Bannon's efforts to contact him. No doubt, Bannon concluded, he was busy running his company.

Bannon next contacted the Team Bravo commander, asking if he was in contact. Lieutenant Peterson, who was commanding that team, reported that he was not in contact but could see the Soviet tanks coming down off the hill to the east. He estimated that there were at least ten, maybe more. He couldn't make out what kind they were, but since they were shooting on the move and hitting, he figured that they had to be T-72s.

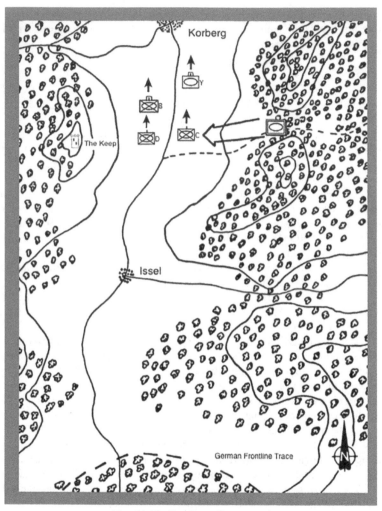

Map 14: The First Soviet Counterattack

It was clear that the battalion, who had been with Charlie, was in trouble, if not already dead. With the S-3 also off the net for some reason, and Charlie Company fighting for its life, Bannon quickly concluded he had to do something and do something fast before things really got out of hand. With Delta Company off the net as it prepared to greet the Russian onslaught, that left Team Yankee and Bravo in a position to respond to the crisis. As he was senior to Peterson, it was up to him to come up with a solution to the nightmare playing out to the rear of his Team before the whole damned battalion was wiped out. As these thoughts were running through his mind, Team Yankee continued to move north, away from the battle, at a steady rate of one meter a second.

∽

The Soviet tank company commander could almost feel the adrenaline running through his veins. They were closing on the Americans to his front. Already a half-dozen personnel carriers were burning hulks while the rest were scattering this way and that, try their damnedest get out of his company's way. All semblance of order was gone. Surprise had been complete. His tanks were reaping the benefits resulting from the speed and violence of their attack.

With curt orders, he directed the fire of his platoons. A report that there were more personnel carriers deploying to the west of the road drew his attention to the ten or twelve that were some three kilometers away. Many of them were already under cover and were dropping their ramps to let their infantry dismount. His company would have to finish the enemy company to its immediate front quickly and reach the second one before they had time to set up a viable defense. Speed and violence were critical! With this in mind, he began to issue new orders to his platoon leaders.

∽

With little chance to think the whole problem out, Bannon began to issue orders. On the battalion net, he ordered Team Bravo to turn east, cross the north-south road, go about a kilometer, then turn south, and take the Soviets under fire in the flank with TOWs and tanks. When Peterson acknowledged those orders, Bannon dropped down to the Team net and ordered the FIST chief to call for all the artillery and close air support he could, then find a position from which he could control it.

Convinced the Soviets had emerged from a gap formed by the two hills to their right and guessing more would follow, he then ordered the Mech Platoon to move to the southeast along the tree line and into that gap. There it was to set up an anti-armor ambush in the woods and keep the Soviets from reinforcing the company already in the valley. His orders to the two tank platoons were simple. They were to make a wide sweep and follow 66.

As Alpha 66 turned east and headed up the hill to the tree line, Bannon explained over the Team net what they were going to do. Once they reached the tree line, they would turn south, following the tree line. When they got to the gap, if there were more Soviet tanks already coming out, they would hit them

Map 15: The Battalion Reacts

in the flank. If, however, Polgar got to the gap first and was able to block it, the tanks would turn west and attack the Soviets in the rear. The Mech Platoon would be left to deal with any follow-on Soviets as best they could.

It was all Uleski could do to hang on. The Team commander had his tank roaring along the tree line at full tilt, with the rest of the tanks in the Team were doing their best to keep up. The Mech Platoon had taken off on its own as soon as it had its orders. To their right he caught quick glimpses of the battle in the valley. A dozen or so tracks were scattered about the area burning. The Soviet tanks were clearly visible as they moved forward, firing as they went. At the ranges the Soviets were firing at, they seldom missed.

Gwent, his gunner, kept the gun laid on the Soviets below. The range was too great even if the Team commander had given them permission to fire. At the rate they were moving, however, that would not be a problem in a few minutes.

Uleski could feel his blood rising as he worked himself into a rage in preparation for the upcoming battle. He stoked the fires of his hatred of the Russians by recalling how his first driver, Thomas Lorriet, had died. The image of the young soldier's body on the ground that first day pushed aside any last shred of compassion he had for the enemy as he cursed the Russians out loud over the whine of 55's engine.

∼

As his tank raced along behind 66, Garger realized that he was thoroughly enjoying himself. Despite knowing full well men were dying in the valley below him, and that he and his crew would soon be in the middle of the swirling melee, he felt no fear. That his luck could run out just as easily as Avery's had didn't bother him.

Somehow the idea that he should be enjoying what he was doing, or about to do, seemed inappropriate. But there was no denying the feeling. He had never felt so alive. Standing in the turret of 31 as it raced along, the image of the US cavalry riding out to the rescue flashed through his mind. The only things missing from this scene were a guidon and a bugler sounding the charge. This was his moment. This was why he had joined the Army. "To hell with it," Garger muttered out loud to himself, "This is great!"

∼

A frantic and incomprehensible report on the radio was the first indication that the Soviet tank company commander had that his company was under attack from the north. He glanced to his right just in time to see an anti-tank guided missile slam into the side of a tank. As if on cue, the second American mechanized infantry company that had deployed along the road loosed a volley of antitank guided missiles. He was trapped. Without a second thought, the Soviet company commander ordered his tanks to turn left and cut on their smoke generators.

They had been lucky. His company had succeeded in wreaking havoc on one American company. But the Americans were now gaining the upper hand. It was time to break off this attack, retreat back to the gap his company had emerged from, and wait for the rest of the battalion before renewing the attack.

Team Bravo was in position and firing just as Team Yankee reached the point where they needed to turn and go into the attack. As soon as Sergeant Polgar reported that he was in place, Bannon ordered the tanks to execute an action right, form a line, and attack. Following 66's lead, the other tanks cut right and began to advance back down into the valley. Team Bravo's fire had been effective in forcing the Soviets to break off their attack and had thus taken the pressure off Delta Company. In a massive cloud of smoke being thrown off by their smoke generators, the T-72 tanks that had survived disappeared to the south.

Without hesitation, Folk switched to the thermal sight and continued to track the Soviet tanks as they fled to the south. Bannon could see that it was now a race, leading him to wonder if the Team would be able to catch up to the Soviet tanks fleeing south. Right now, that didn't seem likely. Team Yankee's grand maneuver had been a bust. It had, by going too far out in front of the battalion, taken the Team out of the fight.

Then it struck Bannon that this disaster, or at least part of it, had been his fault. Had he promptly obeyed the battalion commander's orders, Team Yankee would have been closer to Charlie Company and able to support it when the Russians hit. A pure mech company in M-113s on the move was extremely vulnerable to enemy tanks. Team Yankee should have been able to simply turn around to support the infantry. He had, however, been in a hurry to get out in front and reach the Saale. Not only had Charlie Company and the command group paid for his error, the enemy who'd hit them were getting away.

Just as he finished his self-condemnation, the artillery began to impact to the front of the Soviet tanks. The FIST officer, Plesset, having seen the enemy turn south, adjusted the incoming artillery to where the enemy tanks were headed. He had wanted the artillery to impact directly on the tanks, but had misjudged the enemy's speed and distance. This error caused the Soviets to turn east to avoid the artillery. Their rapid change of direction allowed them to escape the artillery, but drove them straight into the Team. The Soviets had either not seen Bannon's tanks and thought their turning east would be safe or they had decided to take on the Team rather than the artillery.

Whatever the reason, the Team now had a chance to finish the job. Without further hesitation, Bannon ordered the tanks to fire at will before issuing his fire command as he laid 66's gun on the lead tank coming out of their smoke screen.

∽

"ENEMY TANKS TO THE FRONT!"

The Soviet tank company commander snapped his head to the front in response to his gunner's yell. Stunned, he watched as a line of M-1 tanks came charging down off the same hill his own company had come down from and toward him. *It had been a trap. The Americans fooled me and now we are lost.* As improbable as it seemed, that was the only way the Russian commander could explain it.

No matter now. There was no time for maneuver. The only thing left to do was fight it out with the American tanks head-to-head. With that thought in mind, he ordered his tanks to attack and began to direct his gunner to engage the lead American tank.

The scene was more like a medieval battle between knights than a clash between the most sophisticated tanks in the world. Like medieval knights, the two groups of tanks charged at each other with lowered lances. Team Yankee had the advantage of surprise and numbers, nine against five. The element of surprise allowed the Team to fire first. This first volley stopped three of the T-72s, blowing two of them up and crippling a third. The return fire from the Soviets claimed a 3rd Platoon tank.

By the time they were ready to fire again, the Team was right on top of the surviving Soviet tanks. Two of 3rd Platoon's tanks drove past the crippled Soviet tank. The turrets of both US tanks stayed locked on the T-72 as they went by. When the two tanks fired on the Soviet at point-blank range, both rounds penetrated, causing the T-72 to shudder violently as internal explosions and sheets of flames blew open its hatches.

One of the last T-72s, about to be overwhelmed, just stopped. The shock of having so many targets so close was proving to be too much for the crew. With no more Soviet tanks that he could see that weren't already aflame, Bannon watched in morbid fascination as the crew of that tank traversed its main gun to engage a tank, but then in the opposite direction to engage a tank that appeared to be a greater threat before suddenly traversing back toward its first target.

As he watched this bizarre spectacle play out, Bannon wondered why none of the Team's tanks were firing on it. They had all slowed down by now so as not to bypass it. Most of the Team's tanks had their guns trained on the hapless Soviet tank. Yet no one fired. Either they felt sorry for this lone survivor, or they were enjoying making the Russian crew suffer the agony of certain death. Whatever the reason, Bannon ordered Folk to fire. He and four other tank commanders had the same idea at the same instant, giving an effective and spectacular coup de grace to the last Russian tank.

∾

Six kilometers to the east, on the other side of the hill, a Soviet tank battalion commander was in the middle of a raging fit. As the lead tank of his second company raced along the narrow trails to catch up with the company already engaged, it had thrown a track making a sharp turn. Now it was blocking the trail.

At first he was not worried. There appeared to be plenty of room for the other tanks of the battalion to bypass the disabled tank with ease. The fourth tank that tried to do so, however, also threw a track. Not only was the trail now hopelessly blocked, the Russian commander now had two fewer tanks with which to attack. As he was watching of the crews of the crippled tanks and a recovery vehicle struggle with the thrown tracks of the derelict tanks, nervously drumming his fingers on the receiver of his NSVT machinegun, the battalion political officer climbed on board his tank and up onto the turret next to him. Squatting down next to the battalion commander, he watched the efforts further up the trail in silence. The battalion commander tried to ignore the political officer, but found that was not possible. "*The bastard,*" he thought, "*He's come here to intimidate me. He'll not succeed.*"

Both were still waiting for the trail to be cleared when the lead company commander reported they were being engaged by American tanks. On hearing this, the political officer leaned over closer to the battalion commander. "Well, comrade, what are *we* going to do? *Your* attack seems to be failing."

This was a threat, clear and simple. The political officer was telling the battalion commander that if he didn't take action, he, the political officer, would. The commander did not hesitate. At least against the Americans he had a fighting chance. One had no chance with the KGB. Before dismounting, he ordered the three tanks that had already bypassed to continue forward and assist the lead company. Once his order was acknowledged, the battalion commander climbed out of his tank, dropped down onto the ground and made his way forward to personally supervise the clearing of the trail. While there was nothing he could do to speed things up, at least the flailing of arms about and yelling might give the appearance he was doing something. It was worth a try.

∾

For a moment, Bannon drew a blank. The sight of smashed vehicles and the stench associated with burning tanks was becoming all too familiar. The fact that the battalion's predicament was nowhere near what the plan had called for was not any different from other operations. It was the fact that he had no immediate superior to turn to for orders and assistance that threw him. On Hill 214 he had been alone, but at least he was still able to carry on with the order that had been issued. This was different. He had one company that appeared to have been wiped out and two companies that were facing the wrong way, watching the fourth company mill about waiting for him, their surrogate commander, to pull his head out and give them some orders. No sooner had the thought *Why me?* flashed through his mind than the answer followed *Because you're it.* For the moment there was no one else, and if he didn't start doing something fast to get the goat screw he found himself in the middle of squared away, the next wave of Russians would finish them.

With time being critical, he contacted Uleski and ordered him to rally the Team's tanks and stand by for orders. Next he instructed Team Bravo to redeploy his team in an arch facing north. The Delta Company commander was ordered to rally his unit, sweep the battlefield to clear it of any Soviet survivors, and provide whatever help they could to Charlie Company's survivors.

With the line companies well in hand, Bannon contacted the battalion S-3 Air, a young captain back at the battalion's main CP and instructed him to report the battalion's current location, its status, and the fact that it was halted to brigade. Additionally, brigade was to be informed that he had assumed command and would contact the brigade commander on its command net as soon as he was able to. With that, Bannon switched back to the Team's command net and informed Uleski that until further notice, he would command Team Yankee.

Not wanting to sit out in the middle of the field by himself, Bannon ordered Kelp to follow 55. Dropping down to where the radios were, he flipped through his CEOI, found the radio frequency for the brigade's command net, switched the frequency, and reset the radio's preset frequencies.

While the battalion net had been relatively quiet, brigade's was crowded with a ceaseless stream of calls, orders, half-completed conversations, and requests for more information. Bannon entered the net just as the battalion S-3 Air was finishing the report Bannon had directed him to make. Not surprisingly, most of the information was wrong. Colonel Brunn, the brigade commander, came back and asked the S-3 Air to confirm the battalion's current location.

Before he could respond, Bannon cut in, giving the correct location of the companies that were still combat effective and his assessment of the battalion's current situation. He ended by informing the brigade commander that in his opinion the battalion was no longer capable of continuing the attack, running down a list of the reasons why. When he finished, there was a moment of silence on the brigade net while the grim news sank in. Then, without hesitation or a long-winded discussion, Colonel Brunn contacted the commander of the 1st of the 4th Armor and ordered him to pass through the mech battalion and continue the attack north. After this message was acknowledged by 1st of the 4th, Brunn came back to Bannon, ordering him to rally the battalion as best he could and to keep the brigade S-3 posted on its status. For the moment, Task Force 3rd of the 78th Infantry was pretty much out of the war.

❧

As Garger led his platoon through the area where Charlie Company, then the Soviet tank company had, for all practical purposes, been wiped out, he realized that he was seeing another aspect of war that he had so far missed, the aftermath, up close and personal. Up until then, all the engagements he'd been part of had been at long range. Even the run through the town of Arnsdorf with the CO during the defense of Hill 214, where they had been eyeball to eyeball with the Russians, had been but a blur, a frenzied dash carried out at night at high speed.

This was different. The slow movement of the Team through the battle area afforded Garger his first opportunity to bear witness to the carnage left in the wake of a battle up close and personal. Everywhere he looked there were smashed tanks and PCs. Some were burning fiercely, throwing off thick, oily black clouds of smoke. Others showed no apparent damage, almost as if its crew had simply stopped their vehicle and abandoned it. It was the dead and the dying sprawled about in tight little groups near the disabled or destroyed track that were most unsettling. To his left, there was a Russian tank crewman hanging halfway out of a burning tank, his body blackened and burning. Over to his right, a group of dead infantrymen who had abandoned their PC in the middle of the fight only to be cut down by machinegun fire. Here and there the wounded were being gathered by medics who were frantically sorting out those who could be saved from those who were beyond help. Garger didn't want to watch. He wanted to turn away. But that was not possible. Even if he could close his eyes and shut out the horrors around him, the stench of burning rubber, diesel, and flesh would have been enough to paint a picture in his mind that was all too vivid, and all too real.

❧

The time that lapsed between hearing the last shot in the valley to the west and the sound of tanks coming from the east could not have been more than five minutes. Polgar heard the distinctive squeak of tracks being pulled through drive sprockets just as the forward security team he had sent out reported that there were Russian tanks inching their way down the trail toward them. Before he gave them permission to pull back, he reminded the NCO in charge of the security element OP he needed to report the type and number of tanks they were observing. Sheepishly, the NCO informed him he could see three T-72s moving through the thick wood toward the draw where the first group of Soviet tanks had emerged.

Instead of trying to hold them in the open at the tree line, Polgar had decided to deploy his three squads further into the dense woods where they would have the greatest advantages and the tanks would be the most vulnerable, if not downright helpless. The Dragons would be worthless in this fight. The antitank guided missile they fired needed to fly some distance before the warhead armed. There would neither be enough standoff distance for them to arm nor a clear line of sight that the gunner would have between him and the tank he was tracking. This fight was going to be strictly man against tank and at very close range.

Anxious to get his dismounts in place as quickly as possible, his orders to the squad leaders were short and sweet. "Get your men in position and under cover. Fire on my command or when the lead tank hits a mine."

With that, he set out along the trail at a trot accompanied by his driver who was carrying the last two anti-tank mines they had. They'd only have enough time for a surface lay and a quick scattering of leaves over them once they were armed. Hopefully, that would be enough. And if it wasn't, then…

Polgar didn't want to think about the *then* as he hustled down the trail. Hopefully, it wouldn't come to that.

∿

It came as great no surprise to Polgar that commanders of the three tanks were all standing upright and leaning as far forward out of their open hatches as they dared. More concerned about keeping from throwing a track as other tanks behind them had, their eyes were glued to the trail just in front of their tanks. None of them seemed to be too concerned with security. The fact that the lead element had passed through these woods without incident apparently satisfied this group of Russian tankers that the trail was clear. Either that, Polgar reasoned, or they were hell-bent on joining the lead company as quickly as they could. Unable to help himself, Polgar chuckled he watched the T-72s advance. They would be, sooner than they expected.

The men who had been on Hill 214 with Polgar were far more confident than they had been before that fight. They'd seen with their own eyes that under the right circumstances, the big Soviet tanks could be defeated. So rather than being fearful, some saw the coming fight as a challenge of sorts, a test to see how fast it would take them to kill the tanks. The detonation of the first antitank mine was their cue to start the clock.

As the Platoon went into action, there was nothing for Polgar to do. Every man deployed along the trail had been hastily briefed on what was expected of him by his squad leader as he'd assigned a position. Machinegunners and riflemen cut down the tank commanders before they could drop down inside their tanks.

Other infantrymen with light antitank rocket launchers, called LAWs, began to fire. A single M72 LAW with a 66mm warhead is not enough to kill a tank. All of the T-72s would need to be hit multiple times before they were destroyed or rendered combat ineffective. With this in mind, Polgar had had each squad leader organize a three-man tank killer team. Each man in the team carried several LAWs as well as his rifle. It was up to each of the three squad leaders to designate the tank his tank killers were to target and give the order to fire. Once engaged, each man would fire in turn, hitting the same tank repeatedly until the squad leader gave the order to ceasefire or they ran out of LAWs.

The first two tanks were dispatched without much trouble. The driver of the third tank, seeing the plight of the first two, had begun to back up as quickly as he dared. He didn't get far. Two infantrymen, on opposite sides of the trail, pulled a mine attached to a rope onto the trail under the third tank as it was backing up. The detonation severed a track, blew off a set of road wheels and brought the tank to a standstill, but did not kill the crew. Trapped in his disabled tank, with his commander dead, the gunner began to spray the woods indiscriminately with machine-gun fire in an effort to keep his unseen assailants at bay.

Before firing its LAWs, the squad attacking this tank tossed smoke grenades at it. Once the smoke was thick enough, the squad leader maneuvered his tank killer team into position behind the tank where he knew the turret would not be able to be turned on them because of the trees lining either side of the trail. Once set, the LAW gunners waited for the smoke to clear. When they had a clear shot, the LAW gunners began to fire. The squad leader was the first to fire. Then the next man loosed his rocket. Then the third. At the range they were at, no one was missing. The LAWs slammed into the crippled tank one after the other at a measured interval. As Polgar watched, he saw that the third tank was doomed. It was only a question of how many LAWs it would take to do the job.

The crew of the tank knew this as well. Deciding there was no point in dying for the Motherland just for the sake of dying, they opted to surrender. Warily, the gunner stuck a hand up out of the commander's hatch and waved a grease stained white rag. Both Polgar and the NCO in charge of the LAW gunners ordered a cease-fire. This was something new. They were finally going to meet the enemy, a defeated enemy.

After the firing had stopped, the Russian gunner stuck his head out through the open hatch and looked around. Only when he was sure he wasn't going to be shot did he continue to climb out. When he saw the first American, he stopped and waved the white rag at him. The gunner didn't move until the American signaled him to climb down. As he did so, the driver opened his hatch and climbed out and onto the ground.

Both Russians were terrified. Searched at gunpoint, their pistols and anything else that could be used as a weapon were stripped from them. While this search was in progress, a squad leader climbed up to check out the tank commander.

When it was discovered he was still alive, two more infantrymen climbed up and gave the NCO a hand, lowering the wounded Russian down and away from the tank while the medic was called. The Russian gunner and driver, seeing this, relaxed. The horror stories their political officers had told them about Americans killing prisoners were lies. They were safe. They would live.

As he worked on the wounded tank commander, the medic thought how ironic this was. Not more than two minutes ago the Russian he was working on had trying to kill them. Now he was doing his damnedest to save the fucker's life. War was definitely screwed up, the medic concluded. He hoped someday someone would explain it all to him. But not now. He had a man's life that needed saving.

❧

Bannon was in the process of gathering the commanders of Team Bravo and Delta Company when Polgar reported the tanks. As soon as he heard about it, he ordered Uleski to take the Team's tanks up to the Mech Platoon's position. Once there he was to establish a defensive position blocking that trail with one tank platoon and the Mech Platoon, holding the other tank platoon back as a ready reaction force for the battalion.

His meeting with the other commanders was further interrupted by the arrival of Major Jordan. A Delta Company PC making a sweep of the area had found the major and the survivors of the command group in a ditch where they had taken cover when their tracks had been hit. Jordan was covered with mud and bloodstains and shaken, but was otherwise all right.

As soon as he saw the gathered commanders, he smiled. "Bannon, I never thought that I would be so damned happy to see those tanks of yours as I was when they came rolling down off the hill. It was great." Still rattled by his near brush with death, Jordan's eyes kept darting about as he talked fast, without pausing to catch his breath.

Bannon was no less happy to see the major and told him so. "You have no idea how glad I am to see you, sir. For a while we thought the whole command group was gone. Did Colonel Reynolds make it?"

"He's been wounded, badly wounded. The medics have him now. Both our tracks were hit in the first volley. That any of us survived is nothing short of a miracle. As it was, we had three dead and five wounded in the command group alone. How did the rest of the battalion do?"

While the Major sat, drinking water and regaining his composure, Bannon went over the current status of the battalion. "Charlie Company has, for all practical purposes, ceased to exist. I attached the two squads of infantry and their PCs as well as one ITV that managed to make it out unscathed to Delta Company," Bannon informed Jordan. "There are still a number of individual stragglers being picked up, but many of them are wounded. All of Charlie's officers and senior NCOs are dead, wounded, or still unaccounted for. I expect it'll be awhile before anyone can come up with a total casualty count for that unit. Delta Company lost three PCs and one ITV. Their total casualties included five dead, thirteen wounded, and three missing. Team Bravo came out of the fight without a single casualty."

"And Team Yankee?" Jordan asked.

"Not counting the one I lost to the Hinds, just one tank was damaged, Alpha 33. Two of its crew suffered minor wounds that don't require anything more than a Band-Aid."

Still shaken by his experience, it took Jordan a minute to take in what Bannon was telling him. When he did look up, he sighed. "The battalion's lost a lot of good men and equipment."

"By my count, fifteen PCs, three ITVs, and one tank in exchange for ten enemy tanks," Bannon replied glumly. "If you ask me, that's a shitty kill ratio. At that rate, we'll run out of tanks and PCs long before they do."

Jordan simply nodded. "Yeah, that's the idea." Then, after drawing in a deep breath, he rose to his feet. "Be that as it may, it is what it is. Now, you and I are faced with the chore of sorting this battalion out and getting back into the fight."

Bannon was about to say he wasn't exactly eager to get back in the fight, but didn't. Shaken by the by the loss of an entire company and his sudden elevation to the command of a battalion that had just been knocked on its ass, Jordan was in no shape to hear something like that. Instead, Bannon nodded. "Roger that, sir."

∽

Major Jordan was still standing on the side of the road with his surviving company commanders when the 1st of the 4th began to roll past and head north. Bannon watched as the tank commanders of his parent battalion surveyed the devastation on both sides of the road as they went by. When the command group of the 1st of the 4th rolled by Headquarters 33, the S-3's tank broke out of the column and headed over to where Bannon and Jordan were.

Major Shell, the battalion S-3 of 1st of the 4th Armor, climbed down off his tank and asked for a quick update on the enemy situation. Jordan gave him what he had, which wasn't much. After taking one more look around, Shell wished him luck, gave Bannon a quick nod, mounted his tank, and took off to catch up with the rest of his command group.

Uleski's report that there were more Soviet tanks coming down the trail towards Team Yankee's position broke up this impromptu meeting. As he prepared to leave, Bannon asked Jordan if he had any orders for him. Still not completely caught up on the overall picture, Jordan simply shook his head. "No, just hold the flank and keep me posted." With that, Bannon mounted Alpha 66 and moved up to rejoin the Team.

∽

Bob Uleski was still in the process of redeploying the Team when an OP Polgar had sent out further up the trail reported more Russian tanks were coming on and coming on fast. Realizing this new wave of Soviets would be able to see the smoke of the burning tanks the Mech Platoon had ambushed, Uleski was reasonably sure the trick of hiding in the woods and hitting them in the flank would not work a second time. Besides, the Mech Platoon had used up most of the LAWs and the last of their anti-tank mines during the last one.

After a quick consultation with Polgar, Uleski decided on a slight variation. Rather than trying to stop the Soviets before they reached the small open area in the woods, they would yield this small patch of open ground to the Soviets. Uleski hoped the Soviet commander would seize upon any opportunity that came his way to deploy his tanks and attack whatever threat he came across in mass. The problem with this, from the Soviet's perspective, was that the lead tanks would need to slow down in order to allow the follow-on tanks to emerge from the woods at the eastern edge of the clearing and swing out to the left and right in order to get into line before attacking across the small clearing.

To meet this attack, he deployed the 3rd Platoon on either side of the trail right at the tree line on the western edge of that clearing. The Mech Platoon, divided into two groups, deployed on either side of 3rd Platoon in positions that would allow them to cover the kill zone with a deadly crossfire using their Dragons. It was a risky plan, one neither Uleski nor Polgar felt completely comfortable with, for the kill zone was little more than a two hundred meters deep, east to west, and three hundred meters wide, north to south. If the Soviets were quick, they'd be able to overrun the 3rd Platoon and push on into the valley where the mech infantry companies were still in the process of sorting themselves out.

As Polgar was about to leave his side, Uleski put a hand out and stopped him. The XO felt as if he should say something, give the veteran platoon sergeant some last minute advise, or share a word of encouragement as Captain Bannon often did. But nothing came to mind. Polgar knew what to do, Uleski told himself. So did he. With that, the young officer wished him luck before heading back to Alpha 55, which was sitting right in the middle of the trail with its main gun oriented to the east.

∾

The lead Soviet tank slowed, then stopped as soon as it reached the eastern edge of the kill zone. Uleski had no doubt its tank commander was reporting back to his commanding officer. Concerned that the Russian had seen Garger's tanks, which the crews had had no time to camouflage, he gave the order to open fire.

As one, two 3rd Platoon tanks let loose, quickly destroying the T-72 and giving away their positions. As he watched the T-72 burn, Uleski got Polgar on the radio and told him to get his people into position fast. With the ambush sprung before he had planned, the XO knew it wouldn't be long before the Soviets made their next move. As he waited to see what it would be, he reported back to battalion, requesting artillery further east along the trail where the Soviets were probably beginning to stack up.

∾

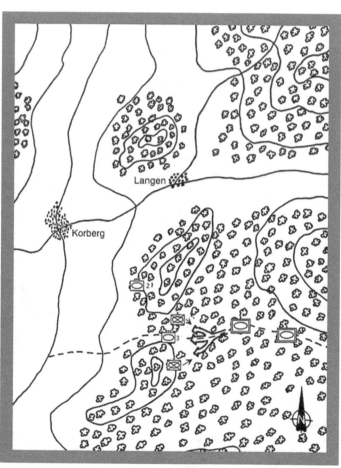

Map 16: The Second Soviet Attack

As unhappy as Uleski was with the situation, the Soviet battalion commander was even more distraught. Every time he thought he was on the verge of breaking out of the cursed woods and into the open, something happened to frustrate him. Even worse, his regimental commander, who was pushing him to attack and seal off the breach the Americans and Germans had made would not listen to reason. With his battalion bottled up on the trail with little room to maneuver, he once more appealed to his regimental commander to allow him to pull back, regroup, and seek out another, more tank friendly avenue of approach. This request was greeted with a hail of threats and abuse, which were followed by a threat the battalion commander knew the regimental commander had every intention of making good on if he failed.

Realizing he had no alternative, the battalion commander ordered his remaining tanks, now down to eighteen, to close up under cover of the woods and wait until he gave the order to advance. When he did, he told the last of his officers they were to rush into the open area to their front, deploy on line as best they could, and attack the far tree line before pushing on and through it. He hoped they would be able to overwhelm the enemy with speed and firepower. He hoped some of his tanks would breakthrough to the open ground beyond even as he was reminding himself that hope was never a sound basis for a plan. Still, with no other choice, he prepared himself as best he could and gave the order to advance.

Major Snow blew up when he was ordered to turn around and fly back to attack the target he had just been told was no longer there. "Those people in flight operations have no idea what they're doing," Snow declared to his wingman over the air and in the clear so that everyone on the net would hear him. "If they wave us off one more time, we're going to go back there and bomb the shit out of them." His wingman, who was just as peeved with the way they were being jerked around, came back with the recommendation that they forget the mission and just bomb the controllers. Still, with little choice but to comply, Major Snow simply shook his head and turned back to the heading they had just left. Maybe, just maybe, he told himself, this time there would be something there.

To Uleski's surprise, rather than pull in their horns and look for another avenue of approach, the T-72s began to pour out of the tree line and fan out to the left and right just as he had hoped. The only problem was Polgar and his people were still not yet in position. With so short a distance and so few tanks to stop the Soviets, Uleski had no doubt that some of the T-72s would make it to them. He knew as they began to fire that it was going to be a hard fight, one he could very easily lose.

∽

During their run in, Snow could clearly see columns of black smoke on the horizon, causing him to wonder if he and his wingman were too late to join the party thanks to the way flight ops had bungled the mission. As they neared the target area, he began to spot numerous vehicles, some of which had already been knocked out, scattered about in a broad valley that ran south to north. But they weren't where he'd been ordered to attack. Further east, in a saddle between two wooded hills marked by several columns of smoke, was where he and his wingman had been directed to.

Banking sharply to their right, the A-10s closed on that spot, which turned out to be a small clearing in the woods crowded with tanks.Neither Snow nor his wingman knew whose they were. Without a forward air controller on the ground to help, the only thing left to do was to overfly them and check them out. Commenting to his wingman that this was a hell of a way to do business, Snow dropped down and went in.

One pass was all he needed. With a firm handle on what was happening on the ground, he brought his A-10 up, circled around, and told his wingman to follow him in on the next run. The tanks lined up on the east-west trail that were spilling out into a small open area were Russians. Finally, they were going to get to kill something.

∽

At first Uleski thought the aircraft that buzzed overhead was Soviet. It had come and gone too fast for anyone to see, not that anyone had been looking. The entire clearing was filled with T-72s. The 3rd Platoon was firing as fast as possible and receiving return fire from the advancing Soviets. When he reported the aircraft, the Team's FIST came back and told him that they should be A-10s he had requested. Not sure, Uleski continued with the business at hand and hoped for the best.

∽

The A-10s came in from behind the Soviets and opened up with their 30mm cannons. In a shower of armor-piercing and HE shells, T-72s began to blow up. As the two A-10s overflew the western edge of the tree line, Snow noticed the American tanks there firing on the Soviets. He cautioned his wingman to watch out for them. There was only two hundred meters between the US and the Soviet tanks. This, he thought to himself as they came around to make another run, was truly close air support.

∽

By the time Bannon arrived on the scene, it was all over.

Pulling up behind Alpha 55, he had Kelp stop. Just past 55, to his front, he could see at least a number of T-72s burning. A quick glance to his left and right told him one of 3rd Platoon tanks had been hit. Dismounting, Bannon made his way over to 55 where he found Uleski, who was just getting over the shock of having been in such a near thing, working up a report for battalion.

As he was waiting for his XO to finish what he was doing, Bannon took another look around. One of Soviet tanks he saw had managed to reach a point less than fifty meters from 55. After a quick update from Uleski, and satisfied the situation was well in hand, Bannon told him to contact Major Jordan and have him stand 2nd Platoon down, that they wouldn't needed by Team Yankee, at least not at the moment.

With nothing more to do at the moment, Bannon made his way back to 66 and waited for battalion to finish sorting itself out and issue new orders. In the meantime, he went over the morning's events in his mind. It wasn't even noon and already the Team had been in four different engagements that had cost it three tanks. "All in all," Bannon muttered to himself, "this is shaping up to be a hell of a day."

CHAPTER 12

"They Came in the Same Old Way"

The Team spent what was left of the morning in its positions, collectively catching its breath and awaiting orders. Slowly, almost unnoticed, a new and unexpected enemy made its appearance, a forest fire. That it happened should not have come as a surprise to anyone. The tracer elements that are part of the main gun and machine-gun rounds, burning vehicles, and flammable liquids leaking from ruptured fuel tanks provided ample ignition sources, the dry, summer foliage, the kindling. Ensconced in a high tech, million-dollar tank, it is easy for soldiers to forget just how much their action and activity affected everything it touched, manmade and natural.

At first no one noticed the burning trees and shrubbery. Fire had become a common sight by now. Only slowly, as the fire in the woods Team Yankee was deployed in began to grow and spread did anyone pay any attention to it. Its epicenter, as best as anyone could tell, was around the tanks that Polgar's men had destroyed in the first engagement. Puddles of fuel, ignited by burning rubber and other onboard consumables set the tree branches hanging over them alight.

Eventually Bannon became aware of the new threat coming from the east. Standing upright in Alpha 66's cupola, he began to study the growing fire. When Uleski, who had been checking the headspace and timing of his M-2 saw his commander warily eyeing the tree line across the small clearing from them, he turned to see what he was looking at. With a single glance, he understood Bannon's concerns. Without using call signs or names, Uleski came up on the Team net, "YOU THINKING WHAT I'M THINKING? OVER."

Looking over at his XO who was seated on top of Alpha 55's turret with his feet dangling through the open hatch of the TC's cupola, Bannon simply nodded before turning his gaze back at the growing forest fire.

After weeks with no appreciable rainfall, the trees and undergrowth was grade-A kindling. Knowing the Team had no choice but to move and move soon, without bothering to call battalion to explain why, Bannon ordered the 3rd Platoon and the Mech get out of the woods. Neither Garger nor Polgar, both of whom had been watching the forest fire as it crept closer and closer to their positions, needed to ask for an explanation.

The move was going to be hazardous. To start, the two platoons could not back away from the tree line and into the woods before turning around. The rapidly spreading fire had, by then, begun to circle around behind them. Instead, they were going to have to move forward into the open and turn, flanking themselves to any enemy force that might still be to their front. Once clear of that hazard, the tracks had to pick their way slowly along the trail leading back to the valley. This would not only slow the Team's displacement, it would be dangerous. One error by a driver or TC could cause a tank to lose its track, blocking the Team's escape route in the same way the Soviet tank battalion had had to deal with. The crew of Alpha 66 already knew about that danger. At the rate the fire was moving, a tank would have little chance of being recovered if it lost a track.

No attempt was made to establish an orderly withdrawal. Bannon ordered the platoons to move on their own using the 2nd Platoon, which was still acting as the battalion's reserve, as a rally point. Uleski in Alpha 55 and Bannon in 66 sat overwatching the Mech, then the 3rd Platoon as they began their move. The air, already oppressively hot from the fire and thick with choking smoke from burning wood, diesel, rubber, and flesh, was filled with tension as the first of the 3rd Platoon tanks rolled into the open. Folk, with his eye glued to his sight as he slowly traversed the turret, watched for any hint of movement from the far side of the clearing. Once Bannon was satisfied that there was no one on the other side who would do anything to his command, he signaled Uleski to begin his move. Alpha 66 stayed in place for another minute, watching the far tree line, before following 55.

The movement through the woods was agonizingly slow for Garger. Even though the platoon had moved forward into positions by creeping along between trees as they were now, it had taken less time, or so it seemed. The idea of being in a tank loaded with ammunition and diesel, surrounded on all sides by a raging forest fire, did not appeal to him. There wasn't a block of instruction taught at Fort Knox that covered what to do in such a situation. Sticking one's ass out to fight the Russians was one thing. Letting yourself get overrun by a forest fire was something else entirely. It was an experience Garger had no wish to embrace.

Following Alpha 32, Garger leaned as far forward as he dared, watching as its crew carefully picked their way through the woods as the lead tank, 32, had the task of blazing the trail. The most difficult part for 31's crew was to maintain their distance and not crowd 32. This was easier said than done. When he wasn't watching where they were going, Garger was glancing between the approaching fire and 32. He had to restrain himself from egging 32 on over the radio. Haranguing SSG Blackfoot would serve no useful purpose other than to add to the growing apprehension everyone in the platoon was feeling. So he held his tongue as he continued to watch 32 plodding along at an unnerving three miles an hour.

The whine of M-113s to his right momentarily diverted his attention. The smaller and more agile tracks of the Mech Platoon were making better time. Their drivers were running at a good pace, weaving between the trees like skiers dashing between poles in a downhill slalom. When Polgar went by, he waved to Garger. The lieutenant returned the wave, then pointed at the approaching fire. Polgar acknowledged the lieutenant's problem with a nod and a thumbs up before his PC disappeared from sight, leaving Garger to wish, for the first time since the war had begun, that he was in an M-113 rather than a tank.

❧

Some say leadership is the art of motivating men to do something that they might not otherwise do. That sounds great in a textbook. As Alpha 66 slowly inched along behind 55 in an effort to escape the forest that was coming on fast, Bannon came up with a few new definitions of leadership. The one that appeared to be most appropriate at that particular moment was something along the lines that a leader was the first man in the unit to put his buns out on the line, and the last to pull them in. As 66 continued its maddeningly slow move through the woods, he wondered if those buns weren't going to get overdone this time.

To take his mind off 66's dilemma, he switched the radio to the battalion net and called Major Jordan in order to inform him of the Team's move. Not surprisingly, instead of contacting the major himself, Bannon found himself conversing with a slow-talking radio/telephone operator who answered for the major. Relaying a message through an RTO can be like getting a new secretary for a major corporation. You know that your message is going to be screwed up even if it finds its way to the right person. His conversation with the major's RTO was a case in point.

First, the man didn't know the proper call signs, insisting that Bannon identify himself fully before letting him proceed with the message. Once he accepted the fact that Bannon really did belong on the battalion net, he couldn't find the major. He had no idea where the major had gone, but said that he would take a message and pass it on. Next, Bannon had to repeat the message twice before the RTO got it down. It wasn't a very long or complicated message. All he had to do was tell the major that a forest fire had forced Team Yankee to displace and that the Team was now en route to the 2nd Platoon's location. Simple. When the RTO finally read the message back slowly and correctly, he made Bannon authenticate to make sure that he wasn't the enemy.

The unusual situation Team Yankee was having to deal with and his efforts to get a message through a slow-witted RTO was all too common, and could be viewed as funny, but only in the past tense. In the present, however, Bannon was finding it to be extremely frustrating and unnerving. There he was, a commander who was in the middle of dealing with a crisis in desperate need of passing an important message over the radio to his higher ups. The only person he can manage to raise on the radio and leave that message with is a class-three moron sitting snug and secure in a command track back in the rear who is just learning how to use a radio. In Bannon's top ten list of frustrating things a commanding officer had to deal with, this sort of thing was near the top.

He had no sooner cleared his mind of the painfully slow conversation with the RTO when the same man came back and told him that his request to displace was denied, that the Team was to stay in place until the major came to the position and discussed the matter in person with him. Bannon was livid. How the RTO had managed to screw up the message even after he'd had the man read it back to make sure the man had it right was beyond him. He didn't give the RTO another chance. Controlling himself, Bannon told the RTO to put the major on the radio ASAP.

By the time he finished with the RTO the second time, 55 was beginning to clear the forest and reenter the valley. It came none too soon, for Alpha 66 emerged from the forest just as the fire began to spread to the tree branches above the tank. A few more minutes would have been a few too many. Once again, luck and timing was on Team Yankee's side.

It was early afternoon before Major Jordan made it up to the Team's new position. By then the two platoons that had escaped the fire had established themselves in the tree line that was not in danger of catching fire on either side of 2nd Platoon. Once there the Team paused to catch its collective breath, unwind, and look after personal needs. It had been on the move or in combat without a serious break for almost nine hours, leaving everyone in a something of a stupor. To a man, the soldiers belonging to the Team were moving with a stilted deliberateness that put Bannon in mind of men who'd had a wee too much to drink. Before the Team could be of any use to anyone, they needed a break. That included him.

Major Jordan found Bannon sitting against a tree a short distance from Alpha 66, stripped down to his tee shirt with his gear in a tangled heap next to him munching on an MRE. Bannon made no effort to stand up or stop what he was doing as Jordan approached.

When he reached Bannon, Jordan stood looking down at him for a long moment. Then, without a word, he dropped down next to Bannon, removed his helmet, unbuckled his LBE, and leaned back against the same tree. When Bannon offered him a canteen, Jordan took it and drank as Bannon continued to eat.

"Sean, it's been a hell of a day so far," Jordan opined after a few minutes "A hell of a day."

Bannon arched a brow as he glanced over at Jordan warily out of the corner of his eyes. "So far? You got some cheery news that's going to make my day even more exciting than it's already been?"

"I just finished talking with the brigade commander. He told me the battalion's done a great job, that he's proud to have it in his command. He then went on to inform me that he had all the confidence in the world that I would do well as its commander."

"Oh-oh. Sounds to me as if the Old Man was setting the new battalion commander up for a hummer of a job. Care to share what it is with this broke dick tanker?"

"I was just about to do that," Jordan declared glumly. "It seems the tank battalion we were hit by is part of a Soviet tank regiment Division believes is still headed our way with the mission of sealing off the breakthrough we've made. The brigade commander feels that since we did such a good job dealing with its lead battalion, we should have the honor of finishing it off when it arrives."

"Bully for us. Did anyone bother to tell you tell you how and where we're to accomplish this martial feat?"

"The where is easy. Everyone thinks they'll attack through the Langen Gap, just north of here. The how is up to us."

"You got any brilliant ideas yet, sir?"

"Not yet. That's why I came here to talk to you. I figure between the two of us we can come up with something."

"Thanks for the vote of confidence, sir. My daddy always said misery enjoys company. Lunch, however, has a higher priority at the moment. Care to join me?"

"Hell, why not. I need some time to get myself together. After spending the last two hours down in the valley sorting out the rest of the battalion, I finally know what General Terry felt like when he came across Custer and the 7th Cavalry at the Little Bighorn."

"Well, if it makes you feel any better, I don't envy your position."

"Sean, stow the saddle soap and pass me some food."

For the next quarter-hour the events of the morning were forgotten, as best they could be, and the chore of preparing for their new mission was set aside as the two officers munched on dehydrated foods. Just as it is necessary for the body to digest a meal, the mind had to be given a break and allowed an opportunity to sort itself out. For most of Team Yankee, the morning events had been nothing new. If anything, some of the men were becoming a little too casual about the death and destruction that surrounded them. For Major Jordan, however, this morning had been his baptism by fire. He was experiencing now what Bannon had gone through during the Hill 214 debacle. No one needed to tell Bannon the major had come to the Team to escape the horror show in the valley as well as in search of someone with whom he could share his new burden. Whether misery really did enjoy company was something Bannon could not attest to. It did, however, need sympathy, and sympathy, in being able to spend time with someone who wasn't staring at him, waiting to be told what to do, or trying to get something from him he could not give was something Major Jordan was in desperate need of at the moment. It was something Bannon was more than happy to give without needing to be asked, or making a big deal of it.

The afternoon was passing quietly. Only the distant rumble of artillery and an occasional crack from a tank cannon to the north broke the stillness. The bright day had given way to clouds and a cool wind coming from the west, foreshadowing a coming storm. In the Team area the crews continued to check their tracks, clean weapons, and redistribute ammunition between tanks in an unhurried, but purposefulness manner. There wasn't much talking or shouting. Very little motion was wasted. A casual observer would have had difficulty determining who was in charge. Officers and NCOs were just as dirty and just as busy, except for Bannon, as the rest of their people. The men knew what had to be done and did it. No one was shouting, no one was rushing about. The Team, through habits born from countless hours of training and drills, was preparing for its next battle.

∿

When they had finished their meal, Jordan unfolded a map and laid it out on the ground before them. Easing into a prone position, Bannon studied the map as the major went over the information he had received from brigade. The Langen Gap was actually a small valley running from east to west, connecting the main valley the battalion was in and the valley to the east where the Soviet tank regiment was located. The town of Langen itself was in the center of the gap with high ground to the north and south.

After studying the terrain, they discussed the various ways the Soviets could come. Both were in agreement they probably would not try sneaking through the woods again. They had already tried that and failed miserably. Odds were, they would attempt to bull through this time using a high speed avenue of approach that would allow them to fully deploy before making contact, hence Division's belief that they would come through the Langen Gap, a conclusion both Jordan and Bannon concurred with. If the Soviets did come through the gap with the intent of maintaining the momentum of their attack, they would be forced to veer north or south of Langen. Thus, the village provided a natural strongpoint and breakwater.

In the gap itself there were few natural positions, other than Langen, from which the battalion could defend. Even if he could, Jordan made it clear he had no intention of putting the whole battalion in the town of Langen or anywhere in the middle of the valley leading up to it. Right off it was decided that Delta

Company, along with the remnants of Charlie Company, would be the only company given the mission of hunkering down in Langen and turning it into a strongpoint. It was deciding where the two teams, Bravo and Yankee, would go that was difficult. There were very few options. If they were deployed on the eastern slopes of the high ground flanking the valley, they would be out on their own and exposed to Soviet artillery and supporting fires. A team deployed on the southern slope of Hill 358 would be masked by the town of Langen and be at too great a range to be of much use.

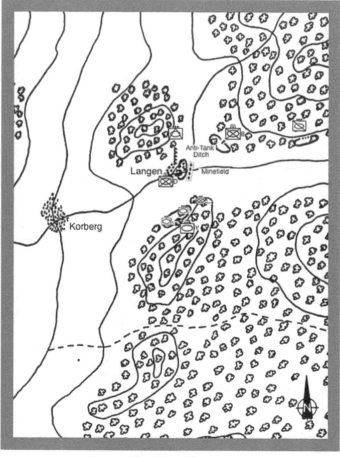

Map 17: The Defense of the Langen Gap

After some discussion, Major Jordan decided that they would go with a reverse slope defense. It would be risky, but there seemed to be little choice. It was the only way they could protect the force and deploy everyone where the entire battalion would be mutually supporting. Team Yankee, with its eight tanks, the Mech Platoon, and two ITVs would deploy southeast of Langen on the high ground facing northwest. Team Bravo, with four tanks, a mech platoon, and two ITVs would deploy northeast of Langen facing southwest. Two ITVs would be positioned on the lower slopes of Hill 358 facing southeast and Delta Company would hold the eastern portion of Langen facing east. In this way, as the enemy force approached Langen and turned either north or south, it would be hit in both flanks. Jordan anticipated that the Soviets would turn south, which is why Team Yankee and the majority of the tanks went there. Just in case they turned north, Bannon was given a contingency mission of being prepared to attack into their flank and rear.

In addition to normal artillery fire support, the brigade was allocating several artillery-delivered scatterable minefields to the battalion. These artillery-delivered minefields, known as FASCAM, consisted of submunitions, in this case mines that were released from an artillery projectile that opened up like a clamshell just above the ground. As soon as the mines landed, they armed themselves automatically. While not powerful enough in most cases to kill a tank, the mines could easily immobilize them by destroying the tracks, slow others that were following, and sow confusion. The plan was to save the scatterable mines until Major Jordan knew for certain where the Soviets were going and were about to be engaged by the battalion's massed direct fire weapons.

The battalion's scout platoon with its five Bradleys would be deployed well forward as a combat outpost line. In addition to warning of an approaching attack, its mission was to engage the Soviets early, stripping away any security elements they might have in front and causing the main body to deploy early. When the Soviet return fire became too intense, they would pull north into the woods and let the Soviets pass. If, in the opinion of the scout platoon leader, his scout tracks could take potshots at the Soviets after they had bypassed his position, they would come back out of hiding and snipe at the Soviet flank and rear.

After dividing the battalion's area of operation up into kill zones and doing some initial plotting of artillery, Major Jordan ordered Bannon to recon Team Yankee's position. He was going to contact the other commanders and have them meet him in Langen. There he would issue his instructions to them and allow them to recon the area. "I want the battalion to be in place and ready by 1800 hours," Jordan concluded as he was preparing to leave. "Do you think you and the other company commanders can manage that without much trouble?"

"We'll be ready," Bannon replied.

"We better be, or I'll go down in history as having had the briefest tenure of command for 3rd of the 78th," Jordan muttered as he gathered up his map.

"Don't worry, sir. The Team will have your back."

Pausing, Jordan regarded Bannon for a moment before giving him a wary smile and a nod. "I'm counting on that."

~

By 1700 hours all platoons were settled in and preparing their positions. Although the brigade could not provide the battalion with replacements to make good its losses in men and equipment, they sent something to them almost as good. A company of engineers with heavy equipment arrived in Langen in the early afternoon. Major Jordan wasted little time in putting them to work digging positions for the two teams and an antitank ditch running from Langen to the northeast. Before the engineers even began the anti-tank ditch, the commanding officer of the engineer company told Major Jordan the chances of finishing it were almost nil. This didn't dissuade the major. In his mind, the presence of even a partially completed ditch might be enough to cause the Soviets to shy away from the northern route and, instead, turn south, where he wanted them to go. In addition to the digging, a squad of engineers assisted Delta Company in setting up a protective minefield in front of Langen.

While Delta and the engineers were busy preparing Langer, Team Yankee deployed along the tree line south of Langen facing the village. Provided the Soviets obliged them, they would be facing the Soviet's left flank as they moved to the southwest. Bannon placed the Mech Platoon on the right at the northern tip of the hill the Team was occupying. From there they would be able to protect the Team's blind side and prevent any dismounted infantry the Soviets might have with them from rolling up the Team's right flank. Next in line was Uleski with Alpha 55, situated between the Mech Platoon and the 2nd Platoon. The 2nd Platoon was to his left. Bannon placed Alpha 66 between the 2nd Platoon and 3rd Platoon. Garger in Alpha 31 tank was on the Team's far left.

During the afternoon, Major Jordan had done some reshuffling of the battalion's task organization based on his recon. The two ITVs Team Yankee was supposed to have were taken away. Instead, they were placed on Hill 358. The major felt the ITVs would have a better field of fire from there. Because the battalion fire-support officer had been killed when the command group had been hit, Lieutenant Plesset, Team Yankee's FIST, was taken by Major Jordan to fill in as the battalion's FSO. As in the first battle, Bannon would have to go through battalion to request artillery. This time, however, it would not be as difficult since the number of options open to the Team and the Soviets were limited and all were well covered with preplanned target reference points.

At 1800, just as the companies and teams were settling in for what promised to be a long and brutal night, a downpour that blackened the sky and came in sheets swept through the area. At first it was a welcome relief. After twenty minutes, however, it started to become a hindrance. The engineers who were still digging the antitank ditch and positions found themselves fighting mud as well as time. The tedious job of emplacing the minefield became a miserable one as well. Hastily dug foxholes rapidly filled with water, forcing the occupants to abandon them and seek shelter in the PCs when they could. They were not the only ones who sought shelter in their tracks. Only Delta Company, with the exception of those people working with the engineers in the minefield, was lucky, for it had been able to take up position in the homes and buildings along the eastern edge of Langen. By the time the last shower passed through at 2000 hours, any joy the men in the battalion had felt over the break in the summer heat had been washed away, replaced by muttered complaints about the cold, the damp, and the mud.

The rain did have one beneficial effect. By coming late in the day, it cooled everything that was not generating heat, thus increasing the effectiveness of the thermal sights. The attacking Soviet tanks would show up as clear thermal images against the cool natural backdrop.

With the exception of the engineers who would continue to work until all light was gone, the battalion was set and as ready as it would ever be. All it had to do now was wait. The tank crews, the infantrymen in the town and on the hills, the scouts, the ITV crewmen, the battalion's heavy mortar men, and the numerous staff and support people that kept the battalion going settled in to wait.

During this interlude Team Yankee, like the rest of the battalion, went to half-manning. The scouts, deployed in the path of any Soviet advance, would be able to give them a good five minutes warning of a pending attack. Uleski took the first watch for the Team while Bannon got some sleep. At first he found staying awake easy. The cold and the damp, coupled with the nervous anticipation kept him alert for the first hour. Boredom and exhaustion, however, soon caught up to him. By 2330 hours he was losing his fight to stay awake and alert. Nothing seemed to be working. Shifting his weight from one foot to another, or shaking himself out made little difference. He even tried slapping his own face. That proved to be just as useless, not to mention painful. Inevitably, no matter how hard he tried, he found he was unable to keep from leaning up against the side of the copula and dropping off to sleep, awakening only when his head fell forward and crashed into the M2 machinegun mount.

Just before midnight, he gave up his efforts and roused his gunner to replace him in the cupola. At the same time, he had the loader replaced the driver. When Gwent was ready, Uleski told him he was going to check the line, wake up the CO, and come back to get some sleep.

As he moved down the line, starting with the Mech Platoon, he was glad to see that the rest of the Team had been able to remain more alert than he had. In the Mech Platoon's area he ran into Sergeant Polgar, who never seemed to sleep. The only way Uleski was ever able to tell that Polgar was tired was to listen to him speak. His slow southern drawl became noticeably more pronounced when he was exhausted, sounding like an old 45 record being played at 33 RPMs.

At Alpha 66 Uleski found Bannon stretched out on top of the blowoff panels of Alpha 66's turret asleep. Looking at Bannon nestled in the middle of the tank's folded camouflage net with the loader's CVC on and plugged into the loader's radio control box, Uleski was at first reluctant to wake him. To have left him alone, even for a little while longer, would have been kind, but ill advised. One of them needed to be awake and alert at all times. Uleski waited until Bannon was fully awake and coherent before he began to update him on the status of the Team and the current situation. This did not take long, as there was little that had changed in the past few hours. Nothing had come over the battalion or team radio nets since radio listening silence had gone into effect. All was quiet.

Bannon was about to tell his XO to go back to his tank and get some rest when a thunderous volley of artillery slammed into Langen and in the saddle between the hill the Team was on and the one just east side it. The flash from the impacts lit up the sky. Division and brigade had been right. The Soviets were coming through the gap.

❧

The men of the Mech Platoon scrambled into their positions as the Soviet artillery continued to crash into the far side of the hill they were on. The water in their foxholes had long since dissipated, but the mud had not. Wherever the infantrymen made contact with the ground, the mud clung to their boots. The added weight, leaving them with the feeling their boots were made of lead rather than leather, slowed them, but not by much as adrenalin and the advent of battle spurred on even the slowest of Polgar's troops.

No one needed to tell them what they needed to do. Riflemen checked their magazines, tapping them against their helmets to ensure that the rounds were properly seated before they loaded their weapons, chambered a round, took their weapons off safe, and placed the barrel on the stake placed along their principal direction of fire. Grenadiers checked the function of their grenade launchers and chambered their first rounds. Machinegunners checked the ammo to ensure that it was clean, dry, and ready to feed. Dragon gunners switched on their thermal sights, checked their systems, and began to scan their areas for targets.

As they were doing so, Polgar trooped the line, stopping at each foxhole, to give each soldier his final instructions, make any corrections that were needed, or offer up a word of encouragement. When he came to a squad leader, he had him to repeat his orders. The image of their platoon leader, illuminated by the flashes from impacting artillery, squatting above their foxhole as he calmly gave them instructions, served to steady rattled nerves and calm fears. His confident and businesslike manner was contagious, binding the platoon into a usable weapon.

The tankers also prepared for their ordeal with a greater sense of urgency, for if the coming battle played out as their commanding officer expected it to, its outcome would be determined by them. The ITVs and the Scout Platoon, firing their TOW antitank guided missiles, and the infantry with their Dragons would contribute. In a battle against a superior and determined foe, every weapon that could be brought to bear counted. In a tank-on-tank engagement, however, the fast-firing M68A1 105mm tank cannon, capable of firing up eight aimed rounds per minute, would decide the issue.

A tank and its crew has but one reason to exist. To maneuver the tank's cannon to a position where it could do the most damage and feed it once it was there. All else takes a distant second. Loaders checked the ammo stored in the turret's ready rack to ensure that the rounds were placed in the order they would be needed. Since they would be fighting tanks tonight, the majority of the rounds fired would be the armor-piercing fin-stabilized discarding SABOT rounds with their long needle-like projectiles. When the loaders were satisfied that the proper ammo was readily at hand, they closed the heavy armored doors that separated the crew from the ammo in the ready rack and checked that the turret floor was clear. In the heat of battle, it would not do to have things clutter the turret. The spent shell casings spewed out onto the turret floor after the main gun fired, rattling and rolling around at his feet, would be more than enough of a challenge to the loader.

The gunners checked their thermal sights, adjusting the contrast and clarity of the image to obtain the best possible sight picture before turning their attention to their computers, checking settings and functions to ensure the fire-control system was ready and operating. Tank commanders, perched in their cupolas, divided their time between watching their crews as they prepared for battle and scanning the tank's assigned sectors. When all was ready, a TC would turn to his wingman and wave until the wingman acknowledged him.

With their weapons ready, the men of Team Yankee prepared mentally for their ordeal, each in his own way. Those who had not forgotten how to do so and still put their faith in God said a prayer. Many of the young soldiers, infantry and tanker alike, weaned on technology, found it so much easier to put their trust in their machines than the concept of a divine being, leading them to check and recheck their weapons. Still, even the most technologically savvy member of Team Yankee could not escape the humbling experience of war, an experience that tends to strip all who survive their baptism of fire of smug pretenses and arrogance. The awesome spectacle of war, and the ever present death tends to bring a man face-to-face with himself. For many of the young men in Team Yankee, it was the first time in their lives they found themselves facing their own mortality. Some found they lacked something, an emptiness. Along the way, a fair number sought refuge and comfort in beliefs long dormant. In the shadow of death, amidst the violence of the coming attack, simple, heartfelt prayers completed the Team's preparation for battle.

∽

Not long after the artillery began pounding Langen, The scouts reported the appearance of the Soviets. They were, as had been expected, tanks, advancing in company columns down the center of the Langen gap. As was their habit, the

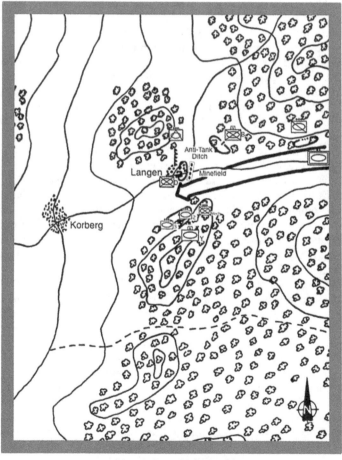

Map 18: Soviet Night Attack

Russian in command of them was waiting until the last minute to deploy. This made it easy for the scouts to divide up the Soviet formation among themselves and engage without needing to worry about the optical tracker of their sights accidently becoming confused with the thermal beacon of a missile launched by another track, a catastrophe that would cause the missile the gunner should have been tracking to lose control of it.

With no need of further instructions from battalion, the scouts began the grim business of the night by engaging at maximum range and calling for supporting artillery fires. The commander of each track focused his full attention on carrying out the battle drill he and his crew had practiced countless times in training, firing, moving, firing, moving.

For his part the Soviet commander, who recognized this threat for what it was, also adhered to his battle drill, doing his best to ignore the scouts. He appreciated the scouts did not constitute a major threat to his regiment. To stop and engage the scouts would not only cost him tanks he could ill afford to lose, doing so would prevent him from reaching the valley and accomplishing their mission in a timely fashion before the enemy could bring additional forces to bear.

The scouts were persistent. Just as a single mosquito can keep a fullgrown man from sleeping, the scout platoon eventually did succeed in drawing some of the Russian tanks away from their mission. A company of tanks peeled off from the formation and began to engage the scouts. In accordance with their instructions, when they found themselves in danger of becoming decisively engaged, the scouts fired a few more rounds to draw their attackers farther away from the advancing regiment. Then, they disappeared into the darkness. The Soviet regimental commander knew they were still out there, waiting to strike again. And though they had done little to impede his advance, they had cost him a number of tanks as well as an entire company that would need to stay behind and keep them at bay.

To the men in Team Yankee, the Soviet advance was an awesome spectacle. Silently they watched as the neatly arrayed horde of Russian tanks bypassed Langen and began to move across their front. The fires burning in Langen provided a perfect backdrop, silhouetting the Soviet tanks as each company deployed from a column of companies into line, with one company behind the other as if they were on parade. As the lead company began to pass to the south of Langen, Major Jordan called for the scatterable mine fields.

Amidst the noise of the Soviet artillery fire that continued to pound Langen, the US artillery-delivered mines arrived almost unnoticed. That is, until Soviet tanks began to run over them. The Soviet officers knew about scatterable mines and their capabilities. There wasn't anything they didn't know about the American military. But to have knowledge about a weapon system does not always mean that you know what to do about it when you encounter it for the first time. The manner in which the Soviets dealt with the scatter-able minefields was a case in point.

As tanks began to hit the mines, shedding tracks severed by the detonation and stopping, company and battalion commanders became confused. Buttoned up and with limited visibility, they at first thought they were under fire and took to searching for the telltale flashes of tank fire or the back blast of anti-tank missile launchers. All the while more tanks hit the mines, stopping them and causing other tanks to slow down or swerve left or right to avoid colliding with disabled tanks in front of them. Belatedly, it occurred to them they were in a minefield.

It was, in the opinion of the regimental commander, an unexpected inconvenience but one that his battalions could deal with. With a single order, the companies began to reform into columns behind tanks equipped with mine plows and rollers. Once he was sure his tanks were out of the minefield, he would give the order to redeploy and continue as before. It was a battle drill they had rehearsed many times before and were able to carry out with little trouble.

It was at this point, when the Soviets were in the midst of redeploying, that Major Jordan ordered Delta Company, the ITVs, and Team Bravo to open fire. The sudden mass volley caught the Soviet regimental commander and the commander of his lead tank battalion off-guard. They had thought that once they had cleared the choke point between the two hills and had begun to bypass Langen there would be no stopping them. It had been, after all, the logical place to stop them as evidenced by the American minefield. Confusion, both in the Soviet battle formation caught in the middle of redeploying and in the minds of commanders faced with an unexpected problem became worse as the Soviet tank company commanders and platoon leaders began to die.

With the Soviets thrashing about in the open, Jordan directed the artillery to switch to firing dual-purpose improved conventional ammunition, or DPICM. Like the scatterable mine, The artillery projectiles were loaded with small submunitions. The submunitions in DPICM, however, were bomblets that exploded on contact and were designed to penetrate the thin armor covering the top of armored vehicles. Confusion quickly degenerated into pandemonium. Some tanks simply stopped and began to fire at their tormentors in Langen or on the hillside to their right. Others tried to carry out the last orders they'd received or simply pressed on. Tanks from the second tank battalion of the regiment which were still in the gap between the hills charged directly toward

Langen. In doing so they ran afoul of the minefields laid by the engineers and infantry. Some tanks, leaderless and commanded by NCOs who possessed a strong sense of self preservation turned toward the woods where Team Yankee was, thinking the silent tree line there offered safe haven.

Sensing that the time was right, Major Jordan delivered his coup de grace. He ordered Team Yankee to fire. The Team's first volley was devastating. Those Soviets headed toward the Team's positions were dispatched without ever knowing what happened. After this first, well-measured volley, the tank crews in Team Yankee began to engage the Soviet tanks in their assigned sectors of responsibility. Firing rapidly, they methodically took out the Soviet tanks starting with those closest to the Team's positions. Above the din of battle, the shouted orders of tank commanders could be heard again and again;

"FIRE!"

"GUNNER, SABOT, TWO TANKS, LEFT TANK, FIRE!"

"TARGET, NEXT TANK, FIRE!"

Like a wolf smelling a crippled animal's blood, the scout platoon swung around to the rear of the Soviet regiment and began to engage, striking the tank company that had been left to guard against it from an unexpected quarter. When the remaining vehicles of that company had all been dispatched, the scouts rushed forward as the battalion began the final stages of its killing frenzy.

ᜎ

The scene before Bannon was staggering. Rising upright in the open hatch of his cupola, he watched the unfolding slaughter taking place in the valley below. Folk no longer needed him to direct his fire. His gunner, the loader, and the cannon they fed and fired were functioning automatically, efficiently, and effectively.

Hell itself could not have compared with the scene in the open space to the front of Alpha 66. Serving as a backdrop was the village of Langen as flames, sent roiling up into the night sky by the impact of incoming artillery rounds, rose high above the village and disappeared in low hanging clouds. From the far left of Bannon's field of vision to the far right and beyond, smashed Soviet tanks and tracked vehicles burned, spewing out great sheets of flames as the propellant from onboard ammunition ignited and blew off whole turrets, sending them tumbling through the air. Burning diesel from ruptured fuel cells formed flaming pools around dead tanks. Tracers and missiles from all directions rained down upon those that were still moving or attempting to return fire, causing stunning showers of sparks when a tank round hit a Soviet tank, or a brilliant flash as a missile found its mark. Soviet crewmen, some engulfed in flames, abandoned their tanks only to be cut down as the chattering machineguns added their stream of red tracers to the fray. Transfixed by this scene, Bannon finally understood what Wilfred Owen was saying when he penned the grim poem, *Dulce et Decorum Est* at the height of the First World War.

❧

As in all the Team's battles, there was no really clear-cut ending. The deafening crescendo of battle suddenly tapered off as gunners ran out of targets. It was replaced by spats of random shooting, usually machineguns searching out fugitive Soviet crewmen trying to escape. No order was given to ceasefire. There was no need to. As before, Bannon allowed the Team to strike down the strays who had somehow survived the destruction of their vehicles. Mopping up is a useful term for this random killing. Team Yankee and Delta Company continued to mop up for the better part of an hour.

When he was sure that the last of the Soviet tanks had been destroyed, Bannon called for a SITREP from the platoons. From his position he could not see any more of the Team than the tanks to his immediate left and right. In the heat of battle, he and the platoon leaders had become totally absorbed in fighting their tanks, often to the exclusion of doing what they should have been doing; commanding their unit. During this engagement, there had been no need to exercise any command or control once the order to fire had been given. It had been a simple case of fire quickly and keep firing. The result was that, although he knew they had stopped the Soviets, Bannon had no idea what it had cost the Team.

At first the replies he received from the platoons were difficult to believe. Though several tanks had been hit, the total cost to the Team had been two men killed and four wounded, all from the Mech Platoon, as usual, and one damaged tank. The positions dug by the engineers, and the fact that Team Yankee had been the last to join the battle after the Soviet commanders has lost control of the situation allowed the Team to come out with relatively light casualties.

Listening to the SITREPs from the other companies being passed over the battalion net, it came as no great surprise to Bannon that Delta Company had suffered far more than either Bravo orYankee due to the artillery bombardment they had been subjected to. Even so, that company was still in good shape and was still able to field three slightly understrength platoons.

By the time Major Jordan got around to calling for a SITREP from him, Bannon's elation at coming out of this last fight as well as the Team had gave way to cockiness. When asked for a report, Bannon took a page of Wellington's book and used the same response he gave when describing the Battle of Waterloo; "They came in the same old way, and you know, we beat them in the same old way."

CHAPTER 13

To the Saale

Dawn of the tenth day of war revealed the full extent of their success. Over eighty Soviet vehicles lay smashed and strewn in the Langen Gap. The largest gaggle of burned-out hulks lay scattered about between Langen and Team Yankee's positions. A few of the tanks had been less than fifty meters away from Team Yankee when they had been knocked out. The battalion, heavily outnumbered and outgunned, by all rights should have paid dearly for holding the gap. But that it had held and had done so cheaply was mostly due to favorable ground, thorough planning and preparation before the battle, and an enemy whose ridged tactical doctrine gave commanders little freedom to deal with a sudden and unexpected crisis.

Yet despite the magnitude of what they had done, there was no visible sign of joy or pride to be found among the tank crews and infantry squads that made up Team Yankee that morning. The efforts of the previous day and night, the emotional roller coaster caused by fleeting brushes with death and brief but intense periods of combat had taken their toll. When Bannon trooped the line shortly after dawn, he was greeted with simple nods or stares by those who were still awake. Uleski, stretched out on top of Alpha 55, was sound asleep. Deciding his XO needed his sleep more than he needed him, Bannon left instructions with Gwent to have him report to Alpha 66 when he woke.

In the Mech Platoon area Polgar had split his men up evenly, with half of them in the foxholes on alert and the rest back at their tracks. Since the mud in the foxholes hadn't begun to dry and wouldn't do so anytime soon, Polgar allowed those men who weren't on duty to stay in their PCs where they could sleep where it was dry. Polgar himself was sitting with his back against a tree, his M-16 cradled in his arms, asleep when Bannon came upon him. As with Uleski, Bannon didn't bother waking him, leaving the same message he'd given to Uleski's gunner with the squad leader in charge.

Only when he was satisfied there was nothing more he needed to do did Bannon make his way back to Alpha 66 where he settled in to enjoy, as best one can, an MRE.

The morning passed quietly. The Team simply remained in position and watched the area to its front for any signs of activity. The chore of sweeping the battlefield after the last of the scatterable mines had self-destructed was left up to Delta Company. This operation gave rise to random shots being fired that no one paid much attention.

Working in small groups, the patrols sent out by The Delta Company commander stopped at each Soviet vehicle to check it. When they were satisfied that the vehicle was harmless, the NCO in charge would mark it with chalk. Those tracks that were still burning were given wide berth. The bodies strewn about the field were also checked. Not many Soviet crewmen had managed to abandon their tanks and tracks when they had been hit. Some had, however, and in spite of the machinegun fire laid down by Team Yankee and Delta Company, a few had survived. When a wounded Russian was found, the patrol would stop and call for medics. An ambulance track darted from place to place picking up those who could be saved. The patrols even came across a few Russians who had managed to hide or play dead through the night. Those who showed even the slightest reluctance to surrender were not given a second chance by infantrymen who were in no mood to be charitable.

∽

Bannon waited until 1100 hours to put word out to the platoons to roust everyone and start checking their tracks and cleaning weapons. When Uleski came around, blurry-eyed and rumpled, Bannon instructed him to compile a complete status of the Team on ammo, fuel, other POL needs, maintenance problems, and personnel needs for each vehicle by noon. At that time Bannon intended to have a short meeting with the platoon leaders to get their current status and give them any news from battalion that he could come up with. Still not quite awake, the best Uleski could come up with by way of response was a sigh, a nod, and a mumbled "Roger, Out" before setting about his tasks.

Kelp and Bannon already had a good head-start on the task of cleaning up and preparing for the next battle. They had spent the morning cleaning 66's three machineguns as well as their own pistols while watching Delta Company's patrols go about their grim tasks in the valley below. Although Kelp had matured a great deal, he was still fascinated by some of the more gruesome aspects of war. Every so often, as he was sitting on top of the turret cleaning a machinegun, he would stop what he was doing and yell out to Bannon. "There goes another one!" Grabbing Bannon's binoculars, he would watch as a patrol stopped to dispatch a Russian who had been hiding and had chosen to flee rather than surrender. After each chase was terminated, usually in a most direct and brutal manner, he would offer his views and critique the patrol's performance, noting that they were using way too much ammunition to bring down the Russians they stumbled upon. When Bannon offered to arrange it so that Kelp could go out there and show the infantry how to do it, he lightened up on his remarks, but continued to watch.

❧

It wasn't until well after noon that Bannon met with Major Jordan, who had been called to brigade headquarters midmorning. On his return, he, in turn, gathered his commanders and staff into Langen for a meeting. He had new orders.

Both the battalion's mission and its organization had changed. Team Yankee, with all three of its organic tank platoons and one mech platoon was being returned to 1st of the 4th Armor. What was left of the 3rd of the 78th was to remain at Langen to cover the Langen gap and serve as a reserve for the Division. Major Jordan explained the reasoning behind all this and what he knew of "The Big Picture."

Division expected the Soviets would renew their efforts to break into the Division's flank even as they were throwing whatever forces they could scrape up between the brigade's lead element and the Saale River. Thus far the brigade had been able to continue the advance, but at an ever mounting cost. At the rate the 1st of the 4th was taking casualties, Major Jordan pointed out, it would soon be combat ineffective.

The problem facing the Division, and the rest of the US Army in Europe, was that it was running out of equipment. Prepositioned war stocks of tanks, personnel carriers, trucks, and all the hardware needed to wage a modern war had run out. Some equipment was arriving from the States, but not nearly enough to replace equipment at the rate it was being lost. Even if the Navy could provide the necessary sealift to carry what was needed and move it across the Atlantic without losing it to Russian submarines, there wasn't enough equipment available in the States to make good the loses being sustained by the United States Army in Europe, known by its acronym USAREUR. At prewar levels, which most of the factories were still operating at, the US could only produce a pitifully small number of M-1 tanks a month. USAREUR was currently losing the equivalent of one month's production of tanks each and every day.

The solution to this problem was simple, but draconian. Since there wasn't enough to keep all units at or near full strength, only those units still capable of carrying out offensive operations or holding critical sectors would be receiving any replacements of men and equipment for the foreseeable future. The 3rd of the 78th, which was no longer capable of offensive operations, was one of those units that fell in that latter category.

"That doesn't mean we're out of the fight," Major Jordan cautioned his commanders and staff. "Our orders are to hold Langen and parry any renewed efforts by the Soviet's to punch trough into the brigade's flank while the balance of the brigade continues to push north."

Major Jordan had no need to elaborate what that meant. Without Team Yankee, the battalion would be down to two understrength mech infantry companies. If the Soviets did manage to find the forces necessary to make a new attack through the Langen Gap, the odds of stopping them were slim. "Division G-2, relying on the old Russian maxim of never reinforcing failure, does not expect another attack here," Jordan pointed out. "Still, they don't discount that possibility."

Needless to say, this left everyone in the room, save Bannon, in a somber mood. After issuing some initial planning guidance to the commanders of Team Bravo and Delta Company, he dismissed them. When they were gone, he gave Bannon instructions on when and where Team Yankee was to link up with the 1st of the 4th. Prior to leaving to return to his Team, Bannon coordinated with the battalion S-4 for rearming and refueling before the Team departed that evening. Then, with no further business in Langen and much to tend to, he too headed out, leaving Major Jordan to huddle with his staff in order to work up a new plan for holding Langen with what they had left.

∾

News that theTeam would be returning to 1st of the 4th was welcomed by Uleski, Garger and SFC Hebrock. Even Sergeant Polgar seemed to be pleased, explaining that as far as he was concerned, it really didn't matter to him where his platoon went so long as it stayed with Team Yankee. When Bannon thanked him for his vote of confidence, Polgar replied that confidence had nothing to do with it. According to him, the chow in Team Yankee had always been good, and good food meant he had fewer complaints to listen to from his men.

Second Lieutenant Murray Weiss, the leader of 1st Platoon, was particularly happy to be back to the Team. He had the honor of being the company's only Jew, a fact that left him open to a great deal of ethnic humor. Fortunately, like Bob Uleski, he had an almost infinite capacity to absorb incoming jokes and return them in kind, a trick he had learned at an early age. Weiss's decision to make the military his career had come as quite a shock to his family. The US Army was not normally something that college-educated Jewish boys were taught to aspire to. But Murray had deep convictions. The Israeli tankers who had fought in the Sinai and on the Golan in '73 had been his childhood heroes. While his friends aspired to be doctors or lawyers, he dreamed of being a tanker like Gen. Mordecai Tal or Avigdor Kahalani. Weiss's performance before and during the war showed he was well on his way to achieving that dream.

The Team had much to do before it began its move shortly after nightfall. As badly as the 1st of the 4th needed them, to leave their positions before dark would telegraph to the Soviets the weakness of the Langen Gap. Though no one at brigade or Division expected it would not take the Soviets all that long

to figure out the tanks were no longer with 3rd of the 78th, no one was willing
to make discovering that fact easy for them.

Even with the move several hours off, the leadership and men were kept busy.
Bannon spent a great deal of time going over his thoughts on what needed to
be done in regards to organization, rearming, refueling, and other such details
with Uleski. He also gave him all the information he had on when the Team was
to move, its route, and final destination. "I'll be taking the first sergeant's track
and going to the headquarters of the 1st of the 4th to get additional information
and, maybe even an operations order," he informed his XO. "If I'm not back in
time, you're to start the move without me. Since I expect 1st of the 4th will be
part of the final drive to the Saale, the sooner I find out what the Old Man has
in mind for us, the more time I'll have to plan and then get the Team ready."

The trip to the 1st of the 4th Armor's headquarters took him back into the main
valley that the Team had advanced into the previous day and through the town
of Korberg. The valley had changed overnight. Roads that had previously been
barren of any traffic save an occasional tracked vehicle were now crowded with
convoys of trucks carrying fuel, munitions, and other supplies forward and empty
trucks coming back. There were also numerous grim reminders of the cost the
brigade had paid for the progress it had made. Along the way Bannon passed
an aid station set up outside Korberg that was drawing ambulances bearing
freshly wounded soldiers like a magnet, keeping doctors and its medical staff
busy. No doubt, he thought to himself, he would soon be adding more of his
own to those already there.

Farther north, he came upon evidence that told him 1st of the 4th had
not had an easy time after they had passed through 3rd of the 78th. M-1s,
PCs, Soviet tanks, and smashed wheeled vehicles of every type and description
attested to the severity of their fight. In the fields on either side of the road
maintenance recovery teams were busy retrieving those tanks and personnel
carriers they deemed to be repairable in a reasonable amount of time. As he
passed a maintenance collection point he recognized several of the mechanics
from 1st of the 4th. They were busy piecing together a track and a set of road
wheels scavenged from one disabled tank in an effort to get another that looked
as if it had hit a mine ready for the next attack. This was no easy task, for each
track of an M-1 tank consisted of eighty track blocks, eighty center guides, and
one hundred sixty end connectors that, when assembled, weighed two tons. Were
it not for the tireless efforts of these people, many of the units that were still in
the fight, including Team Yankee, would have ceased to exist a long time ago.

Bannon found both Lieutenant Colonel Hill and Major Shell at the battalion TOC. Along with the battalion intelligence officer, Capt. Ken Damato, they were discussing the upcoming operation in front of the intelligence map. Having no wish to interrupt them, and eager to find out what they would soon be expecting of his Team, Bannon stood in the background and listened.

Apparently Hill already had a plan in mind and was merely getting an update on enemy units recently reported entering the area of operations and their activities. Damato was pointing out several Soviet battalion-sized units northeast of the Saale that had been located and were being tracked. Never one to miss an opportunity to add a bit of levity to a task that was, by its very nature, grim, across the top of the intelligence map in the area north of the river he had printed "HERE BE RUSSIANS" in large red letters in the same way ancient mariners did when charting unknown waters.

Major Shell was the first to take note of Bannon, "Well, prodigal son returns. What happened? Did the infantry finally get tired of putting up with you and turn you out with the cat?"

"Something like that," Bannon replied as he made his way up to the map where greetings were exchanged. Like Major Jordan and his staff, Hall, Shell and Damato were haggard and tired. Without any further ado, Colonel Hill asked Bannon how much he knew of the upcoming operation.

He informed his colonel that other than the fact that he had been told where and when to report, he knew nothing. Upon hearing this, Hall told Major Shell and Damato to go over the operation with him. When they were finished, he turned back to Bannon and told him he was to see him when the S-2 and S-3 were finished. With that, Colonel Hall headed out to wash up.

The operation that Major Shell laid out before Bannon was nothing more than a continuation of the attack toward the Saale 1st of the 4th had been engaged in since passing through 3rd of the 78th. There were a few new twists to the way 3rd of the 78th had approached the same problem, but basically it was the same. At that time 2nd of the 94th Mech Infantry was hacking its way through a defensive belt the Soviets had hastily thrown up across the brigade's axis of attack. While it was not nearly as impressive as the Soviet defensive doctrine called for, it was proving to be enough to grind down the 2nd of the 94th. Progress was slow and the brigade commander did not believe that there would be enough of that battalion left to make the final push needed to reach the Saale.

That's where the 1st of the 4th came in. Since closing up behind the 2nd of the 94th early that morning, 1st of the 4th had been preparing for a river-crossing operation. All available assets were being concentrated in the battalion for this final push. If 2nd of the 94th's attack stalled by nightfall, brigade's plan called for the 1st of the 4th to pass through the 2nd of the 94th and continue the attack. Once at the Saale, 1st of the 4th would make an assault crossing and establish a bridgehead. As soon as the engineers had a bridge in place, other elements of the

TO THE SAALE

25th Armored Division, now in reserve, would pass through the battalion and continue the drive on Berlin, leaving the 1st of the 4th to protect the crossing point.

The attack of the 1st of the 4th was not the only effort that would be going on that night. The 2nd Brigade would also be attempting to make an assault crossing of the Saale farther to the west. Their mission was identical to 1st of the 4th's. They were to establish a bridgehead, allow the 25th Armored to pass, then protect the flank. It was hoped that both efforts would succeed. The 25th Armored, however, was hedging its bets. The first battalion to make it across and secure a viable bridgehead would become the main effort. The other battalion, if it were still combat effective, would make its way to the bridgehead that had been secured.

Ken Damato went over what he knew of the current enemy situation. Until that morning, the Soviets had been trying to stop the Division's drive through counterattacks, head-on and in the flanks. Like 3rd of the 78th, 1st of the 4th had fought the better part of a tank regiment the previous night after a meeting engagement in the valley. While the Soviet tank regiment had been stopped, so had the 1st of the 4th. That is why the 2nd of the 94th had been passed through it. That battalion had been fighting its way through a series of platoon and company sized strong points since midnight. Progress had been steady, but slow and costly. Reconnaissance of the area immediately south and north of the river showed little indication that the Soviet defense had any depth. "Division believes they've shot their wad," Damato informed Bannon. "The new enemy units G-2 has identified moving into the area are believed to be fragments of shattered units being thrown in as a last resort."

"Kind of like us," Bannon remarked.

"Yeah, kind of like us," the S-2 muttered as if to himself before continuing, "If that proves to be the case, the prevailing belief is that once we're across the Saale, there will be little, if anything, that will keep us from pushing to Berlin itself."

Major Shell took over from Damato at this point. "The plan's simple, Sean. Once 2nd of the 94th has cleared the last of the Soviet positions, or if it finds it can no longer continue, 1st of the 4th will pass through it and make for the river. No finesse, no grandiose schemes of maneuver, just a mad dash for the river at the best possible speed. The battalion has orders not to stop. The brigade commander wants us to vault across and establish the bridgehead on the run. The idea is to establish a secure bridgehead before the Soviets can do anything about it."

"The problem with such a simple plan is that once the battalion starts rolling, the Soviets will be able to figure out where it was going and what it intended to do," Damato pointed out when Major Shell paused. "It won't take them long to figure out what we're up to, if they don't already know."

"What we can do," Shell continued, "is confuse and deceive them as to where the main effort is going. To this end, a reinforced company team will create a diversion for the purpose of deceiving the Soviets as to what thrust constitutes our main effort."

At this point, Shell took to staring at Bannon with an expression that told him that was where Team Yankee came in.

"Team Yankee, with three tank platoons, a mech infantry platoon and the battalion Scout Platoon attached will conduct a supporting attack on the battalion's right," Shell informed Bannon. "Your mission is to give the appearance that Team Yankee is the battalion's main effort by driving hell-bent for leather for a highway bridge on the Saale. While the Soviets will drop the span before you get there, the area near the bridge offers several excellent crossing points. A threat to that area can't be ignored. It's hoped that your attack will draw the Soviets' attention and reserves while the true main effort farther to the west is ignored. With the exception of where you'll be going and that you're to make as much noise as possible on your way there, you have a free hand as to how you go about accomplishing you mission."

Shell stopped for a moment and took a step back, allowing Bannon to take a closer look at the map and consider the task he'd just been given. "Where do you anticipat we'll be passing through the 2nd of the 94th?" was the first question he asked.

The major showed him a point about twenty kilometers south of the Saale. "What will I have in the way of fire support and close air support?" was his next question.

"There are several target areas that will be hit near the bridge by the Air Force at first light in order to support this ruse. In addition, the Team will be supported by the better part of an artillery battalion until one of the other battalions is in a position to begin crossing the river. At that time Team Yankee will lose priority of fire."

Bannon looked at the major, then the map, then back to the major, shaking his head as he did so. "You brought me all the way here to give me this nightmare?"

"What are friends for?" Major Shell quipped. "The colonel thought you'd be thrilled. After all, we're giving you a chance to excel."

At the moment Bannon's reserve of humor was exhausted. He found nothing funny about what the Team was being asked to do. Once more, Team Yankee was going to be on its own, rolling into the unknown. Compared to what he and Team Yankee had been, and were being asked to do, he reasoned the Light Brigade had it easy. They'd only been asked to do the impossible once. Team Yankee was having to do it over and over again. "If you want to give me something, give me four tanks, a dozen trained infantry replacements, fuel, ammunition, and a four-day rest in the rear. Do you know what kind of shape the Team is in?"

Major Shell sensed Bannon's change in mood. When he spoke, Bannon was able to tell he was now being deadly serious "Sean, I'm sure you saw the burned-out tracks along the battalion's route of advance on your way here. We're all in bad shape, with no prospect of getting any stronger any time soon. Our war reserves in Europe have been used up. It will be another month before the

Guard and Reserve units get over here. If we wait for them, the war will be over. We either do it now with what we have, or we lose. It's that simple."

Bannon took to looking down at his boots as he considered what Major Shell had said before sighing. "I know, I know. Major Jordan went over the same thing with me before I came here. It's just that since the war broke out, the Team has been getting the smelly end of the stick every time we turn around. Everyone, including me, is getting tired of putting his nuts out on the chopping block whenever a new mission comes up. So far we have been lucky, damned lucky. That luck isn't going to last, though. One of these times the Russians are going to come down fast and cut us to pieces. Why can't someone else get a chance to excel?"

"Sean, whether or not you know it, your Team has one hell of a reputation. When the Old Man was given this mission by brigade, Colonel Brunn specifically designated Team Yankee as the force to conduct the supporting attack. Everyone agreed that your Team was the one that could pull it off if anyone could. You're it. You can moan and groan all you want, but in the end, you've got your orders."

The rest of the meeting was conducted in a curt, businesslike manner. Shell provided additional details, answered Bannon's questions, and asked if there were anything he needed that he could provide. Bannon decided to end the meeting on a lighter note, pointing out to Major Shell that in the future he could save the saddle soap and come up with easier missions. When he was finished in the TOC, Bannon sought out the battalion commander and talked with him for a few minutes about the condition of the Team and its new mission. There was no point going over arguments he'd already put forth with Shell. The decision was made, and he wasn't going to get it changed no matter what he said or did. All Bannon could do now was give the commander a "Yes, sir, yes, sir, three bags full" and drive on. There was much to be done and not much time.

～

Before he returned to the Team, Bannon stopped by the assembly area the Team would occupy before attacking. He found the scout platoon already in position. The platoon leader, Sergeant First Class Flores, and Bannon discussed the mission and his role. He assigned Flores the task of selecting positions for the rest of the Team in the assembly area and instructed him to provide guides when it arrived. With that taken care of, he started back for Langen and Team Yankee.

The Team never made it to the assembly area. The 2nd of the 94th, in one last push, succeeded in smashing their way through the Soviet's last defensive belt before destroying a half-hearted counterattack by an understrength Soviet tank battalion. This set in motion a change in mission, issued to Bannon over radio while the Team was still en route to its assembly area. Those orders required it to move immediately to a passage point where they were to be met by the Scout Platoon, which Major Shell had sent ahead, and an officer belonging to the 2nd of the 94th who would be on hand to affect and expedite Team Yankee's passage through his unit and a marked lane through a Soviet minefield that had been breached earlier. Once through the minefield, Team Yankee would be on its own.

Lieutenant Weiss' 1st Platoon was the first through the minefield. After giving his platoon the order to deploy into a wedge, he took to surveying the terrain to his front with the aid of his night vision goggles. Upon seeing no sign of the enemy, he glanced over to his right and watched as the Scout Platoon, which had been following his platoon through the minefield, begin to deploy. Like his platoon, it also was forming a wedge. The Mech Platoon was next, followed by Alpha 66. Before turning to his front, he watched as 66 pulled into a position between his platoon and the scouts, waiting to see if his Team Commander signaled him to slow down or change the direction in which his platoon was moving. Only when he was satisfied that all was in order did Murray Weiss leaned back in the cupola and allowed himself a brief moment to relax before focusing his entire attention back to the front and what lay ahead.

Unlike his platoon, the balance of the Team, after spending a relatively peaceful afternoon near Langen, had been on the run ever since the Team commander had returned with its new mission. Pre-combat checks, preparation for the night move, boresighting the tanks, receiving the Team order, and issuing the platoon order had taken up the balance of the afternoon. Immediately after darkness had fallen, the Team moved out for its forward assembly area where it was to wait for the order to pass through the 2nd of the 94th.

Weiss was pleased with the Team's mission and the orders Bannon had issued. In order to create the illusion that it was more than a single company sized element, Bannon had divided the Team into two parts. The XO, with the 2nd and 3rd Platoons, would move along a separate route about one kilometer west of the rest of the Team. Bannon, with the 1st Platoon, the Scout Platoon, and the Mech Platoon took a more direct and obvious route toward a highway bridge on the Saale. The order to bypass all resistance and go flat out regardless of the cost pleased both Weiss and Garger. The two lieutenants were tired of being held in check and having to wait for someone else to get their shit together. Although the Team commander tried to dampen their enthusiasm, explaining that moving fast in the face of the enemy was a recipe for disaster, the lieutenants were thrilled that they finally were going to have a chance to do some no-holds-barred tanking.

The crack of a tank cannon and the blurted contact report from 3rd Platoon jarred Weiss back to the realities of war. The element with the XO had made contact. The Team commander had been right, Weiss told himself as he straightened up in the cupola and began to scan the horizon with greater care.

No one saw where it had come from. One minute there was nothing. The next minute, there it was. It was as if the BTR-60PB had popped up out of the ground less than two hundred meters in front of Alpha 32. Without slowing his pace, and with a single round that went right through the BTR, Blackfoot destroyed it.

The engagement was over before it even registered on Garger his platoon was in contact. He automatically ordered the platoon to go from a wedge to an echelon formation angled back and to the left. This was done without confusion and without breaking stride. After a quick contact report to the XO, Garger turned back to his front and peered into the darkness. Neither he nor any of his tank commanders were able to detect any further signs of the enemy. As best Garger could tell, the burning BTR, now well to the rear of his platoon had been alone, leaving him to wonder if it was part of a forward security screen. If that was the case, then the Russians knew they were coming.

A tank belonging to the 2nd Platoon, to 3rd Platoon's right, fired next, causing Garger to whip around to see what it was firing at. Following the tracers from the 2nd Platoon's rounds, he saw several forms moving away from the Team. A brilliant flash and shower of sparks, followed by an eruption of flames lit up the night. One Soviet tank had been hit and destroyed. A second Russian tank, clearly illuminated by the flames from the one that had been hit, could be seen fleeing north. It did not make it, however. Another tank in 2nd Platoon dispatched it within seconds of the first.

"TANK, TWELVE O'CLOCK, MOVING NORTH!" At first, Garger thought that his gunner was looking at the same tank that he was looking at. Then he realized that the gun tube was still pointed to the left. Dropped down to his sight, he saw the tank his gunner had found. For a moment he hesitated. Bravo Company, 1st of the 4th, was somewhere off to their left. The last thing he wanted to do was fire on a friendly tank.

Garger studied the target in his thermal sight for a moment. He could make out the turret and the tracks. It was definitely moving north. But did it belong to Bravo Company, or was it Russian? Then he noticed that the rear of the tank was dark. The exhaust from an M-1 tank is vented out the rear, creating a tremendous heat signature. If the tank was an M-1, its rear would have been bright green. The tank was Russian. Without further delay, Garger issued his fire command, cutting short the flight of another Soviet tank.

When a quick scan of the area to the left and right of the tank they had destroyed showed no sign of any other threats, Garger stood upright in the cupola. As harrowing as the previous day's engagements had been, the suddenness of these encounters and the unpredictable randomness with which the enemy seemed to be popping up all over was proving to be down right nerve-wracking. "Give me a stand up fight in the open any day of the week," he muttered to himself.

"What was that, LT?" his gunner called out to him over the intercom.

When Garger realized his CVC push-to-talk was keyed in the intercom lock position, he told his gunner he was just thinking out loud before unkeying his CVC.

Having grown used to the strange ways of officers, the gunner thought nothing of it as he went back to searching for new targets.

༄

The young Ukrainian engineer lieutenant was not pleased with his orders or with having a KGB captain at his side watching his every move. The KGB captain and his people were supposed to be at the bridge to gather up stragglers and control movement. The young lieutenant was smart enough, however, to realize that the squat, stone-faced captain also had the task of ensuring that the people defending the bridge and preparing it for destruction followed orders. Why else did the little shite follow his every move and question every order he gave?

At the moment the officer of engineers had nothing much to do but watch elements of the 15th Guards Tank Division as it withdrew across the bridge. Though no expert on tank tactics, the lack of anything resembling order with which the units were crossing left him with an uncomfortable feeling in the pit of his stomach. A tank unit was followed by a maintenance detachment, which in turn was followed by an artillery unit with a field hospital mixed in. To add to the confusion, the KGB captain would halt units at random and demand to see written orders giving them permission to withdraw to the north side of the river. Most of the units did not have these, having received orders over the radio. The KGB captain knew this, but persisted in stopping units anyway.

The thing that bothered the engineer lieutenant the most was the manner in which the KGB dealt with stragglers. When individuals were spotting crossing without their unit, they were taken over to the side of the road and questioned. At first the KGB captain was called in to consider each case. After awhile, however, he tired of this and allowed a young and enthusiastic KGB lieutenant to deal with the enlisted stragglers. The captain only wanted to be called if there was a need to deal with an officer who could justify his need to retreat north of the river.

Justice, KGB style, was quick. The engineer, at the insistence of the KGB captain, watched each series of executions. Once a straggler was determined to be a deserter, he was put into a small wooden shed at the south end of the bridge. When the shed was full, the convicted deserters were lined up next to the road in full view of the troops moving across the bridge. The KGB lieutenant would read a statement outlining the crimes committed against the State and Party before giving the order to fire. The first time he watched, the engineer lieutenant became violently ill. As he bent over to throw up, the KGB captain slapped him on the back and told him he had nothing to worry about. "Officers who follow their orders need not concern themselves with me or my men. It's the miscreants I am here to deal with, the scum who value their own miserable hides above the needs of the Motherland."

The engineer was no fool. He understood the captain's statement was a promise, not a threat. He also knew that if he dropped the bridge without first receiving permission, the next time the KGB captain slapped his back, there would be a knife in his hand.

~

The sudden spat of engagements stopped as rapidly as they had begun. The Team was halfway to the river and making good time. Bannon reasoned that the Soviets they'd encountered thus far were strays, individual tanks and vehicles shaken loose from their parent units who were not interested in offering resistance. Still, after reporting these encounters and his assessment of the situation to Major Shell, Bannon redoubled his vigilance. Things had a nasty habit of changing very rapidly. Half a dozen tanks and a couple of well-placed antitank guided missile launchers in ambush could raise hell with the Team. Expecting to make contact with just such delaying forces at any minute, he put out a net call, instructing his platoon leaders to stay alert and look sharp.

The nearer the Team came to the river, the more unbearable the anticipation of just such an event became. Like Garger, Bannon was beginning to believe an outright shoot-out with the Russians in the open, even an enemy who outnumbered the Team, was preferable to rolling around in the dark waiting to be hit. Despite his best effort to keep from doing so, every time the Team approached a point he had marked on his map he thought was an ideal position from which a Russian delaying force could engage the Team, Bannon held his breath. And each time the Team's lead elements bypassed a point he had identified as an ideal location for an ambush without being challenged, he would let out the breath he had been holding and relax the grip he had on the rim of his cupola. This lessening of tension never lasted very long. Without fail, just as he was managing to calm down some, the next critical point would be reached, causing him to once more tense up in anticipation. Before long he came to the conclusion if they didn't reach the river soon or make contact with the Russians, he'd have a nervous breakdown. It really didn't matter to him which came first. Anything, he told himself, had to be better than dealing with the stress and strain of the unknown.

In an effort to take his mind off his growing fears, Bannon checked his map. The next critical point they would hit was a small town. He would have preferred to bypass it. Going through it at high speed was not only dangerous, but picking their way through the narrow, twisting streets of a German village would slow the Team's momentum. Still, rushing by it without at least checking it out could be even more dangerous. An entire Russian tank company could be hiding in it, just waiting for the Team to bypass it before coming out behind them and whacking them a good one up the butt. Just to be sure, he ordered the scouts platoon to make a quick sweep through it since part of the Team's mission was to be noticed, and running through a town shooting up any headquarters or rear echelon units that were in it was a good way to get noticed.

At the same time, he was ordering the Scouts to go in, he instructed the 1st Platoon and the Mech Platoon to go around the town to the west. If the scouts did run into light resistance, they were to bull through. If the Soviets were present in strength and the scouts got in trouble, they were to back out and follow the rest of the Team.

As ordered, the 1st Platoon veered off to the left just as the scouts were forming up in single file on the road as they prepared to hit the town at a dead run. The lead scout track had no sooner entered the town when the sound of machinegun fire and flashes of light reflected off the buildings of the village lit up the night. A hasty contact report from Sergeant Flores informed Bannon they'd run into a Soviet recon unit in the town square and were taking it under fire as they rolled through. Bannon reminded him that he was not to become decisively engaged, that he was to get out of there as soon as possible to rejoin the Team. With the din of battle clearly audible over the radio as he responded, Flores gave Bannon a curt "ROGER, OUT" before continuing to fight his way through the town.

Though concerned that the scouts might not be able to extract themselves, Bannon was able to take some comfort in the fact that they had finally run into the Soviet recon element. No doubt whoever was in command of it would get a report back to his parent unit that he was in contact with the Americans. In doing so, he would help accomplish part of the Team's mission.

∽

The sound of firing just south of the river startled both the engineer lieutenant and the KGB captain. As one, they looked in the direction of firing, then at each other. For the first time that night, the lieutenant noted a look of concern and uncertainty on the captain's face. Together they began to make their way to the southern end of the bridge in search of the commanding officer of the motorized rifle company who was responsible for its defense.

The firing could also be heard by the soldiers who were attempting to cross the bridge. Not wanting to be caught on the wrong side of the river when it was blownup by the engineers, they began to push and shove their way forward. The impatience of the drivers gave way to anger when they felt the people in front were not moving quickly enough. Truck drivers began to blow their horns and nudge the vehicles to their front in an effort to move things along. This did nothing but add to the confusion and push the mass of troops and drivers on the bridge ever closer to panic. What little order there had been before firing had erupted in the village disappeared.

∾

With the Team now but a few scant kilometers off the bridge, Bannon decided it was time to start making a lot of noise in an effort to give the appearance that they were going to attempt a crossing. He ordered the Team FIST to fire prearranged artillery concentrations on both the north and south side of the bridge. Since the bridge was gone, or would be as soon as the Soviets waiting to drop it saw Team Yankee coming, he figured artillery fire wouldn't hurt anything. It would, however, appear to the Russians that they were firing a preparatory fire as a prelude to an assault crossing. The longer and more convincing his deception was, the easier it would be for those units that were part of the Division's main effort.

∾

With the first impact of artillery, the KGB captain dropped all pretense of being calm and unconcerned. The idea of facing American combat troops terrified him. He and his men knew what would happen to them if they were captured. Yet the KGB captain also knew he and his men could not leave the bridge, not without orders. To do so would be considered desertion. After dealing with deserters all night, he had little doubt what would be waiting for him if he left without orders. His only hope was to secure permission to leave from his superiors.

To this end, both the engineer lieutenant and the KGB captain tried to make it over to the southern side of the bridge where the captain responsible for the security of the bridge had his headquarters. They were, however, fighting the tide, as everyone on the south side was trying to make it over the bridge and to safety before it was blown up. Vehicular traffic had come to a complete standstill. Vehicles hit by artillery, crashed into each other, or abandoned by their drivers were blocking the exit on the north side and the entrance on the south, making it difficult even for foot traffic to pass.

As they pushed their way against the flow of fleeing troops, both the engineer officer and KGB captain noticed their own men had joined the rout. At first the lieutenant tried to stop his, shouting to them or trying to grab them as they went by him. Few paid any attention as they continued to push their way ahead, giving him as wide a berth as the panicked stream of humans allowed. The KGB captain opted for a different approach. Without a second thought, he pulled out his pistol and pointed it at his men. When one of them kept going, he fired several times, missing the KGB private but hitting two other soldiers who happened to be in the line of fire. This, however, did nothing to stem the tide. The other KGB men who witnessed the incident simply did their best to melt into the crowd as they pushed and shoved their way north.

Once on the south side of the river, the lieutenant and the KGB captain found the company commander charged with defending the bridge yelling into a radio mike. When he saw them, he turned to the engineer. "The Americans are only a few kilometers away," he shouted. "They will be there any minute. You must blow up the bridge."

When the KGB captain heard this, he asked the infantry officer if he'd received orders to do so. The commander replied that he couldn't receive any orders because his radio was being jammed. The KGB captain responded that they couldn't drop the bridge until they received permission.

Again the commander told the KGB captain that the radio was being jammed and that he could not contact anyone before repeating his demand that the bridge had to be dropped.

The engineer officer joined in, siding with the infantry officer. "The bridge must be destroyed at once," he insisted. "If you don't give the order, I will."

Flummoxed, the KGB captain simply stood there, staring at the engineer officer. Taking the initiative in such an important matter went against everything he had been taught. He had been trained from childhood to obey orders. Now, when he needed to make a decision that he alone had to make, he found himself unable to. There was no superior to decide for him. There was no one who could share the blame with him if something went wrong. It was only him.

Just as the engineer officer and the commander began to yell at the KGB captain at the same time, imploring that he give them permission to drop the bridge, an American 155mm artillery shell ended their debate.

As Alpha 11 crested a small rise, Weiss caught sight of the Saale. In the clear night air, the light from the half-moon reflected from its smooth surface. They had made it. In a few more minutes, their role in the attack to the Saale would be at an end.

Bringing his tank to a full stop for the first time since passing through 2nd of the 94th, Weiss focused his full attention on the far river bank, searching for any telltale sign of the enemy Captain Bannon expected would be deployed there. All appeared to be calm save for friendly artillery landing on the main road leading to the bridge off to his left. Turning his attention in that direction, he watched as a volley hit right in the middle of a cluster of vehicles attempting to reach the bridge the Team had been heading for. That there were still Soviets on the south side of the river came as no surprise to Weiss. What did was the sudden realization that they were attempting to cross a bridge Captain Bannon told him and the other platoon leaders would be long gone before they got there.

Finding this to be too good to believe, Weiss slew Alpha 11's turret around until the main gun was pointed at the bridge, then dropped down to his sight extension in order to take a closer look. It was still there, whole and complete. It suddenly occurred to him that they had a chance to seize the bridge intact.

∾

"ALPHA 66, THIS IS ALPHA 11. THE BRIDGE IS STILL UP AND I'M GOING FOR IT!"

Weiss' use of vehicle bumper numbers over the radio instead of proper radio call signs was forgotten in the heat of the moment. Like him, Bannon found the news that the Team had not only caught some Russians on the wrong side of the river, but had the chance to seize a bridge intact was more than stunning. Suddenly the need to make a decision that could have a monumental impact on the course of the entire campaign, one he expected he and he alone could make, had been dumped in his lap. Did he let Weiss try for the bridge and risk having it blown up in their face or even worse, with some of his tanks on it? Or did he simply stop on the south bank and let the Russians blow it up? Whatever he decided, it had to be now. The 1st Platoon was well on its way and would, in a few minutes, decide the issue for him.

The Team had been ordered to divert the Soviets' attention from the battalion's main effort. Capturing a bridge intact and establishing a bridgehead here would certainly do that. With that thought in mind, without bothering to inform battalion, he ordered 1st Platoon to go for the bridge. The scouts, coming up fast after clearing the town, were ordered to follow 1st Platoon across. The Mech Platoon was instructed to drop one squad on the south side to clear any charges on the bridge and send the rest of the Platoon across on foot, stopping along the way to clear any and all charges or cut any wires they happened upon. Bannon next ordered Uleski to get up to the bridge as soon as possible and send the 2nd Platoon across to join 1st Platoon and the scouts, then take charge of the south side of the bridge with the 3rd Platoon and the Mech squad there. He concluded his rapid string of orders by instructing Weiss to have his tanks hold their fire until they were on top of the Russians. The way he figured, if his description of the confusion he was witnessing was as bad as he was reporting, the Russians responsible for dropping the bridge might not notice the Team was about to capture it until it was too late.

With nothing more to do, as far as issuing orders, Bannon called out to Kelp. "Kick it in the ass driver and get down there." He needed to be there, with his Team, whatever did happen at the bridge.

∾

Alpha 11 closed to within point-blank range before Weiss finally gave his gunner the order to fire. Falling in behind 11, the other tanks in his platoon followed, blazing away with machineguns at the fleeing Russians before them. With their sudden appearance, all semblance of order disappeared as Alpha 11 pushed onto the bridge.

Going was slow as vehicles of every description that could not be bypassed were pushed aside or simply crushed, igniting fires that spread as spilt fuel from destroyed or disabled Russian vehicles lit up the night, adding a new dimension of horror to an already terrifying ordeal for Russians soldiers still on the bridge. Those who found themselves trapped and unable to reach the safety of the far side of the bridge ahead of the rampaging tanks behind them tried to surrender. Few succeeded. Even if Murray Weiss had wished to take prisoners, tanks in the attack have neither the ability nor the means to collect, disarm, and keep an eye on them. This is particularly true of tanks advancing with a singular, bloody minded purpose.

The men belonging to the Mech Platoon weren't in much of a mood to take any prisoners either. As soon as Sergeant Polgar's track reached the south side of the bridge, he stopped and dismounted. The next track in line did likewise, dropping its ramp and disgorging its infantry squad. As the troops came piling out, Polgar yelled to the squad leader to find and cut every wire they came across. Never having done anything like this before, they began to rip away at every wire they found. In the heat of the moment, one infantryman tried to cut an electric power line with his bayonet, nearly electrocuting himself. Despite this, sporadic smallarms fire from die-hard Russians, and working with nothing but the flickering glow of fires, the infantry managed to keep the bridge from being blown.

Once Uleski had closed up on the south side, the Team went about the task of securing the bridge in a more methodical manner, dealing with whatever resistance remained, and rounding up those Russians who'd had enough, wanted to surrender, and could be accommodated. To provide early warning, Bannon sent the Scout Platoon out as far as he dared to establish a combat outpost line, spreading as much panic and chaos among the fleeing Soviet rear area personnel as they could as they went. The 1st Platoon was deployed to the left of the main road on the north side of the river in a quarter arc extending back to the river. The 2nd Platoon took up positions to the right, also in an arc from the road to the river. One Mech squad was left at the bridge's north entrance, one at the south, and a third sent forward midway between where the scouts were and the bridge to set up a road block. Uleski, still with the 3rd Platoon, remained south side of the river, spreading it in a shallow semicircle to cover an approach from that direction.

When Bannon reported the seizure of the bridge to battalion, neither Colonel Hall nor Major Shell would believe him. They kept asking him to make sure that he was not confusing the Saale River bridge with a smaller bridge that spanned a stream farther to the south. When he finally convinced them that the Team had in fact seized the main highway bridge, they gave him a wait-out while they conferred on what to do. After a couple of minutes, the battalion commander came back on the battalion net and ordered two companies to reinforce Team Yankee at the bridge. The S-3 would continue to drive to the river with the balance of the battalion and conduct a crossing farther to the west as planned while he contacted brigade to recommend they shift the main effort and passage of the 25th Armored Division to the bridge Team Yankee was holding.

∽

As dawn began to break, Team Yankee found itself momentarily alone and out on a limb again. But there was no sign of fear or apprehension as Bannon went about checking on the platoons under the pale blush of predawn light as they prepared for an enemy attack they expected, but would never receive. Unknown to them, far beyond the outpost line established by the scouts, men were making decisions and issuing orders that would start the final, and potentially, most deadly phase of the war.

CHAPTER 14

The Day After

With the arrival of the battalion of commander another company, orders to expand the bridgehead were issued. Those elements of Team Yankee still south of the river were sent north and ordered to move forward and establish a defensive position on high ground five kilometers northeast of the bridge where the scouts were established. Bravo Company established a position four kilometers north of the bridge. The scouts were sent farther out, but had the same mission of seeking out the enemy, providing early warning, and spreading pandemonium wherever they went. Team Charlie was kept south of the river to protect the bridgehead from attack from that quarter as well as mop up any Soviet stragglers that were still running around.

The only action of the day occurred when a company of Soviet T-55s came trundling down the road from the north. The scouts let them pass after reporting it to battalion. It was clear to everyone who heard the scout's report either the Soviets didn't know the bridge had fallen, or they thought that the battalion's positions were farther south. Whatever the reason, Bravo Company, who was ready for them, made short work of them.

By 0700 hours, the lead element of the 25th Armored Division was crossing the river. From their positions, the men in Team Yankee had little to do but watch the endless parade of vehicles and troops stream north. Once the 25th had passed through Bravo Company, it and Team Yankee were ordered to move to new positions farther east, expanding the bridgehead. Team Charlie did likewise on the south side of the river. By noon the entire battalion, minus Team Charlie, was across the river, reconsolidated and again ordered to continue their advance to the east.

It was during a pause brought about by the need to rearm and refuel that word came down from battalion for all commanders to report to the battalion CP ASAP. When Bannon arrived at the roadside gathering, he was greeted with a stone-cold silence by the officers who were already there. They were standing around the rear of the command track listening into a conversation the colonel was having on the radio. Stopping just short of that gaggle, Bannon sighed. "*Great*," he thought to himself. "*Some dumb son of a bitch at Corps has come up with another nightmare of an operation.*"

Inching his way closer, he did his best to listen in on what the colonel was listening to, but could only catch bits and pieces of his conversation with whoever it was he was talking to. When the colonel finished, he put down the mike and stood there a moment. Turning to the S-3, he grunted. "Well, I guess we're fighting a new war now."

Bannon turned to Frank Wilson, the commander of Team Charlie, "New war? What's the Old Man talking about? Did someone pop a nuke?"

Frank looked at Bannon, closed his eyes, and nodded his head in the affirmative. They had crossed the nuclear threshold.

Colonel Hall came out of the track, followed by Major Shell. Stopping midway down the M577 command post carrier's lowered ramp, he looked out over the gathered officers, taking a moment to composure himself before addressing them. "As some of you have already heard, the Soviets have initiated nuclear warfare."

Pausing, he let that statement sink in before he continued. "This morning they launched an attack with a single weapon against a British city, destroying it and causing severe damage to the surrounding area. The United States and Great Britain retaliated by striking a Soviet city with several weapons. Although there have been no further exchanges, we have been told to assume that the Soviets will continue to use nuclear weapons, including tactical weapons. Should they do so, I have no doubt NATO forces will meet every new escalation with equal or superior force."

Once more he paused, this time using the opportunity to look from face to face as if trying to gauge how his commanders and staff were taking the news. "As a result, the battalion has been ordered to increase the distance between the company positions. To make room for this, Team Yankee will be pulled out of the line and held back as a reserve. Bannon, the S-3 will provide you with details. I expect you all to take all measures necessary to protect your force without losing sight of our mission."

With that, Major Shell moved out from behind the battalion commander and over to the battalion operations map where he pointed out where each company and team was to go. Team Yankee was to move back to an assembly area in the center of the battalion's sector. To reduce their vulnerability and present a less lucrative target, its platoons were spread out over a wide area. After some additional instructions, the commanders and staff dispersed and headed off to see to adjusting their units and assets to deal with the new threat.

∿

News that nuclear weapons had been used cast a pall on all activities and conversations throughout the Team. Up to now, despite the horrors and losses they had suffered, the war had been manageable on a personal level. The Team had been in some very tight spots but had, when all things were considered, weathered the storm and emerged from it in relatively good shape. The men had met the Russians face-to-face and found that they could be defeated. In the process, they'd become confident in the Team's weapons, its leaders, and themselves. Their advance into East Germany had even fostered the belief they could win.

The initiation of nuclear war, however, changed all that. Not only was there precious little that the Team could do in the face of a tactical nuclear strike, a nuclear war threatened the United States. Their families and friends four thousand miles away were now in as much danger as they were.

It was this fear of the unknown, accompanied by a feeling of hopelessness that now became Bannon's chief concern and greatest challenge. As soon as the Team was in its new positions, he went from platoon to platoon, gathering its men around and went over with them what had happened and what it meant to them in as much detail as he could. He explained the possible results of an all out exchange of nuclear weapons and what they had to do if that came to pass. For the most part, however, he spent most of his time doing everything he could to keep them from falling into despair, pointing out that they were not entirely helpless. The Team still had a job to do and could still influence the outcome of the war. Most importantly, he was honest with them. They were all hardened veterans by now, men who had the ability to smell bullshit a mile away. This was no time to lie to them or try to blow sunshine up their third point of contact.

By evening the team was settled into their positions and was as ready for whatever came next as it could be. Everyone was in a quiet, reflective mood, with the men talking to each other only when necessary. For the most part, each man passed the night alone with his own thoughts and fears.

Bannon, too, was overcome with a feeling of despair and fear. As part of his training, he had been taught what nuclear weapons could do. He also knew what national policy was concerning their employment as well as the size of the nuclear arsenals that each side had. In Europe alone, the United States had some 7,000 nuclear devices on hand, capable of being delivered by various means, ranging from artillery delivered 155mm rounds to Pershing II missiles.

It was the intercontinental missiles both the US and Russia had that he feared most as his thoughts kept turning to his family. Nightmare scenarios began to play out in his mind, threatening his ability to think straight. The stress of the last few days, exhaustion, and now the fears brought on by the thought of an all-out nuclear exchange were too much for him to handle. With no one with whom he could share his feelings and burden, he sought escape through sleep. Like a child faced with a situation beyond his control, he withdrew from the horrors of the real world and drifted into a fitful sleep.

Stand-to the following morning reminded Bannon of the first day. It was as if the Team had gone full circle and was starting anew. In a sense, this was true. Only the distant rumble of an occasional artillery barrage broke the stillness that smothered the Team like a heavy quilt. As he greeted the men during his morning rounds, they responded in a perfunctory manner. Uncertainty and dread underlined everything they did. The lieutenants looked to Bannon, seeking guidance or inspiration or something. They found nothing. He could see their disappointment when he failed to give them the assurance they were seeking. Even a hot breakfast, the first cooked meal the Team had received in days, did little to raise morale. Something had to be done and done fast, or he feared they would all go crazy.

After the morning meal was over, Bannon called the platoon leaders in for a meeting. In no mood to play cheerleader, he took the "business as usual" approach. When everyone was present, he went down a list of protective measures that should have already been put into effect. These included such things as ensuring every man, including the tank crews, had a foxhole near at hand he could dive into if need be, turning off all but one radio in every platoon, covering all optics when not in use, camouflaging everything, and more. In addition, he warned that the platoons needed to tend to their routine maintenance and personal hygiene.

The platoon leaders either regarded him with blank or puzzled stares. Since the start of the war they had become loose in some of the areas he was now insisting they tighten up on. Rather than explain his rational, he simply returned their stares before telling them they were to inform him when they thought they were ready for inspection. At the conclusion of this meeting, he turned them over to the XO and went to battalion to see if there was any news on the progress of the 25th Armored or intelligence updates.

The news that greeted him at battalion was not at all what he had expected or had prepared himself for. Rather than more grim tidings, word was there had been no further use of nuclear weapons since the first exchange. "Conventional wisdom," Major Shell explained, "is that the Soviets had decided to try to intimidate the Europeans by taking out one of their cities with a nuclear device. Birmingham in England was chosen for this exercise in terror. The prompt retaliation by both Britain and the US against the city of Minsk came as a shock to them, demonstrating that NATO remained resolved and united."

"Even more importantly, the cherished Soviet notion that the US would not risk a nuclear attack on herself to save Europe had been disproved," Ken Damato added. "Just as the leaders of the NATO nations understood the purpose of the Soviet attack, the Soviets understood the meaning of NATO's response. NATO is ready and willing to trade blow for blow."

Major Shell then took to briefing Bannon on the overall situation. "The 25th Armored Division is continuing its attack toward Berlin and is making good progress. So far, the Warsaw Pact units have been unable to slow it down, let along stop it. Furthermore, there are signs the Warsaw Pact is beginning to buckle."

Ken Damato gave Bannon a copy of the Division's intelligence summary to read. "There've been a rash of armed insurrection in several Warsaw Pact Nations," he added when Bannon was finished reading the INSUM. "I expect a number of them are being inspired and aided by US Army Special Forces A teams that have been inserted throughout Poland and East Germany."

The news that Polish units were no longer attacking came as no surprise to Bannon. What did were reports that Soviet units in Northern Germany were beginning to surrender en-masse. Others were on the verge of doing so. Deep strikes by the Air Force were hampering the flow of supplies and the movement of troops. In short, the war was going well for NATO.

"While the loss of Birmingham was a major disaster, it has not interfered with the NATO war effort," Damato pointed out in a manner that struck Bannon as a wee bit too cold and analytical. "The destruction of Minsk, on the other hand, will hampering the Soviets by severing a major communications center. That, and the destruction of key bridges all along the Vistula River are making it increasingly difficult for the Soviets to sustain forces already in Germany, let along bring forward fresh units from the interior of the Soviet Union." As disturbing as the S-2's manner was, what he was saying about Minsk was welcome.

Buoyed by the news he had gleaned during his visit to battalion, Bannon went about the day's activities with renewed energy. He kept telling himself maybe things were not as bad as they seemed. As he went from platoon to platoon, he gathered the men around and passed on what news and information he had concerning the outside world. For the most part, the effect on the Team was about the same as it had been on him. This, and the return to a degree of routine served to keep the men busy and oriented on the job at hand.

In the early evening the battalion was ordered to move farther to the east and establish contact with Soviet forces commencing at 0300 hours the following morning. During the initial phase of the operation, Team Yankee was to remain in reserve. To Bannon's surprise, word of the pending movement to contact was welcomed by just about everyone in the Team he spoke to after he'd issued his own operations order to his platoon leaders. As welcomed and needed as the brief pause had been, to a man his officers and senior NCOs were eager to get on with it. They knew the sooner they got moving, the sooner the issue would be decided. The Team was as Americans have always been, anxious to avoid a war but, when forced to fight, determined to get on with it and finish it.

This new attack began without benefit of prep-fires by the artillery. Not that one was needed, as the battalion's advance encountered nothing but Soviet recon units and troops that were part of the security screen that fired a few rounds before fleeing. Dawn of the thirteenth day of war found the battalion still moving to the east at a steady pace. After an advance of fifteen kilometers it was ordered to halt. While they had not made contact with the Soviets' main forces yet, Division did not want units belonging to its flank guard to go too far. The main effort was still aimed for Berlin. With few forces available to protect the flanks of that drive, no one at Division or Corps wanted to find their lead elements cut off and isolated, not with things going as well as they were.

During this operational pause, the battalion was again dispersed over as wide an area as possible so as to reduce its vulnerability to a nuclear attack. Team Yankee remained in reserve. Once the Team was in its position, it settled in and prepared for another day. Foxholes were dug, camouflage placed, fighting and hide positions for each and every vehicle were identified and improved, platoon fire plans prepared, and numerous other tasks carried out. By noon, when they were as ready as they could be, the Team went to half-manning. When Bannon was satisfied there was nothing more that he needed to do, he lay down in the first sergeant's PC and went to sleep.

At 1700 hours First Sergeant Harrert woke him to tell him that he was wanted at the battalion CP immediately. As Bannon stumbled around, blurry eyed, groggy and still half-asleep, he asked if the first sergeant knew what was up. The first sergeant replied in the negative. "Major Shell didn't say, sir. The only message he gave me was that you needed to get up to the TOC ASAP."

⟞

Bannon's feeling of dread dispersed as soon as he walked into the farmhouse where the CP was located. Everyone was going around the room shaking each other's hands as if it was an alumni reunion. Going over to where Frank Wilson was seated, Bannon asked what was going on.

"Haven't you been told? The Soviets have declared a cease-fire effective midnight tonight. They're throwing in the towel. It's over."

Dumbfounded, Bannon unable to do anything but stand there, staring down at his friend. Just like that, the war was over. It was too good to be true. Something had to be wrong. "You mean they are surrendering?" he asked when he finally found his voice. "They're giving up, just like that?"

"Just like that," Wilson replied. "We don't have all the details yet, but from what we've told so far, the Soviet leadership has changed. The new Premier wants an immediate end to the war."

Before Wilson could tell Bannon anything more, the battalion commander, followed by the S-3 and the battalion XO, entered the room. The XO called the meeting to order. Colonel Hill went over the information he had, adding to it what he thought would be happening in the immediate future. He tried hard to be cautious, to keep from becoming carried away by reminding everyone that the ceasefire wasn't in effect yet and that things could change rapidly. But he, like all the assembled commanders and staff, was optimistic and overjoyed by the prospect of peace.

Colonel Hall was followed by Ken Damato who gave a brief summary on the current enemy situation, pointing out some of the dangers they had to guard against once the cease-fire was in effect as he went along. The biggest one was from sabotage and espionage from line-crossers and the local populace. They were, he reminded them, in Communist East Germany.

Major Shell went next, providing the commanders and staff with a quick overview of the more salient points of the rules of engagement that were to be placed into effect once the cease-fire became official. Warsaw Pact forces were not to come any closer to NATO positions than 1000 meters. Any that did were to be warned. Any that made any gestures that were construed as hostile were to be engaged. "All NATO soldiers have the right to protect themselves and return fire if fired upon," he added with great emphasis before continuing on. "Effective midnight tonight, NATO forces are not to move any farther than the front line trace we have achieved as of that time. The NATO commander had ordered that all operations currently in progress were to continue until then. Once the ceasefire has gone into effect, communications with any Warsaw Pact forces is forbidden unless permission was obtained from Division." Major Shell finished by informing the gathered commanders and staff that copies of the rules of engagement for distribution down to platoon level would be ready soon.

The colonel ended the meeting by again cautioning everyone against becoming too optimistic or letting down their guard. "Remember, even when the cease fire goes into effect, it's only a ceasefire, not a cessation of hostilities. Those other people could decide to say fuck it at any minute and pick up where they left off. So stay alert."

The sun was beginning to settle in the west as Bannon set out to head back to the Team's area. At his back the early evening sky was alive with brilliant reds and purples. The beauty of the lush green German landscape, unfolding before him, coupled with the spectacle of the setting sun and the quiet early night air lifted Bannon's spirit to a height that he had not experienced in months. His driver knew the way back, leaving him free to reflect on the joy of the moment. It was over. His worst nightmare was over and he had survived. There *would* be a tomorrow, a tomorrow he would see. With nothing more weighty on his mind than such thoughts, he relaxed and enjoyed the beauty of the countryside he had not seen before.

∾

The leadership of Team Yankee was waiting at the Team CP when Bannon came rolling in. They had become accustomed to his returning from battalion with grim news or word of a new mission, remaining calm while their commander explained how the Team was about to risk the lives of the men they were responsible for as they went about executing its new orders. This time, like all the times before, they expected no less.

They were therefore taken aback when Bannon approached with a smile on his face. Bob Uleski, sensing that something was afoot, turned to the first sergeant. "Well, either it's good news, or the pressure has finally gotten to the Old Man and he's thrown a track."

As hard as he tried, Bannon couldn't downplay his satisfaction he felt as he told them of the ceasefire as the colonel had. After all they had been through, he found he couldn't hold back. "Men, unless we receive information to the contrary, effective midnight tonight, a ceasefire will take effect along the entire front. Barring anything untoward occurring between now and then, the war is over."

Epilogue

Nothing untoward did happen. The ceasefire held. Over the next few days the Team stayed in place, maintaining its vigilance as they methodically went about the task of preparing for a possible continuation of hostilities. While they were careful not to let their guard down, life began to improve. Regular hot meals became available, as did mail service. The men began to catch up on their personal needs, from bathing to clean laundry. Even the weather improved as they moved from the heat of summer into the cool days of early September.

It was during the first week of September that the Division was replaced by a National Guard unit recently arrived from the States. The job of disarming the Soviets to the Team's immediate front was left to them. Division was temporarily moved back into the western portion of a now re-united Germany where it received replacements of equipment and personnel. By the time this was finished, the Soviet regime that had started the war was no more, and the chances of a new war were, for the foreseeable future, nonexistent.

With the crisis over, the Army bureaucrats began to reassert themselves. Those people who had lived in government quarters in Germany before the war were rotated back to their home station to conduct an inventory of their property, if it was still there, and to prepare a claim for any damages or losses sustained during the war. The decision as to whether personal property that survived would be sent back to the States, or families brought back to Germany hadn't been made yet.

It was strange returning to the military community the battalion had left a little over a month earlier. So much had changed. The community looked the same, empty of women and children, but otherwise unchanged. The MP who escorted Bannon's group verified their names and quarters' addresses before letting each of them into their quarters. Bannon, like most of the others, had lost his keys somewhere along the way.

When he walked into his quarters, he was overcome by a feeling of relief and joy. For the first time he knew it was all over. The horrors, though they would never be forgotten, could be relegated to the past. The life he had known before could resume.

As he was looking around the quarters, he was struck by the way everything was as it had been when he had left. Going over to the dining room hutch, he opened a drawer, took out a family album and made his way over to the sofa, just as he had that night in early August. As he leafed through it, he realized just how much he missed his family. Looking at the pictures of his children, he was secure in the knowledge that they had a chance to enjoy future free of the fears both he and his wife had grown up with. Again, Americans had been called on to pay for their freedom. And again, they had met the challenge, paid the price, and prevailed. Bannon prayed this would be the last time.

But he knew better.

Glossary

9M17: An AT-2 radio controlled antitank guided missile called a Swatter by NATO and Fleyta (Flute) by the Russians. It has an effective range of 0.5 to 2.5 km.

AAA: Anti-aircraft artillery. Conventional gun systems such as the American M-163 Vulcan or the Soviet ZSU 23-4.

A-10: A US Air Force jet designed specifically to provide close air support to ground forces. It is affectionately known as the Warthog.

ADA: Air defense artillery. It can either be surface-to-air missiles or guns.

AH-1: The designation of the Cobra attack helicopter. There are several versions, and armaments range from 7.62mm mini-guns up to TOW antitank guided missiles. Throughout the 1970s and 1980s, TOW provides the main punch of the Cobra.

AK: Short for AK47 or AK74 rifle, the standard assault rifle of the Soviet infantryman.

Armed Forces Network/AFN: The official radio and television network of the US Armed Forces, serving American military forces deployed overseas.

Assembly area: A location normally behind friendly lines where a unit closes into a tight circle in order to rest, rearm, and prepare for further operations.

Autobahn: The German equivalent to our interstate highway system, the autobahns inspired and acted as a model for our interstate highway system.

Auxiliary radio receiver/AUX receiver: Sometimes referred to simply as the AUX, it is simply a radio receiver, unable to transmit. Command vehicles normally carry a radio that can receive and transmit set to the radio frequency of the commander's unit and an auxiliary radio set to the radio frequency of his commanding officer.

Basic load: A prescribed number of rounds or amount of supply carried by a combat vehicle or individual soldier.

BBC: British Broadcasting Corporation.

BMP: A Soviet fully tracked infantry-fighting vehicle mounting either a 73mm gun or a 25mm cannon (in the BMP-2 version), an antitank guided missile, and 7.62mm machinegun. The BMP carries a crew of three and a nine-man infantry squad. The BMP provided the prime motivation for the design and production of the Bradley fighting vehicle.

BRDM-2: Primarily intended to be a wheeled Soviet Recon vehicle, it was modified to carry anti-tank guided missiles.

BTR: A designator identifying any one of several types of Soviet armored personnel carriers from the four-wheeled BTR-152 of World War II vintage to the BTR-70, an eight-wheeled armored personnel carrier now being fielded.

BTR-60: A Soviet eight-wheeled armored personnel carrier. This vehicle comes in several versions, from the original, which has an open top, to the BTR-60PB, which is completely enclosed and carries a small turret mounting a 14.5mm and a 7.62mm machinegun. In addition to the personnel carrier version, the BTR-60 serves as a command and control vehicle, close air support vehicle, and other such uses.

Bradley: An armored fighting vehicle that comes in two versions, the M-2 mechanized infantry fighting vehicle version and the M-3 scout version. Both have a two-man turret that mounts a TOW missile launcher, a 25mm chain gun, and a 7.62mm machinegun mounted coaxially with the 25mm gun.

CEOI: Short for communication and electronic operating instructions. The CEOI contains all radio frequencies, radio call signs, signal information, and passwords and countersigns.

CEV: Short for combat engineer vehicle. This vehicle is a specially modified tank that carries a large caliber demolition gun used for reducing obstacles, a dozer blade for digging positions or clearing debris, and a boom and winch.

Chemical alarm: A small portable device the size of a breadbox that samples the air and alerts its users when a chemical agent, gas, is detected.

CINC: Short for commander in chief, the term is pronounced "*sink*." In this case, it is referring to the four-star general in command of all NATO forces in Europe.

CO: Short for commanding officer.

COAX: Short for coaxially mounted machinegun. This weapon is normally a 7.62mm machinegun mounted next to the main weapon of a fighting vehicle.

Cobra: Nickname of the AH-1 attack helicopter. The Cobra is also referred to as a "Snake."

Cupola: A small, freely rotating turret on top of a tank turret or personnel carrier that incorporates a hatch, vision blocks, and usually a weapon such as a machinegun.

CVC: Short for combat vehicle crewman's helmet. This helmet provides protection to the tracked vehicle crewman's head as the tank bounces around the countryside. It is also wired to the vehicle's radio and intercom, allowing the crewman to hear what is being broadcast and to broadcast over the radio and intercom.

Division rear: Military units occupy terrain. The terrain that the unit occupies is called a sector and is normally subdivided into sectors with subordinate units responsible for the sector they occupy. The division rear is that part of the division's sector that is to the rear of the forward-deployed combat brigades. The division rear is normally managed by the division's support command, called DISCOM, and contains most of the noncombat support elements such as supply units, maintenance units, medical units, etc.

DPICM: Short for dual-purpose, improved conventional munitions. This is an artillery round that contains many small submunitions or bomblets that are capable of defeating the thin armor located on top of armored vehicles as well as being effective against personnel and other "soft" targets.

Dragon: A wire guided medium antitank guided missile launcher, designated the M47. Man-portable, the Dragon is the infantry's medium-range antitank weapon, with a range of 1000 meters.

Executive Officer/XO: The second in command of a unit. In a company, the executive officer, or XO, is a first lieutenant; in a battalion, he is a major. Traditionally the XO is responsible for handling the administrative and logistical matters in the unit.

45: Short for the caliber .45 M1911A1 pistol, the standard side arm for the US Army. This weapon was in the Army's inventory from 1911 to 1985 when it was replaced by the 9mm Beretta 92F.

FASCAM: Scatterable mines that provide a rapid, flexible means of delaying, harassing, paralyzing, canalizing, or wearing down the enemy forces in both offensive and defensive operations. Mines can force the enemy into kill zones, change their direction of attack, spend time in clearing operations, or take evasive actions. FASCAM can be delivered by air, artillery, or by hand using prepackaged and prepositioned containers.

Field phone: Simple telephones that are powered either by sound (TA-1s) or D-cell batteries (TA-312s) and connected by twostrand wire called WD-1.

Fighting positions: The location or position from which a soldier or fighting vehicle fights. This position is usually improved to provide protection to the soldier or vehicle and camouflaged to hide the position until the soldier or vehicle fires.

First sergeant: The senior NCO in a company, normally a master sergeant or E-8. In combat, the first sergeant assists the executive officer in handling the administrative and logistical needs of the company. He is the equivalent to the company sergeant major in the armies of Commonwealth countries.

FIST: Short for fire-support team. This team is headed by an artillery lieutenant and coordinates all requests for artillery and mortar fires as well as close air support. The FIST team consists of four to six men and travels in an M-113, normally within arm's reach of the company commander.

Fifth point of contact/Third point of contact: Paratroopers are taught there are five points of contact their bodies need to make in succession when landing. In order they are; the balls of their feet, the outer thighs, their buttocks, their shoulders, and finally, their head. Hence, when someone has their fifth point of contact firmly embedded in their third point of contact, they have their heads up their ass.

FSO/FSE: Fire-support officer and fire-support element. The fire-support officer is responsible for coordinating all indirect fires, i.e. artillery, mortar, and close air support, for the battalion or brigade to which he is attached. The fire-support element is located at the battalion or brigade command post.

Gasthaus: A small German neighborhood restaurant and pub that may also include a hotel.

GB: A chemical agent, better known as Sarin. A non-persistent nerve agent, it can be lethal even at very low concentrations, with death following within 1 to 10 minutes after direct inhalation due to suffocation from paralysis of the lung muscles. Its last reported use was on 21 August 2013 when it was employed in the Ghouta region of Syria.

Golden BB: In aviation lore a single lucky shot that brings down an aircraft or kills the pilot.

Gun mantlet: The armor that protects a tank's main gun and its cradle.

Halon gas: A gas used to extinguish fires in the M-1 tanks and Bradley vehicles. Automatic fire sensors detect fires and release the halon gas within milliseconds of activation.

Headspace and timing: On a weapon, headspace is the distance between the face of the bolt and the base of the cartridge case, fully seated in the chamber. Timing is the adjustment of the gun so that firing takes place when the recoiling parts are in the correct position for firing. On the M-2 heavy barrel machinegun, proper headspace and time are critical if you want to keep the receiver cover from blowing up in your face while firing.

HEAT: Short for high explosive antitank, a round that depends on a shaped charge explosion to penetrate an armored vehicle's armor. Because the round contains high explosive, it has a secondary role as an anti-material round.

Hind: Nickname of the Soviet MI-24D attack helicopter.

Improved TOW vehicle or ITV: A modified M-113 armored personnel carrier that has an antitank guided missile launcher mounted on a small rotating turret. TOW stands for tube-launched, optically-tracked, wireguided antitank guided missile. The TOW was the heaviest antitank guided missile in the US Army's inventory capable of hitting a tank-sized target out to a range of 3700 meters with a 90% hit probability throughout the 1970s and most of the 1980s.

INSUM: Intelligence summary.

Intercom: Short for intercommunications system. The intercom links all tracked vehicle crewmen together and allows the crew to talk amongst themselves.

IZB/Inter-zonal border: Also called the Inner German Border, this was the boundary that divided the Federal Republic of Germany, (West Germany), from and the German Democratic Republic, (East Germany), from 1949 to

1990 when the two Germanys reunited. Its 1,393 kilometers, (866 miles), of fences, walls, barbed wire, alarms, anti-vehicle ditches, watchtowers, automatic booby traps, and minefields were the physical manifestation of Winston Churchill's Iron Curtain.

LAW: Short for light antitank weapon. The current US Army LAW contains a 66mm antitank rocket that has an effective range of 300 meters. The LAW comes in a collapsible tube that is discarded when the rocket has been fired. It was supplanted by the M136 AT4 84mm Lightweight Multipurpose Weapon in the US Army starting in 1987.

Jedi knights: The nickname given to a graduate of the US Army's School of Advanced Military Studies located at Fort Leavenworth, Ks. The curriculum of the school is intended to teach a select group of junior field grade officers, *"the flexibility of mind to solve complex operational and strategic problems in peace, conflict, and war."*

LBE: Short for load-bearing equipment. This is the web gear worn by soldiers that includes suspenders and a web belt to which equipment is attached, such as ammo pouches, the soldier's first-aid pouch, canteen, grenades, bayonet, pistol holster, etc. LBE was designed, in theory, to evenly distribute the weight of this equipment on the soldier's body.

LOGREP: Short for logistics report. Submitted to higher headquarters to inform them of the current status of ammunition, fuel, maintenance, and supply of a unit.

LP: Listening post. A listening post is an outpost that is used during periods of limited visibility to provide security and early warning to the unit that it is covering. As its name implies, the LP relies on hearing the approaching enemy.

M-1: This is the current main battle tank of the US Army. It has a crew of four, mounts a 105mm main gun, an M2 caliber .50 machinegun, and an M240 7.62mm machinegun. The 63-ton tank is powered by a 1500 horsepower turbine engine and is capable of 45 mphs. The fire-control system incorporates a laser range finder, a solid-state computer, a thermal imaging sight, and other electronics that allow the main gun to fire while on the move with a high degree of accuracy, day or night. Starting in 1986, the tank's main armament was upgraded to a 120mm smoothbore gun, additional armor, an improved fire control system and redesigned the M-1A1.

M-3: The scout version of the Bradley fighting vehicle. See *Bradley* for a description.

M60: A 7.62mm machinegun that is the mainstay of the US Army's infantry squad. It has an effective range of 900 meters.

M-113: Until recently, the M-113 was the primary armored personnel carrier. Weighing 13 tons, it has a crew of two, driver and commander, and the capacity to carry an entire infantry squad. The M-113 is normally armed with a caliber .50 M2 machinegun located at the commander's position.

Because infantry cannot fight while mounted, M-113 is being replaced by the M-2 Bradley fighting vehicle. M-113 still remains a mainstay in the US Army, performing support roles on or near the front. Over 80,000 of these vehicles and derivatives based on it have been produced.

M-577: A specially configured personnel carrier used as a command and control vehicle at battalion and brigade level.

Mech: Short for mechanized or, in the case in this book, mechanized infantry.

MI-24D: A Soviet attack helicopter similar to the US Army AH 1. The MI-24D, named Hind, is heavily armed with an automatic cannon and antitank guided missiles and is well armored.

Mine Roller: An attachment to a tank that clears a path through a mine field for an attacking armored force. The rollers are nothing more than large metal wheels that are pushed ahead of the tank and set off mines as they run over them.

MOPP Level: Short for mission-oriented protective posture. MOPP levels prescribe how prepared individuals are to be to meet a chemical attack. In MOPP level I, soldiers simply carry or have their protective gear available. In MOPP level II, soldiers will don the chemical protective suit and carry their protective masks, gloves and boots. MOPP level III requires the soldier to wear the chemical protective suit, gloves, and boots. MOPP level IV, the highest level, requires the soldier to wear all his protective clothing and his protective mask.

MRE: Short for Meal, Ready to Eat. MREs have replaced the age-old C-rations as the standard combat ration in the US Army. MREs are a combination of dehydrated and ready-to-eat foods that come in plastic pouches.

MTU: A Soviet tank-mounted bridge that can be laid under fire across obstacles such as antitank ditches or small streams.

NATO: North Atlantic Treaty Organization. Founded in 1949, it is a military alliance whose expressed purpose is to prevent Soviet expansion in Europe. Today, NATO consists of Norway, Great Britain, Denmark, Belgium, The Netherlands, Luxembourg, the Federal Republic of Germany, Portugal, Spain, Italy, Greece, Turkey, Canada, and the United States. France is still a member but does not actively participate in NATO maneuvers or exercises.

NBC-1 report: An initial chemical attack report.

NCO: Short for noncommissioned officer or sergeant. NCO ranks are: E-5 or buck sergeant, three stripes; E-6 or staff sergeant, three stripes and one rocker or lower stripe; E-7 or sergeant first class, three stripes and two rockers; E-8 or master sergeant, three stripes and three rockers; and E-9 or sergeant major, three stripes, three rockers with a star between the stripes and rockers.

Night vision goggles: Night vision devices that amplify available light and provide the user with a visible image.

OH-58: Designation of the US Army's current scout or observation helicopter.

OP: Short for outpost or observation post. An outpost is placed well forward of a unit's main position and is intended to provide security and early warning for the unit. An OP can be manned by two or more dismounted personnel or armored vehicles.

Overwatch: A method of maneuvering on the battlefield in which one element or unit remains stationary, ready to support by fire another element or unit as it advances.

Panzer: German for armor.

Panzergrenadier: The German term for mechanized infantry.

Panzertruppen: Soldiers belonging to the German Army's armored branch, German tankers.

Platoon sergeant: The senior noncommissioned officer in a platoon, normally an E-7. The platoon sergeant is the second in command of the platoon and performs the same duties that the executive officer does at company or battalion level.

PRC-77: A small man-portable FM radio used by the infantry.

Protective mask: Gas mask.

REFORGER: A peacetime exercise that practices the redeployment of US forces from the continental US to Europe.

Remote box: Part of the track's radio system, it allows the track commander to change frequencies from his position without having to climb down into the vehicle.

RPG: Short for rocket-propelled grenade. The RPG is the standard Soviet infantryman's antitank rocket, the equivalent to the US Army's LAW.

S-1: The "S" is for staff. The S-1 is the staff officer responsible for all personnel matters in the battalion or brigade.

S-2: The staff officer responsible for gathering, analyzing, and producing intelligence on enemy activities and intentions.

S-3: The staff officer responsible for planning, coordinating, and monitoring combat operations of the battalion or brigade.

S-4: The staff officer responsible for providing and coordinating for supply, maintenance, and non-combat transportation needs of the battalion or brigade.

SABOT: The word is actually French for shoe. Here, it is the name of an antitank round. SABOT is short for armor-piercing fin-stabilized discarding sabot. The round consists of a small tungsten alloy or depleted uranium penetrator that has a diameter smaller than the diameter of the gun tube. To compensate for this, the penetrator is seated in a boot that is the same diameter as the gun. This boot, called the SABOT, falls away after the round leaves the gun, leaving the penetrator to continue to the target.

SHELLREP: Short for shell report. Used to report the impact of enemy artillery.

SITREP: Short for situation report. Subordinate commanders use the SITREP to update their superiors on the current activities, location, and condition of their unit.

SOP: Short for standing operating procedures. A unit SOP prescribes set actions to be taken given in a given situation.

Spot report: A short, concise report used to provide information on the sighting of enemy activity. At a minimum, the report provides information on who has made the sighting, when the sighting was made, where the enemy was observed, how the enemy was equipped, and what he was doing.

Stand-to: A set time, normally before dawn, when all members of a unit are awake and manning their weapons and fighting positions.

Stinger team: The Stinger is a man-portable short-range antiaircraft heatseeking missile. Stinger teams are two-man teams that are stationed well forward with combat units to provide air defense.

T-55 tank: A Soviet tank with a four-man crew and mounting a 100mm gun and a 7.62mm machinegun. This tank is considered obsolete by today's standards but is still found in Warsaw Pact inventories.

T-62 tank: A Soviet tank with a four-man crew and mounting a 115mm smoothbore gun, a 12.5mm and a 7.62mm machinegun. Though considered obsolete, it is still very capable and found in many Warsaw Pact units.

T-72 tank: A Soviet tank with a three-man crew and mounting a 125mm smoothbore gun, a 12.5mm and a 7.62mm machinegun. The elimination of the fourth crewman is achieved by using an automatic loader for the main gun. Special armor and a sophisticated fire-control system make it a powerful foe that is difficult to stop.

Task force: A combat battalion that has both tank and infantry companies. Under US Army doctrine, battalions seldom fight as pure tank or infantry units.

Team: A company-sized unit that includes both tank and mechanized infantry platoons. Unlike a peacetime company, the number and type of platoons in a team can vary according to its assigned mission. In the case of Team Yankee, the Team initially has two tank and one mechanized infantry platoon as well as two improved TOW vehicles.

Thermal sight: A sight that detects the heat emitted by an object and translates that heat into a visible image for the gunner or tank commander.

TOC: Short for tactical operations center. This is where the staff plans future operations and monitors the current battle. The TOC receives and passes reports, relieving the commander of that responsibility so that he may run the current battle.

TOW: Short for tube-launched, optically-tracked, wire-guided antitank guided missile. The TOW is the US Army's current heavy antitank guided missile with a range of 3700 meters. The guidance system provides a high probability of hitting a tank-sized target out to its maximum range.

Trains: A term used to describe the collection of support and service elements that support military units.

Two-and-a-half ton truck: A medium cargo truck with a hauling capacity of two and a half tons. This truck is also referred to as a deuce and a half.

Urah: Traditional Russian battle cry, often shouted when going into the attack.

VC: Viet Cong, another war.

Vulcan: M-163 Vulcan Self-propelled anti-aircraft gun. A 20mm multibarreled short-range antiaircraft gun. The extremely high rate of fire, 4000 rounds a minute, results in a chainsaw-like sound when firing.

Warsaw Pact: A military alliance founded by the European Communist countries to counter NATO. It consists of the Soviet Union, Poland, the German Democratic Republic, Hungary, Czechoslovakia, Bulgaria, and Rumania.

WD-1: Two-strand wire used to connect field telephones or other communications equipment.

ZSU 23-4: A Soviet antiaircraft gun. It has four rapid-firing 23mm guns, (hence 23-4). It is very capable and serves the same mission as the Vulcan in the US Army. The ZSU, sometimes called "Zoo" for short, accompanies the first echelon attack elements to provide air defense for those elements.